THE DRUMS
THROBBED . . .

Yawana gave herself voluptuously to the magic of the dance, her eyes filled with the mysterious night of the senses. Her movements grew more and more frenetic, until she was dancing wildly, twisting and turning, arching her body. . . .

Jonathan never knew quite what it was—the obsessive beat of the drums, the sweat running down the bare body that gleamed so excitingly in the candle-light, or the subtle musky smell that arose from her body. Yawana was watching him from under half-closed lids as he came to her. She threw herself back to take in the white man, and she forgot N'Gio.

Jonathan felt her nails in his back and heard her harsh groan. She had no idea what name she cried, N'Gio or another. All was lost in the thunder of the drums. . . .

NO RIVER SO WIDE

by Pierre Danton

Translated by Jean Raggan

A DELL BOOK

Published by
Dell Publishing Co., Inc.
1 Dag Hammarskjold Plaza
New York, New York 10017

This work was originally published in France by Éditions
Robert Laffont under the title *Antilope N'Tchéri*.
Copyright © 1976 Éditions Robert Laffont, S.A.

Dell ® TM 681510, Dell Publishing Co., Inc.

ISBN: 0-440-10215-4

Printed in the United States of America

First printing—June 1978

CHAPTER 1

The black man slid a slender porcupine quill under the venerable chief's toenail. Delicately, he pierced the skin and scooped out a tiny insect, its pouch bulging with eggs. Flinging it into the fire, where it rolled into a minute, quietly crackling ball, he turned to repeat the procedure, but the quill plunged in too deep and a howl of rage rewarded his clumsiness: "You mangy ape . . . !"

The slave backed away hastily. "It was a mistake, Chief Adende, I beg your forgiveness, it was a mistake."

"Forgive you, forgive you? Imbecile! Be careful, and make sure you don't do that again or I'll skin you alive and feed the remains to the ants."

Onanga's shoulders bowed slightly as he heard the threat. He knew Adende was quite capable of carrying it out at the slightest provocation. The wizened old chief had total power of life and death over him, and all because the men of his tribe had violated Adende's boundaries in their search for bananas. Onanga had been chosen by his own chief to be sent to Adende as a forfeit for tribal war. His right ear had been ceremonially slit, a mark he would bear all his life to indicate his slave status. Since that day he had been at the old man's beck and call, constantly subjected to his tyranny.

Onanga felt himself begin to tremble and shake, and the more he trembled, the more he knew that he would not be able to continue the operation. He was saved by the sudden appearance of a young man.

"A good day to you, Father," called the young man in a joyous voice.

N'Gio ignored the slave crouched at his father's feet as Adende answered, "And a good day to you, my son." The old man realized that his son wanted to talk with him alone, so he shouted at Onanga, "Go away before I beat your brains out, and tell Aziza to come here." Onanga rose and scuttled away as fast as he could.

Adende wore only a straw loincloth which barely hid his skinny, old man's body. He looked penetratingly at his son. "Early today, aren't you, Omwana?" He often called N'Gio by the affectionate name used for very small children. "Well, you are right. The early buffalo gets the best grass. Sit down."

"I really don't have time," said N'Gio, sitting anyway. "The men are waiting for me to go hunting with them. It rained all night so we'll find elephant prints. We need to get at least two elephants, there's no more meat in the village."

Just then, Aziza came in. Young, and ebony smooth, her only adornments were the bronze bracelets jangling at her wrists. She was no beauty, but her youth made up for that in Adende's eyes. He had recently bought her from a neighbor. Her breasts, unusually heavy for her age, did not appeal to N'Gio, who averted his eyes. Anyway, she, like the other concubines, was his father's personal property and would probably be sacrificed, perhaps tortured when he died, and then buried alive with the other wives of the chief—a matter of no concern whatsoever to N'Gio.

The young girl cast a sidelong glance at N'Gio. She knew he didn't like her and was pained by his indifference. She found him extraordinarily handsome, the handsomest man in the village, and she would have much preferred his caresses to the clumsy couplings forced on her by the saggy old man.

"Bring us drink," ordered Adende.

Aziza left, and returned a few moments later with a full gourd. She placed it on the ground and the chief held it out to his son. "Here! Have some beer before you leave. It's made of very ripe bananas, and there's nothing better for speeding the hunter's gait."

N'Gio wasn't thirsty but he didn't want to vex his father, so he took a few sips. His father emptied the gourd in one gulp and Aziza hurried forward to refill it.

The old man sighed heavily. "You are so lucky," he grumbled in his scratchy voice. "I would have liked to go with you, only that fool, Onanga, has almost crippled me. I'm old. My body has become as soft as a crab without its shell."

N'Gio found it hard to hide a smile. He was well aware that since his mother's death his father found every excuse to stay in the village, drinking, smoking herbs, or scattering his energies making love to increasingly younger girls.

"Yes," he said aloud, "you take a good rest, Tato." He pulled himself to his feet. "I will be gone two or three days. I must leave you now."

Adende followed him to the door and watched him move forward to join the other hunters. His son was taller than the tallest. He was magnificently built, and had inherited the proud bearing of his mother, Dowani, an Eshira woman of royal blood. He was the biggest and bravest, and his father's heart swelled with pride as he watched them move away, followed by their wives. Soon, they had disappeared into the dense forest that surrounded the village.

Adende stood there a few minutes, gazing at his domain in the dawn light. It was foggy and the damp air filled the village with a chalky mist. The low huts were arranged in an uneven circle around the central meeting ground. In the middle stood the red trunk of the sacred Olumi tree, towering over a large sprawling structure, the mbanja, temple of the Bwiti, a secret society with frightening rituals. The triangular straw roof was held up by a sculpted wooden post displaying monstrous female genitals, symbol of the creation of the human race. The roof had been damaged by the recent rains and the old man reflected that it would soon need repairs. He glanced up at the sky, now cloudless and limpid, knowing that this meant nothing, and that it might soon rain. He found himself hoping that it would not cause N'Gio too much discomfort if it did. He turned back into his own hut and sat down heavily on the matting. The next few days would be quiet. There would be no one to come and disturb him and he would be able to indulge in his favorite pursuits to his heart's content. He stuffed his pipe with a hallucinogenic herb, lifted the banana-bark pipe, and plunged a firebrand into the stove. The bitter taste of the smoke filled his lungs. He lay back on the mat and knew that he would feel much better in a few moments. Then, Aziza would become impossibly beautiful and he would be as young as N'Gio. "Aziza!" he shouted, "Aziza! Come here at once."

The girl appeared in a few moments, carrying a fresh gourd of beer and some grilled fish wrapped in banana leaves. Adende had finished his smoke and he ate and drank greedily while his companion looked on, knowing what would happen as soon the chief felt the combined effects of the herb and drink. She knew what she was there for. Later, he would undoubtedly take another, younger girl and she would go out to the fields with the other women or serve as a bearer when the tribe was on the move.

Adende had eaten well. He burped majestically, took off his straw loincloth, and drew Aziza toward him. With total enjoyment, he began to knead her young flesh. The scent of it filled his nostrils, intoxicating him, and he plunged his dirty nails into her tender skin.

Aziza accepted his crude attentions without a murmur. She would soon have to stimulate his old man's ardor and the thought repelled her.

A cacophony of voices and dogs barking distracted her from her unpleasant thoughts. Adende grumbled ill-humoredly, wondering who had come to disturb him at such a time. He pushed Aziza away roughly and got up. The sun blinded him as he reached the door, and he raised his hand to his eyes. He could make out some strangely dressed men coming out of the forest and he shouted for Aziza.

The girl ran to his side.

"I can't see a thing with this sun," Adende muttered. "Who are those people?"

Aziza's eyes widened and she stared blankly ahead. "I can't see, either," she said.

A resounding slap almost sent her to the ground. "Silly bird," cursed Adende, "run out there and see who it is instead of gawking with frog's eyes."

Aziza hurried out toward the group standing uncertainly close to the first huts at the edge of the village. The bearers were unloading their burdens. Adende suddenly realized that he was completely naked. He hurried into his hut and tied his loincloth about his waist. Then, grabbing his ebony cane, symbol of his exalted rank, he prepared himself to greet his guests.

Aziza appeared with one of the strangers, an impressively tall man wrapped in a long white tunic. When they drew closer, Adende's face lit up. From the deep ritual cuts carved above the cheekbones he recognized Mouele, the wandering merchant who often passed through the village. He was a Bapounou from the Tchibanga country. He brought precious and exotic goods to the forest dwellers, huge iridescent shells, smoked fish with a stronger flavor than the familiar river fish, and a white powder which he carried in plaited baskets and called salt. The villagers had run out of it a while back and had to make do with the ash of the ombongo grass or dried elephant urine prepared by the Babinga Pygmies.

Adende had often tried to find out where Mouele got hold of all his merchandise, but the Bapounou always managed to avoid his questions.

"Good day to you, Chief Adende," said the merchant. "May the spirits of your ancestors guard and protect you."

"Good day to you, Mouele," returned Adende. "Your visit brings delight."

The two men stooped and went into the chief's hut, and Adende sent Aziza to get them something to drink. He clapped his hands loudly, calling for Onanga: "Where are you, filthy lazy bag of bones?"

The slave appeared at once. "Onanga, see that Mouele's men get something to eat and arrange for the guest hut to be made ready for them for the night," said Adende.

Mouele raised his hand in protest. "No, no!" he said, "that won't be necessary. We won't stay long."

Adende's surprise was obvious. "What?" he said. "You won't be sleeping here, Mouele? But I have a beautiful girl for you."

"I thank you, Chief Adende," the other man responded, "but we still have some distance to cover. However, I shall gratefully accept food for my men, and while they eat, you and I can discuss our business."

Adende frowned, wishing his guest to see his annoyance at having his hospitable intentions thwarted. "Well, well," he grumbled, "I suppose you will do what you choose."

Just then Aziza came in with the beer. She placed it carefully on the ground and slipped away. The two men drank in silence, studying each other before starting to bargain. The old chief was fascinated by the draped tunic Mouele was wearing. He longed to ask where it had come from but felt it would be demeaning for him, as chief, to betray such idle curiosity. He was also well aware that by speaking first he would put himself in a position of inferiority. It was definitely Mouele's place to start the discussion since he was the one in a hurry.

At last Mouele spoke. "I brought salt and pots. What do you need?"

Adende ruminated in silence, as was his custom. Then he said, "I need salt, Mouele. I still have much of it left, but I prefer to think ahead." The lie came out easily and convincingly. "As for the pots," he added, "we really don't need any, but the women of your tribe are so skilled that we take pleasure in buying their work. I'll round up some goats and some ivory to give you in payment."

Mouele didn't answer. He continued to stare reflectively at his feet. At last he raised his eyes to Adende's and said in a honeyed tone, "You know, Adende, times are changing. Prices are not what they used to be."

"What?" exclaimed Adende, "don't you want goats and ivory anymore?"

"Calm down," said Mouele, "that's not quite the question. Let me explain. So far, I have never told you where I get the salt you and the other tribes love so much. Now I shall tell you. I go very far to find it, to a huge lake with only one bank, where the Baloumbou live. They came there long, long ago from the Mongo country, guided by the Pygmies. They draw water from the lake and pray to the sun to turn it into salt." He noticed that Adende was staring at him in obvious puzzlement, then continued, "They don't want goats anymore, Adende. What they want now are slaves. I noticed the one you have, the fellow with the slit ear. If you want your salt, you will have to give him to me in exchange."

Adende continued to look surprised, and Mouele said abruptly, "That's the way it will be from now on, Adende, so you may as well get used to it."

"But Mouele," muttered Adende, "that's the only slave I have. How can I pay you in this manner? I'd need another war with a neighboring tribe, and we are getting along well, right now."

The Bapounou grinned nervously. "It's quite easy," he said. "I'll tell you how it can be done. But first let me show you something." He rose in a fluid movement and left the hut, and the bewildered Adende watched him glide toward a group of men and say something to them. Two of them lifted a huge hamper and followed Mouele, who had turned and was making his way back to the hut. Mouele made them lay the hampers down carefully and then sent them away. He glanced around into the darker recesses of the chief's hut. "Can we speak without being overheard?" he asked. Adende nodded. "Good. Then cover the doorway so that we can be alone."

Adende rose and covered the entrance with a large bark panel. Then he fixed it into place with a twig, so that the only light in the hut was what seeped in through tiny cracks in the walls. As their eyes adjusted to the dimness, Mouele pulled a glass bottle swiftly from the folds of his tunic. He uncorked the bottle and took a large gulp to show that the contents were not poisoned. Then he handed the bottle to Adende. "Here. Drink!" he said.

Adende held the bottle up to one of the slivers of lights, intrigued by the transparency of the liquid. Then he sniffed it suspiciously and lifted it to his lips. The first swallow burned his throat and almost made him choke, but simultaneously he felt an unknown warmth steal through his limbs.

"Drink some more," insisted Mouele.

Adende took a swallow. This time it burned less, so he took a third, deep swallow. He had never experienced anything quite like it. It was delicious, and nothing like the insipid banana beer or palm wine he was used to. The liquid seemed to set each vein on fire and he had a strange feeling that he was becoming larger and stronger. With some regret he returned the bottle to the Bapounou, who pushed it away. "Keep it, Adende," he said, "it's for you. I give it to you."

Adende placed it uncertainly between his legs. "It is good!" he exclaimed. "What is it?"

"Well?" Mouele asked impatiently. "Do I get your slave? You'll get as many hampers of salt as you and I together have fingers on both hands."

It was, of course, far too much to pay for the slave. Mouele was sacrificing his own profit, but he wanted to use this deal as bait to hook Adende once and for all. Adende was in such a euphoric state that he accepted the proposition eagerly and unsuspiciously.

"Yes, yes, of course I'll give you my slave," he said hastily, "but that still doesn't tell me how I shall be able to pay you from now on."

"Relax," said Mouele. "Drink some more, old chief. You haven't seen the half of it yet."

Mouele unknotted the vines that held the hampers closed and opened them to Adende's dazzled eyes. The chief had never seen such a strange and wondrous assortment of objects. Mouele took out a long tube, explaining to Adende that it could kill a man at a much greater distance than an arrow could reach. Next he showed him necklaces of glittering stones and soft, brilliantly colored fabrics. A round flat object returned Adende's face to him, and he touched it, entranced by its magic. His hands wandered in wonder from treasure to treasure as he gazed at them and longed to possess them. Mouele was watching him carefully.

"Do the Baloumbous make all these things?" asked Adende.

Mouele laughed scornfully. "Of course not! The Baloumbou would not know how to make such treasures. White men came from the sun and brought them these objects on their floating villages."

"White men!" exclaimed Adende. "How can there be men whose color is different from our own? You must be mistaken. These creatures must surely be gods or spirits."

"No, Adende," he assured the amazed chief. "They are indeed men, but they have tremendous powers." He paused, his lips curved in an insinuating smile. "If you wish to possess these things, they will give you the powers the white men have. Everyone will respect you and fear you. Your neighboring tribes will do all you ask and follow your laws, and you will be able to have all the women you desire."

Every sly word had its effect on Adende and seemed to plunge him into a magnificent universe, where he saw himself equal to the gods, imposing his will on everyone and reigning over a huge assembly of beautiful girls. "What must I do?" he blurted out, his speech thickened by the alcohol he had drunk. He failed to notice the victorious smile which flickered across the Bapounou's impassive face.

"Why, nothing," Mouele said smoothly. "You will have almost nothing to do. But before I explain it to you, I want to be sure that you have decided to do it, because once I tell you the details, it will be too late to change your mind."

He stared at Adende, who answered impatiently: "But I said I would do it."

Mouele continued in a low voice. "These white men want many many slaves in return for a share of their powers. Now you have told me that all you have is one slave, and that you won't go to war to capture more, so I am going to suggest a very simple plan which will get you all you desire, and more."

He leaned toward Adende and whispered in his ear. As he talked, Adende's expression changed and he leapt up. "You want me to sell my own village?" he cried in horror.

"Don't shout!" the trader answered calmly. "Do you want everyone to hear? You wouldn't really be selling them, you know. You would simply be letting me take them with me. They'll be well fed and rewarded where they go, and as soon as the whites cease to need them they will be returned to you, and they will thank you for what you have done for them."

"Are you sure?" Adende asked doubtfully.

"I'm telling you it's so, am I not?"

Adende didn't speak for a few moments, but huddled on the floor of his hut, deep in thought. Then he looked up and asked in a firmer voice: "You mean I could then have anything I ask?"

"Anything you ask," returned Mouele.

"More of the magic liquid you gave me to drink?"

Mouele smiled. "You'll have more than you can drink," he assured him.

The old chief's eyes gleamed as he envisioned the fantastical treasures that would be his, but a secret flicker of fear prevented him from deciding at once. "I need more time, Mouele," he pleaded. "I need to think."

Mouele sighed. He was aching to push the deal to a conclusion but he didn't want to ruin his efforts by seeming impatient. "Very well, Adende," he said. "I'll give you till the next moon. But I warn you that you are a dead man if you ever say a word to anyone of what has passed between us. Is that clear?"

Adende shrank a little at the other man's biting tone. No one had ever dared to speak to him in such a manner. In the menacing, calculating man before him, there was nothing of the gentle merchant with whom he had had so many pleasant dealings in the past. At last, he spoke in a resigned voice. "Fine. Come back next moon and I'll give you my answer."

"Good!" exclaimed Mouele. "Now bring me that slave of yours and let's get moving."

Adende got to his feet and pulled the panel of bark from the doorway. Seeing that Mouele was calmly packing up his hampers and knotting the vines, he left to find Onanga. The Bapounou finished his task and rounded up his men and all were waiting when Adende arrived with his slave. Several bundles lay about on the ground. Onanga, ignorant of what was going on, stood watching anxiously but without fear.

"There's the salt," said Mouele pleasantly, pointing to the bundles.

"Good," said Adende in a subdued voice. "Now take your pay."

The Bapounou signaled to his men and they threw themselves on the huge Onanga. Before he realized what was happening, his hands were bound behind his back and a vine was wrapped around his neck.

He gave a despairing cry. "Why, Chief Adende, why?" But Adende turned his back on the scene without a word and went into his hut. Onanga's body was racked with huge sobs but he stood his ground until Mouele dealt him a vicious blow with his hippopotamus-hide whip and one of the men pulled the vine tight around his neck, half strangling him. There was nothing for him to do but follow, and the small procession left the village. No one was about, and no one saw them leave. Adende drained the last drops from his bottle and hid it in a corner of the hut. Then he lay down and fell into a deep sleep.

CHAPTER II

The hunters came back two days later. It was early afternoon, and the village seemed crushed under the weight of the sun. The hunters reeked of the blood which crawled down from the haunches of meat they carried on their heads. They placed their burdens near the smokehouse and the women following them hurried forward and lit fires under the tiles. Then they set to work chopping up the huge hunks of meat, which were already surrounded by clouds of flies. They quickly laid out the pieces for smoking before the heat started to decompose them.

N'Gio and his fellow hunters went to the river to wash. He dived into the water, glad to soak off the thick streams of congealed blood that trailed all over his body. He dried himself off with a fistful of grasses and joked with his companions. They were happy to be home, and at last N'Gio left them to their horseplay and went to find his father.

Adende was stretched out on his mats, smoking, his expression beatific. Since Mouele's departure, his mind had dwelt obsessively on all the treasures he was about to acquire and his mood had become one of suppressed exaltation. He had always intended to accept Mouele's proposition, and his hesitation had been only in the interests of shrewder negotiation. No doubts as to the ethics of the transaction had crossed his mind. He saw it as a sort of lending operation, relying on Mouele's assurances that his people would be very grateful to him when they returned.

N'Gio slipped into the hut and sat back on his heels, smiling at his father. His strong, white teeth shone in the dimness of the hut. They had not been filed into points as were those of certain cannibalistic tribes who lived on human flesh. Cannibalism was taboo to the Woumbou tribe his father governed. Adende's face looked puffier than usual and the young man conjectured that his father had used the hunters' absence to drink more than usual and make reckless use of Aziza's firm body. N'Gio grinned with pleasure. The old man was clearly as full of vigor as ever.

"What did you kill?" asked Adende lazily.

"That potion the witch doctor made us drink worked wonders," answered N'Gio. "We came upon a herd of elephants the very first day. Females, their babies, and a huge male. We frightened the females and the male came charging at us in a blind rage." N'Gio started to chuckle as he continued. "That male wasn't very clever. That was exactly what we had hoped he would do and we ran away from him until he blundered into the pit we had prepared, and died on the stake. We didn't even wait for him to die before we leapt on him and began to cut him up. His tusks are enormous. We should be able to buy a lot of salt with them."

Adende, lost in his fantasy world, muttered: "They came two days ago."

"Who came?" asked N'Gio, puzzled.

"The Bapounou," said his father. "They came with the salt."

"Well, I hope you bought plenty," said N'Gio cheerfully. "We don't have a single grain of the last batch left."

"I did," said Adende absently. "I gave them Onanga for it."

N'Gio stared at his father in disbelief. "You mean you paid for the salt with Onanga? But you liked having the slave! And there was plenty of ivory and goats for you to trade with. Why did you do that?"

Somewhat unsettled by his son's reaction, Adende mumbled that Onanga had grown lazy and was no longer useful. This had seemed a good way to get rid of him once and for all. N'Gio said nothing more, but he was surprised that his father should have traded in such an untraditional manner.

The conversation turned to the Bwiti ceremony which was to take place on the night of the full moon. It was a topic of great interest, for this time N'Gio was to be initiated into the legendary sect supposed to have been formed by the Bapindji when the world began. Onanga was forgotten. Adende was a little preoccupied, however, for he knew that on the night of the full moon he would have to give his answer to Mouele.

Soon N'Gio took his leave. The hunt had tired him. As he stepped out of the hut he noticed that the sky had clouded over and was split here and there with jagged flashes of lightning. He was concerned for the meat, and hoped that the rains wouldn't come and put out the fires in the smokehouse before all of it was cured.

N'Gio's hut was built of bark, as were all the huts in the village, but it had added arches around the doorway, made from the spirit plant, a talisman to chase away evil influences. N'Gio had been blessed with a supernatural birth. His mother had borne twins. Since N'Gio was born first, his life was spared, but he learned later that his brother had been killed by the witch doctor—immediately decapitated, as was the custom. The flesh of the small warm body had been thrown into the flames and reduced to ashes, then mingled with his ground bones. Then the witch doctor had gone into a period of isolation. He had mixed the ashes and powdered bones into white kaolin powder to make the paste used as a ritual face makeup in spirit ceremonies. The child's head was buried with much ceremony at the crossroads of two trails in the heart of the forest.

Life trickled along peacefully in the Mounigou village. The villagers spent their days in agricultural pursuits, hunting, and fishing. They were a happy people, and had no inkling of the machinations of the chief they respected. Their mood was optimistic, for they lived in harmony with neighboring tribes and had no fear of raids or wars. To pay the respect demanded by the spirits of their ancestors, the link between this life and the next, they opened the bark containers and meditated over the skulls within. To pacify the Imbwiri, the spirits of air, water, and earth, they often left food in special places, for these spirits were known to be malicious and unpredictable. Adende was the judge where conflicts arose and Moussavou, the witch doctor who had the gift of second sight, took care of any sick villagers. Although he was a cheerful man, everyone knew that it was dangerous to go against him, for he was wise in the language of animals and knew the secrets of plants that could cure or kill.

One afternoon, N'Gio was taking part in the Bwiti temple ceremony when he saw that Yawana had come with her parents. He dropped everything and ran out to greet her. The girl's face lit up when she saw him and she moved away from her parents and came toward him. N'Gio stopped and watched her, enchanted by what he saw. The light straw loincloth she wore hid none of the curves of her young body. Her legs incredibly long, she was as lithe as a

young lad. She had inherited a delicate nose from her father, Isembe, an Akele whose grandmother had married a
Bakola Pygmy. From her mother Ivohino's Akanda ances-
try she had an imperious way of holding her head, counter-
balanced by a charming face, laughing almond-shaped
eyes, and dazzling white teeth in a smiling mouth.

They had long been promised to each other. The tradi-
tional prenuptial gifts had been exchanged before either of
them could walk. They were almost the same age and, as a
child, Yawana often came to Mounigou where she spent
long, joyful days playing with N'Gio.

"Hello, little antelope," said the young man, a rush of
tenderness making it difficult for him to speak. He had always called her by the name of this forest creature, the
most graceful, pretty, and supple animal he knew. He had
even reached the point of asking the village hunters never
to kill an antelope.

She smiled, her eyes crinkling as she looked at him.
"Hello, N'Gio," she said in her gentle voice. "I've come for
a few days. Are you glad?"

"Of course I'm glad," he said, his eyes never leaving her
face. "Come with me, I should greet your parents, and then
we should go to my father." The two young people linked
fingers and went to Isembe and Ivohino, leading them over
to Adende's hut. As they walked in, Adende's eyes lit up. He
had just realized how he would answer the question that
had been bothering him for so many days. If all went according to the plan that had flashed into his mind at the
sight of his guests, he would have excellent news to give
Mouele when he came.

He rose courteously to greet them. After gestures of
warm affection had been exchanged by all, Yawana and
her mother left the men to discuss the problems of daily
living, and went to rest. Aziza brought cool beer and the
conversation turned to fishing, hunting, and the crops. At
last Adende found an opening for what had been on his
mind. "Listen here, Isembe," he said, "the time of games is
over for N'Gio. He will be initiated to the Bwiti at the next
full moon. He is a man now, and he needs a wife to take
care of his home and give him children. Your daughter,
Yawana, is tall and beautiful. It is time for them to marry."

Isembe couldn't hide his satisfaction. This marriage,
planned so long ago, was a final bond of alliance between

his tribe and Adende's, and furthermore, the gifts he was
bound to receive would be welcome. He loved the lavish
feasts that would surely accompany the ceremonies. "Your
suggestion fills me with pleasure," he replied. "I had meant
to speak to you about it myself. The men in my village are
beginning to hang around my daughter. She's at an age to
be taken in love and it is for your son to do it. Let us set a
date today."

This conversation delighted N'Gio. He was eager to
marry Yawana, and had long been waiting for the moment
of approval from the elders. Adende, whose reasons were
vastly different from those that made his son's eyes shine,
was greatly pleased.

"I'll go and tell Yawana," said N'Gio, rising to his feet.
He found her at the other end of the village, sitting on the
grass in the shade of a hut, dreaming, as she watched Ivohino chatting with some women who were piling manioc
into a mortar. As N'Gio came into sight she rose gracefully. She longed to be alone with him, and he, understanding her desire, took her by the hand. They wandered down
by the river. The path they took plunged through a
banana-tree grove, and they walked in silence, filled with
the joy of being together again. Their eyes met often, and
they smiled at each other.

Yawana thought N'Gio was the handsomest man she
had ever seen. He seemed to have changed considerably
since the last time they had been together. She was tall
herself, but he was taller now by at least a head, and his
strong muscles rippled as he moved. A strange feeling overwhelmed her and she pressed close to him. His arm crept
around her shoulders and their pace slowed. He found that
she too had changed. She had ceased to be a tall, gangly
girl and had become a very beautiful woman with a pro-
vocative, languid step.

The path led them through a small wood and opened
onto a sandy beach, golden and luminous in the crook of
the river. The waters had risen because of the rains, and
the river's current was turbulent, but the spot they found
was peaceful. A few women were scouring manioc roots
and some small children tumbled about by the river. N'Gio
pulled the girl a little farther and they sat down on the
sand, hidden from the others. N'Gio didn't understand
why, but he suddenly felt shy. He wanted to touch Yawana

but he didn't dare. And yet it seemed such a short time ago that they had played pembele together, the game where you had to tickle the other person's toes to make them laugh. He looked down at the sand and smoothed the area between his legs with his palm. The girl was peeping at him from under long lashes, her arms tight about her knees. At last N'Gio spoke. "Your father and mine have decided to set the date for our wedding. It is planned for very soon."

Yawana had been hoping for this news for some time, and though she stared at him in feigned indifference, it was hard to contain her delight.

"Why aren't you saying anything? You don't look happy about it," N'Gio said in dismay.

"Well, me, or someone else, what can it matter?" she asked. "What you need is a woman to fix your meals. You'll do as your father has done and take other wives. Why should that make me happy?"

N'Gio was taken aback until he caught the gleam of mischief in her dark eyes. He jumped up and pretended to spank her, and they rolled about on the sand with the exuberance of their lost childhood. Yawana struggled a little and just as N'Gio fell on top of her, she lay still, panting. She had never felt so strange. Her whole body seemed to melt into a pool of wild honey.

N'Gio, startled at her sudden passivity, stared at her. She was looking at him so strangely and her smile was so sweet. A feverish flood of desire swept through him. She soon saw his emotion and her hips began to rotate imperceptibly, adding to his embarrassment. He leapt away and she laughed a joyous laugh, rich with triumph. He was humiliated at first, thinking she was making fun of his desire for her, but her eyes reassured him and he was filled with an intense tenderness.

Adende was right, the time for games was indeed over. Yawana stretched out on her back and answered: "Yes, N'Gio, I am very happy that I shall be your wife." Her voice was low and very sweet.

Their glances met and their hands found each other, and no more words were necessary between them. Time fled by. The sky was streaked with deep pink, and darkness found them still sitting on the sand, holding hands. They watched the moon come out and listened for Aduma, the harpist who dwells in the night and plays for the stars to dance. They didn't hear him, but for the first time in their lives they drank in the pure pleasure of silence.

When they reached the village, much later, the men were gathered comfortably around the fire while the women busied themselves with the evening meal. N'Gio joined his father and Isembe, while Yawana ran to help Ivohino and Aziza. Adende held out a gourd of fresh palm wine to his son, and N'Gio drank the pungent liquor with delight. The three men huddled together talking and waiting for the women to bring them their food.

At last Yawana laid huge leaves in front of them. Grilled fish, sweet potatoes, and ground nuts were attractively arranged on them, and Adende, quite carried away by the thought of the realization of his plans, ate, drank, and talked with abandon.

Once the meal was over, each went his separate way. Adende, mildly drunk, sought out Aziza's animal warmth. He lay awake long after he had finished with her. He was pleased with himself for having set the wedding date. The ceremony was planned for the night of the rising moon, and there would be many guests that day. He ceaselessly rolled around in his mind visions of the immense wealth that he would demand from Mouele.

Yawana couldn't sleep either. Stretched out by the side of her parents, her mind dwelt on the moment when she had felt N'Gio's body full on her own, and the extraordinary sensations that had flooded her. She couldn't wait for the wedding day so that she could give herself to him entirely.

N'Gio had kindled a small fire in his hut to keep away the insects, adding a few ritual herbs to ward off the evil spirits of the night. As he stretched out on his mat, he sank into reveries of Yawana. He had never had a woman, and the young girl's response, as well as his own reaction to it, was a revelation to him. He found himself missing his dead mother, Dowani, and wondering if he would have been able to confide in her had she been there. Her death, a short while before, and the strange sickness that had preceded it, had led people to believe that she had eaten something poisonous, but the witch doctor's examination had revealed nothing unusual. N'Gio remembered her funeral. They had turned aside the flow of a stream and dug her grave in the stream's bed. Then they had laid his mother's body in the grave, covered it with sand, and returned the waters of the stream to their course. All had waited for bubbles to break the surface of the water as a sign that the spirit had left the body. Adende had watched to make sure that no spirit thieves were trying to capture the bubbles in a bowl to set them loose in some secret place. The bubbles had ridden away on the stream, carrying Dowani's spirit to infinity, where it would leave the earth to become a rainbow, symbol of eternity. Sleep came to him as he thought of these things and he remembered nothing more until the sun was high the next day.

Yawana spent a few days at Mounigou. She helped her mother care for Isembe and spent the rest of her time with N'Gio. The lovers couldn't get enough of being together and cherished the new discoveries they made about each other. They bathed in the river often, and under the guise of splashing about in the water took every opportunity for touching each other. Each new day brought more daring caresses and more urgent desires.

The beautiful weather held, except for a few brief thunderstorms, so they were able to range the forest in search of lacy mushrooms or pry out huge purple crabs from among the mangrove roots. When they came upon an ant heap, they drummed on it gently like raindrops and the winged ants came hurrying out, only to be caught and eaten with enjoyment by the two young people.

Adende spent many long hours talking with Isembe. The two men drank and smoked together and exchanged memories of times past. At last the day came for Yawana to leave. She and her parents had to return to their village to prepare for the wedding ceremonies and would not come back before then. The morning of Yawana's departure, she and N'Gio strolled along the riverbank, hand in hand, relishing their last moments together.

N'Gio broke the silence. "I'll be a member of the Bwiti in a few days. Don't you think it would be a good idea for you to be initiated into the Ndjembe, since you are to be my wife?"

Yawana's bright face clouded. She had no wish to become part of this women's secret society. "I don't want to, N'Gio. I'm afraid!"

"Come, come, pretty little antelope," N'Gio said tenderly. "Don't be a silly child. Why are you afraid?"

"I don't know. I've heard things about it," said the young girl.

N'Gio burst out laughing. "Nobody has ever died of it, and anyway, when I take my father's place you will be a chief's wife. You have to join the Ndjembe." Yawana reluctantly gave in to his insistence and agreed to talk to her parents about it. It would have to be done before the marriage, for only a virgin could be initiated into the society.

Back at the village, they found Isembe and Ivohino saying good-bye to Adende. Yawana settled the bundle she would carry for the trip home firmly on her head and N'Gio walked with her to the edge of the forest. He watched them disappear around a bend, and slowly retraced his steps.

CHAPTER III

A steady rain drummed on the straw roofs and furrowed the ground, but it was more than the inclement weather that kept the villagers in their huts that morning. The preceding night had been the grand Bwiti celebration and everyone was sleeping off the effects of the wine and the dancing.

N'Gio lay sprawled on his mat in front of a dead fire, the ashes stirring in the breeze. His face and limbs were still streaked with white clay, and he slept the sleep of the dead, exhausted from the combined effect of his emotions during the initiation and the huge amount of the initiation plant, iboga, which he had eaten. He twitched in his sleep from time to time, as if reliving the terrifying rituals which had preceded his initiation. He was probably dreaming of the horrible statue of Bwiti, the star deity, on its base of human skulls, or the scarlet grimacing creature he had seen in the temple.

Adende was not asleep. He stood leaning against his doorpost, watching the rain beat furrows into the earth. Mouele, the Bapounou, had said he would return on this day, and Adende was hoping that the bad weather wouldn't delay him and that they would have time for their talk before the rest of the village awakened. Suddenly the rain ceased and the sun came out, quickly drying the ground. Adende watched the edges of the village with growing anxiety. At last, he saw what he was looking for. A shape slipped out of the forest and sped furtively toward him. He stepped back to allow the man to enter his hut and saw that he was wearing a tiny straw loincloth that barely hid his genitals.

"Where is Mouele?" Adende whispered urgently.

"Follow me. He's waiting."

"But why doesn't he come himself?" Adende asked in consternation. "Why does he want me to go outside in weather like this?"

The other man made an impatient gesture. "It isn't rain-ing anymore," he said, "and Mouele prefers to meet with you outside your own village. He has his reasons."

Adende stole a glance at Aziza, who was still sound asleep. Pulling his loincloth closer about his skinny hips he took his ebony cane and set out, grumbling to himself. To his relief, the village remained asleep even as he followed the man past the last huts and plunged into the forest. Smooth trunks rose steeply to meet the sky, their leaves tangling high above in a dense matting that almost entirely shut out the sunlight. In the undergrowth it was almost night, a mysterious green night streaked with slanted rays from the sun. Adende followed the guide along a path barely wide enough for one foot to follow another. The capricious terrain kept presenting him with a fallen trunk here, a rock there, or he had to leap over an army of ants advancing relentlessly. Soon they left the trail and entered a patch of thick, twisted vegetation. Out of long habit, Adende broke twigs at intervals so that he would be able to find his way back. The split wood was a gleaming white marker which allowed him to see his route clearly in the dark forest. At last the two men came to a clearing where Mouele was waiting under a leafy shelter set up against the heavy rains. He rose when he saw Adende and they greeted each other with a marked lack of enthusiasm.

"Well? Did you decide?" asked the Bapounou without preamble.

Adende swelled with pride. "I've arranged it all," he said. "It was easy to persuade Isembe and his wife that the time has come for their daughter to marry N'Gio. Only we shall have to respect tradition and wait for the next rising moon. The marriage will take place on the day when the moon will be half-circle, and I can promise you many guests. I hope you are satisfied."

Mouele leered at him. "Well done, old chief," he said. "When it's all over and done with you'll get your reward, I can promise you that!"

Adende had been hoping for a gift, and was disappointed to note that no hampers were lying about in the clearing.

"We'd better separate now," said the Bapounou. "I don't want anyone to see me in these parts. We can meet here again on the day of the wedding to discuss the last details and settle the time." Then without waiting for a word of farewell, Mouele rose swiftly and slipped away, followed by his messenger, leaving Adende somewhat distressed.

The old chief sat on, alone, for a little while before he rose to find his way back to the village. It seemed to him that Mouele had been rather distant, but he supposed that was unimportant. Soon he would own many wonders that would make him the greatest chief in the entire region. As he reached the first huts, he observed that he was none too soon. A few women were about, seeing to their tasks. Adende strode into his hut and shook Aziza awake.

CHAPTER IV

Yawana stared disconsolately at the banana plantation through the only opening in the hut. She had been confined there for several days with two other girls who were about to be married. All were to be initiated. They were only allowed out at night, for they were to be seen by no man. Their only contact with the outside world was an old woman who brought them food, and more food. All three awaited the following night with trepidation, for it was to be the last night of the Ndjembe, the last trial which would open the secrets of the society to them. They had heard many whispered tales of what would come to pass and they were afraid. The three girls were nude except for two banana leaves tied at their waists. Yawana took a fruit and began to eat. It was the only thing she had to do since she had subjected herself to this voluntary captivity, and her shape had begun to fill out from the inactivity and the abundance of food.

"What do you think the priestesses will do to us tonight? Oh! I can't bear it any longer!" cried Dowe, tears welling in her eyes.

"I don't know," said Yawana, "but do not cry. It couldn't be worse than what we have endured so far."

Yawana had been the bravest of the three during the nights of trial. Dowe still bore the marks of one of her trials. One of her hands was swollen, the arm partly paralyzed. The girls had been led, their eyes covered, to the foot of the engokom, the tree of ants. There they had had to grab one of those voracious insects between fingers, and since poor Dowe had been clumsier than the others she had been bitten and the bite had become infected. Another night, the girls had had to endure ritual incisions on the insides of their thighs, and they had also been whipped with nettles. Many things had been done to them to test their resistance to pain.

This day crawled by slowly. Yawana regretted having agreed to be initiated into the Ndjembe, but there was little she could do about it since N'Gio desired it. Already, he

could command her to do as he pleased. Her thoughts
turned to him, and she forgot her fears in happy anticipation of their marriage. She never imagined that the father
of her future husband had plotted to turn that day of joy
into a tragedy that would drag them all into horror and
despair.

The entrance of the Grand Priestess roused her from her
reverie. The priestess was old and withered, as feared as
she was respected by the other villagers. Everyone hated
her, for she was bitter and unkind. Her followers came in
behind her and Dowe let out a moan, knowing that the
time had come. "You are afraid!" exclaimed the Grand
Priestess with evil delight. "Come now! Stop sniveling. It's
time to get ready."

Young Dowe always received the worst treatment because her parents were not rich enough to make large con-
tributions demanded by the Grand Priestess. Even though
her parents had given generous gifts on all occasions, Yawana also received many of the old woman's unwelcome
attentions. The old priestess resented her startling beauty.

"Purify your impure bodies, my girls," continued the
woman, "and then we shall prepare you for the ceremony."

Yawana, always the first, enjoyed her bathing. She
sprayed her whole body with gleaming water and then
carefully rinsed out her mouth as the other women watched
her critically. One of them immediately proceeded to dry
her with a bundle of grasses, while the other two initiates
began their baths.

Outside, day had begun to fade as the three girls were
given a bitter liquid to drink. Yawana grimaced but drank
it up, and she soon felt herself in a new state of consciousness. Sights and sounds took on new and vivid meaning
and her senses tingled. The women then tied wooden bells
about her wrists and ankles and a fringe of pandanus leaves
around her waist. Yawana, in a state of calm euphoria, let
them busy themselves about her body. All her fears had
vanished with the drink. She let them weave green and red
touraco plumes into her hair, and place a crown of ivy on
her head.

The Grand Priestess left the girls alone. Dowe, as if by
magic, had lost all her terrors and was joking and giggling.
The other girl seemed to have fallen into a languorous

dream. Yawana felt a strange sensation take possession of her body, almost like when N'Gio took her in his arms.

When night had fully fallen, a bright light illuminated the banana plantation and two long lines of women bearing resin torches came to either side of the hut's opening. They called to the young girls to come out; Yawana was the first to step out into the night and stand between the two rows of light. The procession moved ahead slowly through the deserted village. Nobody was about, almost as if they were afraid to see. Yawana was in a dreamlike state. The torch bearers sang a low rhythmic chant as they moved into the forest, where their voices echoed in the silence. Their light danced among the trees and made them look terrifying. At last they came to a large clearing surrounded by arum lilies with spotted leaves. A fire burned in the center of the clearing around an earth cone which contained the Supreme Talisman. Yawana noticed that all the women were attired as she was.

Suddenly the Grand Priestess appeared. She was completely naked and there was something macabre about her skeletal body with its sagging breasts. The three girls were pushed toward the earth cone and the others gathered around them. Gourds were passed from one to the other and everyone drank deep of their contents. The Grand Priestess threw a few magic herbs on the flame and sparks flew up. Immediately the drums began to beat and the wild vanilla-root strings on the harps began to vibrate slowly, counterpointing the relentless heavy throb of the wooden drums. The women began to sway slowly and Yawana understood that this was the Bolo, the wild dance where men were forbidden. Her body began to twist with the others as though no longer in her control. Her torso communicated the movement to her legs and feet, setting the bells in motion. All the dancers swayed together, moving in unison to the beat of the music. Dust clouds rose about them, giving the scene a phantasmagoric quality.

Then one of the women began a profane, hoarse-voiced chant glorifying the act of love and the male and female genitals. When she reached the end of the chant she flung off her loincloth and shook her naked body as her voice screamed out the obscene words "Konga, he Konga,!" Yawana found herself answering "Makonga he!" with the others.

The cry seemed to unleash a wild frenzy in the assembled women. Yawana forgot herself. The women were tearing off their loincloths and she found herself feverishly following suit as if to give herself to a lover. Freed of restraining garments, her body leapt and twisted to the call of the music. The firelight gleamed on her sweating skin as she moved in the lascivious dance. Soon, the movements became more hysterical. Hands brushed against her skin, becoming more and more insistent in their caresses. Soon there were lips, too. Tongues searched in her mouth and hands felt for her waist and breasts. There seemed to be more and more of them as the dance accelerated, and soon her passivity gave way to a feverishly aggressive sensuality and she returned the caresses of all who came within her reach. The music entered her, deeper and deeper. The dance had become a whirlwind. Hands reached for the most private parts of her body, and she took a wild pleasure in their touch and began to scream out obscenities she didn't even understand. At one moment, some of the women rushed toward a dark edge of the clearing and seemed to be chasing and cursing a man who had tried to spy on their ceremonies. They were like hellcats.

The ritual dance continued into the dawn hours, and only then did the music cease. The fire was now a mass of dull coals. One of the women took Yawana's hand and led her to the center of the circle, where she made her kneel. Two other women then brought in a catfish, still leaping on its wicker screen, and the Grand Priestess sacrificed this on the cone of earth as a symbol of the fetus and the propagation of life, to the accompaniment of hysterical shrieks. She threw the pieces of white fish meat on the fire and passed in front of the neophytes, stopping a moment in front of each. When her turn came, Yawana felt, from the depths of her delirium, that her head was being pushed forward and her mouth pressed against the vagina of the Grand Priestess. The initiation was over. Drained in body and soul, Yawana fell to the ground in a faint, her body streaming with sweat.

When she came to her senses again, the day was already well on its way out. She was lying in her own hut and her mother was leaning over her washing her face with cool water. Yawana looked at her, and Ivohino gazed back with a mixture of gravity and anxiety. The girl smiled up at her and the mother lost her worried look. Yawana hadn't really understood much of what had happened to her the night before. In fact all she could remember of the wild ceremonies was a vague feeling of pleasure that somehow embarrassed her.

The next few days were spent preparing for the wedding. For Yawana it was a time of enchantment that almost made her forget her melancholy at the idea of leaving her little village of Ombala forever. Everyone made a fuss over her and prepared to represent the tribe with dignity at the approaching festivities.

At last came the day for the grand departure. The preparations had become feverish, as some women had gathered together food for the journey, while others wove skirts from straw or stripped bark from which to fashion loincloths. The men had carefully wrapped their gifts in palm leaves and made sure that they had with them everything necessary for a journey of several days. When they were all assembled in the small clearing at the center of the village, Isembe looked them over to make sure that each man had his assegai, his bow, and his jet knife. It didn't seem likely that there would be an attack, but it was always best to be prepared. Ivohino also went around checking to make sure that nothing had been forgotten. Everyone was in a high state of excitement at the thought of the approaching festivities, and the clucking of hens tied in bunches by their feet and the terrified neighing of goats dragged by children mingled with the steady hum of conversation.

Yawana was proud of being the cause of so much excitement. She waited impatiently for the signal to depart. As soon as her father motioned the group to start on its way she heaved a huge sigh of relief. The women bent to pick up their bundles and poised them on their heads, or let them hang against their backs from a leather thong tied about their foreheads. Small groups gathered and left the village, watched sadly by those too old or too weak to make the journey.

They soon came to the banks of the nearby river, where great rafts made of tree trunks were tied to posts on the shore. Isembe had supervised the building of the rafts. The heavy rains made the trails impossible for his heavily loaded tribesmen to travel. Even if the river voyage took longer, it would not tire them as much, for the village of

Mounigou was only a half day's march from the landing
site.

The hampers were firmly bound to the floor of a raft and
placed so that children could be safely sheltered among
them. Then the goats were tied to posts. Yawana scrambled
onto Isembe's raft with her mother and settled down in the
center. As soon as everyone had piled onto the rafts, men
armed with long poles pushed them out into the river, one
by one.

The narrow river was very muddy and the navigators
needed a sure skill to steer the rafts between the banks.
Isembe, whose raft led the way, was doubled over his long
pole as he circumvented a sand bank or avoided tree trunks
which had been uprooted by the recent storms and drifted
on the current. At the beginning of the ride, men and
women called gaily to each other, and the riverbanks
echoed with sounds of laughter and happy voices. Then
they calmed down and one by one fell silent. Yawana was
too busy watching over the children to notice the forest
that passed majestically in front of them as they floated
down the river. The glaring sun had become very hot, making the travelers sleepy. The day passed without incident.
In the evening, the river had widened and the current was
not so turbulent. Isembe decided to press on. The men took
turns watching over the rafts, their only guide the narrow
ribbon of sky that ran between the towering borders of
trees on the riverbanks.

It was dawn when Yawana awoke.

"It won't be long now," said Isembe. "I know where we
are."

Yawana fed the children and chewed pensively on a
small piece of smoked meat. She was anxious to get there.
The journey was tiring and uncomfortable.

About midmorning, Isembe caught sight of the place he
had been looking for. He shouted orders and the men began to wield their poles with vigor. The rafts turned in a
semicircle and came to rest on a sand bank in the crook of
the river.

Yawana jumped ashore and helped the children climb
down. As soon as everything had been unloaded from the
rafts, they were left to float on the stream. A clear trail
stretched ahead of them. The ground was well-trodden and
dry and Yawana, delighted to be on the move, headed the

procession with her father. She had been allowed to carry only light bundles, articles of clothing for the wedding ceremony.

A few hours later, they came to a clearing where they set up camp for the next few nights. It was close to Mounigou, and Isembe had picked it as a suitable spot for them to spend the night. Huge fires were lit and shelters were built with surprising speed. Posts were dug into the ground for the goats and everyone settled down as best they could. Yawana was exhausted by the long, tedious journey. She lay down and was soon fast asleep.

CHAPTER V

The bush pheasant's cry, dull as the pealing of a cracked wooden bell, rang out again and again, announcing to all forest dwellers that day had arrived, warning the animals to silence until the stars again took their appointed places in the night sky. Only furtive footsteps, branches shaken by clowning monkeys, or the desperate race of a hunted antelope would break the heavy silence of the day, perhaps followed by a wild snarl, a short-lived cry of agony, and the crunching of bones in a leopard's maw.

Ivohino rose and padded softly to her daughter. Yawana pretended sleep, but her mother was not fooled. "Get up at once," she said, "or I'll give you a good hiding. Don't forget you are still my daughter."

Yawana decided to open her eyes and pretend to believe her mother's threat. She smiled at the older women and jumped up from the leafy bed, stretching long and voluptuously. She was fully conscious of the consummate grace of her movements and the beauty of the body which she would soon give to N'Gio. "What a beautiful day!" she exclaimed.

"Yes, yes," muttered Ivohino, making fun of her, "A beautiful day." "But now you must bathe yourself. And hurry. I have to do your hair and help you to get ready."

Hand in hand, the two women headed for the stream that burbled close by. Dawn was spreading a pale silvery cloak across the early-morning sky as they climbed down the gully to the clear water below. They squatted in the water and rubbed themselves vigorously with sand, rinsing out their mouths several times before returning to the encampment.

The icy water had awakened all Yawana's senses and she felt exhilarated. Everyone was up by the time she and Ivohino returned to the camp. The men were scratching themselves or cleaning their teeth with bits of wood while their wives were poking at the ashes to prepare fires for the morning meal. The two women were greeted by happy cries and they ran to join Isembe. Ivohino quickly prepared

her family's meal and with a pleased smile watched Yawana eat heartily. Yawana was hungry; she knew that this
would be her only meal until the feast that would follow
the ceremony, and that was likely to be late in the evening.

As soon as Yawana finished eating, Ivohino set her
down on a tree stump so she could reach her head more
easily and pulled open one of the bundles that held her hair-
dressing equipment. She carefully picked through her
daughter's hair to get rid of any lurking lice, and then she
massaged in some buffalo grease. Next, she separated the
hair into small mounds, which she braided. Finally, she
pulled the braids tight and brought them together to form a
helmet on top of her daughter's head. "Ow! You're hurting!" moaned Yawana. She had no way of knowing that
her mother was having difficulty hiding her emotion and
that by tugging at her and treating her roughly, she was
able to hide her sadness at the thought that her daughter
would soon be leaving her forever. She topped off her
handiwork with ivory pins and circled it with a crown of
blue touraco feathers. Then she stepped back to admire her
creation.

"You look beautiful," she said softly. "N'Gio will be
pleased." Yawana did look beautiful. Although she could
not see herself, one glance at her mother's expression told
her all she needed to know.

Ivohino, satisfied at last, made her daughter stand up
and smoothed her whole body with a scented oil, massaging gently until it soaked in. "Now listen to what I have to
tell you," she said, her voice shaking slightly. "The Woumbou clan that N'Gio belongs to has its own rites. You may
have to do certain things and follow certain customs during
the ceremony which will seem strange to you. But you
must accept it all and do as you are told." Then her mother
told her all that would probably happen, but Yawana, lost
in her own reverie of happiness, hardly listened at all. Her
mind was focused entirely on the moment she most longed
for, when N'Gio would take her. She hoped he would do it
with tender mastery. Although she was a virgin, the widespread promiscuity in her village had shown her the gestures of lovemaking and the intense pleasure they gave, and
now that she was about to experience this pleasure, she was
brimming with impatience.

Once the soothing oil had been absorbed by Yawana's

skin, Ivohino busied herself tying a tiger-skin loincloth about her daughter's waist, leaving her breasts uncovered. She took some sweet-smelling herbs and tucked them into Yawana's hair and behind her ears, slipping ivory and gold bracelets, heirlooms from her own mother, onto the girl's wrists and ankles. She finished by placing a leopard-skin necklace with a fertility talisman around her daughter's neck. Yawana was ready. All this time, her father had been busy devising a stretcher from a huge bamboo branch, with a seat made of intertwined vines.

It was time to move on. Yawana, heavy with adornments, climbed into the chair with her father's help, and two men grabbed the bamboo branch and placed it on grass cushions on their heads. Everyone picked up their bundles and Isembe led them on. An hour later the travelers could hear voices and smell the scent of wood fires. In moments they could see straw roofs through the banana plantation. Isembe signaled for the procession to stop. Yawana stepped down from her chair and everyone stood waiting for the signal that would inform the young girl that she could enter the village to become N'Gio's chosen bride.

The Mounigou village had also risen very early. Fires were still smoldering, and blue wisps of smoke hung just above the ground. A line of women were on their way to the river, empty gourds dangling from their arms. Their graceful silhouettes disappeared around a bend in the trail, and their cheerful chatter faded. They were probably giggling about lewd Ombwiri, who was supposed to dwell in the huge kapok tree and who sometimes attacked women passing his lair.

Soon the children appeared and filled the village with their games and shouts as they waited for the morning meal that the women prepared when they returned from the river. Old, wrinkled women crept out of the farthermost huts and began to sweep the compound, chasing hens and pigs in all directions. They worked silently, bent double, their limp breasts swinging with their movements.

N'Gio was awakened by the children's voices. He jumped up from his mat and scratched at the insect bites, yawned, stretched, and squashed a centipede with his heel, glancing at the silvery trail it had left on the floor of the hut. Then he slipped the bark door-hanging aside and stepped out into the gathering place. His father's house was already open. The old chief was sitting cross-legged on his mat, drinking, a grumpy look on his face. Aziza, curled in her corner, was still sound asleep.

Adende had slept badly. He had not been disturbed by any scruples, but merely by the excitement and anticipation of concluding the deal he had planned so carefully. He was impatient and couldn't quite suppress the anxiety that gnawed at him.

"Good morning, Tato," said the young man.

"Good morning, N'Gio," returned his father. "Would you like some palm wine?"

"No," said the young man, "it's still too early for me. I'll go and bathe and then get ready."

"N'Gio!" exclaimed the father suddenly. N'Gio turned and looked inquiringly at him. "N'Gio, I've been thinking," the old man continued. "After the ceremony you should take your bride over to the hunting camp across the river. You'd have more privacy there."

N'Gio looked puzzled. "No, Tato," he replied, "I'd rather stay with all my friends. They wouldn't understand if we slipped away before the festivities are over."

"That really doesn't matter," scoffed Adende. "They'll never even notice that you're gone."

The young man protested vehemently, "We couldn't do that. Yawana wouldn't want to do that to her family and friends either. They've come a long way for these festivities. Perhaps we can go across the river after it's over." He turned and hurried away without noticing the flash of fear that crossed his father's wrinkled face. Even if he had noticed, he would not have understood it. Adende realized that however much he insisted, his son would not want to change his plans.

The sun streamed through the branches and bathed the clearing in light. The women were filing back from their trip to the river with full gourds of water and they smiled as they passed the young man. The young ones threw brazen glances at him. N'Gio answered their greetings absently, hurrying toward the river where he found the other men. He liked to be alone when he washed himself and he slipped along a trail edged with rosebushes to the riverside, where the tall trees dwindled into mangroves. Pulling off his loincloth, he leapt into the water. The water, swollen by the recent rains, had a brackish taste. He reveled in the feel of the cool liquid against his flesh, and watched a duck drying off its wings as it perched on a dead tree stump while small creatures darted about in the high grass. N'Gio was bursting with happiness. The beautiful Yawana was to be his wife this evening and he shivered with joy at the thought of making her his own. At last he paddled back to the bank and strode toward the village.

The village was in turmoil. Everyone was hurrying about their tasks preparing for the evening's festivities. The hides, hung on the walls to dry out, had all been removed and hidden away, and carved masks, grinning and smooth with age, adorned the doors. Nobody knew anymore who had sculpted them. They had been part of the tribe's heritage since living memory. They were made of soft and hard woods painted red and black, encrusted with bits of metal or covered with a thin layer of bronze. Some were attached to mysterious talismans with unknown powers. N'Gio beamed when he saw them, for they were certain harbingers of some major event. They were not dance masks, nor were they supposed to accompany merrymaking. They were brought out for wars and other important occasions, and N'Gio remembered once having asked Moussavou what they meant.

"They have great power," the witch doctor had said. "Those masks represent obscure gods and are linked with the forces that govern the invisible world. You must never offend them." N'Gio had been enormously impressed by these warnings and had asked how long the masks had been in the village. The witch doctor answered solemnly: "Nobody knows. Perhaps we could know if we read the parchment of silence hidden in the sky, but that is a secret one should not try to discover." N'Gio had been even more puzzled, and had not understood that Moussavou's obscure answers were intended merely to mask his own ignorance.

The ground in front of the temple had been swept clear, and a huge area had been prepared for the feast. Large mats were spread on the ground around a mound of dry wood ready for lighting.

There was still time, so N'Gio drifted to the corner of the village where the food was being prepared. Every single one of Mounigou's pots and other cooking utensils had been gathered in one place. Drawn by the appetizing aroma drifting from them, N'Gio stepped cautiously to-

ward the earthenware cooking pots sitting on the flat stones
before the houses. Some women were cutting up meat, others were scraping vegetables or grating palm nuts. Isengo,
whose great skill equaled her great age, was busily melting
lamantin fat. As soon as it began to sputter, she dropped in
pieces of pork and sprinkled them with salt.

"Good morning, Isengo," N'Gio said politely. "Mmm!
That smells good!"

The old woman nodded her greeting and wielded her
spatula, turning the pieces of meat as they browned.
"You'll have a magnificent feast!" she said, grinning toothlessly.

"Have you thought of the ancestors?" asked the young
man.

She waved her stick at a small pot bubbling in a corner.
"There you are," she said. "There's meat, fish, and bananas
for them. As soon as it's ready the children will take it and
pour it onto the tombs."

"Ah!" exclaimed N'Gio, relieved, "that's good, Isengo.
Their souls will be appeased and everything will go well."
He noticed the uncertain gait of the old woman and teased
her: "Did you drink too much palm wine this morning?"

She was suddenly angry and raised her stick. "The
kitchen is no place for men!" she screeched, pretending to
strike out at him, "and particularly not for urchins like
you. You'd better go and get ready."

N'Gio ran off laughing, and the other women joined in
teasing Isengo. She was furious and grumbled vague threats
as the young man left. It was indeed time to get ready.
Soon the guests would arrive.

Once back in his hut, he took off his loincloth and
scrubbed his body with mangrove bark to prevent scabies
and lice, as he did every morning. Then he boarded up the
entrance to his hut and began to get ready in the dim light.

CHAPTER VI

"Ten fathoms . . . twelve fathoms!"

The sailor chanted monotonously, counting the depth from the plumb line as he leaned over the prow. Next to him, another sailor repeated the information for the benefit of the man on the bridge.

"Seven fathoms . . . watch it! Sand bank right ahead!"

The helmsman wrenched the wheel sharply to starboard, missed the reef, and straightened the ship. The huge three-masted vessel had tacked all night, waiting for the tide, and was now slipping through the shoals at the entrance to the lagoon. Her sails were furled to make the approach easier and at last, slowly, she entered the lagoon, her stem cutting clearly through the small yellowish waves. The ship's silhouette was etched starkly against the low dark clouds that seemed to be resting on the tops of the trees, presaging stormy weather.

The low bank lay drowned in early-morning mist, its curves obscured by stretches of papyrus plants and sprawling mangrove roots. A few fishermen's huts squatted in the tall grass. The whole area was quiet and peaceful this early in the day. A few native canoes glided alongside the banks, drawn by sails of woven leaves. A few pelicans in the tall trees were fluffing their feathers in search of lice and an occasional white flash announced the presence of an egret as it fell like a stone past the sails and flew up again, a quivering silvery prey in its beak.

The ship moved on a little, weaving through small islands until it finally hove to and dropped anchor near a tiny promontory. *The Sea Witch,* frigate of the Royal African Company, was a three-hundred-ton vessel. She pulled on her anchorage and floated on her bulging hull as the Union Jack, the three crosses of Saint Andrew, Saint George, and Saint Patrick, ran up the main mast and fluttered at her prow.

The crew members warily took up battle positions. The gun crew had lifted the portholes and were grinding out the guns slowly, dark menacing mouths protruding toward the

shore, while the sailor in the top mast scrutinized the promontory with painful concentration.

Suddenly Jonathan Collins, captain of the vessel, appeared
on deck. He was a young man, taller than any of his officers. Leaning on the deck rail he took a good look at the
new country before him. The officers and crew followed
suit, gripped by a strange unease.

The storm was blowing toward the east and the cool
wind had given way to heavy, humid heat. The brilliance of
the day seemed to have flattened out the countryside, elimi-
nating contrasts and giving it a monotonous gray look. On
the port side of the ship, the lagoon narrowed and fed into
the mouth of a big river. A lesser chain of mountains but-
tressed a steep mountain range to the south.

Captain Collins, silent and immobile on the deck, found
himself thinking that it seemed a joyless, depressing country. The river ahead rose steeply toward the Portuguese
outpost and he could glimpse a small fort built to withstand
attack from native tribes, its walls made of baked mud and
fortified by bamboo stakes. Protruding from it was a large
gun, its mouth pointed toward the ship. The entire enclave
was surrounded by a stake fence, beside which plants and
flowers had proliferated, softening the menacing structure.
One corner held a lookout post, but it seemed as if the
conical structure had no one in it. There were other struc-
tures on the left, also stockaded, while the banana leaves
and palm fronds waved gently in the distance.

A path led from the fort to the dock where a few canoes
were moored. Only the distant crow of a cock pierced the
intense silence of the place and announced the presence of
living creatures.

Jonathan Collins pulled a small gold snuffbox from his
waistcoat pocket, carefully laid a pinch of snuff on the back
of his hand, and sniffed it up his nose. He was very puzzled. The post's obvious inactivity worried him. He was
tired from the journey and dreaded complications. Turning
to his first mate, a tall red-headed lad with an alert expression who was surveying the bank with his spyglass, he
asked, "Do you see something, Mr. Adams?"

"Not a living soul, sir," said Gregory Adams, calmly
continuing to sweep the countryside with his spyglass. "Are
you sure the fort is still in use?"

"Quite sure," said Jonathan Collins. "I have it from our

shipowners that it's one of the best outposts in the territory. We'd have been sent word if it had been abandoned."

"It looks as though they're all dead, then," said the other.

Jonathan grinned. "You mean they're all dead drunk," he retorted. A shadow of doubt had begun to cross his mind. He turned and called, "Tell the lookout to let us know if he sees anyone there."

Adams hurried off and was back at his side in no time. "Nothing, sir," he said. "The lookout can't see a soul either, but he thinks there's a column of smoke."

"Very well," said Jonathan. "Tell the men to shoot a round of musket fire at the walls. That'll wake them up if they're asleep. The men are not to leave their combat posts, and tell the gun crew to hold ready to fire a salvo. If we don't get any reaction to the muskets we'll see if the cannons will get a rise out of them, and if that doesn't work either, we'll have to go over there and see what they're up to."

Gregory barked out the orders and ten sailors gathered on the foredeck. Jonathan was anxious to avoid any risks. The fort's garrison might be asleep, but there was always a possibility that they had all been massacred. This was a land of savages and there was no knowing what might have befallen them. Many an incautious ship had paid for impulsive action with the lives of its crew. Jonathan knew that it would not be pleasant to fall into the hands of savages.

A sharp order was shouted and a volley of gunfire rang out, stirring up billows of dust about the fort's walls. Men appeared immediately. The turrets were suddenly bristling with muskets.

"Black or white?" Jonathan asked.

"White," said Gregory, his eyes glued to the spyglass. He handed the instrument to Jonathan. "Here, see for yourself, Captain."

Captain Collins took the glass and counted about twenty men at arms lining the upper ramparts of the fort. He was relieved to see that they were white men, not because he feared a fight with the natives who could do little against his trained sailors and fortified ship, but because he had business to transact and no time to waste in fighting. He could not afford to return without his cargo of slaves. The Portuguese fort had been recommended to him as one of the best on the coast and he knew that if the inhabitants had been massacred, he would have had to drag along the shore for weeks, perhaps months, trying to fill his quota. His shipowners were expecting a good cargo. They had little patience for manpower losses and less for expensive expeditions.

"Show the colors," ordered Jonathan.

The observers on the fort sent out a cheer as they saw the Portuguese flag run up the halyard. Clearly, these were friends, and the delight of the fort's occupants was echoed in the sailors who rejoiced that they would at last be able to land without fearing for their lives.

"Mr. Adams, leave half the men from the starboard watch where they are and have the rest get the boat ready before they take a rest," ordered Jonathan. "I'm going down to my cabin to change, because unless I'm much mistaken, we can expect visitors. Tell the other officers to come to me there when they've washed and shaved. No one is to leave the ship without my express permission."

"Yes sir!" Gregory said smartly. But Jonathan had already turned his back and was soon bending his head to enter his cabin. It was a large cabin, and his taste for comfort had led him to furnish it as luxuriously as possible. One corner held a huge chest ringed with iron. A long table with silver candlesticks filled the center of the room. A mahogany desk stood in an alcove with shelves all around, a map table laden with navigational instruments beside it. A large armchair, some wooden chairs, an iron bedstead, and a low chest made up the rest of the furnishings.

Jonathan loved his cabin. It was his refuge. Son of a noble family, he had completed his studies brilliantly, and had entered the Royal Navy, where he was assured a rapid rise. Nothing in his background prepared him for the vile trade he was now engaged in. Unhappily, his affair with Aurelia, an admiral's wife, had ruined his career. They had met during a royal hunt. She was much younger than her husband, and her dazzling, fragile beauty had completely captivated Jonathan. He saw her often, and their affair might long have continued in secret if Aurelia had not made the mistake of telling her best friend about it. Aurelia's best friend turned out to be her husband's mistress, and as such was delighted to cause trouble between husband and wife. She triumphantly told her lover all about his wife's infidelity. The admiral, an illegitimate son of the Elector of Hanover and a lady-in-waiting to the Queen, which made him half brother to King George I, had seen to it that Jonathan was ignominiously banished from the Royal Navy. His very life would have been in jeopardy had not the King himself intervened. The incident left him destitute on the pavements of Liverpool, without a future, rejected by his mistress. The offer of the command of a slave vessel had been miraculous. The shipowners were not too particular about the backgrounds of the officers they hired as long as they knew how to captain a vessel and were good navigators. The Royal African Company did not like to lose money. It was not prepared to risk the sale at auction of an entire vessel complete with valuable cargo, as had happened to a French ship whose captain had only the vaguest notion how to navigate.

While Jonathan was changing, two sailors came in with a red copper bathtub, into which they poured large buckets of steaming water. While they were filling it up, Jonathan stared at himself pensively in the mirror. His light blue eyes stood out in startling contrast to his smooth face, marked now by the life of adventure he had led for the past three years as captain of *The Sea Witch*. Although he was only thirty-eight, silver hairs graced his temples and added to the look of distinction that made him irresistible to women.

The sailors left and Jonathan slipped his large sinewy body into the soapy water. He closed his eyes, savoring the relaxing heat of the bath. This was his second trip to Africa, and he hoped it would be his last. His earlier trip had taken him from the Gulf of Guinea to the island of Jamaica. The wind had helped him on like a steady friendly hand, and it had been an uneventful journey. Since Britain had signed the Triple Alliance Pact with France and Holland, dangerous encounters on the high seas had lessened considerably, except for those with the Spaniards, with whom the British were at war. There had been few losses of either crew or cargo, and sales had been so good that he had returned to England with a hold crammed with sugar.

This time his contract was bringing him to the Gabon, where agreements had been made with the Portuguese who had settled this part of Africa. Jonathan's assignment was to take on as many slaves as possible and ship them to

Louisiana, the new French colony whose tobacco planters were desperate for slave help on their plantations.

Soon after contracting for this expedition, Jonathan had decided it would be his last. He hated the trade that his ill fortune had made necessary, and now that he envisioned having some money, he planned to settle down far from the country where so many friends had turned away from him at the moment of his greatest need. His own family had disowned him because of the nature of his work. The slave trade was widely accepted and considered a fairly normal occupation, and the Liverpool shipping companies, London banks, or Lancashire industrialists involved in it were not frowned upon. They were accepted into society, but nobody wanted anything to do with the captains of the slave ships, whom they considered the dregs of humanity. Jonathan's life had taken such a negative turn that his only hope was to start a new one in a distant land where nobody knew him.

He climbed out of the tub, dried himself, and shaved. The temperature in the cabin was pleasant, with a fresh breeze coming through the open portholes. He daubed on some eau de cologne and vigorously rubbed himself all over. Tying back his long blond locks with a ribbon, he pulled on white linen trousers, boots of supple black leather, and an eggshell open-necked shirt. He had barely finished buttoning the cuffs when there was a knock at the door and Pierre, the ship's French cook, came in to get his orders. Pierre was a small man, round and somewhat childish, with a bald pate and a small mustache. His chubby hands fluttered about rapidly as he spoke. Pierre had joined the merchant vessel as a result of mysterious circumstances which Jonathan had thought it wiser not to investigate. His cooking was excellent and that was enough. Jonathan also enjoyed Pierre's inimitable accent and the amusing twist this gave to the simplest phrases.

"Pierre, I shall probably be having a guest for dinner," the captain said, "and Mr. Adams will undoubtedly join us. Can you scramble something good together? Wines, too?"

Pierre bowed, a bright smile illuminating his face. He loved Captain Collins, whom he considered very kind, and a real connoisseur of fine cuisine. He had never told him that he had left France in a hurry because he had taken a cleaver and killed the owner of the inn at Honfleur where he had been cook. The innkeeper had dared to make a remark about some inadequacy in the sauces and Pierre had not considered the reprimand deserved.

The small round man was sweating profusely. "You can count on me, Captain," he said. "There is still enough food to make a feast fit for a king."

"I'm sure you can do it, Pierre," said Jonathan.

Pierre hurried back to his pots and pans. He had barely stepped out of the captain's cabin when Gregory came in. He had changed and shaved, and brought with him three men who were clearly not crew sailors.

"Gentlemen," said Jonathan as they came in, "we are finally here. I do thank you most heartily for all your help and I thought we could drink a toast together to celebrate our arrival."

A cheer greeted his suggestion and the cabin boy, who had followed the officers in, filled the glasses with wine from Málaga and passed them around. Jonathan lifted his glass and announced, "Gentlemen, I drink to our journey home."

"The King!" returned the others simultaneously.

"Hm. Well, if that's the way you want it," muttered Jonathan, who felt that the King was in fact responsible for many of his own problems. "The King!" he repeated, not wanting to seem to dispute the loyalties of his staff.

The five men drained their glasses and held them out to the cabin boy, who refilled them.

Jonathan sat at the table and gestured to the rest of them to join him. "I'm expecting the captain of the garrison to have dinner here. I'm sure he'll turn up any minute," he said. He turned his head to look at Gregory and continued. "You'll stay with me. As for the rest of you, I must ask you to be sure to do everything I tell you." He drained his second glass.

"Now, Doctor," he said, "how many sick people do we have on board?"

Simon MacLean turned in response. He came from Glasgow, from a poor but respectable family. He had boarded *The Sea Witch* on his twenty-second birthday in the hope that his savings would enable him to finish his medical studies. He had not had time to learn much about medicine and knew even less about surgery, but Jonathan had been impressed with him, and with the doctor's bag he had spent the last of his meager savings to buy. Jonathan had been aware of his lack of experience and had worried about it, but a good ship's doctor for a slave vessel was almost impossible to find and he had had to make do with the earnest young man. MacLean had spent most of the journey in an absentminded haze, his head buried in his books except when Jonathan made him fill in the log.

"No sir," the young man said, shaking his blond mane, "nobody sick except for a few cases of colic."

"Well, I hope that lasts," Jonathan sighed. "We may have some epidemics on the way back. I want you to examine all the men, and see that they wash. You must never forget that from the moment we set out, the life of a slave on this ship is more important than the life of a sailor."

Simon nodded eagerly, intent on winning the five-hundred-pound bonus paid to ships' doctors who managed to keep the death rate among the cargo to a minimum, even at the expense of the crew.

The captain turned to the other two. One of them, John Woolcomb, was the chief petty officer. He was a giant of a man, bearded and taciturn. This was the first time he had sailed further than the Bristol Channel. The other, William Clark, gunnery officer, was a rough lad, but kind. It was his first time aboard a ship, but he was skillful when it came to pointing a gun.

"As for you, gentlemen," Jonathan continued, "it's up to you to clean this ship and make all repairs before we load up for the return journey. The gun crew should always be ready in case of attack. This country is full of ambushes, and don't be fooled by the fact that this has been an uneventful voyage so far. You'll see that the rest of this trip will be no picnic. We may have mutinies on board or attacks to repel. Go to it!"

Jonathan rose, indicating that he had finished, and the officers left, except for Gregory, who stayed on, a questioning look on his face.

"I'm counting on you, Gregory, to keep an eye on those rascals," concluded the captain. "They're good men, but they lack experience."

Jonathan always called his first mate by his first name when they were alone. Gregory Adams was the only person he trusted. Like himself, Gregory was an old Royal Navy man, but he had left the navy of his own free will, finding it far more profitable to engage in the slave trade than to manage on the pittance he received from the royal purse.

The two men chatted quietly for a while, until a sailor came to tell them that a boat had left the shore and was heading toward the ship.

CHAPTER VII

There was not a cloud in the sky when Jonathan and Gregory stepped out on deck. The crew was assembled, leaning against the railings watching the maneuvers of a long canoe as it approached the vessel. The canoe was manned by about a dozen black men wearing nothing but light cloths about their waists. They were paddling to the solemn rhythm of a chant repeated again and again. Three white men were sitting in the center of the boat, but they were too far away for the intent observers to draw any conclusions about them.

Captain Jonathan Collins had slipped a white silk scarf into the neckline of his shirt. Defying the intense heat, he had dressed himself in a black three-cornered hat and a blue coat, generously decorated with gold braid. His sword hung by his side and he wore a pair of pistols in his belt. The other officers were also decked out in their best finery. They carried sabers in leather sheaths instead of swords.

Jonathan seemed to be looking for someone. "Where, for God's sake, is our wretched chaplain?" he burst out at last. "I haven't seen him all morning."

A man struggled out onto the quarterdeck at that moment, as though in answer to his question.

All that identified the Reverend Frank Ardeen's ministerial office was a cross of wood and bronze attached to a string about his neck. His coat was bedraggled. Once a rich brown, age had faded it to a greenish tint. His thin legs ended in socks which bagged about his ankles, and low-heeled shoes with rusted buckles. His eyes bloodshot and tearful in an ill-shaven face, he was clearly drunk. He gave a shamefaced grin which turned into a witless grimace baring uneven teeth. When he had finally heaved himself up onto the deck, he grabbed hold of the rail and balanced there, swaying foolishly, not quite sure what he should do next.

He had not boarded *The Sea Witch* to save lost souls or because he liked going to sea. He had been forced to leave his parish at Chester, having tried to rape one of his flock behind the altar of the church. His victim's shrieks had alerted other parishioners, who had tried to slash him to pieces, but he managed to grab a passing mule and so saved his life.

He had no illusions and realized that his safety depended on the number of miles he could put between himself and his outraged parishioners, so he had signed up on the first ship to put to sea.

Jonathan had felt sorry for him, and since the law demanded that he have a chaplain aboard, he agreed to take him along. As it turned out, Ardeen was a devotee of the bottle. By the time Jonathan realized it, it was too late to leave him behind. Jonathan had tried to forbid him any liquor, but the minister was wily as a serpent and nosed out what he needed. When Jonathan had made a remark about his vice, he had lapsed into a state of offended dignity and locked himself into his cabin. He had hardly come out since.

"May God bless the King, *The Sea Witch,* the captain, the niggers, and every whore in this godawful bitch of a life," invoked the Reverend Ardeen in a devout tone.

A shout of laughter greeted this strange prayer.

"I've a good mind to make you pay for all the liquor you've drunk out of your salary," said Jonathan, when the mirth had quieted.

Frank Ardeen stared at him with dull eyes and Jonathan could see the threat slowly making its way to the center of the befuddled brain. At last it seemed to get through, and a wave of sadness washed over his features. He seemed to vacillate, wondering what to do and how to react, but suddenly he decided on a course of action and collapsed against a heap of rope, snoring heavily.

Jonathan shrugged his shoulders and turned back to the canoe which was now very close. The oarsmen ceased their chanting and pulled in alongside the hull.

A portly white man rose, and placing his hands on two of the blacks to give himself leverage, he gave some orders to the two other whites in soft-spoken Portuguese. Then, grabbing the rope ladder hanging from the ship, he began to awkwardly climb the wooden rungs while the canoe turned and regained the shore.

Jonathan went down to the deck to greet his guest. The man, helped by a couple of sailors, set foot on deck and faced the captain, puffing and blowing from his exertions. He was wearing a big-brimmed felt hat, a yellow buttoned jerkin without a collar, and white cotton trousers tucked into fawn-colored boots. A red sash was wound around his large waist with two pistols and a powder horn tucked into it.

Jonathan disliked him immediately. The man's face was pockmarked, with a broken nose, and a mild squint that made him look sly. He was fat and dirty and had a thick mustache that drooped on either side of his mouth. He bowed and uncovered his head in an ostentatious gesture and held out a thick hairy hand.

"My name is Gomes, Captain," he said in an obsequious voice. "Theophilus Gomes at your service, sir."

Jonathan thought with distaste that he must be a draftee who had landed in this godforsaken spot as the result of obscure problems in his mother country. Nonetheless, his innate courtesy came to the rescue and he took the outstretched hand.

"Pleased to meet you, sir," he replied. "I am Captain Jonathan Collins, captain of *The Sea Witch*, and these are our officers, Master Adams, and Woolcomb, Clark, and our medical officer, MacLean."

The Portuguese executed an elaborate bow at the sound of each name, and then shook hands with the man it belonged to.

"And that," concluded Jonathan, pointing to Frank Ardeen lying in a heap in the corner, "is our chaplain, the Reverend Ardeen, but I fear he is in no state to greet you. The crossing has—how shall I put it—been a little too much for him."

"No surprise, no surprise," returned Gomes, "the good Lord don't make reverends so that they can travel about on this kind of skiff."

Jonathan started at the scornful tone Gomes had used in mentioning his ship, but he restrained himself, promising himself a sound clout at the first possible opportunity.

"Would you care to follow me to my cabin?" he asked politely, then turned to Gregory with, "And Mr. Adams, please join us."

Soon the three men were settled around the big table, their weapons cast aside. Pierre had put out a linen tablecloth, fine Bristol china dishes, and crystal glasses trimmed with silver. Cahors wine sparkled invitingly in two delicate decanters.

Gomes drank appreciatively and muttered to Jonathan, "I'm no stickler for manners, Captain, but I'm under my country's orders. I know I can trust you and all that, you look like an honest fellow, but I have to ask you if you have your landing papers in order. Now, Captain, I don't ask you to show 'em to me. I just ask you to tell me if you have 'em. That's good enough for me."

"Don't give it another thought," answered Jonathan, "all my papers are in order."

Gomes went on, insisting, "Now no offense meant at all, Captain, but there are all these contraband situations and I . . ." He paused and grinned, then continued, "If your papers are not in order I won't make no fuss at all, not for something like that. I'm a peaceful sort, I am, and then I have so many blacks that I just don't know what to do with 'em. They're expensive to feed, y'know, and if you make it worth my while, y'understand, I'll make sure you get everything you want."

"I said my papers are in order," repeated Jonathan dryly, disliking the Portuguese's sly tone more every minute. "Gregory, would you be so good as to get the contract and show it to Mr. Gomes?"

Adams rifled in a drawer and pulled out a parchment which he held out to Theophilus Gomes. It was a contract made out in the name of the Royal African Company, authorizing Captain Collins to deal with the Portuguese administration. Gomes took it and looked at it closely, ill put to hide his disappointment that it was indeed a genuine document in good order. He had hoped for a fraudulent operation that would have netted him some extra profit. He gave the parchment back to Gregory without hiding his sulky expression.

A cabin boy came in bearing steaming platters of food which he placed on the table. The three men helped themselves, and the atmosphere became a little more relaxed. The cabin boy poured the wine. It was a plentiful meal. There was chicken with rice, smoked eels, eggs and bacon and cheese. The Portuguese ate greedily. He didn't seem to know what to do with the knives and forks, and grabbed at the food with his fingers, wiping them every now and then on the cloth.

Jonathan could hardly hide his disgust at his guest's manners. He and Gregory exchanged several exasperated glances. He knew the man must be entertained as was the custom, but he swore to himself that he would never again have this ill-bred person at his table. The meal ended and Gomes burped majestically.

"Haven't eaten like that in many a day, Cap'n," he said, his mouth still full of food. "I'd say you have the devil of a fine cook on board."

"He's a Frenchman, that's why," Jonathan said with a notable lack of eagerness.

The cabin boy cleared the table and the three men pushed their chairs back, stuffing their pipes and lighting them from the candle held out to them by the young sailor, who then poured a glass of rum for each and departed.

Gomes took up his glass, sniffed it appreciatively, and drank. "Darn good!" he said enthusiastically. "What is it? I've never tasted nothing like it!'

"It's Barbados rum," explained Gregory, who had been silent throughout the meal. "They make it out of cane sugar."

"Yes," added Jonathan, "it's new. I brought a few barrels back with me from my last voyage to Jamaica."

Gomes seemed to find the drink wonderful. He drained his glass and held it out to Gregory for more.

"Where're you going to deliver your niggers?" he asked. "Would it be to Cuba?"

"No," Jonathan said. "We're headed for Louisiana. It seems the planters there are in great need of field hands."

"I'm asking, because most of the slave traders who come here plan to leave off their black meat in Cuba," said the other. "I don't know why. Maybe it's the climate."

Jonathan had winced at the term "slave trader." He knew that he was one, but every time someone called him that he felt insulted. Gomes' manager had hardly improved matters. He answered him with pronounced distaste, "No, as I told you, we are going to Louisiana."

"A shame," sighed Gomes, pursuing his own train of thought. "If you'd be heading for Cuba, I'd ask you to bring a couple of hounds. I hear that over there—an Englishman like you came from there recently—that over there in Santo Domingo they have 'em brought over. They use 'em to hunt down blacks, and to get them used to it they make them eat a couple so they can get a taste for the meat. That way they are sure to find them. Sometimes I get one here who turns *marron*."

Jonathan raised his brows in astonishment. *"Marron?"* he asked.

"Cimarron, if you prefer," Gomes replied. "That's what we call the hogs that escape and become wild again. If the word is good enough for hogs, it's good enough for blacks, don't ya think? I'd even say we were flattering them!"

Jonathan's face had turned a dangerous shade of purple and Gregory was afraid he would burst. He quickly changed the subject.

"Mr. Gomes," he asked, "how many blacks could you get for us quickly?"

"That'll depend, Mr. Adams. How many can you cram into your holds?"

"Mr. Gomes," said Jonathan in a calm voice that barely masked his fury, *"The Sea Witch* is neither a skiff nor a slaver. She is a *ship,* if you have any idea what that means."

"See here, Captain," said Gomes, "I'm really sorry if I got you all riled up. No offense meant, if ya know what I mean. But so many blacks die in those tomb-ships that there's no other word for 'em."

Jonathan was annoyed with himself for having let his anger show. After all, this Portuguese, despicable as he was, had a point. How could he know the terrible reversals of fortune that alone had been able to propel Jonathan into such a trade. He turned back to his guest and continued in a milder tone, "Yes, I know. But as far as I am concerned, I care very much how these men are treated while they are aboard my ship and I plan to lose as few as possible."

He turned to Gregory. "How many did we lose last time, Master Adams?" he asked.

Gregory thought for a few moments and then answered. "Well, we had taken in four hundred and six, as I remember it. Thirty-eight died of dysentery, and so did two of the crew, and there were four blacks who committed suicide shortly after we left."

"I'd say that proves you take real good care of your blacks, that's what I'd say," said Gomes.

"I don't see why they shouldn't be treated decently. I make sure that all the rules of hygiene are strictly observed on board ship, and I feed them well. My job is to sell them when I get there, not to kill them on the way. You asked me how many my ship would hold. Well, it will take four hundred pieces of India. That would make four hundred head, because I take mostly adult males."

"I've already got about a hundred in my barracks," said Gomes, pleased, "and with the new arrivals I expect that should bring it up to four hundred. I'll fire the guns to alert the catchers."

"Catchers?" queried Jonathan.

"Yea, the catchers. Ya know what I mean. That's what I call the blacks who bring me the slaves. Some of 'em went off on an expedition a month ago. They should be back soon."

Theophilus then expressed a desire to get back to the fort. He left an invitation to Jonathan and all his crew to a welcome feast that night. Jonathan accepted with resignation, knowing he couldn't go against tradition and that his men needed to stretch their legs a little.

The three men left the table and headed for the bridge. Gomes climbed down into his canoe, which had arrived to fetch him, and was rowed back to land.

Jonathan and Gregory spent the rest of the day touring the vessel to make sure that all their orders had been carried out. Then the captain called the crew together and announced the plans for that evening. Only ten sailors would stay aboard to guard the ship, and he entrusted the guard to John Woolcomb.

"I count on you, Mr. Woolcomb, to maintain a watch at all times," he urged. "Light torches all along the railings and see that they stay lit. Should there be an attack, fire the guns and we will return at once.

The petty officer reassured him that nothing would go wrong and the rest of the men rejoiced at the idea of going ashore and cheered Jonathan with gusto.

Later, as the day began to wane in a haze of rich color, Jonathan noticed some smoke puffing out of the fort's cannon. Men had appeared beside the cannon and were scurrying about. There were several salvos and the message of violence echoed out beyond the mountains to tell the hunters that the hour had come.

CHAPTER VIII

N'Gio was ready. He had tied on a short straw skirt and since the occasion did not prescribe any ritual face makeup, he had simply placed a crown on his head, ornamented with scarlet parrot feathers.

He had opened the bark box that contained the talismans and had wound them around his arms and neck to make sure that all was on his side this memorable day. The talismans were small leather pouches or tiny antelope horns stopped up with wax. Some were a protection against poison, others were intended to make him an indomitable hunter. His favorite was a necklace made up of his ancestors' teeth. It had been given to him by his father on the day of his circumcision. Its powers protected against the ruses of enemies and enabled him to escape from the spirit-snatchers.

He had also hidden a talisman in the folds of his straw loincloth. It was made from a snail's shell with herbs inside, and had been given to him the day before by Akere. "Wear it on your wedding day," she said. "It is the igola talisman, the talisman of love. As long as you have it, your wife will remain strongly bound to you."

As he thanked her, she slipped a small leather pouch into his hand. "Take this too," she said, grinning toothlessly. "It's mouvava bark. Chew a tiny piece before you make love to Yawana, and your strength will double."

N'Gio had heard about this powerful aphrodisiac and suspected that his father often made use of it. "Thank you, Akere," he said, "but I feel sure I shall be strong without it."

"Tsk, tsk," muttered the old woman, "you never know. Listen to old Akere. You should honor your wife several times tomorrow night, and you might find that the ceremonies tire you more than you imagine."

N'Gio was ready, but there was nothing prescribed for him to do just yet. He would have to wait for everyone to get ready and assume their places before he could appear outside his hut. He could hear lively conversations and laughter sifting through the cracks in his hut's walls, and he could see the streams of guests arriving and settling down. Most of them were from neighboring villages whose chiefs were on friendly terms with Adende. They had been summoned to the marriage by the sad mellow tones of the horns, sounded for several nights past.

They greeted and complimented each other with pleasure, feigned or real, it was hard to tell. N'Gio was able to recognize some of the tribes they belonged to by the clothes and headdresses they wore: the Bateke smiths, the Eshira from the huge plains, the Tshogo from the mountains, and the Shimba from the forests.

They were all massing in a circle in front of the Bwiti temple, leaving a huge empty space. Loud cheers greeted the arrival of the musicians, hand-picked from all over the surrounding region for their outstanding skills. They settled down in the temple and began to tune their instruments, harps, and drums covered with the skins of antelope, or sheep's or elephants' ears. One of them even sported the neck skin of a huge sea turtle. A musician tried out his pipe, made from a tiny gourd, the ends plugged by the delicate skin of bats' wings. He played it by blowing air through his nose into the upper hole of the instrument.

Two young men placed a low stool covered in fur and a second, simpler one in the center of the open space.

Adende, who had been waiting for this moment, advanced toward the temple majestically, and sat down on the smaller stool. He was decked out in his handsomest garments. A leopard skin covered his front, and ivory and bronze bracelets encircled his wrists and ankles. A crown of gorilla teeth was perched on his head and he wore a necklace of black panther fangs purported to have been dipped in the blood of the gods.

Flapping regally at himself with a buffalo tail fly switch, he glanced about him with a possessive smile. He knew Mouele would be delighted with his catch, for there were more guests than even he had dreamed, and it was hard to hide his glee. The innocent victims of his greed had done all they could to honor him. The men were in full war apparel; furred helmets, bamboo bells, and brass bracelets; and the women, with their loincloths of braided leaves or woven bark, had expended a wealth of ingenuity and imagination on their elaborate flower-ornamented hair. The

young boys wore only a narrow belt, their genitals caught
up and hidden in a band of decorated dried banana leaf.

One by one, the chiefs of the various tribes paraded in
front of old Adende to congratulate him and then take their
places standing by his side. Their tiger skins and the large
ebony canes they held in their hands marked them as the
leaders of their tribes.

Adende shook a large wooden bell and tapped the earth
with his cane several times. The chattering ceased as if by
magic. All eyes were on the Olumi, the sacred tree. They
did not have long to wait. The sun was exactly at its zenith
and the tree called "incomparable" because of the respectful fear it invoked cast a perfect vertical shadow. Olumi
was as vivid as the rainbow, and it rang with a hollow
sound when tapped. Its immense purple trunk was pierced
about thirty yards up from the ground by assegais bearing
baskets filled with offerings. Nobody would dare to cut
down such a magnificent tree.

The drums began to beat dully, sending a shiver through
the assembled villagers and their guests. They were calling
to N'Gio, and he came out of his hut at once, to be greeted
with a loud shout. He made his way toward his father,
knelt in front of him, and rubbed his forehead in the dust
at his feet. Adende placed his cane on his son's spine, and
N'Gio rose and went to stand beside the old chief. The
drums throbbed continuously. Slowly, a man lifted a large
antelope horn to his lips and blew several long, mournful
blasts.

Yawana, while she awaited this signal, had settled into
the prepared seat, and her family and friends started to
walk alongside as she was carried toward the village. Soon,
the crowd parted, and the bearers slowly advanced and deposited Yawana in front of N'Gio and Adende. Helped by
her parents, she carefully climbed down and walked toward
her future husband, her eyes lowered. She stood silently in
front of him, her head bent in an attitude of submission.
Yawana was superbly graceful. The women twittered in
jealousy as the men admired her exquisite features, the
pure lines of her body, and the elegance of her bearing.
Her hands were crossed on her breast, but the dark nipples
were visible. She looked so desirable at that instant that
N'Gio was afraid his emotion would overpower him.

Isembe came forward to greet Adende and signaled for

the gifts he had brought to be laid at Adende's feet. Adende was overwhelmed by the generosity and magnificence of the gifts, which demonstrated to the assembled crowd how highly he was esteemed by Isembe.

The murmur of appreciation from his tribe proved their excitement. He thanked Isembe and signaled to two young men who came over and brought gifts he had chosen for Yawana's parents. The two men bowed to each other again and then Isembe took a small stool he was wearing slung across his waist and sat down beside Adende.

While these ritual exchanges were taking place, Yawana stood watching N'Gio from under her long lashes. She saw him look at her tenderly and then glance proudly out at the crowd, as though calling them to witness the beauty of his bride.

Once more, Adende shook the bell, and Moussavou, the witch doctor, came out of the temple where he had been hiding for the early part of the ritual. He was wearing his most magnificent talismans and did not notice Adende's envious glance rest on them as he appeared. First, he rang an iron bell with a twisted handle, meant to chase away evil and call on beneficent spirits to bless the couple with fertility.

Yawana winced, as if hearing the evil spirits whirling about her and fading away. Moussavou moved forward, fanning the air with the rattan switches he carried on his arms and banging the earth with his heels. He danced back and forth and the small wooden bells tied to his white- and red-painted calves jangled and tinkled.

Still dancing, he made his way to the two young people. Adende and Isembe both rose and came to stand beside the wedding couple. Ivohino and her brother, Mangouka, also joined them. Moussavou stood still and began to speak in a thunderous voice that reached the outer circle of the assembled crowd.

"You, N'Gio, son of great chief Adende, and you, Yawana, daughter of great chief Isembe, you will unite as the hurricane unites earth and sky. But whereas the hurricane destroys all in its path, you will create life. May Yawana's womb be fruitful and may vigor swell N'Gio's loins."

Yawana trembled slightly as she felt N'Gio's eyes on her during this incantation.

"Last night," continued Moussavou, "I consulted the

skulls of the ancestors and I read the secrets hidden in water, and I saw. I saw that you, N'Gio, will be as brave as a man with five hearts. But you must never forget that the bird always seems larger with its wings spread. You must never try to grasp the sun. Be happy warming yourself in his rays and do not be carried away by pride."

The crowd was hushed, listening religiously to the wise words of the witch doctor. All were amazed at his wisdom. An approving rumble came from the people, but Moussavou nipped it in the bud with a stern, compelling glance. Silence fell again and he continued, "You, Yawana, you will often know the joys of giving birth. But remember, Yawana," and here his voice grew menacing, "remember that N'Gio is the son of a chief, and that if you were thoughtless enough to commit adultery you would be subjected to the most horrible tortures. Of course, your punishment would be milder if you gave yourself to another man in the forest rather than in your husband's dwelling, but the man who takes you will be strangled and thrown in the fire. And you will be tied naked to the ant tree for half a day. If you are unfaithful a second time, your vulva will be slit and you will be buried alive. This lover will have his mouth slit and will be tied to a wooden plank and thrown into the river where he will be eaten by fish and crocodiles."

Yawana shuddered violently as she listened to the horrible tortures the witch doctor was describing. She knew about them, for she had once seen them perpetrated on an unfaithful wife in her own village. N'Gio listened to the diatribe without emotion. Many of the women present, consumed with envy of the girl's loveliness, reveled in the thought that these tortures would destroy her arrogant beauty. The crowd waited impatiently for what would follow.

"However," Moussavou continued in a gentler voice, "I am confident that your soul is pure and that you have nothing to fear. N'Gio, you are an initiate of the Bwiti, and you know that you must never—and I mean never under any circumstances—reveal the secrets of your brotherhood to your wife, and she must not tell you about those of the Ndjembe of which she is an initiate. It will be your duty to obtain meat and fish for your household and Yawana will care for the plantations to bring you fruits and vegetables to eat. Now, since you are not of the same village, nor of the same tribe, there is nothing to prevent your union in marriage. Yawana, you will leave the Akele tribe forever to enter N'Gio's tribe. You must submit to the laws and customs of this tribe you have adopted as your own. If you do not, the most dire calamities will befall you and your family and village."

Moussavou's long speech was over. He placed his hands on the shoulders of the two young people and said, "Now, my children, I shall unite you by blood. Hold out your wrists."

N'Gio and Yawana held out their wrists and Moussavou pulled a small knife from the folds of his belt and made shallow cuts in the two right wrists. As soon as a faint line of blood appeared, he pressed them against each other and held them there.

"May your spirits mingle as the blood is mingling, and may death alone have the power to come between you," he intoned. For the first time, Yawana raised her eyes to those of her husband and their joy swelled beyond earth to find its place among the stars.

Moussavou then pulled out a tiny pouch from his leopard-skin cloak. He extracted some dried herbs from it and gave them to the parents of the two young people. He asked Mangouka if he was indeed Yawana's maternal uncle, and Mangouka, a frail little man who lived in awe of Ivohino, said that he was.

"Then," intoned Moussavou, "bless Yawana before she is given to N'Gio."

Mangouka came to Yawana and the girl walked around him three times as a sign of respect. She circled both of her parents in the same way and came back to stand near her uncle.

He looked deep into her eyes and called on the spirits of his ancestors as well as those of all the Akele in his village. Yawana bowed her head, and Mangouka spat some of the juice from the herbs he had been chewing onto her hair. Isembe, Ivohino, and Adende did the same and all wished her the greatest possible happiness.

At last, I belong to N'Gio, thought Yawana. But she knew that first she would have to be adopted by the new tribe. The ritual to follow, which her mother had described, was terrifying to her.

N'Gio stepped away from her and went to sit on the small stool in the center of the open space. Ivohino took Yawana's hand and said gently, "Come, come, my little daughter."

Yawana, her legs trembling, followed her mother docilely as she led her to her husband. She didn't know if her emotion was fear or excitement, or perhaps something else.

"Kneel down," said Ivohino, "and put your head on N'Gio's thighs."

N'Gio smiled at her and the girl did as she was told. Her mother pressed her shoulders slightly to make her kneel. Yawana placed her two arms on the young man's sinewy thighs and laid her head between, her face turned toward him. N'Gio gently caressed her face and laid his other hand on her back. He was not too happy about what was to follow, but there was nothing he could do about it. It was the custom.

Then Ivohino lifted her daughter's loincloth and uncovered her buttocks, more rounded than usual because of the position she was in. The drums, which had been silent for the ceremony, began to throb again, as all the men in the village of Mounigou formed a long line, headed by Adende.

Yawana lifted her eyes to N'Gio's face, bent over hers.

"Don't be afraid, little antelope," he whispered tenderly.

Adende was already behind her. He knelt on one knee, fixed his eyes on N'Gio's, lifted his loincloth, and passed his penis along the furrow of the young girl's exposed genitals. She shivered at the touch and jerked in distaste, but N'Gio's hand on her back held her firmly in place.

All the assembled men followed Adende's example. But this repeated touching of her private parts began to arouse her. In spite of her humiliation at being subjected to the gaze of the entire assembly, she could not control her rising excitement. She could feel the effect her beauty was having on some of the men.

N'Gio watched his wife as the line shortened. Her eyes were closed, and he saw her bite her lips to still the moans that even the throbbing drums might not have drowned.

Yawana was having difficulty enduring her rising excitement in silence. Her hands were clawing at N'Gio's thighs. Finally, the last man moved away. N'Gio took her hand and helped her gently to her feet. Her ordeal had left her in such a heated state that she would have liked him to carry her off and take her at once, but she knew this could not be. Custom did not permit her to show N'Gio what she was feeling, and she knew that they would have to attend the festivities that followed together.

The music had stopped and the villagers and their guests were milling about in the compound, heading for the place where the banquet had been laid out. Women would be allowed to attend, since this was a very special day. N'Gio sat on a mat at his father's side and Yawana, sitting between her parents, faced him. The others sat wherever they wished. Everyone was thirsty from the long wait in the sun. Women moved among the guests with gourds of palm wine. Soon, the coconut shells, antelope horns, and other receptacles were all filled with a yellowish liquid, bubbles foaming to the top and bursting on the surface.

As soon as everyone was served, Adende poured a little of his wine on the ground to propitiate the spirits and then drained his cup. All followed his example and the receptacles were again filled to overflowing. Soon, the acid wine had produced a state of euphoria in the gathering and the talk rose in volume. Adende, however, drank far less than his guests.

Foods were then brought out and placed before the villagers. Fat river shrimps were accompanied by tiny mangrove crabs, followed by a soup in which giant snails floated. In the general ebullience, nobody noticed that Adende looked preoccupied. If they had looked closely at the old man they might have observed that his smile was forced and his conviviality strained.

Between mouthfuls, his lips dribbling sauce, he said to his son, "Look at your wife. Her eyes are shining. She longs for you to take her. Don't wait, N'Gio, leave the village as soon as the meal is over and take her far from here. You need to be alone."

N'Gio had forgotten that his father had suggested the same thing earlier that morning. He was watching the dainty way Yawana dealt with her food.

"I'm also impatient to take her, Tato," he said, "but why should I go and do it in the forest like an animal? We can't leave the festivities before the dance."

"The dance! The dance!" grumbled Adende. "Is that all you can think of? You'll have the rest of your lives to dance."

"Oh yes, yes!" exclaimed Yawana, who had only heard the last part of the sentence, "I'd like to dance!"

"You see, Tato," said N'Gio, smiling, "I can't deprive her of that pleasure."

Adende stopped insisting. He was furious, but he couldn't show his anger. He would just have to make quite sure that the Bapounou understood the situation. He was willing to sell his village, but he was not willing to let his son go.

His thoughts were interrupted by the arrival of the next course. There were porcupines roasted in their own blood accompanied by tiny fried bananas, boiled river turtles, elephant meat tenderized in papaya leaves, delicious roast pheasant, lacy mushrooms, and many other savory dishes. Even the Bwiti members were able to eat their favorite food, anteater meat, baked in ashes.

Everyone ate voraciously, stuffing themselves as full as they could. The gourds, flowing with palm wine and banana beer, were passed constantly. Yawana and N'Gio ate little. Love and passion had replaced their hunger. The girl was happier than she had ever been and N'Gio was floating on a high plane of ecstatic joy.

The meal ended with mountains of ripe fruit, especially papayas, whose sweet pulp helped the digestion. Some of the guests, their stomachs swollen with food, went off to rest in the shade of huge mango trees. N'Gio left his place and went to sit near Yawana. Everyone was satisfied, drowsy with food and drink.

That was when Adende quietly disappeared. N'Gio did not notice him leave, although had he done so he might have observed that his father's intent gaze was not that of a man about to take a nap.

Adende made his way to his hut. He went in, took a gourd hidden in one of the corners, and left by the back door. He hurried quietly toward the last few huts on the edge of the village, and paused for a moment to make sure he was not noticed. As soon as he was satisfied that he was alone, he slipped off into the trees.

He approached two guards who had been posted at the outskirts of the settlement to alert the villagers in the improbable event of an attack. They were chatting animatedly, leaning on their assegais.

"Here you are, my friends," said Adende. "Drink. You must be thirsty," and he held out the gourd.

"You are most kind," replied one of the guards, gratefully. "They're all having fun out there, and we're stuck here."

He drank avidly and passed the gourd to his companion, who drained it.

"I'm going for a stroll," said Adende. "I won't be long. As soon as I get back I'll have them bring you food and more drink."

He hurried away. The drug he had concealed in the wine had an immediate effect, and soon the two guards were deeply asleep.

Displaying incredible agility for a man of his advanced age, Adende disappeared into the forest.

CHAPTER IX

By now the forest was so thick that Adende could no longer hear the sounds of revelry from the village. Some light filtered through the heavy foliage and lent a mysterious atmosphere to the surroundings. The trail became narrower, twisting and turning. Adende stopped to remove his ceremonial dress. He laid his headdress, robes, and jewels on the ground and rose, clad only in a small triangular loincloth. He felt much freer and better able to move now that there was no danger of snagging his trappings on the dense undergrowth. After listening intently to make sure that he had not been followed, he continued on his way.

A jabbering tribe of monkeys passed high above his head among the blue and green orchids, branches swaying and snapping with their weight. Suddenly Adende stood stock still. He thought he scented gorilla and felt a thrill of fear at the idea of meeting one of those huge manlike creatures, particularly some old male whom lack of female had made aggressive. Adende had no intention of having an arm or leg ripped from his body by giant talons. Wishing he had brought a weapon with him, he peered into the darkness, sniffed several times, and continued on his way, reassured by what he saw and smelt.

The trees were streaked with fungi and other decaying vegetation. Adende climbed across a huge tree trunk spanning a deep fissure in the ground and hurried on, anxious not to be late for his meeting.

At last, he reached the spot, but no one was there. He stared about him, intensely disappointed, wondering what could have happened to spoil his carefully laid plans. Ready to turn back, he froze as he heard a sudden rustle behind him. He turned in one swift movement, ready to grapple with whatever wild forest creature was about to attack him, and found himself face to face with a very tall man wearing an ample white tunic belted with leather, a double-edged saber protruding above the waist. A necklace of human teeth ringed his throat and he was holding one of those strange weapons Adende had seen and coveted during his meeting with Mouele. Peering at him, Adende realized that here was one of the Bapounou he had met before, and he felt relieved. Nonetheless, he greeted him with displeasure.

"Where is Mouele?" he asked. "Why isn't he here to meet me? Is this the way to greet the great chief Adende?"

The man leered unpleasantly and answered, "Mouele is waiting for you, old man. Only he didn't trust you not to lay an ambush for him. He's not far from here. Follow me!"

It was more an order than an invitation and Adende raged inwardly that the man should have addressed him in such a fashion, but there was little he could do except follow his guide through the underbrush.

The other man sped along without a backward glance to see if the old chief was having difficulty keeping up. Branches slapped Adende's face as he tried to keep his guide in sight. Only the thought of fulfilling Mouele's magnificent promises drove him on and persuaded him to forget his indignation. He had sunk too low to have the right to be offended.

The two men soon came to an open, freshly cleared space in the midst of the underbrush. A fire leapt cheerfully in the center of the clearing and hastily built branch huts were scattered about. Adende counted about thirty men in the open space. Some were asleep, others were eating and chatting among themselves. They all wore tunics and Adende, who was almost naked, felt rather ridiculous and vulnerable. His head shrank slightly into his shoulders as he saw their fierce look. They all stared at him with the same cold, greedy expression, but he was so intent on the gifts he expected to receive, which would make him as strong and powerful as they, that he ignored his growing sense of unease.

Mouele was sitting alone. He rose and came over to Adende, saying in a sarcastic tone, "Welcome, old chief, welcome! Forgive me for your discomfort, but I must be very careful. I must take all precautions."

Adende's smile was stiff as he answered, "Good day to you, and to you all."

The men acknowledged his greeting gruffly as he shook hands with Mouele.

"I don't begrudge you your precautions," said Adende,

"but let's get to the point. I have to get back to the village
in time for the dancing. Everyone will notice my absence
and wonder about it if I stay away too long. They might
even come looking for me."

"I understand, Adende," Mouele said in a placating
tone. "But why don't you sit down for a few moments all
the same."

Adende sat, and Mouele signaled to one of the men to
bring him a drink. The man brought a bottle like the one
the old chief had already seen, and filled a coconut shell.
He held it out to Mouele, who took it and drank, to show
his good faith. He even took care to hold his thumb up
from the rim to show Adende that there was no poison
hidden under his nail. He then held out the cup to the old
chief, who also drank and handed it on to the others, re-
peating Mouele's careful gestures. Only the last man to
drink did not lift his thumb.

Mouele suddenly spoke in a sharp tone: "Well, Adende,
I hope everything has been organized."

"Yes," answered Adende, "everyone has arrived. There
are more than I expected. Many people came from the
neighboring villages, just as I promised you. You will be
pleased. I hope you have brought what you promised me."

Mouele silently gestured toward hampers in piles a little
further into the clearing. "It's all there, as you can see," he
said. "A promise is a promise and you will be paid as soon
as the raid is over."

Adende stared at the heaped hampers with greedy eyes.
He wanted to ask to have them opened so that he could see
what treasures they held, but he didn't quite dare.

"Is everything in there?" he asked anxiously. "The liquor, lots of liquor? Necklaces and loincloths? Those strange
weapons you call guns?"

"Of course, old fellow," soothed Mouele. "Stop worrying
about it. Now. When can we attack your village?"

The undisguised question gave Adende a shock. It put
him suddenly face to face with the realities of the situation
and he felt his resolve slipping for a moment. He was about
to refuse to go through with the deal when he noticed the
eyes of all the men fixed coldly on him. He knew that to
turn back now meant certain death.

"I hope you aren't going to change your mind now?"

Mouele asked in a menacing tone, as if reading his thoughts.

"No, no, of course not," Adende said firmly. "But we must wait for the dancing to be over, and for everyone to be asleep. And I also want you to promise me one thing."

"Speak!" Mouele said.

"I want my son N'Gio and his bride Yawana to be spared," Adende said, "and I also want the bride's parents and all my wives to be spared too."

Mouele gave another signal and they filled the coconut shells again. Adende drank and burped loudly.

"I also want," he continued, "the small children and old women to be left unharmed."

Mouele patted his shoulder reassuringly. "Don't you worry, old chief," he said. "All will be done as you wish it. We'll attack at cock's crow in the morning and we'll only take the strong men. As I told you last time, when they come back to you, they will be grateful."

Adende was distressed despite Mouele's convincing tone, but the drink was beginning to take effect and his suspicions abated as he was lulled into a pleasant stupor.

"I think you'd better go now, old man," said Mouele, and Adende rose and followed his guide out of the encampment. The man slipped away, and he found himself alone.

By this time, Adende was congratulating himself on having obtained the promise that N'Gio would be safe. He hadn't been able to persuade him to leave the festivities early, but at least he knew that nothing would harm him. Soon, he was thinking about his reward. His mind dwelt on the weapons and the fine treasures that would soon be his. He would be able to shower his wives with gifts and they would be even more eager to fulfill his desires and cater to his whims.

He soon found the spot where he had left his clothing. Putting it on quickly, he made his way back to the village. The guards were still sound asleep, and he slipped unseen into Mounigou, reaching his hut without incident.

CHAPTER X

Yawana stepped out of the hut set aside for her parents. She was wearing only a light bark skirt and wooden bells at her ankles. Crossing the empty space in the center, she stared toward N'Gio's hut to see if he was ready. The clearing was now free of its trappings except for a huge fire which crackled in the golden light of dusk, heralding the end of the day. Adende sat there, surrounded by his concubines, talking to Aziza who crouched at his feet.

Yawana passed groups of dancers. The women were dressed as simply as she, but the men were painted red and white and wore headdresses decorated with parrot feathers and monkey fur. The bells tied to their ankles tinkled pleasantly as they moved. N'Gio came out of his hut, clad in a short loincloth. He saw Yawana and took her in his arms. "We'll come back here during the dancing," he whispered. "Are you happy?"

Her answer was to burrow into him, her stomach grinding against his.

"Be patient, little antelope," he said, laughing. "You won't have long to wait now."

She gave a disappointed pout, then smiled. N'Gio took her by the hand and led her to join the others. The musicians were readying themselves, the harpists plucking their strings, and the drummers holding their instruments close to the fire to tauten the skins.

There was expectancy in the crowd as they waited for the dance to begin. Women were bringing around palm wine mixed with iboga to strengthen the dancers for the night-long festivities.

At last, a man blew a long, drawn-out wail on his trumpet, which was followed by several piercing nasal notes from the flute player. Delicate sounds came from the harps, and gradually the drums came in one by one with a steady rhythm. Soon there was a full-blown unbridled outburst of sound. The dancers began to sway. Their feet tapped the ground faster and faster, echoing the beat of the drums with the faint pealing of their bells. Suddenly, they all began to clap, raising their voices in a chorus of praise for the young lovers.

Adende, his eyes on the scene, drank steadily. All the alcohol he had imbibed since the morning was beginning to produce a drunken euphoria. Every now and then, a flash of reality permeated the barrier and he felt a shudder of anguish. He was no longer clear in his mind whether or not he had done the right thing with the Bapounou.

N'Gio, taller than anyone else, was dancing almost without moving, while, opposite him, Yawana leapt and contorted her body with uninhibited frenzy. Her body twisted more and more sensuously, exuding an almost tangible eroticism.

The shadows were lengthening and the sky had taken on a crimson tinge, streaked with purple and black clouds. As the day faded, the flames of the great fire leapt with brighter and brighter splendor and red shadows flickered across the sweat-streaked bodies of the dancers.

By now, the only sound was the relentless beating of the drums in a fury of insistent rhythm. Suddenly a harsh explosion broke through their beat. It was muffled and seemed to come from very high above the forest. Its reverberations were lost in the loud crash of the explosions which came again and again at regular intervals. The musicians stared at each other, and one by one they stopped playing. The dancers stopped too, realizing that their accompaniment had ceased. One last set of bells tinkled forlornly, and then there was silence. All stood still, heads turned toward the north, listening for a repetition of the strange sound. The crashes suddenly sounded sharper. Adende bounded to his feet, completely alert. Somehow he guessed that the noise had something to do with his treachery. N'Gio grasped Yawana's hand tightly as though aware of a mysterious danger. Others also seemed aware of it. They had heard the sounds before and had no idea where they came from. They were so deep in the forest that all strange sights and sounds were immediately attributed to genies and evil spirits. Nonetheless, they did remember that the strange crashing sound had not been with them for more than a few rainy seasons, and stories had begun to spread which were repeated in whispers, after dark had fallen. It seemed that entire villages had disappeared overnight, and those who had gone to find out what had hap-

pened had also disappeared, never to be heard of again.
The villagers wondered uneasily if they were to be the victims of evil spirits, or whether their neighbors had met with
a god who had taken them away with him.

Silence fell on the gathered tribesmen. The old chief
glanced around at the tense faces, and in an imperious gesture ordered the musicians back to their playing.

Yawana, to whom the incident had meant nothing more
than an interruption, began to dance again and pulled the
others in to join her. None were aware that the rolls of
sound they had heard were like the agonized thud of a
dying heart, pumping out its lifeblood, the lifeblood of
their country.

Night fell. Yawana and N'Gio only paused long enough
in their dancing to drink some more palm wine. Gradually,
the dancing took on a new aspect. The iboga began to take
effect, and the chanting degenerated into hysterical clamor.
The fire, disturbed by the dancers' violent movements,
flung great scarlet tongues at the sky and sent up showers
of sparks that melted into tiny red stars as they fell. The
frenzy had reached such heights that even the straw roofs
of the huts seemed to be dancing.

Without any visible signal having been given, men and
women separated into groups and faced each other. Loincloths were flung aside, and the dance became an orgiastic
mime of the gestures of love.

Yawana and N'Gio danced a few moments longer, coming closer and closer to one another. Yawana was beside
herself with desire. She grabbed her husband's hand and
drew him away from the dancing. He had barely pulled the
covering over the door of their hut, when she grabbed him,
pressing her body against his, biting at his shoulder. He felt
her nipples harden against his strong chest, while her hands
sought him feverishly.

Gently, he pulled her hands away and laid her down on
the mat.

Yawana opened her thighs and dug her nails into
N'Gio's back She pulled him down to her without waiting
for him, and N'Gio held back for fear of hurting her. He
watched her rising pleasure through half-open eyes. She
was staring at him intently, a tiny frown on her smooth
forehead, her small teeth biting at her upper lip. He kissed
her, and abandoned himself to his own pleasure. Yawana,

lifted beyond pain by her intense pleasure, clung to him. Streaked with sweat, their two bodies gave off a musky scent and their passion unconsciously followed the wild rhythm of the music still beating outside. They held back until they could restrain themselves no longer. Then they let themselves be carried far far out by their senses until they wondered if they would ever come back. Yawana's shriek tore out of her throat and mingled with N'Gio's roar.

She was drenched with joy. The peak of pleasure she and N'Gio had reached simultaneously was more wonderful than anything she had ever imagined. They lay still, their eyes wide and luminous, as they slowly came back to earth. Then N'Gio whispered words to her that would have been nonsense at any other time, but soothed her like a beautiful melody. His hand softly caressed her breast. She wondered if he liked her breasts firm or preferred them flattened with a straw band to make them more like those of women who had borne many children. Then she thought that she would have many children herself, and it was not necessary to ask. A deep desire to have a child immediately welled up inside her. She wanted a daughter first, and then more. Then N'Gio would be proud of her and would keep her always. She knew that when she was old he would take young and beautiful women, and then she would be left to work in the fields, but she didn't care. All women ended their lives as beasts of burden. What mattered was to be with him as long as possible. She timidly placed her hand on his body and, worn out by the ecstasies of dancing and passion, fell instantly asleep.

The two eager bodies found each other many times during the night and came together with the same unrestrained passion and delight. The music faded, one by one the dancers disappeared to fall asleep in their huts or to lie down and make love in the dust, often falling asleep before they had fulfilled their desires.

Just before dawn, Yawana woke up, alert and listening. The village was wrapped in an intense silence. She felt very tired, but she needed to go and wash her body. Gently, she moved the arm with which N'Gio held her in his sleep, and he slept on as she rose from the mat, wrapped her loincloth about her hips, and crept out.

The fire was still flickering; the musicians were asleep at

their instruments. Yawana stretched, tingling with a sensuous delight in the early-morning air on her body. She
hurried on silent feet, and as she passed the last hut, she
thought she heard a slight crackling in the underbrush at
the edge of the forest. She stood stock still, turned slightly,
and listened with every inch of her body. She heard nothing, and blamed her imagination or some couple making
love in the bushes. She resumed walking languidly toward
the river.

Adende was also awake. He turned and twisted on his
mat, waiting for the fatal moment of action. His anxiety
grew as the moment came closer, and he found himself
envying Aziza's peaceful slumbers as she lay close to him.
His vague unease was turning into a state of acute tension
as he sensed that he might have been duped. It was, however, too late.

CHAPTER XI

Captain Collins had not changed. He felt it unnecessary to wear a coat, in view of the intense heat that weighed on the lagoon. He had already succeeded in showing vulgar Theophilus Gomes how a naval officer should behave, and the coat was now no longer necessary.

His sword proved a nuisance, so he had limited himself to two pistols slipped into his belt. He had checked to make sure the powder was dry and that the flints were tightly wedged in the hammers. He had added a horn of powder and a bag of bullets. The bone handle of a slim dagger protruded from the top of his boot, and he wore a plain black tricorn on his head.

The officers he joined on deck were as lightly dressed as he. Predictably, Reverend Ardeen was not among them. No doubt he was hidden away in some dark corner near the storeroom, sleeping off his drunken stupor. The sun had almost set and a gray twilight surrounded *The Sea Witch*. The ship's lanterns sent shifting streamers of light onto the dark waters, meeting the shimmering lights from the fort. John Woolcomb came toward Jonathan.

"All in order, sir," he said. "The men of the watch have eaten and are at their posts."

Jonathan nodded gravely to John Woolcomb and replied, "Thank you, Mr. Woolcomb. We can now leave."

The crew had gathered on the main deck, waiting for the order to board the three longboats. The oarsmen had their poles raised. All were heavily armed, as they had been ordered.

Jonathan called for silence.

"Don't forget that you are in dangerous country," he warned. "Be constantly on your guard and move in groups of two. Never wander far from the fort, and in any case, never move without your weapons, whatever you may be doing." He paused and grinned, adding, "You know what I mean! Don't overdo the drinking, and be back aboard this vessel in the morning at the latest, every man of you. Come along."

A loud cheer greeted the order to move as Jonathan began to descend the length of the hull. He settled in his boat, where he was soon joined by his three officers. The men then climbed into the other longboats. The men left aboard to stand watch gazed on enviously, leaning over the rails to observe the departure.

Gregory took the helm and signaled departure. Jonathan's longboat moved away from the side of the ship and the men pulled on their oars. It slid through the water at a fine speed. Fish leapt and splashed in its wake. Ahead, they could see a garland of torches advancing toward the landing dock. The two other boats followed Jonathan's closely and the sailors' voices rang out in chorus, drowning the swish of the water.

Jonathan stood in the prow of his boat. His face was grim. To him, the evening ahead was a duty he could not avoid. He had no idea how long he would have to live here, and he knew it would be a tactical mistake to alienate either his crew or the Portuguese. He vowed to himself that he would get back on board as soon as possible, and limit his visits ashore to strictly professional ones. As for the men, he knew their feelings were different. They were in sore need of relaxation after their long crossing. They had seen no women for weeks and he was sure that Gomes would have something lined up for them. Of course they ran the risk of catching yaws, the African form of syphilis, but there was no way of avoiding these encounters. He could not forbid them their women. To do so would be to risk mutiny, or a mood of barely contained discontent at the very least, and that would not do. He knew he would have more than enough problems on his hands with the slave cargo. A grumpy, undisciplined crew was the last thing he wanted. He found himself fervently hoping that all would go well.

While he was worrying in silence, William Clark was joking with Dr. MacLean. They were indulging in all kinds of fantasies as to how black women made love, and their ribald remarks were making the sailors roar with laughter.

The three boats docked. Jonathan jumped ashore and the rest of the crew followed with much banter and cheerful clatter.

Before the two groups met, Jonathan turned to his second-in-command and said, in a low tone, "I want two men permanently stationed by the longboats. You can see that they are relieved every two hours. Tell them to keep their eyes peeled, I don't feel at all comfortable about the men from the fort."

As Gregory gave his orders, Jonathan moved toward Gomes. The torchlight flickering across their faces made the men accompanying the Portuguese look ferocious and confirmed Captain Collins in his suspicions.

Gomes held out his hand.

"Welcome to my humble domain, Sir Captain," he said. "I have prepared a royal welcome for you."

"I thank you, Mr. Gomes, it's really too kind of you," Jonathan said politely.

Gomes continued: "Your men must need some relaxation after their arduous voyage, don't you think? They must not be disappointed. Would you do me the honor of accompanying me?"

Jonathan, flanked by two of his officers, made his way to the side. The torch bearers spread themselves out to give light along the path.

"Everyone has to walk single file," Gomes said in a loud voice. Then turning to Jonathan, he explained, " 'S better to be careful with all these niggers around. They're scoundrels. I fight 'em with their own weapons, it's the only way. All around the fort I had poisoned straw laid on the ground. One of their own recipes." He let out an evil laugh. "You dip it in a rotting corpse and it's deadly. That way if they come snooping around here at night they scratch their feet. It helps prevent surprise attacks. As for us, we don't risk anything. We wear boots. But I see that many of your sailors don't have shoes and I don't want them to get hurt."

"Did you get that, fellers?" shouted Gregory, who had heard the Portuguese's warning. "It's full of nigger traps here. Better watch out where you put your feet."

The sailors of *The Sea Witch* huddled together at once and a long, intent serpent of men wound its way upward along the path that led to the fort.

They soon came to a high fence of wooden stakes bound together by tightly woven creepers. An armed man opened a doorway. He closed it as soon as everyone had entered, and secured it with a heavy iron bar.

Night had fallen, and it was now hard to make out anything, but there was a fire on the left which shone on a

man sitting, his rifle between his legs. He was guarding the
entrance to a long low building, from which muffled groans
escaped. A heavy fetid smell hung about the area.

"That's where I keep my nigger meat," explained
Gomes as Jonathan raised his handkerchief to his nose.
"I'll show you in the morning. I got a good bunch in there
already. All top pieces of India, tradeable as can be. I only
touch the best. That—there is where I keep my males. The
females are further on. I always separate 'em, y'know, all
they ever think of is fornicating like animals. They're as
treacherous as can be and I don't want 'em cooking up any
plots."

Jonathan gave no answer beyond a grunt. He was fighting the mosquitoes that were battering him without letup,
undeterred by the delicate fabric of his shirt. He wished he
had worn his coat after all, despite the hot, humid weather.

A hundred yards farther in, the Portuguese welcomed
their guests into the fort proper. The gateway was open,
guarded by two men. The walls were of dried mud
crammed into bamboo lacings and a good yard wide. It
wouldn't last long against bullets or cannonballs, but it was
sufficient protection against arrows and assegais. Holes had
been bored through, here and there, for guns to poke out.
The cannon that had boomed its message earlier rested on
a square wooden platform, and a curved path ran around
the top of the fortification.

There was a wide-open space in the center surrounded
by the men's quarters. Gomes' quarters, complete with
storage rooms, kitchen, and servants' quarters, stood a little
farther back. A fire in the center of the fort was the only
light.

Gomes climbed the few steps necessary to reach the veranda which jutted from the pyramidal roof. Bowing ceremoniously, he invited Jonathan and his crew to join him
inside.

Jonathan's glance swept around the room where he
found himself. It was immense, and very comfortable. A
huge table lit by chandeliers stood in the center. The mud
walls were punctuated by heavily barred, small windows,
and huge beams supported the straw roof. Some benches
lay along the wall and around the table, and there was a
door at the end of the room opening onto a passage. Oppo-

site the entrance was a large painted wooden figure of Christ nailed to the wall, the face reflecting infinite sadness.

The room was surprisingly cool and refreshing after the heat outside. Mayflies darted about candle flames, losing their wings, and falling into the steel goblets and polished wood bowls; gray lizards chased insects among the straws on the roof.

The Sea Witch's sailors were grouped near the door, somewhat intimidated by the scale of their surroundings. Jonathan and his officers waited for Gomes to push his way through the assembled crew and reach the head of the table. He pulled up a cane chair, opened his arms wide in a gesture of welcome, and invited his guests to take their places at the table.

Turning to the officers, he said formally, "You, Captain, and you gentlemen, seat yourselves at my side." Then he addressed the crew, calling out, "Settle down, my friends. There is room for everyone here."

The sailors lost their timidity and scrambled for the table, anxious to find a seat. At last, everyone was seated and the men from the fort then sat themselves in the remaining places.

Jonathan contemplated his host. Gomes seemed to have washed and shaved in his honor. He had even waxed his mustache. He was wearing a clean shirt and his greasy hair was carefully combed into place. The other men from the outpost had not taken such pains. They were dressed in dirty faded cotton shirts and trousers cut raggedly above the knee. Some had gold rings in their ears, and their long hair was tied back with a scarf at the nape of the neck or crammed into a silk or wool bonnet. Their rough beards hardly inspired confidence and Jonathan was sure that they must be outlaws at the very least, possibly wanted for murder or desertion. They paid no attention to the sailors from *The Sea Witch*, hardly addressing a word to them. They talked amongst themselves in their own language throughout the meal, with sly conspiratorial glances that Jonathan found disturbing, and which confirmed his decision to be constantly on his guard.

Gomes clapped his hands and a man entered. He was magnificently built, about twenty years of age, with sharp features. His dark skin and flattened nose indicated a mixed racial heritage, though he dressed like the Portuguese and wore a whip tucked into his belt. His shifty blue eyes stared at Gomes.

"This is Vasco, my overseer," explained Gomes. "He's part Pahouin, part Portuguese. The captain of a ship shot a little honest Christian juice into some black wench on one crossing, and he kept the female and child with him in Lisbon for a while. He sold the mother in the end, but he kept the boy with him until he died of smallpox here. There was an epidemic on his vessel. He really liked the little ape, and before he died he begged me to take good care of him. I use him as an interpreter to explain the language of those beasts, if you can call it a language. And he knows how to make good use of a cudgel. He obviously has a little human blood in his veins."

Vasco stood behind his master in a seemingly respectful pose throughout this tirade, but Jonathan read deep hatred in the eyes that gazed at Gomes.

"Get them to bring us something to drink, you big ape," ordered Gomes, "and then serve the dinner. These gentlemen are hungry."

The half-breed nodded silently and left the room.

The excited cacophony of sound around the table died down as a flood of curses came from outside the room, heralding the arrival of three young blacks bearing pitchers, naked except for rags tied about their waists. Vasco, flourishing his whip, was abusing them roundly.

"Get a move on, filthy niggers," he shouted. "The whites are waiting. You know you must never keep the whites waiting. I'll tan your hides until there's no skin left." The poor blacks were hurrying to pour the drink, trembling in all their limbs. In his anxiety, one of them spilled a little wine on the table and stood there, eyes rolling madly, terrorized by his own clumsiness. The half-breed grabbed the pitcher from his hands and lashed at his face with a stroke that sent him rolling onto the floor in agony. Without a word, the young black got to his feet and ran for all he was worth as Vasco took his place and finished the task of filling the goblets. When everyone had been taken care of, he left, grumbling under his breath.

"Did you see that, Captain?" asked Gomes. "Did you see how I have to be after them? There's no other way to teach 'em manners. All they understand is the whip. You have to know how to hit hard, too, because they have a tough hide."

He raised his goblet.

"Gentlemen, may the Holy Mother keep you in her protection," he said solemnly.

Jonathan raised his glass and the others followed suit. Vasco came back with pitchers full to the brim, which he ordered placed on the table as blacks brought in steaming platters of food. Gomes, his raised eyes on the painted Christ figure, clasped his hands and murmured a faint grace. The other Portuguese, Dr. MacLean, and some of the sailors joined in. The invitation to begin did not have to be repeated, and the hungry sailors fell on the food.

Despite Jonathan's fears of the contrary, the food was varied and excellent. There was roast pork with a highly spiced sauce, banana bread, a guinea-fowl stew with pureed palm cabbage. The meal ended with huge baskets of guava pears and oranges. The Englishmen did full honor to the meal, as Gomes tried to show off to the officers at the head of the table. His half-breed stood behind his chair throughout the meal, careful to attend to all his needs, removing the insects as they fell onto his plate, and making sure that his goblet was always filled.

"See, we discovered this Godforsaken country here," expounded Gomes proudly. "Yes sir. Yes, Mr. Captain, we Portuguese were the first to venture so far from home, and to discover Africa. All the rivers have Portuguese names, you know. The lagoon here, for instance, is called Fernan Vaz, you see. He gave it his name. Before that the lagoon was called N'Komi."

Jonathan was quite irritated by the Portuguese's pontificating manner, but the details interested him.

"N'Komi was the name of the niggers who was here when we came," explained Gomes. "They had lived here for a very long time. They're still here. That wasn't their name before, but I couldn't tell you what they called themselves. I don't know. All I know is, they took that name because it's the name of the west wind that blows here from the sea." He paused reflectively, and concluded, his speech slurring from the drink, "Perhaps they didn't have no name at all, they're so primitive."

"But perhaps you could tell us where they came from?" asked MacLean, always avid for new information.

"No," returned Gomes. "I couldn't tell you that. Maybe Vasco knows the answer. Vasco! Tell the white man where those poisonous apes come from originally. And you use your best manners when you're talking to a white, now. Did you understand, you lazy bastard?"

"Yessir, Mr. Gomes, I'll be polite," Vasco said humbly. "Mr. White Man, these blacks were called Etimboue N'kombe. They told me that they used to live near a large lake and that men on horses chased them away. They didn't say if they were white or black. But anyway, that's why they came here, Mr. White Man. They're the ones who make deals for us with the Poutous."

"Can't you say Portuguese instead of Poutous?" demanded Gomes in a rage. "What's the use of trying to teach you to speak right? You're just a Pahouin idiot!"

"Yes, Mr. Gomes, sir. Forgive me. Yes, Mr. White Man, I'm just a Pahouin idiot. I don't know anything more," stammered the half-breed. He didn't say another word, but fury seethed in his pale blue eyes as he calmly went about his tasks.

"Well, I can tell you," said Gomes, "that those niggers— the N'Komi, I mean, they're a little more civilized than the others. They know how to make canoes and work with iron, but that's about all you can say about 'em."

The fat little man drank some wine and let out a loud belch.

"I make my nigger deals through them," he explained. "I need them because they know how to trap 'em. When I first came, they used to bring 'em to that island opposite. It is called Nengue Sika, which means Island of Money, because that's where I used to pay 'em. Now I do the whole thing from here."

The wine was beginning to take effect, and Gomes went into a long monologue about his past. He told Jonathan and the other officers that he was the son of a poor fisherman who had chosen to become an expatriate. Africa provided him with the comfort, the money, and all the women he wanted, whereas in Portugal he had lived from hand to mouth in a tiny seaport.

Jonathan was sure he was hiding something and that other reasons had led him to this hostile land which all maps marked as deadly dangerous to Europeans, but he was careful not to reveal his suspicions. Every man there had something to hide, he not the least, and it was no-body's business.

Gregory realized that it was time to relieve the guard left with the longboats and, rising, he tapped two sailors on the shoulder as they whispered to each other at the foot of the table.

"Smith, and you, Fleming, come to the dock with me," he ordered.

The edge of the dock was feebly lit by a torch, and the two guards were sitting on the wooden boards, their legs dangling over the water. They were wrapped in light cotton as a protection against the mosquitoes, and were talking quietly to each other, their glances constantly sweeping the area. The slightest sound sent their hands to the pistols at their belts.

One was very young, barely twenty, his smooth face childlike. He seemed frail, and coughed frequently. His companion was older, with strong features that seemed to indicate an early knowledge of the seamy side of life. The younger was saying in a dull, discouraged tone, "They told me that if I joined the navy I'd have a good salary, and that if I managed to smuggle in a couple of stowaway slaves I could sell them for a lot of money in the Americas. Then they gave me lots to drink, and next thing I knew I was out at sea."

"Sons of bitches!" cursed the other softly. "Sons of bitches, all of 'em." He added seriously, "Now listen to me, Matthew, they had you on, they did. Don't you realize that even if you could hide your niggers, and I'm not saying that you could, they'd likely die on the way?"

"Why would they die?" asked the other, discouraged even more by these comments.

"Listen here, young 'un. You'll see what it's like on *The Sea Witch*. They're going to be stacked so tight in there, there won't be room for them to move a foot or a finger. So where do you think you could hide some?"

The young sailor looked disconcerted.

"Well, I had thought of the anchor cable pit . . ." he said hesitantly.

"The pit? It's the pit, is it, eh?" The other let out a hearty laugh. "Think o' that, now. That all you could find, son? Let me wise you up a little. Everybody thinks o' that pit. You'll have to do better'n that, m'lad."

Matthew looked stunned. "You seem to say that there's nothing to be got out of these niggers, then," he said. "So why are you on that rat trap out there?"

The older man threw a pebble into the water and watched it splash, his gaze stony. " 'Twere different for me," he answered. "I didn't have no choice in t'matter. I prefer the stink of nigger flesh to a dungeon in the floating Liverpool pontoons."

"What if I deserted here?" asked Matthew. "Perhaps I could get in with those Portuguese." His voice broke and there were tears in it as he continued. "I'm really afraid of dying on that ship. I know if I stay there I'll die. I feel it. I just know I will. I've always heard tell there's lots of death in them ships."

"You talk a lot of nonsense, lad," said the older man. "First, you are not going to die. Second, what would you do if you stayed here? Answer me that. You say you're afeared of dying. Well, you can be sure you won't live long in this place. If the blacks don't get you, one of their infernal diseases will. Or perhaps the captain will search you out and then you'll swing for it, with your tongue all purple, dangling from the topmast . . . not a pretty sight, I can promise you that. No, son, don't you think of that. I'll tell you what you must do. Wait until we're in America, and there we could get took on some pirate vessel or even a Royal Navy ship. If they take you on, you ain't considered no deserter, y'know. They think that any sailor who's done a stint on a nigger ship is real tough. They say it's the best character-forming experience a sailor can have."

Their discussion was interrupted by voices. They stared toward the sound and saw a glimmer of light coming toward them.

"Adams, it's me!" called Gregory. Knowing how trigger-happy guards could get in strange country, he preferred to identify himself well out of range of their pistols.

The two sailors were delighted to see him. They were famished, and heartily sick of the insect bites. Their talk of escape forgotten, they greeted the relief with eagerness as Gregory repeated his cautions to the new guards.

"Nobody is to board the longboats," he reminded them. "Shoot, if you have to. And come and get me at once if you see the men on *The Sea Witch* in any difficulty."

Leaving them, he climbed back toward the fort with the

others, who eagerly settled down at the table and tucked into the excellent food.

Jonathan lit his pipe. He was tired. "I'd like to go aboard now," he said to Gomes.

"Really?" asked the other in surprise. "Won't you stay? There's going to be a dance by the women. I've reserved a beauty for you, Captain, not fourteen if she's a day, and breasts like ripe melons."

"No thank you," said Jonathan courteously but firmly. "I do need some rest, Mr. Gomes. It has been a long journey and I have much to do. But I leave you my men and my officers."

"If you don't mind, sir," interjected Gregory, who had sat down beside him, "I would prefer to ride back to the ship with you."

"As you wish, Mr. Adams," said the captain.

Gomes seemed disappointed by Jonathan's refusal to stay on, but he didn't insist.

"Vasco!" he called, "accompany these gentlemen with torches."

Gregory picked out the six crew members who seemed the least drunk and asked them to go back on board ship with them. MacLean and Clark, euphoric though they were, seemed quite lucid.

"Have a good time and watch out for the men," Jonathan cautioned as they left. "I want everyone back tomorrow morning before dawn and I hold you both responsible." He turned toward his host. "Mr. Gomes," he said, "I have greatly enjoyed your hospitality and have been most honored by your kindness. I shall be back to see you in the morning. We have many details to iron out and I want to take a look at the blacks you have down there."

"The honor was mine, Captain," answered Gomes, not to be outdone. "I'll see that they're washed up a bit so that the smell isn't too bad. Sleep well, Captain, and you too, sir, and may the good Lord keep you. I'll see you tomorrow."

"Coming, Gregory?" Jonathan asked somewhat curtly, and they set off, led by the half-breed, the six sailors bringing up the rear.

As soon as the two officers had left, the atmosphere lightened considerably and the sailors relaxed. The presence of MacLean and Clark didn't put a damper on their high spirits, for the doctor was too young for them to be impressed by him, and his role on board ship was not to keep order. As for the gunnery officer, he had already drunk quite a bit and was far from stopping anyone else. The drinking continued in full force.

Gomes had also had his share of liquor. As long as Jonathan was at table with him he had exercised a certain restraint, but now that he had left there was no need to exhibit a moderation so alien to his nature.

The remains of the feast still covered the table, mingling with grease from the candles and spilled wine, when Gomes rose abruptly and pushed his chair back.

"Let's go and have some fun, friends!" he exclaimed. "What do you think of that?"

Thunderous applause, whistles, and shouts greeted his suggestion, and he stood, swaying slightly, until there was silence again.

"I thought a little music and dancing might divert you," he said. "Vasco! Go get the musicians. Move it, you black nigger monkey."

The half-breed hurried away and was soon back with a group of young blacks, their eyes rolling with terror. They were carrying musical instruments, mostly drums. Vasco herded them toward the end of the room and sat them down. He took a pitcher of wine, handed it to them, and went out.

"That's so that they play better," said Gomes to Clark apologetically. The sailors lolled in their seats and settled themselves more comfortably as the musicians began to play. At first, the sound was tempered by their fear, but as the notes took hold and lifted them from their harsh reality, they began to play a strange music, wild and incredibly beautiful. It filled the farthest corners of the room and the men from *The Sea Witch* fell silent.

The rhythm and tempo of the music increased and became very turbulent as Vasco again appeared, this time accompanied by about twenty young black girls. They must have been no older than twelve or fourteen, but they were beautiful, with well-rounded figures. They were completely nude except for two tiny squares of fabric joined by a thin cord. The sailors greeted their appearance with breathless expectancy. Having seen no women for many a long week, they were so excited by the smooth bare black bodies that they remained silent as the girls, pushed by the half-breed, grouped in the center of the room and began to dance. One of them seemed to be holding back, and Vasco switched her shins and ankles until she joined the rest. The sailors sat, their eyes popping out of their heads, watching the most suggestive contortions they had ever seen. They found themselves wondering if the music or the nature of these primitive young girls caused them to be so openly erotic. Gomes, watching the faces of his guests, allowed himself a small satisfied smile.

"Pretty, eh?" he leered, leaning toward MacLean, who had come out of his drunken stupor and was watching the girls avidly. "It's a shame about the music. I tried to get 'em to play the trumpet, but those blacks only know how to bang on drums or tap pieces of wood."

The drinking went on unabated. The young dancers gyrated and leapt, their sweating bodies gleaming in the candlelight. Their violent movements often lifted the thin fabric of their skirts and exposed them to the staring eyes of the fascinated sailors. Gomes sensed that the moment had come to offer the girls to his guests. He got to his feet with difficulty and moved into the center of the dancers, who continued their movements as if nothing in the world counted for them but the steady throb of the music.

"Friends," he said loudly, "these girls are for you. Take one each!" And he laughed suggestively.

The sailors hardly waited for the end of the sentence. They leapt forward and fell on the girls. The room was the scene of total confusion as each sailor sought the girl of his choice and the girls tried to escape in a cacophony of shrieks and shouts of victory. Sometimes two sailors leapt on the same girl and tried to pull her in two different directions. At last each sailor had found a companion. The girls knew what was in store for them. This was not the first crew that had come to the fort, and they knew what was expected of them. They had no objections to having sex with white men, other than the disagreeable fishlike smell they exuded. They knew that this was a temporary respite to being chained and sent off on one of those enormous vessels that disappeared from sight and was never heard from again, and from which no one had ever returned. They really had no choice. Escape was impossible, and if they were caught it could end in torture or death. If they refused to do what was expected of them they would be treated to the Portuguese whip or to the half-breed's cudgel. How they hated Vasco! His cruelty was far greater than that of the whites. He seemed to revel in torturing those who were almost his own people, as though he hated them the more because he himself was not entirely white. He took all the girls he wanted and they couldn't do a thing about it. The luckiest were those picked by Gomes for his own personal pleasures. They sometimes had to submit to some revolting practices but they were at least assured plenty of food for as long as he cared to keep them.

The sailors had dragged the young black girls to the table and were forcing liquor down their throats, to the accompaniment of giggles and much horseplay. The evening degenerated rapidly. Gomes had gone to his quarters to sleep or to disport himself with his companion of the moment and the girls were thrown down on the table and assaulted there on the rough wood, amid the dirty plates and tumbled glasses. The floor was littered with drunken sailors whose prey had profited from their collapse by fleeing. MacLean, an expression of ecstasy on his face, caressed a young Negress with a naive affection that caused her to stare at him with huge, startled eyes. She was little accustomed to such consideration. At last he decided to take her out of the room, carrying her in his arms. Clark had disappeared earlier, as soon as he had made his choice.

It was still dark when the longboats regained *The Sea Witch*. The sailors rowed languidly and out of time, cutting ragged wakes behind them. They were singing hoarsely in a tired dissonant chorus while those who were dead drunk slept in the bottoms of the boats where they had been dumped by their companions.

The Sea Witch was immobile, her anchor chain loose. Awakened by the din, Jonathan was standing aft, leaning against the poop rail. He reflected that it would not be much use to ask much of the men that day. He acknowledged a deep feeling of utter contempt. His officers were no angels, but they wore haloes compared to his crew. Most of them had been pressed into service from gaming houses from which they would have had to go to prison. They had been forced into signing up, or their drunkenness had been taken advantage of. Jonathan knew that few would ever go back to their country. Some would die during the crossing, and the rest would go to swell the motley population of the New World, where they would undoubtedly end as pirates or dangling from the gallows.

Jonathan's mind dwelt nostalgically on the iron discipline he had known in Her Majesty's Navy. This was a far cry from his past. He knew that he, too, would probably never see England again. He would never again see the smiling Cornish girls or chase a fox through the Norfolk countryside.

Suddenly he thought of Aurelia, his reason for finding himself on a slave ship, in a country that bore a close resemblance to Hell itself. He remembered how it had felt to have her soft hands on him, and her lips seeking his. He could still conjure up the feel of her caresses with painful reality. God, how he had loved her! He still loved her passionately. He knew he would probably never see her again, and his heart plummeted as a huge wave of loneliness washed over him. His eyes moistened.

The men hauled themselves up onto the deck one by one, and stumbled to their bunks, or simply lay about, sleeping where they fell. Silence gradually returned to *The Sea Witch,* the steps of the guard sounding hollow on the deck and the rigging squeaking gently in the background.

"Everyone has come aboard, sir," said a voice at Jonathan's elbow, and turning, he saw John Woolcomb.

Wrenched from his painful reverie, he moved away from the rail, acknowledging the information with a grunt. He turned his back quickly for fear the other officer might see the intense emotion under which he was laboring, and hurried to his cabin.

CHAPTER XII

At the exact moment that Captain Jonathan Collins hurried into his cabin aboard *The Sea Witch*, somewhere far beyond the curves of the great river, a man rose up in the depths of the forest. Like an evil spirit, his tall figure stood in the center of the clearing. Mouele the Bapounou gazed at the sky and read in the stars that the time for action had come.

He woke the men who were stretched out beside the dying embers of the fire, and they got ready without enthusiasm.

"Come on! Up with you!" ordered their chief. "We must get started if we are to make best use of the dark."

As soon as they were all up they began to load the flintlocks while those not fortunate enough to carry guns took up assegais, sabers, or jet-handled knives. For them, these were as efficient as the guns, which they were not practiced in handling—their awkwardness was offset, however, by the sheer terror caused by the loud noise of these weapons. Each man also carried a whip, a lash made from buffalo or hippopotamus hide, and a cudgel.

Mouele made them gather round to listen to his instructions.

"This operation must succeed," he said. "You must do exactly as I tell you. Any man who disobeys will be killed."

By now the small band of men was completely armed and wide awake. They were impatient to slake their blood lust, and listened avidly to their chief's words.

"We'll go to the edge of the village," continued Mouele. "I don't want the slightest sound. We'll wait there till dawn before we attack. We'll get rid of the sentries first and then we'll close in on the villagers. The most important thing will be to surprise them. Those idiots will be sleeping off their drunk and it will be easy. I forbid you to kill any strong men. If they put up a fight, knock them out but don't wound them. As for the young women, take them all, even the pregnant ones. The infants and old men must be killed." He glanced at their intent faces. "Understand?"

The men mumbled in unison and he gestured toward the forest. "Let's get moving now. Be very quiet. Ah! I almost forgot! No one is to touch Adende and his wives. I made a deal with him." The tall Bapounou gave a mirthless laugh.

The men finished taking up their weapons and some settled heavy hampers on their heads. Had Adende, whose acquisitive mind was filled with dreams of splendid gifts, known what they contained, he would have been astonished. There were no sumptuous fabrics and intriguing trinkets. The hampers were packed with iron chains, leather thongs, and iron collars for fettering the prisoners.

Mouele stepped to the head of the column and the others fell in behind. He didn't really expect the villagers of Mounigou to put up much of a fight. He had taken a good look at their defenses and had concluded that there were few. He was delighted to think of the profits this expedition would bring him. He, too, had heard the cannon the previous night as it boomed its message that a ship was in port. He knew that it meant his prisoners would soon be sold, and his chief, King Minga, would be pleased with him.

Advancing in total silence, the Bapounou reached the trail that led to Mounigou. Mouele stopped them and ordered them to hide, and keep very quiet. Then he moved away, signaling to one of the men to follow him.

With infinite precautions, the two men crept through the banana plantation and reached the two guards, who lay in a drugged sleep, thanks to Adende. A sign from Mouele, and his companion had a short dagger out of his belt. There was a flash, a smothered gasp, and a gush of blood. The second guard was dispatched just as quietly. The killer wiped the bloody blade on his tunic and followed his chief, now crawling on his stomach toward the first huts. The crackling of the fire was the only sound. Everywhere, men and women were sound asleep, their arms about each other, lying exhausted on the ground from the combined effects of dance and liquor.

The two Bapounou exchanged a satisfied grin. All was as they had hoped. They slid backward the way they had come and hurried to rejoin the others. In spite of all his care, Moucle snapped a twig, but the slight crack was not loud enough to wake the sleepers. In his haste he failed to notice Yawana, who had come out of her husband's hut and was peacefully walking toward the river.

As soon as he reached his band of ruffians, Mouele told them what he had seen. They were champing with impatience. Rape, pillage, murder, and hoards of loot were theirs for the taking and they were more than ready to obey their leader.

"Absolute silence until you reach the first huts," cautioned Mouele. "Then you await my signal."

They got to their feet and slipped through the plantation. As soon as they were all at their posts, Mouele rose to his feet and, throwing caution to the wind, gave the signal for attack, yelling the death cry, "Yona, yonani, kill, kill!"

The men all picked up his cry and hurled themselves forward, firing the guns to intensify the panic. Yelling at the tops of their voices and brandishing their weapons, they burst into the huts. The villagers and their guests, surprised out of a deep sleep, were thrown into total disarray by the curses and the loud explosions they did not understand. Gunshots rang out everywhere, forcing them out of their huts. Any who tried to escape were killed immediately.

None was swift enough or alert enough to seize a weapon in defense, except N'Gio. Like the others, he had awakened in alarm. Hearing the chaos, the shrieks of terror, and the gunshots, he put out a hand to touch Yawana. Stunned and disoriented at finding her gone, he didn't know what was happening, and leapt instinctively for his spear. He had barely reached it when two ruffians burst into his hut. Without pausing for thought, he hurled himself forward and pierced one of them with his weapon. The man crumbled, but his companion rushed forward. N'Gio felt an agonizing pain in the back of his head as he lost consciousness.

Old Adende was awake when the attack began. He hadn't expected such chaos. The sounds of the carnage outside terrified him. Although he had provoked the attack himself, he was appalled by its brutality. He huddled in the farthermost corner of his hut, surrounded by his wives who pushed against him, moaning and wailing in terror. When a giant shadow darkened his doorway, he feared all was lost, but in an instant he realized that his visitor was Mouele himself. Limp with relief, he stared at him, incapable of uttering a single word.

"Stay where you are, old man," cried the Bapounou. "Don't move out of here under any circumstances. I'm setting up a guard in front of your hut." The tall man left, and Adende felt reassured as he saw a man take up his position in front of the hut, thinking that this would undoubtedly protect him against a possible mistake by the attackers. There was nothing left for him to do now but await the end of the attack. The biting remorse that had begun to torment him earlier in the evening faded as he realized that Mouele intended to spare him and his family.

A little later, the villagers of Mounigou and their guests were all brutally herded into the center of the village. A gray dawn lit the ghastly scene. The Bapounou tribesmen stood around their captives, shouting curses and orders, poking at them with assegais and forcing them into a tighter and tighter group of terrified creatures. Those who tried to escape were stopped by the weapons and forced back into the circle. N'Gio, dragged by his feet out of the hut, was thrown in with the rest. He gradually came to, his nose in the dust, and heard the shrieks of his tortured tribesmen in an echoing jumble of sound. In the midst of his confusion, he wondered again what could possibly have happened to Yawana. He could not understand this attack. There had been no recent provocation of neighboring tribes. He wondered if his father had managed to escape, and who these men were. He wondered about the terrifying explosions he heard all around him. His head ached unbearably with pain and terror.

Mouele stood watching his helpless captives with a sneer. "Dogs!" he cried in a harsh, cruel tone. "I've been waiting for this moment for a long time. You won't argue about the price of salt anymore. You are my prisoners and you won't escape me now. I am your chief from now on, and I will kill all those who try to rebel."

Furious insults rained down on him in answer, but he merely laughed.

Then he turned to his men. "Separate the men from the women!" he ordered.

Sticks and whips separated them without more ado. The men were left where they were, and the women were dragged to one side. Small children clung to their mothers, screaming and crying. Old women, paralyzed with fear, were roughly pushed about with goads.

N'Gio watched in horror, too weak to move. All the old people were systematically removed from the two groups and massacred immediately. Small children were snatched from their mothers, their agonized shrieks ringing in the early-morning air as they watched the Bapounou's dreadful games. They hurled infants into the air and caught them on the points of their spears, or seized them by the feet and flung them full force against trees until their skulls cracked.

The prisoners were sick with horror at this extermination. Even the ones old enough to have fought wars could not remember such cruelty. They could not understand what evil force had burst in to break the ancestral rhythm of their days. N'Gio realized that his days of freedom were over forever. In a desperate effort, he tried to get up but he was seized immediately, and his hands were bound behind his back. He was clearly one of the strongest and most dangerous captives. All the strong male prisoners were bound by twos in a double fork of wood tied tight about their necks with leather thongs. As soon as they were immobilized, their captives took away all their clothes and their festive adornments. The huts were being searched and pillaged, and anything useful or valuable was piled onto the hampers on the ground.

N'Gio had been shackled to Ozengue, the fisherman, a small timid man who was sobbing hysterically. N'Gio had no words with which to console him. What was there to say?

Then came the women's turn. The Bapounou had reserved special treatment for them. Their hands bound behind their backs, they were also stripped of clothing and jewels, and then their torturers threw themselves on them without preliminaries and raped them on the spot, ignoring their shrieks and pleas for mercy.

The Bapounou continued as long as they wanted while N'Gio searched for Yawana with desperately fearful eyes. She was nowhere to be seen. He began to hope that she had managed to escape these monsters and, in spite of his discomfort, an immense joy welled up in him. He could not have borne to see her subjected to such treatment.

When they had finished with the women, the Bapounou tied them in groups of ten bound at the waist by ropes short enough to prevent any attempt at flight. Some had their hands free so that they would be able to carry hampers.

Móuele had every reason to be satisfied as he gloated over the excellence of his prize. It had been a brief attack,

and he had lost only one man, the man killed by N'Gio.
Most of the captives seemed young and strong. He was well
pleased with himself.

Adende had seen nothing of what was going on outside,
but the horrified shrieks had left him in no doubt about
how his people were being treated. The man at the door
came into the hut. "You can come out now, old man," he
said. "You and your wives. Mouele wants to see you."

Now that at last he would receive his reward, Adende
felt a shock of pleasure course through him as he hastened
to obey, followed by Aziza and his other trembling wives.
N'Gio, when he saw him, thought his father had been captured. He never wondered how the old man had so far escaped the attackers. All he knew was that the man for
whom he had unbounded love and admiration was about to
suffer horrible tortures and degradations. He was amazed
at Adende's courage. The old chief advanced, head high,
as though nothing was wrong. N'Gio reflected that his
father might try, with his customary daring, to save them
all from this band of ruffians. Perhaps he would negotiate,
whatever the price. Seized by the same insane hope, the
others fell silent and ceased their moaning. In the midst
of deathly hush, Adende advanced toward Mouele.

The Bapounou stood with his legs apart, waiting defiantly, surrounded by his men. Adende stopped a couple
of paces away from him, his wives crowding behind him in
terror.

"You see, Mouele," he said proudly, "I didn't lie to you.
I hope you are satisfied. Now you must pay me, and take
your captives away."

The words pierced N'Gio's heart like an arrow. The
blood left his brain and he almost lost his senses. He could
not believe that he had heard correctly. In his distress, his
father must have said the wrong thing. But the talk continued and shattered the last of his hopes and illusions.

"No, you didn't lie," answered the tall Bapounou in an
oily tone. "You have deserved your pay, old man." And he
began to laugh silently, his lips curling in derision like a
hyena's. Adende, his mind reeling with the blind pleasure
of having his greed finally assuaged, failed to read the menace in the words.

Mouele turned to the prisoners. "Did you hear that?" he

asked. "It's this old cur who sold you all. He arranged his
son's marriage just to trap the lot of you."

A storm of curses greeted his words. The captive tribesmen suddenly understood the enormity of Adende's treachery, but he watched them with disdain, certain that he had
nothing to fear from them now. A few lashes would soon
quiet them. N'Gio felt a wave of icy cold reach his limbs.
How could it be possible that the father he had so loved
had become this despicable creature, who had not hesitated
to betray his tribe, his friends, his son. He could not bear
the thought that the marriage had been set for no other
purpose. In a last gasp of loyal disbelief, he shouted, "Tato!
Tato, no! It's not true!"

Adende turned in shock at his son's voice.

"Don't you be afraid, N'Gio," he soothed. "You will be
freed." Then he noticed how ignominiously his son was
bound and he hurled himself angrily at Mouele.

"What does this mean?" he cried. "Why is my son tied
up like the others? That's him! That's my son! It's N'Gio,
don't you understand? You promised he would be safe.
Free him this minute!"

The Bapounou pushed the old man roughly. He fell
backward, taking Aziza down with him. Mouele and his
men burst into raucous laughter as Adende rose with difficulty and stared at them in horror. The thought that all
was not going as planned was beginning to pierce his euphoria. He still shouted, but his tone had lost its convic-
tion.

"Pay me at once and let my son and his wife go," he
roared, his voice hoarse with anger. "And get out of here!"

Mouele stopped laughing.

"Listen to that!" he exclaimed to his men. "The old ape
isn't pleased."

He stepped closer to Adende and put his hand on his
shoulder.

"Come, come, old chief," he said with emphasis, "calm
down. You will be paid. You will be very well paid indeed."

Removing his hand, he said to his men, "Seize him!"

Four men rushed at Adende and threw him to the
ground despite his roars of rage and desperate resistance.
They kicked and punched him remorselessly, keeping him
pinned to the ground in the dust and tearing off his clothes.

Mouele pulled out his saber, bent between the victim's legs, and sliced off his testicles in one short stroke. Adende opened his mouth wide to let out a howl of agony, but the pain was so tremendous that he could make no sound at all. His torturer stuffed the dreadful trophy in the old chief's mouth and forced it shut with a kick on the jaw. He and the others then set about the old man with their knives and soon he was nothing more than a mass of torn, quivering flesh. Then each man crouched over him and soiled his body with excrement.

Stunned into total horror, Aziza and the other wives watched what was happening to their master. But as soon as he was dead they could no longer pity him, for they were thrown to the ground in their turn by the Bapounou, who raped them viciously. Then they were pushed toward their companions in misfortune and tied in the same way.

Mouele came over to inspect the captives. He looked worried. Passing in front of Aziza, he took the opportunity to wipe his saber, dripping with her husband's blood, across her stomach. The young woman's revulsion made him roar with laughter. Moving over to his men, he muttered something to them but they shook their heads. He left them and approached N'Gio.

"Where is your wife, son of a bitch?" he asked. "Where did you hide her? Answer!"

N'Gio, still speechless from the overwhelming horror of his father's death, stared at him disdainfully.

"I don't know," he answered, his voice barely audible, "and even if I did, I wouldn't tell you, filthy murderer." He spat in Mouele's face. Mouele blanched under the insult and slashed at his lips with the lash. N'Gio fell with the force of the blow, dragging down this companion in the collar.

"Find her!" hissed Mouele through clenched teeth. "She can't be far."

Ten men left the group and sped in all directions in search of Yawana.

N'Gio, his mouth bleeding profusely, managed to get up with difficulty as Ozengue, whose throat had been violently bruised in the fall, whimpered quietly.

All the captives then turned the force of their insults on the young man, piling on him the incredible treachery of his dead father. N'Gio tried not to listen. Their insults hurt

him far less than his father's betrayal. All he had left in the
world was Yawana. He now felt certain that she had managed to escape. He couldn't imagine how, or when, but she
was free. If only she could stay out of the clutches of those
monsters. He hardly dared think what would happen to the
girl if she was captured. At the mere thought of the brutal
rape she would probably have to endure, large tears such
as he had not felt since childhood ran down his cheeks, and
he realized the depth of his love for Yawana. After what
seemed an eternity, the men came back empty-handed
and a huge sigh of relief escaped N'Gio's wounded lips.
Mouele, furious at this setback, gibbered with rage. He
came at N'Gio and covered him with lashes, but N'Gio,
lost in his joy and relief, hardly felt them.

Foiled in his intent, the Bapounou shrieked his orders.
The whips and cudgels thudded against the bare spines of
the prisoners and the column began to move forward under
blows and curses. Meanwhile, some of the men lit resin
torches and set fire to all the huts. The peaceful little village of Mounigou instantly became a flaming beacon.
N'Gio and his companions left their little universe to begin
the long march along a trail that would lead them very far,
toward a world they would never leave.

CHAPTER XIII

Yawana splashed water all over herself in joyous abandon. She was excited by the new life which was opening out ahead of her. She lay in the clear water and rubbed her body with fistfuls of sand, then satisfied and totally relaxed, she gazed up into the sky. Fireflies, tiny love symbols, gave off flashes of green light as they darted about in the dark. The haunting cry of a lemur echoed in the silence, fish leapt out of the water in gentle splashes, and the muffled swoosh of a bird's wings fanned her face.

Farther down the river there was a sudden agitation in the water followed by frantic shrieks and then silence. Yawana shivered as she recognized the grunting of crocodiles. She was in a spot protected by high bamboo clumps, but still, she thought, she had better get out. She climbed onto the bank, her body glistening with the bright water, and she giggled as she thought of N'Gio's surprised awakening when she slipped her damp body beside his. She found her loincloth and fastened it about her waist.

She was preparing to return to the village when an outbreak of terrifying noise turned her to stone where she stood. There seemed to be cracks of terrible thunder and then shrieks and screams. Tiny pearl-gray herons flew agitatedly out of the grasses around her, and other birds soared to the sky, squawking shrilly in fear. There were now cries of terror and roars of rage mingling with the thunder reverberating from behind the curtain of trees.

An attack, it must be an attack! thought Yawana in panic. "Oh, N'Gio," she whispered to herself, half-sobbing. "N'Gio! May the spirits help you to escape. Come and find me!"

There could be no doubt as to what was happening in Mounigou. An enemy tribe must have attacked the village and she prayed that the inhabitants had been able to defend themselves. There was nothing for her to do but wait for the carnage to end, and she fled in terror along the riverbank. Thorns and brittle leaves scratched her skin, trailing vines clutched at her feet and made her trip and fall in the

mud. The insects, awakened by her panic, stung her mercilessly, black wasps whose sting turns men mad before drug-
ging them to sleep, huge yellow flies with green eyes, and
millions of tiny gnats, their bites burning like fire. She ran
and ran until she fell from exhaustion. With her scant remaining strength, she crawled into a mass of papyrus leaves
and let them close over her. Lying there in terrified immo-
bility, her heart beating great loud beats, she placed her
hands over her ears to shut out the distant shrieks and explosions that still echoed through the forest.

For a long time she sat and trembled, listening and
trying not to hear. Sometimes the noises seemed to be coming closer. The shrieks of pain turned into long, drawn-out
death howls. Day came up over the river and the fog lifted
with the first rays of the sun. All living creatures had fled,
the birds, the rodents, the crocodiles. The explosions became fewer and farther between. There was a long silence
and then a dreadful scream that rang out longer and
louder, more terrible than any that had preceded it. Then
the silence fell again.

No other sound came from the village. Yawana reflected
that the fight had ended at last and that she should risk
going to see what had happened. She was getting ready to
leave her hiding place when she heard voices close by.
Peering through the papyrus stalks she saw two men approaching. They were carrying strange metal rods, and
they wore long tunics that covered their entire bodies. Nothing about them identified them as members of any
tribe she knew. They were beating about in the tall grass
and seemed to be looking for someone. They came so close
that for a moment she could hear them breathing and was
afraid she was doomed, but they moved away, to her great
relief, and their voices faded. She wondered what had happened to N'Gio and to all her family, whether they might
be dead, or whether they had been taken prisoner. She
found herself hoping for the latter, unless this meant torture
or unless the attacking tribe was of the Pahouin race who
sometimes ate their prisoners of war, the worst horror of
all.

One last rumble broke the silence, and then nothing. A
huge cloud of smoke, pushed by the wind, rolled over the
river. It reached Yawana and made her cough. She stayed
in her hiding place as long as she could, almost asphyxiated

by the fumes and not sure whether her discomfort or her
suffering were causing her to weep.

At last, unable to bear it any longer, she crept out of
concealment. She was sure that the danger had passed at
last. Without a sound she crawled to the trail and listened,
all her senses on the alert, but the only sound was the crackling of the fire. She stood upright and ran madly toward
the village.

The fire had spread beyond the bounds of the village,
but had begun to die out, having nothing but damp bushes
and healthy trees full of sap to feed on.

Blinded by the smoke, Yawana stumbled over a body
lying on its stomach, a gaping wound in its back. In spite
of her horror, Yawana had the courage to turn it around,
and she recognized Adiadine, the old hunter so beloved by
N'Gio. She could still read the agony he had experienced in
his staring eyes.

The smoke became more and more suffocating. A little
further on she found Noge, the woman who told such
beautiful tales, her throat slit. Her tiny infant, its face a
mess of blood and bones, was still clutched in her arms.

Nothing remained of the huts. The roofs had caved in
and the posts were no more than flaming firebrands, almost
burned to the ground. Shaking with horror, Yawana stared
at the devastation that surrounded her. A stench of death
was carried by the heavy rolls of smoke that hung over the
ruins. The earth was red with blood, and the heat had already caused the corpses to swell. Vultures circled silently
above the treetops, and rodents and fierce forest dogs
lurked in the nearby undergrowth. Armies of ants, roused
by some primeval instinct, advanced toward the village
from far away in interminable columns. All were preparing
to gorge themselves on the carnage.

Yawana fled from one corpse to another, hunting for
N'Gio. Many were horribly mutilated. She found the soiled
body of the old chief, Adende, in the center, where he lay
in all the degradation his assassins had inflicted on him.
Yawana did not know that he was entirely responsible for
the tragedy that had overtaken his village, and that the revolting mutilation hanging out of his mouth was payment
for his treason. Had she known, she might have felt differently. As it was, she crouched in pity and agony over the
body of the man she had loved as a father.

Close by, she found Ivohino, her skull crushed by a blow, fallen across the body of Isembe, who lay there with half a face. It was too much for the young girl. Her head in her hands, she fell on her mother's corpse, and rocked back and forth, wailing her pain and despair in a long continuous sound until she fainted away.

A vulture, encouraged by her stillness, passed so close to the corpse that its wings touched the girl, and revived by the revolting incident, she leapt to her feet. Scavengers all around her flew up from the carrion with shrieks of noisy rage and landed a little further away.

There was nothing left for her to do here. Yawana now knew that N'Gio was still alive, and since nothing in the entire world remained to her except him, she decided to find him. Rummaging in the ruins, she was able to find a little food, and she ran into the plantation and took some bananas, which she packed into a small straw basket that had miraculously escaped the flames. She felt a surge of joy as, in the ashes of his hut, she came upon the little ivory horn that N'Gio liked to wear about his neck. Clutching it against her heart, she felt protected.

She had not realized how long she had been in the deserted village until she saw that day was waning fast. She knew she must hurry to catch up with the kidnappers. Hanging her basket against her back from a sturdy vine around her head, she took up a glowing brand. She knew how to make fire by rubbing two pieces of dry wood together, but preferred this, which would enable her to make fire as soon as she needed it. She chewed on a bitter nut for strength and, following the trail of the party, she turned her back to the river and plunged into the forest toward the setting sun. Without a backward glance at the little village of Mounigou where she had expected to live so happily, Yawana set out, her body bent under the burden she carried.

The forest seemed more silent than usual. The explosion of violence had frightened away all living creatures except the scavengers, who were in their element. The screech of a blue touraco, harbinger of disaster, echoed from the treetops. Yawana took no notice of a cry that would ordinarily have alarmed her, for what disaster could the touraco announce that had not already happened?

She walked as fast as she could, her eyes fixed on the trail the others had left. She had never gone alone so deep

in the forest. She knew nothing about its density, nor even
if it ever ended. Only her determination to rejoin N'Gio
was able to erase the awe she usually felt toward the crushing vegetation that encircled her. Enormous bamboo met to
form an archway above her head, stirred by the movements
of huge multicolored butterflies.

Suddenly it was night. Yawana was exhausted and reluctant to continue for fear of getting lost, so she decided to
stop where she was. With the smoldering firebrand she had
taken from the village, she managed to light a fire to chase
away insects and keep the wild beasts away. She ate a little
smoked meat and some manioc and stretched out between
the roots of a giant tree. She was a tiny graceful figure who
had ever been afraid of the night. Safe in her parents' warm
hut, she had always been aware of the night panting on her
doorstep outside the bark barricade, presided over by the
eater of souls, Ngwyakinda. Now wrapped tight in her loincloth, the little forest bride fell asleep immediately.

Her sleep crawled with nightmares. She woke up very
early the following morning, startled to find herself in such
an unfamiliar setting. But the preceding days' events came
to her like a flash of lightning and she doubled up in agony. A faint column of smoke still curled up from the
dying embers of the fire she had made. Her basket lay on
its side; all the food had been devoured in the night except
for a few bananas and a little manioc. She shivered as she
thought that she herself might have been some wild night
creature's meal and vowed to be much more careful in the
future.

She decided to leave the hamper, and taking up the little
that was left of her provisions in one hand and a new firebrand in the other, she set out, the smoldering branch leaving a tiny trail of blue smoke behind her as she walked.

She stopped by a stream to rinse her mouth out, but fear
of leeches kept her from plunging her body into the cool
water. Traces of the kidnapping party now converged with
an elephant trail, so the walk became easier. Elephants always chose the best trails and avoided steep terrain. The
huge creatures had left enormous footprints in the humid
earth. They must have passed only a short while before, for
Yawana plunged a finger into their droppings and found
them still warm.

About noon, she reached a clearing where the captors

and their prey had certainly spent the preceding night. The ashes from their campfire were scattered about. She was about to take a rest, when she noticed two corpses lying at the edge of the trail. The heads had been cut off and lay beside the bodies, whose hands were tied together. They were unrecognizable, their flesh crawling with voracious scavenger ants. She stared at the bodies, wondering what to do, when she felt the ants begin to climb the side of her leg, planting their sharp mandibles in her flesh. Shuddering with horror, she fled, brushing them off and then stamping her feet to make sure none remained on her body.

Both corpses had been too small to be N'Gio, and comforted by the thought, she wondered what they could have done to deserve such a terrible death. Those tortures, in her tribe, were reserved for sorcerers. She had once seen a sorcerer convicted of vampirism. He had possessed the body of an ancient woman of the tribe and escaped at night to commit horrible crimes. He had had to prove his innocence with the iron ring test. The witch doctor had thrown an iron ring into some boiling palm oil, and the sorcerer had had to plunge his hand into the boiling oil and retrieve the ring. Everyone knew that he would not burn if he were innocent. But his pain had been too great and he had not managed to pass the test, so there could no longer be any doubt as to his guilt and Isembe had immediately ordered that his head be chopped off.

He had been led to the center of the village, a prey to the stones and taunts of the furious villagers. Then he had been forced to sit on a stool and his feet had been tied to two stakes. Stakes also held his arms and legs rigid alongside his body, and a long brand had been plunged into the ground in front of him. A creeper at its tip had been used to bend it into an arch and the creeper was then tied around the sorcerer's neck so that his neck was stretched to its maximum. The executioner had been placed behind him, and had decapitated him with a large cutlass. It had not been very sharp and he had had to make several attempts to sever the victim's head as the poor creature shrieked in torment and the crowd squealed with delight. At last, the head left the body and was lifted high in the air by the released arch, which made it swing from side to side. The head and body had been left exposed for several days as an example to the rest of the tribe. When they were finally taken away, the body was burned, the ashes scattered in the forest, and the head was flung into the river so that the dead man would not survive in the world of shadows.

But Yawana could imagine no way in which the two creatures she had just seen could have merited so terrible a punishment, and a realization of the senseless cruelty of the captors began to dawn on her.

She walked valiantly ahead all day, almost giving in to despair now and then, but always finding the strength and courage to continue. By evening, she heard the sound of many voices from far away. She crept to the edge of the forest, taking infinite precautions, her hand shading her eyes from the brilliance of the setting sun. Out on the plain, she saw the fires that surrounded the men she was following.

She was too far away to see if N'Gio was among the prisoners, but somehow she was certain that he was and she experienced a glimmer of happiness in the thought, in spite of the fear that almost overwhelmed her. She moved carefully away from the trail and hid again in the forest. Before night fell, she crushed the last of the fire from her firebrand, afraid that the smoke might betray her whereabouts. She ate what she could find, and climbed a tree to avoid all possibility of attack. She settled herself as best she could between the large branches of a fork and tied herself in with a creeper around her chest. She could just see the encampment from her perch and hear the sound of voices through the branches. She planned to watch for the moment when the group would start on its way the following morning. She was much too tired to try to figure out how she would get to N'Gio. That would be for tomorrow. Closing her eyes, she fell asleep at last.

CHAPTER XIV

Jonathan Collins hurried down the wooden blocks leading from the hull. He was so used to them that he had no need of help from the knots in the ladder rope.

The chaplain tried to do the same thing, but almost missed a step, and had to catch onto the rigging to save himself from a plunge into the brackish waters beneath. He managed to get his balance and noisily took his place in the longboat next to Jonathan.

Frank Ardeen had insisted on going ashore. He had come to Jonathan's cabin in the morning, and the captain had been stunned to note that he was shaven and neatly dressed. It was the first time since their departure from England that he had seen the man sober. Even his speech, usually slurred with liquor, was precise.

Jonathan had been about to finish his breakfast of fried fish and biscuits, and he said in surprise, "By God, Reverend, I never saw you so elegant. To what do I owe the honor of this visit?"

Ardeen had seemed embarrassed. He coughed and murmured, "Captain, I mean to say . . . well, that is, I thought I might be of some use to you. I heard from Mr. Adams that you were planning to go ashore. I'd like to accompany you, and walk on something other than a ship's planks for a change. So, if you will allow me . . ."

Jonathan couldn't get over the change in appearance and attitude, but he supposed that it was not inconceivable that Frank Ardeen should also harbor a desire for terra firma. Moreover, the idea of finding himself alone with Gomes did not enchant him, and he was pleased to have company.

"Very well," he said. "Come along with me. We'll leave the ship before lunch."

Ardeen had bowed ceremoniously and left the cabin, not without a squint toward the flask of Madeira glittering on the table. With difficulty he restrained himself from asking Jonathan for a glass.

Actually, his motive was less a desire to be of assistance than a driving passion to see for himself the things the

young sailors had told him about their orgy. They had
raved about young, passionate women, liquor by the gallon,
and more, until he shuddered with anticipation. Lately,
Pierre the cook had become more and more careful about
letting him have liquor from the storeroom and the men
were also becoming more reluctant to give him part of
their daily ration on credit. As for women, the long abstinence of the crossing had been hard for him to bear.

The oarsmen pulled fast and rhythmically despite the intense heat, and the boat slid forward in smooth rushes. The
sailors aboard were those who had stayed on the ship the
night before and they were in a great hurry to feel something other than lurching ship's planks under their feet.
Jonathan and the chaplain sat side by side in the rear of the
boat, sweating profusely, blinded by the glare.

Behind them, *The Sea Witch* was quiet as a result of the
previous night's revelry. Most of the men slept under
large tarpaulins. The only movement on board was that of
a few sailors scooping up buckets of lagoon water to pour
on the overheated lathing of the decks.

Seeing the state of his crew, Jonathan had decided to
accord them a day of rest. He knew they were incapable of
any good work, anyway. The only thing that he had insisted upon was that Gregory should come with him to verify that the twenty-eight pieces of eight of the battery and
the eight pieces of four on the castle were loaded, the plugs
removed, and the guns protected from humidity.

Canoes came close to the ship, but none dared come too
close. The natives knew from experience that few of those
who had gone on board one of these vessels had ever returned alive. As a seafaring man, Jonathan was lost in admiration for the pure lines of the light skiffs.

Floating islands of papyrus, wrenched from the shore by
the current, drifted slowly on the water, rising and falling
in the wake of the ship. An old woman, impassive in her
tiny canoe which was half submerged from overloading,
crossed their path. She stared at them as they passed, puffing on her clay pipe. Jonathan wondered if her eyes held
scorn, curiosity, hatred, or simply indifference. He said as
much to Ardeen, but the chaplain, who was lost in fantasies
of sex and flowing alcohol, replied with an unintelligible
grunt and Jonathan gave up trying to have a conversation
with him. The shore was close now, and they could see a

certain agitation there. Women were washing clothes on
the riverbank, and little naked children ran and played in
the water. Blacks, bundles balanced on their heads, were
making their way to the fort, where a guard, rifle at the
ready, stood in the watchtower. Other Portuguese walked
along the ramparts.

Jonathan guided the boat toward the beach rather than
the dock, and they stopped on a sand bank. Two sailors
lifted the captain and chaplain on their shoulders to help
them out of the water.

Soon after, Collins and Ardeen were climbing the steep
path bordered with red tulips that led to the fort. The gate
was open and the Portuguese greeted them with a certain
listlessness.

"They don't look very welcoming," remarked the chaplain.

"That's putting it mildly," Jonathan replied, "but we
shouldn't look for friendship from this scum. I can't help
feeling suspicious toward them. They have such unpleasant
faces."

"Oh, come now," Ardeen exclaimed, "you're exaggerat-
ing! One can hardly be full of high spirits, living under
these conditions." He was ready to find any excuse for anyone who might be able to provide him with women and
liquor.

"You may be right. I sincerely hope so," sighed Jonathan, chalking up the chaplain's kindness to Christian charity.

By now they had reached the inner fort. A group of
blacks in ragged military garb, with wigs and hats, was
entering the porch. They parted with ill grace to allow the
two men to enter.

"Those are the worst of all," grumbled Jonathan.

"They don't seem to be as wild as the rest," said the
chaplain.

"I'll soon be thinking that you are more befogged dry
than drunk, Reverend," said the captain. "Can't you see
how arrogant they look! They are the middlemen. They
massacre and pillage. They and their kind are ready to sell
their own fathers for the price of some colored glass or a
swig of rum."

Ardeen was more astonished than hurt by Jonathan's

comment. "What have the Portuguese to do with all this, then?" he asked.

"They just wait for the slaves to be delivered to them. They regroup them, feed them, and wait for a ship to come in and take them over. While they're waiting, they get drunk and sleep with the black girls."

Here, Jonathan paused, for they had reached the stairway that led to Gomes' quarters. The two men climbed the stairs and entered. Gomes had been alerted to their arrival. He had just got up and was unshaven and bleary-eyed. Very young black girls, completely nude, were vigorously cleaning up the mess left over from the previous night's revelry, and Ardeen stopped short as he saw a naked rump immodestly wiggling before him. He was so fascinated by this that he failed to see the hand Gomes held out to him in welcome. At last, sensing the silence around him, he dragged himself away from his fascinated contemplation and shook the outstretched hand. The fat Portuguese seized it, kissed it humbly, and genuflected before him.

"You honor us, Reverend," he said with evident sincerity. "Welcome to my humble abode." Ardeen drew his hand away in embarrassment and laid it on the Portuguese's head. "Bless you, my son," he said hurriedly. "By all the saints, I am dying of thirst and I doubt if the Lord would object to our taking a small drink together."

"Right away, Reverend, right away," said Gomes, rising and shouting for Vasco. The three men were seated by the time the half-breed arrived.

"Where were you, good-for-nothing son-of-a-bitch," grumbled Gomes. "Get us some food and drink in a hurry. The whites are hungry." Turning to the young black girls, he growled at them, "Get out! Get out!"

They slipped away, giggling, to the chaplain's great regret. He raised his eyes heavenward and met the gaze of the wooden Christ figure on the wall. His face clouded immediately and he was sullen and withdrawn until Vasco came back with the drink. Ardeen preferred hard liquor to wine but after two glasses he felt more himself. The three men attacked the pâté of boar's head with relish, also enjoying the fried breadfruit and grilled carp, and the rich wine from the banks of the Tage. Ardeen ate and drank greedily, and Gomes, already disconcerted by the lust in the chaplain's eyes as he stared at the young Negresses, was stupefied to see a clergyman take such undisguised delight in the pleasures of the flesh. His profound religious beliefs were shaken.

Throughout the meal, Vasco filled goblets and served the guests. He was particularly attentive to Jonathan. The English captain in his elegance and distinction made a sharp contrast to the grubby vulgarity of the Portuguese. The half-breed hated his master, and the English officer reminded him a little of the white man who had brought him to these shores and who had treated him rather like a family pet. As for Ardeen, all Vasco saw in him was a man like all the other whites who came ashore to load up on slaves.

Jonathan was not conscious of the half-breed's particular attentions, and Vasco was disappointed. The conversation turned to the blacks.

"I'm telling you, Mr. Collins, those animals have no soul," expounded Gomes. "They are just flesh, crammed with vices. What do you say to that, Reverend?"

Ardeen nodded vigorously.

"Absolutely," he said, his speech already slightly slurred. "You are right, Mr. Gomes, and that is why the Lord came to me one night. He told me I must come here to save the souls of all these creatures from burning in Hell. It was the good Lord Himself who took me by the hand and guided me to Captain Collins' ship."

Jonathan, who knew well that the reasons that had precipitated Ardeen's involvement with his ship had nothing to do with the good Lord, was impressed with the chaplain's aplomb. As for Gomes, he was overcome at the idea of sharing his meal with a clergyman in whom the good Lord took such a very personal interest.

"Yes," continued Ardeen, by now too far gone in his cups to care about the effect of his words, "that's how it all happened. The good Lord, He said to me, 'Frank Ardeen, you leave all your comforts and go to seek all my poor lost lambs in the remotest parts of the world.'" He drained his goblet. "You see, Mr. Gomes," he continued, "if I had enough time I would settle here and baptize all the Negroes. God's truth, I would."

"What fine work you do," said Gomes admiringly. "Those animals are truly lucky, Captain, to have a fine man like you to lead them far from here to a country where they will be happy doing good Christian work. That's what I think."

"Absolutely," said Ardeen heatedly, delighted to agree with a man whose hospitality was so lavish. "Absolutely. We are doing as the Romans did with the Gauls, and their descendants, the French, have never had anything to complain about, have they?"

"Your work, Reverend, is to wash their souls of all their sinfulness and savage instincts. Did you know they eat each other? First thing you must do is burn all their idols. They dance around them for days and do revolting things, so I'm told."

"There you are. We must burn everything!" exclaimed Ardeen enthusiastically.

And as if to emphasize his convictions, he looked at the glass, lifted it, and drained it in one gulp.

Jonathan had remained silent for most of the meal, but he suddenly seethed with anger. "And what do you call that?" he asked, pointing to the wooden Christ figure. "That is the God you are offering them in exchange for theirs. Fine example of truth! A white God, come to save the souls of the whites, who hurried to nail Him to a cross like a wretched barn owl. What the hell do you think they're looking for in their sculpted tree trunks? They're looking for the same God you have, but they represent Him in their own way. Sell the poor devils! Beat them to force them into working for you and doing work you don't want to do yourself! Kill them if you must, but leave them their beliefs. What if God Himself were black . . . ?"

Ardeen and Gomes were surprised by Jonathan's unexpected diatribe, and his last sentence totally shocked them. They leapt up at such a heresy. Even Vasco, who was filling up the goblets, dropped the pitcher and stared at the captain with horrified eyes.

The chaplain and the Portuguese would have had to know a great deal more than they did about Jonathan's past to understand his explosion. He was raised in a Lutheran family and rebelled at a very early age against doctrines that seemed unreasonable to him. Although the massacres of Catholics had taken place a century earlier, they had made him hate religion. He could not understand how a God, if one existed, could accept for His people to kill one another in His name. He had read and reread the story of the execution of Mary Stuart and had been repelled by it. He could not understand how anyone could have killed such a beautiful, sensuous queen, killed her because a sterile queen was jealous of her dazzling beauty. He read about how regal and disdainful she was until her death, and how she walked to greet that death dressed as if for a ball. The executioner had tried three times before he finally decapitated her.

A heavy silence fell on the room. Jonathan, uneasy about the shock he had caused, pushed back his chair violently.

"That's not the reason for my visit," he said placatingly. "God is the chaplain's affair, not mine. I have to load a ship, and we have much to discuss."

Gomes took his cue from the captain and said, "Vasco, stop standing there like an idiot, and fill up these gentlemen's glasses. Can't you see the goblets are empty?"

"Could I visit your little encampment?" asked Ardeen, glad that the subject had been changed.

"I'll give you Vasco to take you around. Vasco! Come here!"

The half-breed, having finished serving, came to his master, who whispered in his ear.

"Yes, Mr. Gomes," he said. "Yes, Master, I understand."

"There!" exclaimed Gomes. "Follow him. He'll show you everything." And Gomes allowed a small enigmatic smile to play across his features.

Ardeen did not have to be invited twice. He drained his goblet, got up, and hurried after the half-breed. As soon as they had left, Gomes and Captain Collins lit their pipes and went over to sit in the shade of the veranda. Pigs and goats ambled about and chickens pecked contentedly at the ground. Women were busy in the kitchens, their voices muted by the crushing heat. The guard slept in his watchtower, his gun propped against a bamboo pole. Ardeen had vanished.

Jonathan's pistols felt uncomfortable after his copious meal. He unfastened them from his belt and placed them on a small table within easy reach. He leaned back in the rattan chair and stretched his legs out comfortably. "Before I go and see your blacks," he said to Gomes, "I'd like to

ask you if you could put up about half my men and officers
here on shore. That would make about twenty in all."

"Why not all of you, Captain?" asked the Portuguese.
"I'd be happy to have you all as my guests ashore for as
long as it takes to get you the rest of the niggers you need."

"No, thank you. It is most kind of you, but I always
prefer to have some of my men stay aboard ship," returned
Jonathan shortly.

"But how about you, Captain?" pressed Gomes. "There's
no reason for you yourself to stay on board, is there? I'd be
glad to put my own quarters at your disposal. It would be
an honor."

Jonathan managed to conceal his intense distaste for
Gomes' company, though he was firm in his resolve to
sleep in his own cabin; he said he preferred the fresh breeze
that whistled through his porthole and kept the mosquitoes
away.

A vague unease showing in his eyes, Gomes was spong-
ing his face while Jonathan was speaking. He seemed almost asleep, and Jonathan was surprised to note his sudden
alertness when he asked for a safe place to store the merchandise he had brought with him for trading, since it was
taking up most of the hold and prevented him from making
the changes necessary for housing the slaves. A brief glimmer of greed pierced Gomes' murky stare, but Jonathan
was so engrossed in the practical side of the arrangements
that he missed it, hearing only that Gomes was promising a
guard posted day and night over the merchandise. Gomes,
in fact, promised everything he wanted. Seeing a note of
suspicion in the Englishman's clear blue eyes, he thought to
dispel it and suggested, "Why don't you choose one of my
black girls, Captain? I have some lovely ones, very young,
some of them have never known a man. You can take several of 'em with you if you want to have a good time on
board ship."

"I appreciate your offer, Mr. Gomes," said Jonathan,
"but it would be impossible. You see, I expressly forbid my
men to bring a woman on board, and it would be giving
them a bad example." That was not his real reason for refusing the offer. He carried the picture in his heart of a
young woman he had held in his arms during a foxhunt,
who later had given herself to him without shame or re-

serve. His thoughts turned to Aurelia and his deep desire to find her again one day.

Gomes was staring, and Jonathan feared that he might see how moved he was. He rose in one brusk movement and took up his pistols. "Let's go and take a look at those blacks," he said gruffly. He eased his weapons into his belt and started down the stairs. Gomes rose from his seat with a sigh and followed.

Ardeen was having his own troubles, while the two men were making their way to the slave quarters. Vasco was trying to follow his master's whispered instructions to the letter. He made a quick tour of the fort and surrounding plantations with the chaplain in tow, and then hurried toward the compound where the women were kept. It was surrounded by tall, pointed, closely driven stakes, and there was no sound from within. Vasco muttered a few words in Portuguese to the guard who was standing at the entrance, and the latter gave the chaplain a sly look and burst out laughing. Then he lifted the bar that held the heavy door in place and bowed ironically as the men went in.

Ardeen tried to ignore the insinuating grin and entered the enclave with what dignity he could muster, followed closely by the half-breed. He came to a sudden halt, mesmerized by the unaccustomed sight of naked black female bodies sleeping under straw canopies around the walls. The women lay on the ground. The older ones wore an iron collar which was chained to a post, and one who seemed taller and stronger than the rest also had shackles on her hands and feet. Some very young girls were left unshackled, and these in particular drew Frank Ardeen's gaze. He had never seen so many naked women. They sat about in total abandon in positions that emphasized their grace, and he shuddered. The euphoria induced by the liquor he had drunk was replaced by a wave of desire that left his throat dry, and he had to make a violent effort to prevent his body from trembling visibly.

Vasco's voice penetrated his agitation. "Mr. Gomes, he say that Mr. White Man should take a girl."

"The good Lord placed you in my path, my son," he said to Vasco. "I shall remember you in my prayers and pray that He will allow you to enter His glorious kingdom."

Vasco stared at him, not quite sure what he meant. He couldn't understand what the White Man's God had to do with it all. When he wanted a girl, he took one whether she wanted to go with him or not, and the only accounting he had to give was to Mr. Gomes.

Ardeen drew close to a group of three young black girls, reflecting that Gomes was indeed a man of distinction and tact who knew how to receive his guests. "I'll take that one," he said gruffly, pointing to a graceful, young creature. Vasco bent and shook her arm and she leapt up in fear and tried to pull away, but a strong slap across her buttocks made her docile. She began to sob, thinking that she would have to go with him, but the chaplain, his face congested with lust, pushed the half-breed to one side and ran his hands over the girl's body in a fever of excitement. She was really very pretty, with her tiny smooth face, her budding breasts, and boy's buttocks. Without a whimper, she let Ardeen feel her all over. The years of frustrated desires flooded Ardeen's senses.

"You want her here, or in a hut?" asked Vasco anxiously, but the question did not distract Ardeen, who was now leaning over another very young girl. She was just waking up, and stared at him in terror. He grabbed her hand and pulled her to her feet. At last he was going to be able to live out the fantasies that had so long tortured his nights. "Give me a hut," he said, his voice thick. "I'll take these two."

As he passed in front of the guard, holding the two girls by the hand, the man spat at his feet. But Ardeen was already in another world and didn't even notice the insult. Vasco led him to an empty hut and left him there. Then he made a wide detour and came back to hide behind the little bark hut. He got great pleasure watching how the white men diverted themselves with the black women.

While Frank Ardeen was exorcising his demons, Jonathan and Gomes had come to the men's quarters. A stench, strengthened by the heavy heat and lack of wind, hung around the mud walls of the buildings. Muffled moans reached Jonathan through the narrow ventilation shafts near the roofs. Close by, huge copper cauldrons simmered on an open hearth and some blacks leaned over them, stirring a thick soup with sticks.

"The males are here," explained Gomes, who seemed quite oblivious to the stench. "We'll get them out here so you can look them over."

He turned to two Portuguese guards who were walking up and down in front of the building and called, "Diego! Lopes! Open the doors and let the apes out!"

The two men moved slowly to the door and unbolted the heavy locks. They pulled the door open and went inside. Hoarse shouts came to Jonathan's ears, followed by the whistle of a whip, shrieks, moans, and the rattle of chains.

Soon, dark shapes emerged, hesitantly. Handcuffed together in pairs with chains binding one man's left leg to the right leg of the other, they were prodded by the two guards who made them advance in some sort of order. Blinded after days in semidarkness, and weak from their inactivity, the men appeared shaky on their feet and winced at the brilliant sunshine.

The guards forced them into a circular procession as soon as they were all outside, and made them trot around and around by flicking their calves with whips. They seemed in good physical condition and Jonathan reflected that they must be well fed, although their lack of exercise probably contributed to their rather flabby bodies.

"Aren't my niggers fine?" asked Gomes proudly. "They're all free of defects, and see what a fine rich brown color they are. Even that one over there with the bluish skin don't have any deformities, but maybe he's not of pure nigger blood."

Jonathan had to admit that Gomes was right. The black men parading before him were mostly between fifteen and twenty years old, superb black gold that would bring an excellent price in Louisiana.

"Why don't you take 'em aboard right away, Captain?" suggested Gomes. "They might as well be on your ship."

"Oh, I couldn't do that, Mr. Gomes," protested Jonathan. "That's impossible. The ship has not been made ready to receive them yet. Anyway, I can't keep them cooped up like that until we leave. It's much better for them to stay here."

Gomes didn't insist. He knew that Jonathan was right, but it would have suited him had the captain accepted his suggestion. Some ships did things his way and it meant fewer mouths to feed. Moreover, once they had boarded the ship, his own responsibility ended.

Jonathan insisted that the men be left out in the air all day and only confined at night until such time as he was ready to load them on the ship. He offered his sailors to guard them. He was afraid that the conditions under which they were imprisoned would permanently damage their health and he wanted them in excellent shape for the crossing. Gomes was reluctant at first, but finished by accepting. They left the blacks to their sad roundabout and went toward the women's quarters.

All this time, Vasco, enthralled, had been watching the chaplain's antics with the two young women. If the black girls had hoped that the white man would be gentler than Gomes, they soon found out otherwise. Ardeen's method was to push them to the limit of endurance and extract cries of pain from them. Vasco, watching, had to admit to himself that Ardeen was blessed with incredible sexual strength that far surpassed his own. The poor girls felt they had been thrown into the merciless clutches of a wild beast. They tried to defend themselves at first, but a rain of blows delivered with sadistic precision soon made them submit to the chaplain's perversities. After a while, their moans and cries began to take on another sound that was not one of pain.

Watching this refinement of sensuality, where violence gave way to pleasure, Vasco began to believe that the white man's god had indeed given his representative on earth incontestable powers. His admiration for Frank Ardeen grew, and he swore to make sacrifices to the god with the sad expression who was pinned to the wall in Gomes' quarters.

A sound snatched him from his thoughts. Jonathan and Gomes were advancing toward the women's quarters, and he slipped away as fast as he could.

Jonathan was very satisfied. If the new prisoners were as good as the ones he had seen, he would have a cargo far superior to that generally carried by most slave ships. The women he had just seen seemed to be in perfect health. Ten of them were pregnant, which greatly increased their value. Only one of them was too close to delivery to make the trip. As for the children old enough to sell separately, there were enough of them to round out the cargo.

As they passed the hut, Ardeen recognized their voices. He made the young girls keep completely silent and became as still as a statue himself. One thing he knew he didn't want was for Jonathan to find him like this. As soon as they had passed, he drew a deep breath and began to settle down to more of the same, but the girls no longer felt hatred as they fixed their liquid black eyes on him.

Much later, Ardeen and Collins sat silent as the longboat drew close to the ship. Ardeen was still immersed in the wonderful experience he had just enjoyed, and Jonathan was lost in pity for the poor beings he was about to tear away from their rivers and forests and customs forever, to transplant them into a hostile world where even the sounds and scents would be eternally strange to them. He felt very close to them in his own exile, knowing he had lost everything except his honor, and that he would never return to his own land. In the solitude of his cabin he got as drunk as a lord, cursing the Portuguese, the blacks in Africa, his native land, and his own stupidity.

CHAPTER XV

A brutal kick woke N'Gio, jerking him from the drugged sleep of total exhaustion.

"Get up, son of a pig!" shrieked a furious voice.

N'Gio had trouble opening his swollen lids and he could barely make out the standing figure peering down at him. He was still so groggy that he didn't realize where he was or what was happening to him. He tried to move, but thongs bound his wrists and a split stake held his ankles immobile. A whip lashed cruelly at his chest and brought him back to consciousness and the horror of his situation. A second kick jabbed at him and the whip continued to sting his skin.

"Get up, I said!" A gob of spittle landed in his face. Making a superhuman effort, and ignoring the agonizing pain that lanced all his limbs, N'Gio managed to roll to his side and lean on one elbow. Then he got to his knees, and stood up. He couldn't see well and could just make out some shapes moving about in a muddle of sounds. He recognized the man who had spat on him and brutalized him as one of his kidnappers. The man held a sharp blade at his throat and unbound N'Gio's hands from behind his back. The blade continued to cut into the tender skin of his throat as his hands were brought around in front of him and fastened again with handcuffs joined by a short chain. In spite of the cuffs, N'Gio hands felt freer and less cramped. The blood began to circulate again in his pained fingers. He was left there, his feet still immobilized, swaying with the effort to stay upright.

A pale light had spread over the plains where the caravan had spent a second night of horror. The Bapounou were hurrying among their captives to the accompaniment of cries and groans, blows and curses, removing the bonds that had kept them totally immobile all night. N'Gio, who was by far the strongest, and therefore considered of greatest danger, was bound more tightly than the others and was a butt for redoubled cruelty from his captors, as his swollen face attested. They were trying to smother all thoughts of revolt in him and the leader of the group was holding him responsible for Yawana's disappearance.

As soon as all the bonds had been loosened, water and small portions of food were distributed. N'Gio was given a tiny portion of manioc and a ladle full of water. He fell on the food and drink while the men were removing the iron chains that bound his ankles together. As they had done the previous day, they pushed Ozengue forward and made him crouch before N'Gio. He squatted there without a glance at the other man while their captors fixed the double yoke about their necks. N'Gio picked up the block, and then the two men were able to get up.

The Bapounou were in a hurry to get back on the road and they forced all the captives into a long column. Lashes and cudgel blows rained heavily on them, and the line formed quickly, to the accompaniment of moans and curses.

Mouele gave a guttural command and the column moved forward.

N'Gio, with Ozengue, was at the head of the procession, followed by the other men yoked two by two in the same way. Their hands were chained behind their backs or in front, depending on whether they were carrying a burden or not. The women followed. They had been less brutalized than the men and their bonds were looser. They were able to help the children who tired easily on the long march, and they had to be available at all times in case one of the kidnappers suddenly wanted to couple with one of them, without untying her from her partner.

The children were tied to their mothers, and the very tiny ones were left free. They were often the appalled spectators of their mothers' rapes and, at first, many of them had wept long and loud. But the horrible threats of the Bapounou had stilled their cries. Blows also rained on them, and N'Gio often heard their shrieks of pain following the sound of a slap or the hiss of a whip.

It was an agonizing march. Ozengue's legs were short, and N'Gio had to bend almost double and take tiny steps to meet his rhythm and prevent the yoke from cutting at his throat. The physical agony N'Gio was suffering was nothing, however, compared to the despair he felt and his anxiety for Yawana.

His blistering, tearing, blinding obsession was what had

become of her after she returned to the devastated village
and saw her massacred relatives. He remembered with a
rush of tenderness that she found it hard to catch a fish,
and he worried about what she would find to eat. She must
think he was dead, too.

During the day following the kidnapping, he had heard
shouts of triumph coming from the rear of the column and
his knees had almost given way under him as he thought
with horror that she had been caught. He had tried to
catch a glimpse of what was going on, but the yoke had
been tightened so that he could barely breathe and could
not turn his head at all. He tried to persuade Ozengue to
slow down and fall behind to where the women were walking, but Ozengue was unwilling to cooperate, and the Bapounou, observing what he was trying to do, forced him
back to the head of the column with lashes and cudgel
blows. Now he could only pray with all his heart that Yawana had managed to escape in spite of everything.

The plain had almost merged into the forest again. Its
menacing borders were a dark shadow, and its twisted
trails meant more arduous and painful marching. The
block hurt N'Gio's shoulder, and, lost in his enormous agony, he was denied even the solace of friendship. All his
closest friends had insulted him following the raid, in desperate revenge against his father's unbelievable treachery.
Ozengue, to whom he had been bound for the entire journey, was locked into an obstinate silence and refused to say
a word to him. He was deeply alone, but he couldn't blame
the others for their scorn and desertion. N'Gio wondered
what the Bapounou had promised Adende. He had
watched his father's torture and death without feeling anything at all. He could not reconcile his beloved Tato with
the Adende who had coldly sold all those who had trusted
him. In his wounded soul, N'Gio felt a deep agony in
knowing that his father had tried to save him from the tragedy. The fact that his father had several times counseled
him to leave the village and spend the night at a distance
was no comfort at all. He, N'Gio, the bravest, proudest
warrior of them all, had had to bow his head to the sting of
the whip like everyone else.

Ahead of him, Ozengue's shoulders shook with sobs.
N'Gio realized that he also must be plumbing the depths of
despair and tried once more to get him to answer.

"Ozengue," he murmured, "listen to me! Listen, and answer me. I'm your friend, Ozengue. Why do you resent me? Why do you hate me as if I were some evil beast? I suffer more than you because of my father's treachery. Do you think I would be here, sharing your yoke, if I had been in league with him over this?" He stopped. Ozengue's sobs had quieted, so perhaps he was listening at last. "I beg of you, Ozengue!" pleaded N'Gio.

Ozengue's voice replied at last, halting, barely audible. "Yes, I do believe you, N'Gio," he said. "I've tried to hate you because I needed to feed my hatred for your father on someone alive. But I saw how they treat you. I know you are innocent." N'Gio felt a comforting warmth spread through him.

"Thank you for your answer. We must try to escape as soon as possible."

"No," answered Ozengue, sadly. "There's no way. We are lost." And his voice broke. A guard approached them and N'Gio stopped talking to avoid more blows. He waited until the man had gone, and then continued: "Do you know what tribe they belong to? Their tattoo marks look like Bapounou, but I don't recognize the robes they wear or their sticks that spit out flame."

"You are right, N'Gio, they are Bapounou. I recognized some of the men who came to sell us salt, at Mounigou."

"Well, I understand even less," groaned N'Gio. "We are on peaceful terms with those merchants. We aren't at war with them or I would have heard about it when I was fishing; such things always float on the current of the rivers. Why did they attack? It is madness to cut off the hand that feeds you, isn't it?"

Ozengue said, "Don't forget, N'Gio, that the Bapounou used to be called Bayaka. And only recently took the name Bapounou, which means 'warrior.' Perhaps they are trying to live up to their new name."

N'Gio thought about it, but this explanation didn't make sense to him. "No, Ozengue," he said. "There's something else. Something I don't understand. No tribe treats prisoners of war the way we have been treated. Prisoners of war are treated with respect, and even sometimes marry the women of the conquering tribe. No, Ozengue, I have a premonition that a terrible destiny awaits us. You were right when you said that everything is lost."

Ozengue bowed his shoulders, and N'Gio thought again of Yawana.

"You were with the others last night," he whispered. "What did they tell you? Has anyone seen Yawana?" His voice broke.

"Don't cry, N'Gio," said Ozengue. "You should rejoice that she has escaped these murderers. You've seen what they do to our wives and daughters. They don't even spare the youngest among them."

N'Gio was about to reply that he was well aware of that when the guards came up the column toward them. The long curling leather lash fell without pattern or reason. N'Gio and Ozengue got their share and they were obliged to fall into silence.

The young man felt obscurely comforted by the few words he had been able to have with Ozengue. He was still in as dreadful a position as before, but at least the scorn of his friends seemed less. However, despair gave way to a terror of an unknown danger more dreadful than the wrath of the skies or the forces unleashed by Nganga. He shivered as he wondered if they would all be tortured, or eaten, or even something worse than that, something too terrible to imagine.

He knew well the path they were taking. He had often traveled it with the men of his tribe to hunt assalas, the small aggressive black elephants. He remembered the trail when it had echoed with the happy cries of hunters laden with fresh meat. N'Gio knew all that was gone forever. Each step he took dragged him farther from his youth. The life that had seemed so filled with promise of joy was over. He would never see Yawana again. He was the son of a traitor. And furthermore, he knew in some obscure way that the trail led to dreadful events over which he would weep tears of blood. Yells from the back of the column dragged him out of his gloomy thoughts.

The men beating at the head of the column began to run toward the back and the march came to a halt. Ozengue walked around N'Gio in a semicircle so that they could both see what was happening. The Bapounou seemed to be running after someone. Then they held their sticks to their shoulders, and smoke and explosions roared out of them. The noise of the guns brought N'Gio to the point of panic, for he had seen what devastation they had brought before.

The Bapounou came back dragging a man by the arms. One of his legs was almost severed from his body, and blood spurted from the wound. The men who had caught him attached his hands and feet to a thick bough and made two of the other prisoners carry it on their shoulders. The man was shrieking in pain. N'Gio was too far away to see who it was. The guards came running up and started the column moving again and Ozengue pulled on their yoke.

At last the plains ended and the forest opened into a long dark tunnel. The column had to wind about to follow the faint trail and N'Gio's wounds from the yoke reopened although Ozengue, now that they had spoken, was doing his best to make it easier on him.

One of the guards had gone ahead and was opening out the path by swinging his saber like a sickle among the matted branches. Even so, tough creepers and sharp leaves tortured the bare skins of the prisoners. Insects, awakened by the turmoil, feasted on the helpless prey, and N'Gio, his hands chained, could do nothing to fend them off. But even this physical torture did not make him forget how hungry he was.

Toward midday, they unyoked him from Ozengue to enable them to step over a large tree trunk spanning a deep ravine. Then they allowed the prisoners to go down to the bottom of the ravine and wash themselves off in the warm water. But it was only a brief respite and the long march soon started again. A herd of gorillas, disturbed by the noise, scattered in all directions uttering strange yelps, then silence followed again.

When daylight began to wane, the column stopped at a plateau that rose above a river.

Scuffed earth, ashes, and the remains of huts bore witness to earlier encampments here. Even before the guards gave the order to rest, the prisoners had all collapsed onto the ground, exhausted. No one spoke. Even the children had no strength left to complain. The past few days had robbed them of their childhood forever.

Men and women were grouped separately, as on previous nights. The women assigned to fire-making put down braziers they had been carrying and gathered up twigs and dried branches, and soon high flames leapt up in the center of the clearing.

The yoke was removed from Ozengue's neck, and he

went and joined the other men. N'Gio was alone. A guard fastened his ankles into the two pieces of wood again, not sparing the lashes and imprecations as he worked, but N'Gio showed nothing of the pain he felt. He had reached a state of detachment where blows meant nothing to him anymore. He knew that his captors were afraid of his strength, in spite of all the bonds they piled on him, and he managed to retain a sense of pride in the midst of it all.

He knew now that they would not tie his hands behind his back until after he had eaten, so he took advantage of his freedom to scratch himself and flex his cramped muscles. It would be hard to sleep once the meal was over.

The Bapounou seemed in no hurry to feed the prisoners. There was sudden activity in the center of the encampment and the man who had earlier tried to escape was thrown to the ground. He was still tied to the branch and seemed only half-conscious in spite of his moans. N'Gio recognized him as Kowe, a boy from Mounigou, about his own age.

Mouele approached Kowe and stood gazing at him. He kicked him assiduously for a time and then turned to the other prisoners.

"Now listen here, you creeping lice," he screamed, "I had to behead two of you who tried to escape last night, but it seems that was not enough! Look at him, this piece of stinking flesh, this putrid carrion. He tried to escape too. He hoped to escape while the guards were busy elsewhere. But you have seen that there is no escape. He will be punished, and you will all watch. He will have a very slow death, and I hope it will be an example to you all. I will not tolerate any attempt at revolt, and if you refuse to understand this, each one of you to be caught will be tortured longer and more horribly than the last. Each time, your bonds will be tightened, you will be deprived of food, and you will be beaten. This time, in the greatness of my heart I shall allow you to eat. You will even be given meat." As he said the last words, he began to shake with vile laughter.

Then the men cut Kowe's bonds and the boy lay there, motionless but moaning. N'Gio knew that a horrible death awaited the lad and he was not mistaken. Kowe was laid out on the ground with his arms and legs spread-eagled. Some of the men held him firmly in this position, while others hammered sharp wooden stakes into his hands and ankles. Brought to full consciousness by the terrible pain,

Kowe roared like a wild beast and his body reared into an arc, then fell, and reared up again. Then he ceased to move and his lips opened in a terrible endless wail. The Bapounou took firebrands and burned the most sensitive parts of his body. His shrieks and contortions amused his torturers and spurred them on to greater atrocities. When they were finally bored with their sport, they left him for a while and drank some palm wine, and another liquid which they carried in transparent containers. But they had not finished with Kowe. After they had drunk a great deal they came back to where he was lying. They turned him over and all the men urinated on his face and body, laughing raucously. N'Gio and the others were filled with compassion for the poor young man's suffering and humiliation, and yet they knew the punishments their own tribes reserved for criminals such as the leopard-man. N'Gio could remember seeing a woman's body far from Mounigou when he was little. The breast had been opened and the lung hacked to pieces. The severed head had disappeared and the entire body was slashed all over. It must have been a crime perpetrated by a traveler who had taken the head to feed on the brain. The leopard skin and the iron claw had been found in the man's hut and were proof of his guilt. The villagers had rubbed his eyes with pepper and then cut off all his fingers and toes, but he had only admitted to his guilt after they cut off his genitals. Then he had been tied to a log, dowsed with boiling palm oil, and burned alive. It was a horrible death, but well-deserved, whereas Kowe had merely attempted an escape.

Mouele picked up a heavy rock, and standing between the prisoner's legs, he smashed his genitals with one blow after another, until a river of blood flowed from the body. Kowe had already screamed so much that only a faint muted agony escaped his lips. Then the other men took up cudgels, and beginning with his legs, they broke all his bones one by one until the body was nothing more than a revolting pulp. Kowe had already been dead when a last blow fractured his skull.

One of the Bapounou opened Kowe's stomach and pulled out the entrails which he hurled over the seated prisoners. Then they cut up the body and threw the pieces on the smoldering braziers. The smell of burning flesh spread over the encampment and N'Gio suddenly understood what Mouele meant when he sardonically promised the prisoners meat for their evening meal. Without even waiting for it to be cooked, the guards were distributing the pieces among the captives, and it was the only thing fed to them that night.

N'Gio was too hungry to respect his tribe's taboo against the eating of human flesh. He, like all the rest, threw himself avidly on the flesh of his childhood companion. The women and children were spared from this macabre feast, not because of any compassion, but because there was not enough meat to go round. They were given a few bananas to share among themselves.

After they had eaten, the prisoners were bound up for the night. As he had anticipated, N'Gio's hands were chained behind his back more tightly than before. The thongs bit into his swollen flesh. Trying to find the least painful position, he laid his head back against a tree, and closed his eyes.

But sleep was elusive, despite his overwhelming exhaustion. The songs and dances of the captors rang out into the forest late into the night. They had untied the women and were forcing them to dance before raping them. It seemed to N'Gio that their screams and cries gradually faded into hoarse moans and sighs. He couldn't help thinking of the sounds he had drawn from Yawana's passionate body and his blood began to throb. It was long after the noises had died down that he finally found sleep.

CHAPTER XVI

The cool damp air woke Yawana long before day broke. Her scantily clothed body was stiff from her uncomfortable position. She was shivering uncontrollably and acute hunger gnawed at her insides.

The voracious night insects had left her little time for sleep, and animal rustlings and growls had kept her alert. A pack of wild creatures had prowled around her tree in the deep of the night, and she had heard the panting of their breath as their muzzles reached upward toward her. While she had congratulated herself on being out of reach of the gluttonous, gaping jaws, she shook with fear of the spirits who might want to punish her for invading their domain.

She untied the creeper carefully, trying to make as little movement as possible, and pulled a bitter nut from the folds of her skirt. There was something reassuring about its sharp taste and Yawana soon felt revived. She had nothing left to eat, and she longed to creep to the encampment and seek out some odds and ends of food that might have been left behind by the bandits. She rubbed herself vigorously for warmth as objects began to take shape out of the gray mist that covered the plain. Voices and clatter came to her ears as the day dawned, and the mist whitened under the rays of the sun and suddenly vanished, revealing the encampment in a flurry of activity.

Suddenly her heart began to beat very fast, as one of the prisoners rose to his feet. She was sure it was N'Gio; that magnificent silhouette could belong to no one else. "Oh, N'Gio," she moaned, "you are alive! My friend, my love, I have found you at last. N'Gio. N'Gio." Her lips continued to mumble his name as though he might hear, and a wave of happiness suddenly engulfed her. She was no longer a poor little lost girl. Anything could happen now, she didn't care anymore. She could already see herself freeing him and fleeing with him far from the horrors they had both experienced. Her small face was wet with tears.

As she built her fantasy world from her distant perch,

she watched the prisoners eat and make preparations for departure. She could see that they were tying N'Gio to a much smaller man and that the prisoners were massing into a long file. Then she saw the guards raise their hands and hit them, and each time she heard the agonizing groans of pain. Her husband, too, took his share of blows. The prisoners picked up the bundles laid on the ground beside them and the column began its march in a chaotic fervor, the shouts of the kidnappers mingling with the cries of their captives.

She was longing to follow them, but she knew she must wait until they were far enough away. The trail of men and women disappeared in the distance and the sounds ceased, but Yawana didn't move, for fear that one of the kidnappers might have stayed behind. A small flying lizard leapt from a branch and came to rest neatly on a large blue butterfly, using his membrane to slow his landing. He swallowed half his prey immediately and then ate the rest slowly, one blue wing trembling from his mouth. A cloud of brilliant green parakeets swept by noisily and the harsh screech of the toucan broke their chirping.

Then the forest fell silent. The column was now no more than a series of black dots in the tall grass. At last, Yawana decided it was safe to come down from her perch, and as she moved a bird of prey, frightened by the noise of her descent, flew heavily away. As she had often seen her parents do, the girl ran to where he had been and found a half-eaten bird, as she had hoped. It was a guinea fowl. Delighted with her good fortune, she wrapped it in a leaf and left the edge of the forest. When she reached the encampment, she gathered up some scattered manioc and a few fruits. There was still a fire smoldering, and she roasted what was left of the guinea fowl. The flesh was somewhat tough but she was so hungry that she almost swallowed it whole. Her courage returned as she assuaged her hunger. She picked off the elephant ticks that had settled in her skin during the night and began her march along the path taken by the prisoners.

The huge plain stretched as far as the eye could see, blending at the very edge into the purple haze of the forest. The grass was a silvery green, reflecting the rays of the sun. Here and there ant heaps made black stains. Yawana couldn't see the column anymore but she knew she wouldn't lose them. Their trail was easy to follow now. Although the tall grasses hid her, she thought it might be wiser to take a parallel path, so she swung to the left and made a wide detour before continuing.

The sun was high, and sweat trickled down the small of her back. She had no idea how many days this march would last or where it would lead, but she was fiercely determined to find N'Gio. Now that she had seen him alive, a new fervor replaced the debilitating despair that had filled her days and nights since the tragedy. She hardly felt her exhaustion or the rigors of the terrain she was covering with her small bare feet.

The route led her to the edge of a lake bordered by heavy twisted mangrove roots. She bathed and drank, as pelicans and pink flamingoes stared at her. The nearby buffalo must have judged her harmless, for they continued to plunge about in the cool mud surrounded by the white flash of the cattle egrets which fed off the bugs on their backs.

The swampy lake spread far, and Yawana had to head toward the center of the plain to get around it. A shuddering of the grasses made her tremble, and then there was a herd of prairie dogs rushing past her, yelping loudly. They were inoffensive, and for the first time Yawana forgot her sorrows long enough to laugh at their antics, and at their long ears and tufted tails which vanished into the grasses.

The ground was flat, and rocky plateaus rose from the grass here and there. The young girl advanced at a fast pace. She didn't realize that because she was weighed down by no burdens and was driven by an anxious longing, she had come too close to the column. Suddenly, as she was about to walk across a clearing, the sound of voices broke into her reverie and she quickly squatted in the grasses, her heart pounding with fear. She could hear raucous laughter and moans coming from very close by, and at last her curiosity overcame her fear and she parted the grasses and stared at two men in white tunics raping two young girls still bound together by thongs. They were indulging in every possible brutality and the girls wept and moaned as the men exchanged foul jokes at their expense. She could almost reach out and touch their bestial faces. Yawana was suspended in a sort of paralyzing, almost fascinating horror at the sight of the entwined bodies on the ground and the

sounds they were making. She made a great effort and
drew back, letting the grasses fall back into place. She
crouched low and hardly dared breathe.

All of a sudden there was a flurry of noise and activity
and she heard the whistle of whips and the screams of the
young girls who were being forced to run under a rain of
curses and insults, to catch up with the column. For a long
time, Yawana remained where she was, trembling and silent.

Much, much later she dared take up her pursuit again.
She knew that this was what awaited her if she was caught.
She was not so much terrified at the thought of rape as she
was at the idea of being treated with such cruelty. She had
never felt the sting of a whip against her fresh young skin,
and the prospect repelled her. She promised herself to be
doubly careful, knowing that she wanted desperately to
save N'Gio and that her own capture would ruin all
chances of his escape.

Later, she heard thunderclaps from far away echoing the
ones that had so frightened her during the massacre at
Mounigou. She hoped that they were not aimed at N'Gio.
The plain had narrowed and the trail led again toward the
forest. Yawana had no difficulty finding the path and she
hurried in among the trees.

Crossing over a large tree trunk that spanned a deep ravine, she walked and walked. Night was almost upon her.
She had no idea how far she was from the column. At last
she decided to stop where she was rather than risk a deadly
surprise. She nibbled on a bit of manioc, and climbed a
tree as she had done the night before. She chose the most
hidden branch, tied herself on securely, and lay waiting for
sleep.

Much later, in the midst of a black night, she could hear
Kowe's tortured screams echoing from far away through
the forest vaults. The scream did not sound human and
Yawana was sure it must have come from wild beasts fighting in the underbrush.

Early in the morning, she bathed in a narrow stream.
Fat land crabs scuttled to their holes as she came upon
them, but she was able to catch one. She shattered the
gleaming shell and gobbled up the tender flesh. The pale
meat had little taste, but she was half starved. Some mushrooms helped to round out her meal and she drank won-

derful great swallows of cool water from the palms of her hands.

The forest was a tough tangle of sinews and roots. Yawana advanced cautiously, starting at every sound. A rattlesnake undulated across the trail and she stopped to let it pass. She knew that the slightest alarm would turn its poison against her.

By midmorning she had reached the clearing where N'Gio had spent the night, but to her great disappointment, there was no food left lying about. To her horror, she found a shattered skull and some half-burned bones lying beside the ashes of one of the fires. Suddenly she understood the screams she had heard in her sleep, and it dawned on her in a flash of revulsion what the prisoners' meal had been the previous night. Conquering her disgust, she picked up the skull and examined it, and a huge sigh of relief escaped her lips. The teeth were worn down and decayed, and she knew this could not be N'Gio, whose magnificent healthy teeth she had so often admired. She almost felt a rush of happiness, and she never even wondered who the victim might have been. Nothing pierced her emotions any longer. The unbearable horrors she had seen had built a permanent shell about her sensitivity. She had even lost her fear of the forest's deep mysteries.

CHAPTER XVII

Yawana's agony in her determined pursuit was great, but N'Gio's was worse. Whips cracked ceaselessly on bare spines to force the prisoners to speed up their painful progress, and the young man shuddered each time the humiliating pain bit into his flesh. A new day of martyrdom was beginning, and it promised to be harder than those which had preceded it, for the cruelty had doubled in intensity.

N'Gio wondered how many more days he could bear this long march toward death. If he had guessed that Yawana was so close he might have felt even more courage in facing the day. As it was, he was determined to continue on and see what lay at the end of the march. Whatever it might be, he did not see how it could be worse than what he had already endured. He had no wish to be beheaded like the two guests from his wedding, or eaten by his friends as Kowe had been.

Few words passed between him and Ozengue. The small man had reached the limit of his endurance. He kept stumbling, and each time he tripped, the yoke slammed hard into N'Gio's throat. N'Gio murmured to his friend to try to bear his exhaustion with courage.

"But I can't take any more," groaned Ozengue.

"Whatever you do, don't stop!" cried N'Gio, urgently. "If you do, they'll kill you like they did those others."

"N'Gio," sighed his companion, "don't you understand? I've had enough of these brutes and their whips."

"I do know how you feel, Ozengue," N'Gio responded compassionately, "but we are all like you. What is there to do? You saw what they did to Kowe."

Ozengue seemed to shrink into himself and didn't answer. Although he felt very sorry for the man, N'Gio was too immersed in his own suffering to think of anything else for long, and he too fell silent.

They marched on all day, slowing down now and then to let the stragglers catch up. N'Gio had no strength left for

thought. His one aim was to keep walking, to keep putting
one foot in front of the other. While they were marching,
one of the Bapounou suddenly raised his metal stick to his
shoulder and thunder issued from it, throwing the man
back to where N'Gio stood. There was a sound of snapping
branches and a large monkey fell like a stone. The others
yelled with delight and laid the animal on the shoulders of
one of their captives. N'Gio stared with fascination at the
man who fired the shot. He saw him pull out a small sack
from his belt and pour some black powder into the hole of
the metal stick, and he wondered what witch doctor had
devised such a powerful poison. Then the man carefully
pushed in a small metal ball and wedged it with a thin
stem. In spite of his disgust and fear, the young man was
unable to keep himself from feeling a certain respect for the
power his captors seemed to possess. Later, he saw another
Bapounou kill a wild pig in the same way.

The trail rose and fell ceaselessly and, much as N'Gio
was relieved when it rose, he suffered when the path led
downward, for he had to walk bent double to match
Ozengue's height.

At last they arrived at an open space, but Ozengue was
not strong enough to make it to the evening resting place
and he stumbled and fell, dragging N'Gio down with him.
The others continued marching around the two men collapsed in the mud. Ozengue wa .ot moving, and N'Gio,
entangled in his bonds and nailed to the ground by the
weight of the yoke, could do nothing to help him. The
shock of the fall had deprived him of breath and he
couldn't even speak to tell Ozengue to get up.

A guard approached with a lash and brought it down
savagely on the two men. "Get up, you swine!" he shouted.

Ozengue turned a haggard face toward his torturer and
spat with his remaining breath. "Get back into the vagina
of the pig that bore you!"

Mad with rage, the Bapounou fell on him, but the renewed attack seemed to stimulate Ozengue. Without even
trying to dodge the whip, he got to his feet, followed by
N'Gio, and as soon as he was standing he lashed out with
his hands at the guard's face. The man collapsed with a
shriek of pain and Ozengue fell on him and pummeled him
with fevered blows.

The yoke had cracked in the fall and N'Gio was suddenly free. It was no use for him to interfere now. Ozengue was past saving and if he joined in the fray it would mean certain death for him too. Without a backward glance toward his friend, who was now surrounded by guards, he followed the others.

As soon as the camp had been made and the fires lit, the Bapounou started to cook the animals they had caught along the way, and then turned to Ozengue's punishment.

Three men dragged him toward the edge of the clearing, among them the guard whose face Ozengue had attacked. His face was still bleeding, and he was eager for revenge. They forced the small man to his knees, laughing at his pleas, then tying his arms straight out with creepers.

N'Gio and Ozengue's other friends could do nothing but watch. The Bapounou began their systematic beating, insulting him and covering him with spittle as they lashed. Ozengue never uttered a sound. He knew that this was just the beginning. It was when they forced slivers of wood and porcupine quills under his fingernails that Ozengue began to scream with pain. Next, they cut his nose and lips, broke all his teeth, and gouged out his eyes. Ozengue's screams were ghastly. One of the men brought out a bucket of honey and smeared his entire body with it, particularly the genital area, and the wide nostrils and mouth. Then he spread more honey on the ground around him. Ozengue knew what kind of death awaited him. Words twisted incomprehensibly from his mutilated mouth as he begged to be killed instantaneously, but all he got in response were loud jeers and laughter.

N'Gio watched helplessly as his friend suffered this terrible torture. He could not even put his hands to his ears to shut out his cries. All the captives were paralyzed with horror.

Ozengue was left to his unbearable agony and N'Gio and the others were each given a piece of wild pig or monkey, barely cooked. Ozengue's shrieks had blended into an endless moan.

Suddenly he let out a long, shrill howl. Fierce scavenger ants, drawn by the blood and honey, began to climb his legs. In no time at all, his body was covered by a revolting, heaving, black layer. It was deep night, and the fire danced on his shining silhouette writhing against the creepers that bound him.

Little by little, the screams grew fainter. When they ceased altogether, N'Gio knew that the ants had gone in through the nose, the eye sockets, and the ears, and that their voracious mandibles were at work on the brain.

Exhaustion took its toll, and despite his agony of soul and the pain of his tightly bound limbs, the young man fell into a nightmare sleep.

CHAPTER XVIII

Yawana walked in a daze, like a sleepwalker, drawn on by her determination to rejoin N'Gio. Even the turbulent eruption of a gorilla family from their midday nap failed to provoke any emotion in her. Their angry cries would normally have terrified her, but now she hardly noticed them.

As she walked, her eyes glued to the ground, something sticky slapped against her face. A large black and yellow spider dropped in front of her and disappeared among the leaves. Yawana automatically tried to wipe the thick yellow mess off her face with the back of her hand.

She hurried on, but she had fallen behind and night caught her unawares. She pulled together a bed of leaves and this time lay on the ground, indifferent to the dangers that lurked about her.

This night, neither the fear of the dark nor the howls of wild creatures kept her from sleep. Her body flamed with desire for N'Gio. She couldn't keep her mind off what she had seen that day on the plain. The young girls' moans and cries echoed in her ears, provoking troubled half-dreams with N'Gio as the central figure. Unconsciously, her hands crept down her belly and, soon afterwards, she lay still, panting and exhausted.

Next day, Yawana started out well before dawn, determined to find her husband before dark, no matter what. She longed to touch him, to kiss him, to hear the sound of his voice. Her own miseries seemed small next to what she was sure he must be suffering at having been so cruelly snatched from his village, after witnessing his beloved father's brutal death. Had she known of Adende's treachery, she might have had a better idea of how tremendous were the burdens of pain and sorrow that N'Gio bore. But she had seen how brutally the kidnappers treated the girls and what indiscriminate sadism they inflicted on their prisoners, and she was terrified that he would have to undergo similar horrors at their hands.

As soon as she saw the light of day, she hurried on, crossing a region of undulating hills and valleys. On either side of the trail huge craters overgrown with vegetation opened out. They looked like giant lion-ant nests. On a plateau to the left, warm ashes showed her that the kidnappers had not been gone long. She was luckier than the previous night, for she found the bones of a big black monkey and a wild pig, and there was enough meat left on them to make a substantial meal. But her most precious discovery was the big cutlass someone had left behind. Now she could protect herself if she was attacked. She took advantage of her find to crack open some big nuts that lay on the ground and to hack down a strong creeper from whose stem she drank the clear plentiful sap which was as refreshing as water.

A few steps farther on, she came across a horrifying spectacle and leapt back, trembling. The skeleton of a small man was tied to a tree on the edge of the trail. His bones were picked absolutely clean and the strong smell of formic acid floating about the skeleton left no doubt as to how the poor creature had met his death. The girl shuddered spasmodically at the thought of such torture and tried not to think of the man who had felt his flesh eaten alive by hordes of voracious insects.

By midday she was very close to the column. She could hear the yells of the guards as they prodded the captives to march faster. She redoubled her precautions and kept well behind, judging the distance by the loudness of the voices.

The forest had changed. Tall trees had given way to bamboo groves, blossoming forth in huge sprays, alternating with the shade of leafy palms. The trail had widened. A motionless fisher eagle and a flight of honking ducks informed Yawana that she was approaching water.

As the day faded, a buzz of voices announced that the column had halted to prepare for the night. Yawana slipped into the tufted undergrowth and crawled forward as fast and as quietly as she could. Soon, she came to a large body of water. The kidnappers had seated themselves on a strip of land, and prisoners were sprawled about, lost in total exhaustion. A few of them, prodded by guards, were wearily gathering wood for a fire.

Yawana had never come so close. She could actually

recognize tribesmen from her village and from Mounigou, and she reflected that they must curse the day of her marriage, which had so brutally ended the lives they knew.

N'Gio was alone, leaning against a tree which had been uprooted in a recent hurricane. His feet were locked into a split piece of wood and his hands were bound. Yawana couldn't take her eyes off him. He looked so vulnerable. Tears poured unheeded down her cheeks. She wanted desperately to fling herself against him, to console him and help him.

With a last look at her lover she moved a little further away, trying to keep the encampment in view so that she could observe what went on until night had fallen.

When it was pitch dark, Yawana came back to the edge of the camp, and saw a huge fire blazing in the center. Hidden behind a bush, she saw the mass of prisoners tightly bound to each other. N'Gio was still leaning on the uprooted tree, and he seemed to be asleep.

The kidnappers were stark black silhouettes against the flames. Bats darted about, drawn by the shifting light. The men were talking in low voices and passing gourds that they emptied rapidly. At a brief order from Mouele, two of them got up and went to check on the prisoners' bonds. They grabbed a quick moment of pleasure with two drowsy girls, talking to each other all the while, and then went to stretch out in comfort. Yawana waited for a long time, long after silence had spread throughout the camp and the only sounds that broke the stillness were the snores of sleeping people.

At last, taking her courage in both hands, her heart beating madly against her breast, she began to crawl toward N'Gio. She moved with agonizing slowness, taking care to stay outside the area lit by the flames of the fire. Every time one of the guards twitched in his sleep, she froze, and then with infinite caution, began her steady progress again.

She came so close to N'Gio that she could hear his heavy breathing. He lay on his side, his legs bent. His feet were separated by the piece of wood and his hands were tied behind his back. He was sound asleep, his head resting against the rotting tree trunk.

Yawana crossed the few yards that separated her from

her love. With one last glance she made sure that everyone was sleeping, and then she got up swiftly and pressed her hands against N'Gio's mouth.

"N'Gio, it's me," she whispered. "It's Yawana."

CHAPTER XIX

The day following Ozengue's death, N'Gio had to walk alone. Fearful that he might try to escape, the Bapounou had tied an iron collar around his neck, fastened to his ankles by a chain. The yoke no longer rubbed at his throat, but he would have preferred the discomfort to the pain of knowing his friend dead.

The day passed without incident. The prisoners seemed finally subjugated. The women had ceased to fight and let the kidnappers do what they wanted, sometimes even seeking out their caresses in the hope of wheedling a little extra food for themselves and their families.

They camped on the borders of a wide river that night. The rains had not made the river rise very high on the bank; it formed an elbow at this spot and a wide beach of golden sand had settled in the crook.

As usual, N'Gio was placed at a distance from the others. He was tied to a dead tree half buried in the sand, at the edge of the encampment. Later they brought him some meager victuals which he ate without relish, and he was soon fast asleep, his head resting on the tree trunk.

One after another, the guards fell asleep, and silence spread over the sprawled bodies. Suddenly, N'Gio started. It seemed as if the night was whispering his name. He woke up, startled, but a delicate hand clamped firmly against his lips. He opened his eyes, and saw Yawana's anxious face close to his own. It took him a few minutes to realize that this was no dream, it really was she, and it really was her hand on his mouth. Yawana gradually released him, and he whispered on a sigh, "Yawana."

He couldn't believe that they were together at last. Yawana saw such pain in his eyes that she thought she would faint, and she fell on him, her face pressed against his. The emotion of being so close to each other made them pant and gasp for breath.

"Oh, N'Gio! N'Gio, my love! I thought I would never see you again," sighed Yawana. She went on whispering his name over and over again, sobbing silently against him.

Her gentle voice in his ear filled N'Gio with a tremendous joy. He longed for his hands to be free, so that he might hold her to him.

One of the guards turned over, grumbling in his sleep, and the two lovers froze, their breath rising and falling in unison. They stayed clutched together in this way until the camp fell silent once more. Luckily, the fire was dying down and they were in shadow.

Yawana reached out to untie his hands, but N'Gio rolled onto his back to stop her.

"No, Yawana," he muttered, "don't do that."

"But I want to free you, we must run away."

N'Gio shook his head sadly. "Not now," he said. "They'd find us easily and the punishment would be torture and death. If you only knew in what horrible way they killed Ozengue and Kowe, my friends . . ."

"I do know," she whispered. "I saw them. But what can we do?"

She stretched out against him again and rested her head on his chest.

"Let's wait until we reach the forest again," said N'Gio. "The right moment will come and we'll be able to hide more easily."

The girl was lost in thought, saddened to see how weak he had grown in so short a time. She realized that the kidnappers wanted to destroy his vigor and kill his courage. She did not insist, however, for she knew he was probably right. The area where they were was too open, and they should wait for a better hiding place.

"I'll do whatever you want, N'Gio," she said.

"Then follow us, but keep your distance," urged N'Gio. "Whatever you do, don't get caught, or we are both lost."

"I know how to look after myself," she said belligerently, and she showed him the cutlass hidden in her skirt.

"You couldn't do a thing with that," said N'Gio sadly. "They have terrible weapons that have a talisman that kills from far away."

The two young people fell silent. In spite of their desperate plight, they could feel desire swelling in their bodies as they lay together. Yawana's hands began to move slowly. She caressed N'Gio's shoulders, and then stroked his breast until she felt the muscles contract. She went on until she heard his breath come faster.

Then she placed her lips on her husband's and as their tongues sought each other in a fever, she continued to caress him, her hand circling lower and lower, her fingers clutching at each of the muscles of his abdomen. When her hand closed about his penis, she crushed his lips with hers to smother the cry she knew she would provoke. Then, very gently, she squeezed the strength in him that rose toward her. Her lips replaced her hands and she continued her caresses until at last she placed herself tenderly on his body.

They were carried away in a whirlwind of emotion, as though a barrier had suddenly been removed. Their spirits rose to meet the winds above and they forgot all about their unhappiness and the cruelty of men.

Yawana sat on him, her torso poised, her breasts outthrust, her hands behind her head, like a hardwood idol. When the fire reached her stomach she fell in a warm heap against her vanquished lover. Her nails dug into N'Gio's shoulders and she bit him to stifle the deep cry that was rising from her throat.

N'Gio's body was encrusted with sand, his bound hands were crushed, he was in pain, but he dared not move for fear of spoiling this wonderful moment.

Yawana could no longer contain her tears and they ran down N'Gio's chest, mingling with his own, and replacing the words they could not find to express their feelings.

N'Gio was the one who noticed that a faint light heralded the dawn. He moved to wake the young woman and Yawana opened her eyes.

"Off you go, Yawana!" he said tenderly. "It is almost day."

Yawana detached herself from him regretfully, kissing him with passion. "Yes, I'll go," she said. "But now you know that I shall follow you everywhere. We shall soon be free."

Very quietly she rose to her feet and disappeared into the night. N'Gio rolled onto his side and lay with his eyes wide open, awaiting the day.

CHAPTER XX

In the distance, lightning split the sky in brilliant patterns. A violent wind had arisen. A flight of parakeets hovered over the waves, and deep troughs split open under the raging gusts of wind.

Captain Collins stood in his cabin listening to the rain beat on the deck in a frenzy. It fell so heavily that he couldn't see the land, even though it was very close by. Every now and then, to starboard, the lightning showed him the island of Nengue Sika, the island Gomes had talked about. It was an island of money, an island where brandy and geegaws served to pay off the treachery of a people who had sold their own into slavery.

Jonathan swallowed the tumbler of hot sweet grog that Pierre had brought him. He was bathed in sweat but his body shook with chills. Nonetheless, the fever that had held him in its grip since his last visit to the Portuguese several days ago had begun to fall. Young MacLean had wanted to prescribe a bloodletting and a mustard plaster, but Jonathan had preferred the cook's remedy, far tastier, and surely as effective.

His endless worries had helped him to overcome the brief moments of despair he had felt when they arrived. His character was firm, fashioned of the stuff that had made Queen Elizabeth's seadogs famous and had enabled them to search out these remote outposts two centuries earlier.

There was a knock at the door and Gregory appeared, his trousers soaked and his bare torso gleaming with rain.

"Ah! Good day, Gregory!"

"Good day, Captain. How do you feel this morning?"

"Much better, I thank you. Here, have a drink. There's nothing like this fine Barbados rum to warm your innards."

Gregory accepted the glass with pleasure. He drank deep and stretched, while Jonathan stuffed his pipe, rubbed a tinder to light it, and puffed on it comfortably. "God, I hope this lousy rain lets up!" Gregory grumbled.

"Come now," Jonathan soothed, "there's nothing for you to worry about. It's very good for the ship. Do one thing for me, though. Go down to your cabin and dry yourself and then come up here, and on your way back you can tell Pierre to serve us luncheon. You might also tell Woolcomb and Clark to join us, and of course we mustn't forget the doctor and the reverend."

Gregory disappeared, then returned a short time later dressed in a blue linen shirt and white pants rolled up to expose bare legs. A black cotton scarf was wound about his head.

"Woolcomb and MacLean went ashore," he announced. "But Clark will come. As for the chaplain, no one's seen him since yesterday. He must be at the fort."

Jonathan enjoyed his lieutenant's company, and the two men sat down while a cabin boy prepared the table for the meal. The rain continued to fall remorselessly. The windows showed a smudged blanket of shifting gray which changed with the vagaries of the wind, as *The Sea Witch* creaked and shifted on her anchors.

"Well, Gregory, where do we stand?" asked Jonathan. "This fever left you with all the responsibilities."

"The ship's in order, sir," Gregory responded. "The sails badly needed attention, and they've been repaired. I've changed the frayed ropes and washed down the hold and decks. All I need now are your orders for how to set it up."

"What about the merchandise we brought for trading?"

"I've had it removed from the foredeck and stored on land in the building you told me about, with a good guard on it night and day. You can rest easy about that."

"I hope you haven't unloaded the guns, the lead, and the powder?" Jonathan asked anxiously.

"Don't worry," said Gregory with a chuckle, "I followed your instructions. We'll only bring those out at the last moment. Here, let me give you the lists the doctor made."

Just then William Clark came in. He greeted the two men cheerfully and helped himself to a glass of liquor without waiting to be asked.

"All well with you, Clark?" asked Jonathan.

"Yes, Captain. All's well. I had the armorer look over all the weaponry, and he also got all those chains and things ready for the Negroes. Everything has been greased and cleaned. They'll have some beautiful collars and bracelets for the journey," he said with a wry chuckle.

Just then, luncheon was announced. Pierre had taken a

trip ashore to bring back fresh foods and the three men sat
down to a repast of roast suckling pig garnished with fried
breadfruit, roast duckling, and mangoes.

Jonathan ate without appetite, but the others did honor
to the fine feast and drained large mugs of cool, light beer.

"How are the men, Mr. Clark?" asked Jonathan. "Any
sickness?"

"No sir," returned the other. "So far they're doing pretty
well. The only one that worried me is that lad Matthew.
They pressed him aboard, you know, and now he sits for
hours without saying a word."

"I know what you mean. You'd better watch him closely
and make sure he doesn't try suicide. Where is he right
now?"

"He never moves outside the big cabin."

"Make him go ashore, and see that he gets off work.
He'll find something to amuse him there, like the others."

"Well, that's what I wanted to talk to you about, sir. I've
made a schedule, as you suggested, but when the men go to
the Portuguese fort they get very drunk and fool around
and fight."

"Let them, let them, Mr. Clark. A little relaxation won't
do them any harm."

"Yes," Clark said seriously, "but their work is suffering."

"Well," Jonathan said, "that's your problem, Mr. Clark.
If you have to, keep them aboard, but don't be too hard on
them. They have a long hard voyage ahead."

"I hope we won't have a revolt on the way back," Gregory said.

Clark gave a mirthless laugh.

"What would you do, Gregory, if they dragged you from
your own country one fine day and sent you to die in God
knows where, wouldn't you want to revolt?"

"Don't compare me to these Negroes, Clark. They're animals. They aren't human. If they revolt, it's from sheer
nastiness, nothing else."

"Well, my friend, I disagree," Jonathan said gently,
pushing his plate aside. "I did think like you at first, I
thought of them as merchandise, but I see a glimmer in
their eyes sometimes that looks amazingly like intelligence.
You see, Gregory, when we load them onto our ships, we
have no idea where they come from. Perhaps they have left
a village, a family, a god behind. Perhaps they are capable

of loving one another. Don't underestimate these Negroes. Despair could push them to the worst."

"Whatever you say, I find it dangerous to load the vessel as we do," Gregory replied. "It would be much easier to keep control over smaller cargoes."

Jonathan smiled. "I agree with you, Gregory," he said, "but unfortunately our contract specifies that we must furnish large numbers of slaves to the French colonies, and we also have to bring them to the others."

Did they give you any trouble on your last crossing?" Clark asked.

"No," Jonathan said. "I had a cargo of Ibos and Mandingues. Ibos are not dangerous, but they are highly emotional, and I had several suicides. As for the Mandingues, they have a thieving disposition, but they're good workers and if they're well fed and well treated they behave themselves."

"Anyway," concluded Clark, "I shall see that some strapping pieces of four are brought down and I'll set them up on the maindeck. Any sign of rebellion, and I'll plug their legs full of a mixture of salt and sand. It won't take them long to get the message."

The cook's arrival put an end to the discussion. He was cheerful, as usual.

"Well, Captain," he asked, "how was the dinner, good?"

"Delicious, Pierre," Jonathan said. "Unfortunately, I wasn't very hungry."

"You're sick, my poor Captain," Pierre said with comic solicitude. "What you need is a good hot toddy to get rid of your misery and set you up. It's all the fault of those damned flies!"

"You're clearly out to get me drunk," said Jonathan, laughing. "But I'll accept, anyway. These gentlemen are not ill, but I should think they'll take some, too."

Pierre sent the cabin boy scurrying to the storeroom.

"Sit down a moment, Pierre," the captain said cordially. "Any problems?"

"No, Captain, no problems. Pierre never has problems," answered the cook firmly. "I have enough stockfish and flour to feed the entire Royal Navy, and there's enough wine to satisfy a horde of thirsty chaplains."

Everyone burst out laughing at this reference to Frank Ardeen.

The cabin boy came in with steaming tumblers for all, including Pierre. He placed them carefully on the table and went to stand in a corner of the cabin. It was an honor for the lad to serve the officers and he stood there solemnly, all ears.

The four men drank appreciatively and Jonathan enjoyed the hot, soothing liquid going down his throat.

He turned to Pierre and said, "I'd like to have your opinion on the deal."

The small man puffed up with importance at having his opinion sought out by the captain. "Captain, I'll tell you something," he said. "To be honest with you, the slave trade leaves me cold. All I care about is that we make a living out of it, we, the smiths in Birmingham, the bankers in London, the sailmakers in Bristol, and the rest. As for the Negroes—well, someone has to cut all that sugarcane, right? And it can't really do them any harm. It can only be good for them. At least over there they'll give them some clothes to wear, they won't have to go naked. I've even heard tell that they get freed, some of them. I wouldn't be surprised if they get as clever as whites one of these days. And the ones who sold them into slavery, they'll still be here, killing with their assegais and banging on their drums. Anyway, they're prisoners of war, I say, and as far as that goes . . ."

Pierre paused, breathless from his long tirade.

"They *were* prisoners of war," Jonathan corrected. "Before, they used to take prisoners because there were wars. Now they make wars so that they can take prisoners to sell."

Pierre looked confused. He hadn't thought about it quite like that.

"You may be right, Captain," he admitted, "but if you want my opinion, you should watch out for those Portuguese. They're devils incarnate, you mark my word."

"I know, Pierre. I know," said Jonathan. "But there's nothing we can do but trade with them. They are the first settlers in this country. They discovered it. There's nothing we can do to get them out, for the moment."

"Well, you watch out, anyway. They look like the worst band of ruffians I ever saw."

With this last caution, Pierre bade them farewell and returned to his ovens. Jonathan prayed that all would go well. He was in a hurry to load his cargo and leave this ugly low-lying region.

The rain ceased as suddenly as it had started. The last clouds sped westward, leaving a leaden sun in a blue sky. Jonathan rose.

"You come with me, Mr. Clark," he said. "Let's take advantage of this break in the weather to go ashore. I'd like to see how that merchandise has been stored and talk to that Gomes."

"Aye aye, sir," said Clark, and the three officers went out on deck. The deck was smoking from evaporation; it was almost dry already. Some men were closing up the drains which had been opened to catch the rainwater. Some sailors came out on the bridge where they had gone for shelter from the storm and the vessel became a hive of activity again, under Gregory's direction.

On the ground, the torrential rains had dug deep channels in the ground. Mud stirred up and turned the lagoon yellow near its banks. The heat was stifling. When they came to the fort, Jonathan and Clark went to Gomes' quarters without waiting to be announced. Gomes leapt from his chair, frantically adjusting his trousers and sending away the little black girl who had been kneeling in front of him. She ran out with an insolent glance toward the English captain and his gunnery officer.

"Good morning, Mr. Gomes," Jonathan said with a touch of sarcasm. "I hope we are not disturbing you."

"Good morning, Captain, sir," the fat man returned sulkily, furious at having been caught at his private pleasures. "What can I do for you?"

He was as dirty as before. His huge stomach overlapped a pair of linen trousers spattered with stains, and a cotton shirt that once had been white opened onto his fleshy chest which gleamed with sweat. He headed toward a basin of water on a table and plunged his head in. Jonathan and Clark seated themselves.

"I came to check out the merchandise we have stored with you," said Jonathan.

Gomes, who was rubbing his face with a towel, gave a formless grunt in reply. A sailor from *The Sea Witch* came in and placed a keg of brandy on the table.

"I brought you a keg of the best French brandy, Mr. Gomes," said Jonathan. "I thought it would please you."

Gomes had finished drying his face. He stroked the keg complacently and thanked Jonathan profusely, touched by the thoughtful gift.

"Vasco!" he shouted, "bring us some goblets."

The half-breed came in at once. He bowed slightly to the guests and placed tin cups on the table. Gomes ordered him to open the keg and pour a generous portion of the brandy for each of them. Clark, in the meantime, had pulled a sheaf of papers from his shirt and laid them out in front of Jonathan. The three men raised their goblets but paused as a staggering figure detached itself from the shadows near the door. Reverend Ardeen was roaring drunk and his attitude had lost what little dignity it had previously aspired to. He came weaving in, calling in a slurred voice, "Good day to you all. Good day to the distinguished representative of His Majesty's Royal Navy and his best gunner."

"Well, Reverend," Jonathan exclaimed, "you seem to be in a sorry state. I would ask how it is that whenever liquor is to be served, you miraculously appear, but it would be a pointless question, would it not?"

"Mr. Gomes has been very kind to me, gentlemen," volunteered Ardeen. "Yes, indeed, Mr. Gomes knows the true meaning of Christian charity."

"I have no doubt," Jonathan replied sarcastically, "that his devotion is as great as your capacity for drink."

Ardeen ignored the remark and turned to Vasco.

"I'm thirsty, angel of darkness," he cooed drunkenly. "Don't let a poor pastor be dry. This land burns like the gates of Hell." And he fell mumbling into a chair.

Vasco hurried to do his bidding and Ardeen grabbed the goblet with shaking hand and raised it to his lips. He drained it and laid it empty on the table, nodding off to sleep almost at once.

Jonathan ignored him and pulled a wooden container from his pocket. He took out his good clay pipe and stuffed it with cut tobacco. Then he turned to Gomes.

"Mr. Gomes," he said, coming to the point of his visit, "I cannot stay in this country forever. When can we expect the rest of the cargo?"

"Won't be long now, Captain," Gomes assured him. "You can't get so impatient. They have to be trapped y'know, and it's not always easy game. I think my catchers will be here in a day or two at the most."

"Your what . . .? Oh, yes, I forgot." Jonathan's hands smoothed the papers laid in front of him by Clark. "Well, while we wait let us go together to check on the merchandise we unloaded from the ship."

"Yes," said Gomes with interest, "I heard you unloaded a lot of good stuff, but those men of yours are damned disagreeable. They won't let me anywhere near."

"Orders, Mr. Gomes, orders," said Jonathan, smiling. "Until we have taken an inventory no one is to go near the storeroom. That's why I came today, you see."

Gomes looked less disgruntled.

"I thought you didn't trust me," he said. "And it made me sad that two whites far from home, lost in a dangerous country, should find it so hard to trust their brother."

"That had nothing to do with it," said Jonathan, annoyed by the whining tone of the Portuguese. "That merchandise is for paying the slaves. As soon as we have both checked out these lists, we shall put one of your men and one of mine on guard, and no one except you or I will be permitted entry. If anything has disappeared by the time I must pay up, I would have to return the lost goods in slave value. This procedure was not meant to offend you. That has always been the way we do things. You know the customs as well as I do, and I think it best we should stick to usual procedure, don't you?"

The Portuguese scratched at his huge stomach which protruded from his unbuttoned shirt.

"You're right, Captain, and it'll be done just as you say. Shall we go now?"

Soon they were outside under the blazing sun. Two youths were wrestling and they landed smack against Jonathan's legs and started up, staring, not quite knowing what to do or say to the tall Englishman. They wore only tiny loincloths. Their skin was light, almost white, and their hair was long and curly.

"You go and play somewhere else!" cried Gomes, his hand lifted to strike at them. The two boys ducked the slap with incredible agility and ran as fast as their legs would carry them.

"Two of my sidekicks. I got 'em off a N'Komi female.

You have no idea how vicious they are. You'd think they had white blood in them."

Clark and Jonathan exchanged meaningful glances, their reflections on the incident clearly the same.

Gomes was leading them to a storehouse set a little to one side. Its door was soundly fastened with a heavy lock.

Two *Sea Witch* sailors, armed to the teeth, were playing dice under a straw shelter. They stood up as the three men approached. They were young, and magnificently built, their arms and bare chests covered with tattoos. They wore hats woven from straw to keep the sun off their heads and were both heavily bearded below smiling faces.

"Hi, Tracy! Hi, Rand!" said Clark.

The sailors saluted smartly in reply. They unlocked the door at the officer's orders and Jonathan went in with Gomes, while Clark asked where the doctor could be found.

The storehouse consisted of one long windowless room. It was surprisingly cool, and the space between walls and roof allowed some light to penetrate. Barrels and crates and piles of miscellaneous objects lay on the floor.

Simon MacLean, roused from his nap, came in half asleep.

"Got something to write with, Doctor?" asked Jonathan.

"Yes, sir, I always have," answered Simon.

He took a small leather pouch from his belt and carefully extracted goose quills, a metal inkwell, and a powder sprinkler. He laid it on a crate and pulled it close to the door. Jonathan held out the sheets of parchment to him.

"Mark a cross by each article," he said. "As soon as we have verified its presence and quantity."

Captain Collins and the Portuguese began the inventory. There was something of everything—Manchester cotton, the large copper basins called "neptunes," colored linens, glassware, copper nuggets, iron bars, bottles of tafia rum, cauldrons, Sheffield knives, and a myriad of other objects.

As each item was counted out, MacLean put a cross beside the name in the margin and carefully dried the ink with ivory powder.

When the inventory was over, Gomes turned a distressed face to the captain. "I don't understand, Captain," he said. "Where are the weapons, the gunpowder, the lead? I don't see any of that, and I could never deal with you like this."

"The guns and the rest are on board ship," replied Jonathan dryly. "I'll have them brought ashore when we make our deal. I don't intend to take any risks. I know that your fort is well guarded, but one can never tell. It would be most dangerous to attract the greed of your neighbors out there on the lagoon."

Gomes was not able to hide his disappointment. "I suppose you're right," he conceded with bad grace. "The main thing is to know that you actually have them. For a minute there I thought you were not going to trade according to custom, and I thought I'd better warn you at once."

MacLean put away his writing equipment and everyone left the storeroom. A sailor locked the door behind them and a soldier from the fort came to take the place of the sailors who had been on guard. Gomes and his guests went back to the living quarters, where refreshments awaited them on the veranda.

The chaplain was still sound asleep inside. His drunk's sixth sense must have warned him that the drinks were nothing more than fruit juice and that it really wasn't worth his while to wake up.

Jonathan agreed, at Gomes' insistence, that some of the merchandise should be given to him immediately to facilitate his preliminary negotiations for the new batch of slaves.

"Understand me, Captain," explained Gomes. "I am just the last link in the chain. Those blacks, before they get to me, must pass through several different sets of hands. The ones who catch them, now, they have it the hardest of course. After that, they sell them to another tribe, the Baloumbou, who live on the coast a little further south. The Baloumbou sell them again, to the N'Komi and the N'Komi bring them here to me to get them onto the ships. You can see that it's not as simple as all that. As for me, if I don't give them a little merchandise ahead of time, they will never bring me their blacks. That's why I also need the guns and powder, y'see."

"Well, I do agree with all the rest, Mr. Gomes," said Jonathan, "but I will not budge an inch on those guns. You'll get them in the end, and that's what you can tell your traders, and if you can't convince them, do you know what I will do, Mr. Gomes? I shall take my crew and go and hunt out the blacks myself, and they won't get anything at all."

Gomes was quick to placate the captain. "Fine, fine," he said hurriedly. "You have the final word. I'll do just what you say. I'll tell them exactly what you told me, but don't you go out there yourself, man. That would be the end of my trading with this country. As God is my witness, if you did that, all that would be left for me to do would be to climb on board your ship with my men, and leave this country once and for all. They would kill me, Mr. Collins, I tell you, they would kill me for sure, and I don't like to think about how they would do it."

Jonathan didn't want to think about it either, but only because he had no interest whatsoever in Gomes' fate, whatever it might turn out to be.

The two men came to an agreement, and decided how the advance merchandise would be counted in terms of the final deal. Following the instructions of the owners of his ship, Jonathan then asked about products other than blacks that he could take as subsidiary cargo.

Gomes, his English stiff and awkward, told him of the other riches the African coast had to offer.

"As far as that goes," he said, "I have the best you can find anywhere along the coast. I have coral wood—it's good stuff from the swamps, not the wood from the hills. Mine is a fine color, red as it comes. I could also give you some good ebony, I have plenty of that, and ivory. I don't have very large pieces here, but it's all a good white color. Then of course there are spices and wax. And I want to be paid in gold coins for anything other than the Negro flesh, Captain. As for the loading of fresh victuals you may need for the return trip, you can pay me for that with cannon powder and white powder."

Gomes had resumed his arrogant tone by now, certain that Jonathan would not try to bargain him down, as in fact he did not. He had what he needed to pay, and he was prepared to buy everything the Portuguese had to offer, knowing that he would find an eager market for his cargo in the Americas. Gomes undertook to have the merchandise carried down to the dock, from which Jonathan would have it taken to the ship little by little.

Shadows lengthened on the mustard-colored earth and the colors of the scenery deepened. The throbbing of drums drifted across the lagoon, carried by the waters, and the melancholy wail of a horn announced the preparation of a feast.

Jonathan took advantage of Gomes' absence to tell Clark to replace Woolcomb on shore that night. "Be very vigilant, Clark," he cautioned. "I may be wrong, of course, but I have a sort of presentiment that these Portuguese are not to be trusted. Pierre is quite right. So be sure that you order your men to stay grouped and close to their arms at all times. Fire at the slightest provocation."

"Just as you say, Captain," Clark promised. "Like Pierre, I am uneasy myself."

The two men stopped speaking as the Portuguese came up to them.

"Ah, well, Mr. Gomes," Jonathan said, "I think it's time for me to go back to my ship."

"Why don't you stay for supper?" Gomes asked. "What's your hurry? You can leave after you eat."

Jonathan shook his head regretfully. "I'm afraid a million tasks await me on my ship," he said. "I will have to be there to see that everything gets done as it should be."

John Woolcomb arrived just then and announced, "I'm leaving for *The Sea Witch* with a group of sailors, will you join us, Captain?"

"I'm with you, Mr. Woolcomb," Jonathan said. He turned to the young doctor. "What about you, Mr. Mac-Lean? Will you be staying?"

The young man had been immersed in his own thoughts, but he now turned and answered, "No, no, Captain. I'm with you. I have some notes to work on. What of the chaplain? Do we let him stew out his drunk here?"

"He's fine where he is," Jonathan said. "We don't need him for the moment, and I have every confidence that Mr. Gomes is taking good care of him for us."

They went out to join Woolcomb, who was standing on the dock. Their longboat passed the boat taking a new batch of sailors ashore to relieve the guard crew. The setting sun cast a surreal glow on the landscape and Jonathan was forced to admit that there were moments when this was truly a country of exceptional beauty.

The guard on deck *The Sea Witch* was reinforced and Jonathan repeated his instructions that no native canoe be allowed closer than a cable-length from the ship. Turning to MacLean, he asked him to bring news of young Matthew and to advise him the next day if his behavior continued to be strange and withdrawn.

He was still a little stiff from his recent fever, so he took a bath and dined on lentil soup. Then he stepped out on the poop for a breath of fresh air. A sailor, leaning against the railing, was standing the watch in silence. The barrel of his gun gleamed in the lantern light. When he saw Jonathan, he stood to attention. He spat a long stream of yellow tobacco into the black waters and pushed his wad into the other side of his mouth with his tongue. His cheek swelled with the tobacco, and he said indistinctly, "I dunno if the good Lord created the blacks at the same time as the whites, all I know is, he chose the country well. This Africa ain't made for Christian souls, I'm telling you. I wish we had left here, and I ain't alone."

"No, you aren't alone," said Jonathan, smiling. "I'd also like to be gone from here. Don't worry, it won't be long now."

Some of the men were playing out on the foredeck, and the rattle of bones rang out in the night. Others stood around gravely watching the casting of lots while they sang a mournful song about a country they would never see again and a girl who would not wait for their return. The song rose into the night and the words caught in the air like tears.

Jonathan stood there for a long time, thinking of the things he had lost forever.

CHAPTER XXI

Yawana could no longer remember how many plains had followed forests, and how many valleys had alternated with hills. She even lost count of how many days she had been walking, but she never lost her courage or resolution. Her love sustained her: It was as huge as the overwhelming forest. Her courage was all the more extraordinary because she was not really equipped to undergo such an ordeal. Her physical strength had never been tried in this way before. Her feet were a bleeding pulp, and her body was covered with scratches.

She was haunted by the almost unbearable pleasure of the night when she had been able to get close to N'Gio and lie on his fettered body. She couldn't understand why, but the dangers she was running and the events she had lived through seemed to have sharpened her senses. From the moment of her arrival at Mounigou the morning of her wedding, there had been nothing but eroticism, blood, and violence. The rites she had had to undergo, and which had so distressed her during her marriage ceremony, N'Gio's caresses, the massacre of her family, and the rapes she had witnessed flashed through her mind constantly and plunged her into a confusion which was almost pleasurable.

After leaving N'Gio, she had stayed hidden in the papyrus, numb to the incessant mosquito bites. She watched the awakening of her tortured friends and waited until they crossed the river. Herons came out and settled on the bank, and woodcocks emerged from their shelters. The men had clearly gone far enough away that they were no longer to be feared.

Reassured, Yawana came out of her hiding place. She was exhausted from hunger, but there was nothing left for her at the encampment. However, her luck had not let her down, for she saw a long trail of footprints that led her to a whorled spot in the sand. She dug her hands in and came up with some gavial eggs. She gathered up as many as she could find, and cooked the round soft shells under the

ashes. The taste was nauseating, but they restored her
strength. After a long bath, she started to walk again.

Many days passed. She had never gone so far from her
village and there was no way she would ever be able to find
her way back. All her life she had known the forest, with
its pattern of wooded areas and brief flatlands, but suddenly the landscape had begun to change. There were only
a few leafless trees, and they stood stark and white as bones
against the sky. The spongy ground was covered with short
grass. The mountains had disappeared and the short grass
stretched across a monotonous landscape. Because of this,
Yawana had to keep very far behind the column so as not
to be seen.

Her thoughts clung to N'Gio. She wished desperately
that the life force he had deposited in her body would bring
a child. She knew she must free her husband, and together
they would flee to a place where they could make love to
each other and be together, and no one would be able to
separate them, ever.

She ate what she could find, crabs, lizards, and snails.
She ate the snails raw, for fear a fire would make her presence known to the kidnappers. She looked constantly for a
chance to approach N'Gio again. If only the accursed plain
would close into dense forest again, she would dare anything
to save him. The atrocities she found along the way served to
strengthen her resolve. The day before, she had come
across a man impaled on a stake, vultures scrabbling and
shrieking over his flesh. The face was intact, and she recognized Mawga, a friend of N'Gio's. The trail was dotted
with half-eaten corpses, probably of those who had collapsed from exhaustion. There were women, men, and even
two children from her own village. She wondered if all of
them would die in this way. She wondered, too, how long
she could go on.

Days and nights melted into one another for N'Gio,
highlighted by the blows he received or was spared. The
agony of the long march had even erased the memories of
his capture itself. His entire past had vanished into a vast
blankness, like scent from a dead flower.

They had yoked him again, to a distraught young lad
named Bokou, from the Akele tribe. He had come from
the Ombala village with the other wedding guests. He had
watched his wife's rape and was fast losing his reason. Like

Ozengue, he was short. The kidnappers wanted N'Gio's march to be as painful as possible in order to weaken and shatter his will to survive and revolt against them.

N'Gio was incapable of revolt. He was worn to a shadow of himself. His throat ached from the bruising yoke, his limbs were mangled from the chains, and he had to continue walking, walking, walking, day after day along the trail that led to the last lap, where he sensed that something tragic awaited him.

Like him, his fellow prisoners were beaten, insulted, and harassed. If they stopped for a minute, they were whipped mercilessly. If they fell, they died. The column straggled more and more pathetically. Only the youngest and prettiest of the women were spared some of this ill-treatment and given relatively generous freedom, for their captors wanted to keep them in good shape. All they had to do besides serving the men was take care of their needs at the night stops.

As he walked, N'Gio thought of the night Yawana had come to him. The memory of her hungry young body obsessed him. Now that he knew how close she was, he trembled and agonized for fear that she would do something silly and be caught in full daylight. His love grew in depth and strength to an intensity he had never suspected himself capable of, for he realized the dangers she was braving for his sake. In spite of the pain of the yoke, he couldn't help looking back from time to time to see if he could catch a glimpse of her.

A wordless prayer to the sheltering souls of his ancestors rose to his lips. "Protect her!" he whispered to them. "Protect Yawana from the evil spirits of these wicked men. Keep wild beasts and snakes from her path. Help her to find a way to free me."

He held on to the insane hope that they would be able to escape and run away together. He didn't know where they would go, although it would surely not be back to Mounigou. He never wanted to see that place again. He had lost his freedom there, and his love for Adende, his father. No, he was determined that they would go and hide in the forest, as far away as possible, to mend their shattered lives.

For some time now, there had been no reason to hope for escape. The terrain had been too open, and he knew that Yawana would have to wait for a suitably covered spot. Some of the men had tried to escape and had been caught very quickly, and killed. The cruelty of the captors seemed to grow as the journey continued and N'Gio shuddered at the thought of the death that had been meted out to his childhood friend Mawga, who had managed to untie his bonds one night and escape the watchful guards. He had broken a leg in his escape and had soon been caught. The Bapounou, beside themselves with fury, had impaled him on a stake without more ado. N'Gio knew that he did not want that kind of death, nor did he want to die along the way. From the moment Yawana had come and lain with him so joyously on the beach, he wanted only one thing: to live at all costs.

One night, the column stopped in an abandoned village. The huts were dilapidated, but had not been destroyed by fire, so N'Gio assumed that the village had not suffered the same fate as Mounigou. Small mounds stood in front of the huts, surrounded by curved stems of spirit plants. Clearly, these were the graves of remarkably skilled hunting dogs, and N'Gio realized that it must be a Mitsogo village, for they were the only tribe that made this kind of grave for animals. The Pahouin tribe were reputed to pay more attention to their dogs than to their women, but not to the extent of conducting death rituals for them.

Huge screens for smoking game seemed to point to the fact that it had been a hunting camp. But N'Gio hardly cared, anyway. All he knew was that this night he would have a roof to shelter him from the rain, for the sky was frequently torn by lightning and a storm was brewing.

It was almost as though the guards were comforted by the huts, for their behavior was less brutal than it had been, and the prisoners were fed a hearty meal of fresh-killed buffalo.

Yawana came as close to the village as she dared, and watched the evening meal. She hid in a nearby field and before it grew completely dark, she saw the captors chain up N'Gio for the night and push him into one of the huts. Black clouds were massing in the sky. The wind shaking the banana leaves made her shiver, and flashes of lightning alternated with menacing rolls of thunder.

The storm raged in a fury of rain and thunder, terrifying the girl. She pulled down some banana leaves and made a rickety shelter, where she huddled, shivering. Her teeth chattered and she mumbled and shook with fear and cold.

"I must see you," she muttered, "I must touch you. I want to feel you inside me. N'Gio, don't cry. I'm here, very close. I'll come and see you and we'll love each other again."

It helped her to talk like this. It helped her to forget the cold and the rain a little. As the night advanced, the storm abated and the wind died down. Only a thin rain continued through the night, rattling on the leaves in a continuous clatter of sound.

Yawana waited until there was no further sound from the village before she dared move. When she was quite sure that everyone was asleep, she crept up to the first huts. The kidnappers had lit a huge fire in front of the central hut, where they had congregated for the night. She made a wide sweep around it and came back toward the hut where she had seen them lead N'Gio earlier in the evening. She couldn't get in through the door that opened onto the central clearing, for fear of being seen. She crept behind the hut, only to find that there was no other way to enter.

She glued her ear to the wall. N'Gio must be asleep. She could hear his labored heavy breathing so close, so very close. Taking every possible precaution, she managed to lift the outer layer of the wall to reveal a tracery of branches through which she could glimpse N'Gio, sleeping on his side.

"N'Gio," she called in a low murmur, "N'Gio!"

The young man was too exhausted to hear her. She was afraid to go on calling, it was too risky. She worked at making a larger opening and passed her arm in. The branches were tightly woven and she had to ease them apart. At last she was able to touch his chest. She had not counted on his extreme nervousness. Her light touch woke N'Gio, who sat bolt upright with a strangled shriek.

"Don't make such a noise," whispered Yawana, appalled. "It's only me!"

Just then, she heard the sound of feet hurrying toward the hut. Although the cry had been muffled, it had woken one of the guards who was rushing to see what was happening. Yawana fled to the clumps of bush that bordered the village and ran as far away as she could. Before she disappeared, she heard a furious altercation.

The Bapounou had erupted into the hut with a resin

torch in his hands, and the first thing he saw was N'Gio sitting in front of a hole in the wall, so he concluded immediately that the prisoner had tried to escape. N'Gio, still half asleep, stared at him in bewilderment.

"Ah, you tried to get away, you filthy creature!" the guard yelled in a fury. Before the young man could utter a word, he rained cudgel blows on him, kicking him repeatedly and shouting insults. Then he called for help, and N'Gio was dragged out to the fire, where they all beat him. Then they left him in the light of the fire, so that they could keep a close eye on his activities.

N'Gio was still bewildered. He had been having a nightmare when he was suddenly awakened with a start, thinking he heard his name. Then a light had suddenly blinded him and blows began to rain on him, and now he was collapsed in front of the fire, surrounded by his captors, who were threatening the worst torture imaginable because he had tried to escape.

He was gradually coming more fully to his senses. He could taste blood in his mouth. His lower lip was cut and bleeding.

He guessed that Yawana must again have come to try to save him, although he had begged her to be careful and not to try anything unless she was certain that they could manage to escape. He wondered sadly why she had not listened to him. Now the guards would redouble their precautions and be on the lookout constantly. They were already more wary of him than of the others, and now he realized that he would be the butt of even more cruelty and pain.

He was too close to the fire and felt the flames begin to burn him, but he didn't dare move for fear of getting hit again.

And, Yawana, my little antelope, he thought, you'll get caught yourself, if you go on taking risks.

Now he was suddenly happy that the kidnappers had thought he had tried to escape, and that he had been able to tear apart the wall in spite of his manacles. If they thought for a moment that it could have been the girl, they would have rushed out immediately in search of her, and there was no way that she could have escaped them.

He spent the rest of the night in such agony and fear for her that he forgot his own pain.

Yawana could hear all the commotion from far away,

NO RIVER SO WIDE163

and she realized that N'Gio had to suffer the consequences
of her thoughtlessness. She was petrified at the thought that
they might come after her, and ran as far as she dared,
until she fell to the ground, exhausted, and lay there weeping hopelessly until morning.

The rain continued to fall, sometimes a light mist, sometimes a heavy downpour. When it stopped at last, it had
considerably delayed the departure of the kidnappers and
their prisoners.

The sky was washed clean of clouds. Yawana, hidden in
a grove, dared not come out into the open to dry off in the
sun. She was drenched and shivering, but she preferred to
wait. She wanted to be sure that the village was empty before she ventured into it.

It was already late in the day when she finally crept out
of her hiding place, waded through the mud, and struggled
toward the huts. She hadn't eaten for many hours, and she
felt faint and feeble. She knew she must find something to
eat at once. She was about to enter one of the huts when
she leapt back and hid, shaking. Two bodies were lying
inside, moaning in a way that left little doubt about what
they were doing. The walls were not well built, and Yawana was able to watch the couple from where she hid.
One of the kidnappers was stretched out on one of the
woman prisoners, her legs wide open, her every movement
demonstrating the intense pleasure she was experiencing.
Her head rolled from right to left and back again, and a
long, drawn-out wail of pleasure came from her lips. Suddenly her mouth opened wide and she gave a loud cry. The
man got up, said a few words, and left, followed by the girl.
Yawana recognized Ilali, the wife of Mawga, whose tortured body she had come upon a few days earlier, impaled
on a stake.

She shuddered to realize that the kidnappers were not
content with assassinating the prisoners, but that they also
reduced their wives to willing mistresses. How, she wondered, could Ilali give herself with such obvious passion to
the man who had perhaps been responsible for her husband's horrifying death? She puzzled over this for a long
time.

Two more days went by. The rain had not come again
and Yawana was lucky enough to find food in the deserted
camps. She made no attempt to approach N'Gio. She felt

abandoned, infinitely alone. Her courage defied the bounds of human resistance as she trudged on, refusing to give up and let herself die. Whenever she almost gave in to despair, the thought of N'Gio set her back on the trail.

In spite of his fears, N'Gio had not been treated worse than usual, although the guards were more careful to shackle him within sight at night. The prisoners dragged on, more and more slowly. No one tried to escape anymore. They had neither the desire nor the strength left. N'Gio, too, succumbed to his destiny and ceased to pull against it. All he wanted now was for the relentless march to end one day, so that he could sleep.

Clumps of trees, small woods, and plains gave way to a dappled forest. Then more and more cultivated fields began to appear. The trail widened, and there was evidence everywhere of a good-sized settlement nearby. Sometimes a couple of inhabitants came out of an isolated hut, to cast terrified glances at the depressing column straggling by before hurrying back inside.

The changing scenery seemed to have brought about a change in the Bapounou's attitude. They joked amongst themselves but pushed their prisoners to walk faster and faster. It was clear that they were nearing their destination and were in a hurry to reach it.

More and more signs of life began to appear along the way. Women worked in the plantations and groups of them crossed the column. Some even left what they were doing and ran to watch them pass. They chattered animatedly with the kidnappers, and often walked some distance with them.

Yawana, who was following at a discreet interval, was finding it harder and harder to hide. She slowed down and went off the trail to make use of the bushes along the side. By keeping beside the trees she could advance without being seen. When she reached the edge of the forest, there was no possibility of going on. She saw the column snaking into a large bamboo enclave and disappearing within. She could see many straw roofs above the bamboo fence and then she heard a din that grew and grew and she stuck her fingers in her ears. It was more like the sound of wild beasts at the kill than of human beings.

As they entered the enclave, the kidnappers announced their arrival by shrieking and whipping their captives. They were glad to be back and wanted to show their tribesmen the importance of their catch. At last they were returning to their families. They would be able to rest, and leave the constant surveillance of their prisoners to others.

When N'Gio and his companions, shoulders bowed under the whips, entered the clearing, the huts spewed out their occupants and the huge crowd milled about, shouting and gesticulating. They came from every direction, young and old, running to line the column's path.

Soon there was a solid wall of people, screaming welcome to the kidnappers and cursing the prisoners with hatred.

They were now collected in the center of the enclave, terrified by the chaos, and not knowing what to do. The village children, armed with sticks, prodded the prisoners and screamed with laughter. One threw his stick at N'Gio's legs, and N'Gio fell heavily, to the accompaniment of jeering laughter. He got up, helped along by a rain of kicks and blows.

The women were the wildest of all. They set on the women prisoners like harpies. Their rage was sharpened by the knowledge that their husbands had no doubt had full use of them during the journey. They pinched them with sadistic glee, slapped them, and pulled their hair. The poor women, horrified by these attacks, couldn't get away from them. They were obliged to endure the harassment and shrieked with pain, to the great delight of their tormentors.

The guards seemed to have lost interest in the prisoners and were indulging in rowdy reunions with family and friends.

This incredible confusion might have continued indefinitely had not a sharp order rung out.

"That's enough!" snapped a hard, authoritative voice. "Silence!"

Everyone became quiet at this command and turned their eyes in the same direction. N'Gio saw a huge man advancing toward them. He was even taller than N'Gio. He wore a short tunic and a leopard skin pinned to his shoulder with ivory pins. A crown of wildcat skin and egret feathers adorned his head. His wrists and ankles were ornamented with brass bangles and a whip hung from his belt. He kept flapping at his shins with a buffalo-tail fly switch.

He smiled scornfully as he looked long and hard at the

captives, and his teeth showed, blackened, and filed to sharp points. He came closer and closer and the silence thickened. He was clearly chief of the tribe. At last he came to a stop in front of the terrified prisoners.

"Mouele!" he shouted. "Come here!"

Mouele hurried over to him. He fell to his knees and rubbed his head in the dust at the chief's feet. Then he got up.

"Yes, King Minga," he said humbly.

"You seem to have done well, Mouele," said the big man. "I shall reward you well. Let's take a look at what you have brought."

The two men slowly circled the prisoners, none of whom dared move. One by one, they were carefully examined by King Minga.

"Good, good," he kept murmuring, "very very good."

When he reached N'Gio, he stopped for a moment to stare appreciatively at his broad frame. The young man stared straight back at him until a glimmer of rage grew in the king's eyes. Then N'Gio's shame overwhelmed him and he lowered his eyes. He was so very tired, and he had been whipped and beaten so much.

Minga gave a nasty little laugh and went on with his inspection. He came to the women prisoners and muttered with interest, "Ah, their women. Are they beautiful, Mouele? Yes, they are, very beautiful, I must say."

"Yes," said Mouele, "and there are many young ones."

"I hope you amused yourself?" asked the king, and the two men laughed uproariously. Minga waved toward three of the youngest girls.

"I'll have those," he said, his voice suddenly hoarse.

Mouele knew his king's taste and was not surprised by his choice. He gave a gruff command and two of his men pulled the young girls out of the group and dragged them to the king's hut. They went, their heads bowed. In spite of all they had endured, their bodies were still graceful, and Minga followed their supple walk with a look of intense greed on his face. He turned to Mouele.

"See that the prisoners are settled in the guardhouse, and let them be given a copious meal. After that, you and your men go take a rest. You certainly deserve it. The men of the village will take over the guard."

"Yes, King Minga," Mouele said obsequiously.

Minga returned to his hut and Mouele began to bark out a series of orders.

The inhabitants of the village returned to their huts. They knew what would happen now and they had to prepare a fine feast in honor of the conquerors.

N'Gio and his companions were pushed unceremoniously toward the edge of the village where a tall fence stood around a giant shelter, made from a straw roof resting on stakes. A partition divided the shelter in two, and more stakes were driven into the ground at intervals, with chains and iron bracelets and collars fixed to them.

The Bapounou separated the men from the women and made them go into the separate halves of the shelter. Their yokes were removed, and their bonds fastened to the pickets by means of the chains and collars. The chains were only long enough to permit them to lie down. They could not move at all. In addition, N'Gio had a huge iron ball fastened to his ankle.

The women were chained at the waist so that they could take care of the children, who were left free. The pregnant women were driven toward a small closed hut at the edge of the enclave.

When they had all been settled, the guards took up their posts outside.

N'Gio had no idea what awaited him, but one thing was certain: he would be able to sleep at last. Some old women brought gourds filled with cool water. Then generous portions of boiled elephant meat, smoked fish, and grilled yams were doled out to the prisoners. N'Gio was so famished that he swallowed everything he could lay his hands on, and everyone around him did the same. Nobody spoke a word. It was the first good meal they had had for many days. They were so weak that many of them fell asleep before they even swallowed the meat they were chewing. N'Gio was one of the first to drift into sleep. His last thought before his eyes closed was of Yawana. He didn't hear the songs and dances that were swelling outside.

Two huge eyes sunken with exhaustion spied on the movements of the villagers from behind the walls of the enclave. Yawana was still waiting for the moment to save her husband and she had waited until the plantations were empty before she dared approach. Nothing, it seemed, could diminish her obstinate determination and no amount of tiredness could destroy her delicate body.

Her face fell as she watched. She would never manage to get him out from here. She was too tired to move, and clutching at the bamboo fence with both hands, she watched the feast eagerly as shadows grew about the leaping fires.

CHAPTER XXII

"Gentlemen, I bid you good night," said Jonathan, barely able to suppress a yawn.

His officers left immediately, not sorry to go and take some rest themselves. The sailors in the big cabin were also dead to the world. There was no one left on deck other than the watch, although the hour was not late.

The crew on board was almost complete, for Jonathan had insisted that everyone return to the vessel to work on the repairs and alterations necessary to prepare *The Sea Witch* for the slaves. Reghan, the quartermaster responsible for guarding the storeroom, had stayed ashore. So had young Matthew. Following Jonathan's orders, William Clark had taken him there to help him over his melancholy.

Jonathan was barely able to pull off his boots before throwing himself fully dressed on the iron bed that groaned under his weight. He was dead tired. The past few days had been particularly trying for both officers and crew, and the frequent thunderstorms had not helped preparations on and below deck.

Everyone had been roped in, including the Reverend Ardeen, who had temporarily put aside his bottles and his lustful activities in order to give MacLean a hand with the fever cases that had broken out among the crew. There were plenty of sharp tongues aboard who found good reason for his sudden solicitude, and William Clark was the first to remark that the doctor often used alcohol in his ministrations, which explained the reverend's sudden zeal for his fellow man.

Captain Collins had spent a good part of the day with Gregory, inspecting the ship. He noted that his orders had been carried out thoroughly. *The Sea Witch*, a peaceful trading vessel, had been transformed into a formidable prison ship in just a few days. The hold had been scrubbed fore and aft and prepared to hold water and food for the journey. The battery had been prepared for combat and provision had been made to store live cattle. The ship's carpenter and his assistants had built false decks, and iron bars weighted with chains ran the length of the partitions, with huge tarred basins placed at intervals for use by the slaves. The pen for the women and children had been similarly equipped under the quarterdeck, and the entire ship had been thoroughly disinfected with quicklime.

A heavy partition had been built on the maindeck around the center hatchway, making an enclave with a small piece of artillery in each of its four corners. Pierre had installed a kitchen there for the blacks with two brass cauldrons resting on brick ovens. Boarding nets were lying ready to be fixed along the edge of the deck to prevent any attempt at suicide during the voyage.

The English captain should have slept easily, and yet he could not find peace. His large frame, damp with sweat, turned and twisted on his bed, and sometimes a moan escaped his lips. Aurelia, so haughty, so uninhibited, Aurelia managed to cross the seas and torture his flesh without the benefit of a ship. The same dream always haunted his nights. She would appear before him in the park surrounding her castle, superb and naked, her black hair undone. She would let him kiss her, caress her, and then with a harsh laugh she ran away, and then returned again to torment him.

The ship was wrapped in silence, broken only by a man coughing and the creak of the rigging. The bell rung the hour, and its dull clang mingled with the ghosts in Jonathan's sleep.

He woke suddenly to the sound of running footsteps on deck. His cabin door flew open and a man stood framed in the doorway. Jonathan leapt up and seized the pistol he always kept hidden under his pillow. He relaxed when the light of the oil lamp showed him Gregory Adams.

"Captain," said Gregory breathlessly, "get up! I think we are about to be attacked!"

Jonathan leapt to his feet.

"We can hear boats coming from far down the lagoon," said Gregory, "and it sounds as though there are large numbers of them."

"Sound the alarm at once and see that everyone takes their battle posts in total silence," cautioned Jonathan, pulling on his boots. "I'll meet you on deck."

Gregory ran out of the cabin and Jonathan slipped his

pistols into his belt. He had expected something of the kind for some time, and he congratulated himself on having taken every precaution against it.

When he stepped out on deck he was greeted by a pitch-black night. There was no star to be seen and no ray of moonlight pierced through the heavy clouds. The attackers had chosen their moment skillfully. Jonathan realized as he climbed the ladder to the bridge that they would have been trapped had they relaxed precautions and guard of *The Sea Witch*.

Pierre was already standing there, a hatchet in his hand. His face showed excitement at this unexpected diversion. Jonathan surveyed the ship with narrowed eyes. Furtive shadows crept about the decks and men stood silently all along the bulwark. The ship's lantern, its reflection dancing about like a long yellow serpent in the water, was the only light on board ship. The dim, still shapes and the sensation of tension filled the air with menace.

Jonathan leaned over the starboard rail, peering into the dark. A faint sound of oars dipping in and out of the water came to his ears from the bank opposite the Portuguese fort. Gregory came up and leaned beside him, shoulder to shoulder.

"All set, sir," he whispered. "The men are all at their posts."

"Good, Gregory," Jonathan replied in an undertone. "We'll give those sons of bitches a welcome they won't forget. Have the starboard cannons loaded with chained bullets and three measures of gunpowder. Might as well do the port ones too, in case those savages decide to catch us unawares."

"Do you think they'll try to board, Captain?" asked Pierre, his eyes gleaming with excitement, and his meat cleaver waving in agitation.

"I don't think we'll give them time to do that," Jonathan assured him.

Pierre looked disappointed as Jonathan left him and made his way to the deck. He could feel the tension in the men, but he also sensed their fierce determination to stand up to whatever action came their way. He warned the crew not to open fire until he gave the signal with a pistol shot, and then to fire all possible weapons immediately. Then he went down to the battery. William Clark was there, super-

vising his gunners. Jonathan gave them instructions and
then returned to the bridge.

Woolcomb and Adams were waiting for him there, and
the three officers tried to pierce the darkness with their
eyes. Now they could barely distinguish a wavering line
advancing toward them. Beneath them, the opening portholes squeaked gently and, one by one, the mouths of the
guns protruded from the hull.

The assailants advanced with infinite caution; the sound
of their oars was hardly discernible above the wash of the
waters. They were still too far for Jonathan to guess their
numbers. He reflected that they would soon learn that
greed did not pay. Not content with selling their brothers
into slavery, they were trying to kill the very hand that fed
their greed. Their behavior was so outrageous in this con-
text, that Jonathan gave up trying to understand it. He
merely shrugged and waited.

The enemy boats began to loom out of the darkness.
They seemed very heavily laden and were about thirty in
all.

"I'll give the signal in good time," Jonathan reassured
Gregory. "These must be the N'Komi Mr. Gomes told us
about. I wonder if . . ."

But he never finished his sentence. He couldn't let fall an
unprovable accusation that could well provoke the undying
fury of his crew. Nonetheless, he himself did not discount
the possible involvement of the Portuguese in this attack.
He swore to himself that he would get to the bottom of it in
due course. He had more urgent matters to attend to now.

"The lanterns!" he yelled, suddenly deciding that matters
had gone far enough.

The starboard side of the ship sprang to light in an instant, illuminating the line of attackers. Seeing that they
were discovered, they threw prudence to the winds and began to paddle forward at top speed toward the ship, uttering fierce war cries. Their bodies were painted white from
head to foot and they wore strange headdresses of white
feathers. Their remarkable garb did not fail to astonish the
sailors who were used to more subdued uniforms.

They did not know, of course, that long ago the N'Komi
had dressed like this to attack their enemies and that their
enemies had taken them for birds and been easily con-

quered. No doubt they thought the ruse would work as well with white men.

A volley of arrows, assegais, and knives spurted from the boats and fell into the sea short of the vessel. Jonathan, seeing that they were now close enough, sent a signal pistol shot into the air.

Immediately *The Sea Witch* let go with a heavy salvo that swept away most of the blacks standing in their boats. Shrieks and howls of pain and rage filled the night as bodies splashed into the water. But despite the brief confusion, the boats continued to advance, and the sailors quickly reloaded. A second volley of assorted projectiles came from the boats, and this time at least one reached its destination, for a sailor fell to the deck, an arrow in his throat. Woolcomb's shoulder was cut by a jet knife, and MacLean leapt forward to help the wounded.

Clark's muffled orders rang out from the battery, "Consign your souls to the Lord, and fire!" A huge burst of flame shook the ship as all the starboard guns went off simultaneously, sending out a rain of bullets attached two by two by a short chain. They hit the oncoming boats full force, shattering them and scattering corpses. Panic reigned. The triumphant cries of the sailors mingled with the death rattles of the natives. The guns poked out again and a second murderous salvo took care of the remaining boats. They sank as a new salvo from the guns sprayed the battlefield.

The N'Komi who had escaped death were flailing about in the water, swimming in all directions, not knowing where to turn. Some swam toward the ship, and it looked as if they were begging to be taken aboard.

Jonathan ordered longboats put out to sea. Soon after, the sailors reached the survivors and killed every one with their sabers and hatchets, cutting the hands that reached out to the boats and shattering the heads that bobbed about in the waves. Pierre had taken a position in one of the longboats and was having the time of his life.

The lagoon was soon red with blood and covered with mutilated corpses floating under the torchlight. At Jonathan's orders, two of the attackers were spared. They were hauled out of the water like fish and thrown into a longboat where they were immediately knocked unconscious with blows from an oar.

The longboats prowled around a while to ensure that all the attackers had been killed, and then they regained *The Sea Witch*.

The two prisoners, their faces grotesque and bleeding under the white paint, were dragged between decks, where they were fastened to the fittings that had been made for others and left there to regain consciousness.

After the fight, Jonathan gathered his officers together. Woolcomb's arm had been bandaged and he joined the rest. His wound, happily, had not been a grave one. The wounded sailor had been less fortunate. The iron-barbed arrow had been poisoned and he died almost instantaneously. The chaplain, sober for once, was with him in his last moments.

"Gentlemen," said the captain, "as you can see, we must redouble our vigilance. This vessel is attracting too much envy. This time it went well, but if we had not been on the alert, and our enemies obviously hoped that we would not be, we would all have been massacred. So until we leave I must declare a permanent alert here. Have you all understood?"

An indistinct murmur greeted his words.

"Doctor," Jonathan turned to MacLean, "take good care of Mr. Woolcomb. We shall bury the sailor tomorrow. His possessions can be put up for lottery among the rest of the crew. I plan to ask Mr. Gomes to lend us Vasco tomorrow, without telling him that we want to use him to interrogate the prisoners. Now, all of you go and get some rest. Pierre, please give a ration of liquor to all the men, they certainly deserve it."

The Sea Witch stayed illuminated until dawn, and the sailors spent the rest of the night discussing the battle.

CHAPTER XXIII

Captain Collins had been trying to consign some of the preceding night to the log. He laid down his quill and turned to the man who was respectfully awaiting his attention.

"What can I do for you, Reghan?" he asked.

The quartermaster, who had been guarding the storehouse at the Portuguese camp, twisted and turned his wool cap awkwardly in his fingers. "I had to see you, Captain," he said. "I had to tell you that the lad, Matthew, that Mr. Clark left with me, disappeared two days ago."

"Well, that's hardly a serious matter, is it?" Jonathan was annoyed at having been disturbed. "He's probably holed up somewhere with some wench. Don't make such a fuss of it."

"Well, I've had him hunted everywhere, Captain, and I can't help worrying. The lad didn't seem in a normal state."

"Listen," said Jonathan resignedly, "if he doesn't turn up this evening we'll put on a search for him. I don't like deserters, particularly right now. Did you hear that we had some activity here last night?"

Reghan shuffled his feet. "I also wanted to see you about that, Captain," he said. "I don't like to tell tales or encourage rumors, but there are some things I don't understand."

"Really?" Jonathan's interest was suddenly aroused.

"Yes, sir. My men and I were waked up last night by all that firing. I ran to the fort to see what was going on, and those Portuguese, they seemed to be enjoying every minute of it, no doubt about it. I couldn't understand a word they said in that damned lingo of theirs, but that's what it looked like to me. And they looked at me with an odd look, too. When our guns began to hit at the attackers, their whole mood changed. They didn't look too pleased, I can tell you. I hurried right back to my lads and I told them to watch it, because there might be a bit of a fight before dawn. But God be thanked, nothing happened. All the same, Captain, I do think we should watch the bastards, begging your pardon. I'm not saying they was a part of it, but they wouldn't one bit mind taking over our ship and all what's in it."

"Was Gomes there?" asked Jonathan tersely.

"No, I didn't see him, Captain."

"You did well to tell me about this," said Jonathan. "I had my own suspicions about all that. I'm going to send some more men along to reinforce your group. Right now, you'd better get back ashore. Tell Gomes that I invite him to dinner. And tell him to bring that half-breed bastard, Vasco. If he asks why, you can say that you don't know."

Reghan left and Jonathan let his thoughts wander. He was wondering what he would do to the Portuguese if it turned out that he had really tried to betray them. In any case, it would be best to wait for all the slaves to be loaded before acting, and in the meantime to be constantly on the alert, although he was sure that Gomes would not attempt another attack after such a total failure. He wiped his pen, dipped it in the ink, and set to work again. He was determined to finish before the sailor's funeral rites.

On deck, two sailors greased their huge needles constantly in the suet horns they carried at their waists as they finished sewing a shroud for their dead companion. They tied him up with rope and added a large stone. Then, keeping him horizontal, they lifted him onto a plank balanced against the taffrail. Obviously, he could have been buried at the fort, but the men had heard tales about the tombs of the whites being robbed of corpses for use in secret rites, so Jonathan had decided on a sailor's grave.

The Reverend Ardeen arrived, steadied by Clark, who had gone to fetch him. The crew were lined up on deck and Jonathan joined them, accompanied by MacLean, and Woolcomb with his bandaged shoulder. Gregory followed almost immediately.

Ardeen stopped in front of the shroud, an absent expression on his face. He realized suddenly what was wanted of him, and slurring the words, he intoned a sermon on the spot, more of an exhortation than a funeral oration.

"You were born of mud . . . er . . ."

"Coolidge," whispered Woolcomb, "his name was Coolidge."

"Thanks," Ardeen returned in a stage whisper. "Yes, Coolidge," he intoned at the top of his voice, "you were born of mud, and you will end your days in mud." He staggered a little and seemed to be struggling to find the right words. "Only Hell can receive you into its open arms," he continued emphatically, "unless your hero's death compensated for all your sins here on earth. In that case," and here his voice became reassuring, "you will perhaps be lucky, and not have too long to wait around in . . . around in . . . in Purgatory," he ended triumphantly. He caught hold of the plank to save himself from collapsing as Jonathan and the others listened in horror to this strange farewell.

Arden started to pummel frantically at the corpse with his fists. "Leave us, miserable sinner," he screamed, "may the abyss swallow you and may you find eternal rest in the stomachs of fish. Hup! Over you go," and he ended roguishly with a hiccup. Worn out by his own oratory, he fell down on deck and began to snore heavily. As amazed at his fall as they had been at his speech, the sailors trembled with nervous laughter, and the poor dead man slid to the deep in the midst of general merriment.

The morning passed peacefully until Gomes' arrival. He had scrubbed for the occasion. He was wearing a startlingly white shirt and red cotton trousers tucked into high boots. In his desire to prove his peaceful intentions, he had left his weapons behind. Vasco was with him, dressed in white trousers cut raggedly above the knee, and an old sleeveless jacket which had known happier days on the back of an officer of the Royal Navy.

Gregory greeted the two men on deck. He invited Gomes to follow him and turned the half-breed over to Pierre, asking him to see that he had plenty to eat and drink. The cook gave Jonathan a heavy wink to show he had understood and dragged Vasco to the galley. A huge pot steamed on the maindeck under the tarpaulins. The sailors stood in single file, waiting to receive a bowl for each group of seven.

Jonathan received Gomes with feigned cordiality. He had no intention of revealing his suspicions. As for Gomes, the invitation had taken him by surprise, and he was also intent on hiding his feelings. However, in spite of his forced good cheer, it was clear that he was not at ease.

Gregory left the two men to themselves. Two of the crew

set the table while a cabin boy poured the drinks, and talk turned naturally to the battle.

"It's hard to believe what happened last night, Mr. Collins," Gomes said with an innocent air, putting down his empty glass. "They were really savages. I hope none of your men were hurt."

Jonathan caught him in a hard stare.

"I did lose one man, Mr. Gomes," he returned, "and one of my officers came near to being killed. Of course it would have been worse had we been caught unawares."

The cabin boy placed a cheese dish on the table, with oyster fritters, and refilled the tumblers.

Gomes helped himself generously and said, "When I heard all that shooting I put all the fort on emergency alert. I was just about to have 'em join in when it all stopped."

"That's not quite the way I heard it," Jonathan said coldly. "Your men were, in fact, ready to intervene, but hardly in the way you have just told me. It seems they were vastly amused by the incident. As for yourself, I heard that you were not even there."

Gomes swallowed his drink and grew pale. "Oh, Mr. Collins," he said in a shaky voice, "who ever could have told you such a thing?"

"My quartermaster," Jonathan said evenly. "He was guarding the storeroom on shore. He had the distinct impression that your men looked at him in a very unfriendly way."

Gomes couldn't eat. He was nervously pleating his napkin between fat fingers. "That's impossible, Mr. Captain," he cried. "It's really impossible. I was there, I swear it, and I was worried sick. What did they tell you my men were saying?"

Jonathan saw where the wind was blowing. He sighed and answered: "My man couldn't tell me exactly what they were saying, Mr. Gomes, my man doesn't speak a word of Portuguese."

"Ah! You see?" Gomes said triumphantly. "You shouldn't accuse people like that. I swear to you that they were all about to come to your aid, and I with them. I swear it on the Virgin and all the saints," and his voice shook as he made the sign of the cross.

"I'm an honest dealer, and I can't see any reason why I

should be pleased to see you go under. Who would I sell my blacks to, then? You tell me, who?"

He had a point, and Jonathan realized that he was getting nowhere with the discussion. He hoped that perhaps the confrontation between Gomes and the two prisoners would give him a better idea of who had hatched the plot, and he decided to let him off with a warning for the time being.

The cabin boy arrived and placed a magnificent roast kid with fried squash in front of them. After he left, Jonathan said abruptly, "I warn you, Mr. Gomes. That must not happen again. You have enough influence on these tribesmen to exercise some control over them, and I shall hold you personally responsible for any new incident involving them."

Annoyed, Gomes attended to his food, without bothering to answer.

"All right, now let's forget all that," Jonathan said at last in a conciliatory tone. "I'm sorry. I let my temper get the better of me."

The wine and excellent food that Pierre had prepared soon warmed the conversation. Jonathan asked Gomes if he had any idea where the lad Matthew might be, but the Portuguese assured him that he hadn't. He expressed some astonishment that they should have asked him to bring his half-breed valet along, and Jonathan explained that he had thought Vasco would like it. This seemed to satisfy Gomes and he let the matter drop.

By the time the meal was over, peace had again fallen between Collins and his guest. Gomes was eager to prove his goodwill and promised Jonathan his full help in supplying the ship. He assured the English captain that he would be watching out for the safety of his crew, although he continued to insist that he had no knowledge of the tribes who had attacked the ship. The two men emptied a last tumbler of wine and went out on the bridge. A slightly misty sky announced the end of the season of rain. The sailors went about their tasks, and the decks of *The Sea Witch* hummed with activity.

On the maindeck, the two black prisoners were chained to a tall mast. A few gaping sailors watched them, occasionally sending a well-aimed kick or a string of angry curses in their direction. The N'Komi, the only survivors of the massacre, were gray with fear. They were sure that their fate would be the same as the one they themselves were in the habit of meting out to prisoners: torture, death, and then to be eaten. They lay there, naked, writhing under the jeers.

Gomes observed this from up on the bridge and gave a start.

"Those are two of our attackers," said Jonathan. "They must be N'Komis. The rest died." Then he added in a mild tone, "See here, since Vasco is aboard, could we take advantage and ask them a few questions? He could interpret for us."

He watched the Portuguese closely to observe his reaction, but Gomes accepted at once, eagerly. "Of course, Mr. Captain."

Jonathan stepped aside to let him descend the ladder to the deck and followed him down. The half-breed was just stepping out of the galley. Pierre had done a good job: Vasco was dead drunk.

Gomes frowned when he saw him. He walked up to him and slapped him across the face. Then he let out a stream of curses, but since Jonathan couldn't understand Portuguese, he had no way of knowing if he was angry that Vasco had drunk too much, or if he was threatening him with what would follow if he failed to watch his words during the interview with the prisoners.

Vasco seemed to come to his senses. He stared at his master with a hangdog expression. "Yessir, Mr. Gomes," he whined, "yes, Master."

He followed the two men to where the prisoners were tied, and the crew, fascinated by what was coming, formed a circle around the tall mast.

With a swagger, Vasco untied his whip from his belt, but Jonathan stopped him. "No, Vasco," he said, "not on my ship. On shore, you can do as you wish, but these men are mine."

The half-breed frowned and replaced the whip.

"Ask them where they come from and who their chief is, and ask them who ordered them to attack us," said Jonathan.

Vasco turned to the two blacks. He began to talk very fast in a guttural language interlaced with musical sounds. One of the men answered, and the other nodded agreement. Vasco started off again and as he became more and more vehement, the two prisoners seemed to shrink in on themselves, throwing furtive glances in the direction of Gomes, who was gazing out to sea as though he had no interest in the matter at all.

When Vasco stopped, Jonathan asked him, "Well? What did they say?"

Vasco paused for a moment, then spoke, his gaze shifting from Gomes to the captain.

"Well, you see, Mr. White Man, what they say, these blackies, they say they are N'Komi. They are from the village of Assewe at the end of the lagoon. That's what they say to me, Mr. White Man. It's their witch doctor who bewitched them. He made them drink the water women wash in and told them that nobody could kill them. Then they danced the mbunda and became birds. They wanted to eat you and take your ship. But now, you see, they think that the gods were not with them and that their witch doctor, he make a mistake in the medicine. That's all, Mr. White Man." Then, seeing Jonathan's skeptical expression, he added quickly, "I swear it."

There was no question that Vasco must have invented the entire story. Jonathan could have sworn that the real story was vastly different but he had no proof. All he had to judge by was that Gomes had regained his confident expression by the end of Vasco's story. Jonathan accompanied him to his boat and saluted him coldly, though with his customary politeness.

"I think you are right, sir," exclaimed Gregory. "They must all have been in league."

"Yes," said Jonathan thoughtfully, "but they know now what it costs. We'll take care of them before we leave, but not sooner. Get the prisoners back below decks for now. I want to keep them as my own personal trophies, and we should separate them from the rest of the slaves during the voyage or they'll be torn to shreds."

"Fine, sir," said Gregory, "I'll see to it, and then I'll take the relief guard ashore."

CHAPTER XXIV

In the prisoners' area there was total silence. The grueling march that had brought them to this unknown place and the despair they had lived with for days had emptied them of all resources. They sprawled on the sandy ground and slept as they had fallen. Flies crawled on them, buzzed around their heads, and stuck to their closed eyelids—and they never even twitched.

The bark huts of the Bapounou were also silent. They were tired out from the festivities. They had danced and drunk all night. The entire village had listened to a detailed account of the kidnappers' expedition. Stories of their courage, the violence of the resistance, and the incredible strength and stamina they had to muster to control their victims grew with each tale. What had been nothing more than a cold-blooded act of vandalism and massacre became a glorious epic in the retelling.

Yawana's night seemed interminable, the worst she had endured so far. She was unable to sleep and silently prowled about the enclave, trying to peer through cracks and determine where N'Gio was chained. She heard the hysterical clamor and beating of drums that heralded the return of the kidnappers, and an immense desire to scream and cry also welled up inside her. She wanted to shout out her hatred, cry the name of her beloved husband for all to hear, and wail out all her sadness.

At last, heartbroken, she dragged herself back to the outlying plantations to hide. She was desperately hungry, but she had neither the strength nor the courage to gather up the fruits that lay around her. She lay in a heap, hidden as well as possible, not knowing what to do. The thought that she should abandon her hopes and retrace her steps crept unbidden into her mind, but her intense loneliness, the promise she had made to herself to try to save N'Gio wherever that might lead her, and not knowing where she might go alone were enough to convince her to stay. She tried to imagine, for comfort, that everything had merely been a nightmare and that she was really in the arms of the young man she loved back there in Mounigou, sheltered by their own bark hut. Her nerves took over and she lost all sense of time and of the dangers that surrounded her. Her eyes closed, burning with unshed tears.

Cocks crowed joyously, and the dogs awoke in an uproar of barks and howls. The village came to life immediately. Fires were lighted, and the bustle gave a pleasant appearance of normalcy to the early-morning scene. There was nothing to indicate that this was the headquarters of the most revolting trade carried out under the most unpitying circumstances.

The prisoners were awake, though groggy, and puzzled that for once they had not been lashed and insulted out of sleep. The men who came into the enclave were well armed, but they treated them without cruelty. They untied the women and took them and their children in small groups down to the river to bathe. Then they came for the men, N'Gio among them.

Three of the male prisoners went down to the river, surrounded by four guards. Bokou, who had been yoked to N'Gio after Ozengue's death, was among them. N'Gio did not know the third man and when N'Gio asked him his name and his tribe he refused to answer. N'Gio wasn't surprised by the silence. The prisoners had long since given up talking to one another. There was nothing left to say. They couldn't talk about the fish they had caught or the health of their plantations. They couldn't boast about the size of the game they had hunted or comment about the virtues of their wives. There was nothing to be said about the wind in the forest or the rain that left deep ruts in the red earth. The misery was the same for all, and now that their gods and spirits had rejected them they had nothing left to say. It was almost as if they didn't exist anymore.

The guards led them across the village. The villagers had satisfied their curiosity the night before, and the children playing in the sand took no notice of them. They were used to seeing people in chains being led about the village and then leaving one day, like a herd of cattle, for an unknown destination. They were convinced that these must surely be inferior or cowardly tribes to have allowed themselves to be captured and herded about in this way.

Further on, women were stuffing wood into the stoves, while others were rolling out long clay forms, which they then twisted into spirals to give them the shape of bowls, smoothing them with wet hands before putting them in to bake.

They passed the end of the enclave and came to a wide, well-trodden path leading to a peaceful river bordered by papyrus. Women crouched on the banks, beating manioc roots to rid them of acid. The young ones fished for small fry in the reeds. Some small children splashed about in the water between large hollow trees. N'Gio stared at them in astonishment, not sure what their use could be. Nobody paused or seemed to notice the prisoners at all. The guards prodded them into the river. N'Gio had forgotten how wonderful it felt. The cool water soothed his aching limbs. The countryside was incredibly peaceful. It was the first pleasure he had known for a long time and had his hands and ankles not been tied together, the delight he took in the bath might have obliterated the heavy weight of his present pitiable condition.

It was a short respite. The guards ordered the three men out of the water and they started back to the village. At the entrance to the enclave, they saw young girls crouched in front of the abaos, miniature huts where they were leaving offerings on the shrines of past chiefs of the tribe. They were certainly preparing a feast in the village, for N'Gio had time to see men placing sacred masks above the entrances of their huts, before he was led into the prisoners' shelter. The ritual objects, he noticed, were very elaborate and were topped by plumes. He was impressed by the delicacy of the carving and the richness of their decorations.

Back at his stake, N'Gio was again chained into an iron collar. The bath and rest had broken the captives' apathy. They were getting used to their misery, and that day no one had waked them with kicks and cudgel blows to make them march to the point of total exhaustion. With rest they were regaining hope; hope for what, they did not know. They whispered among themselves in an undertone for fear of attracting the attention of the guards.

"What can we do?" muttered Bokou. "You, N'Gio, are the strongest among us. You are now our chief. Don't you think we could try to escape?"

"You are now our chief." N'Gio's mind flamed with relief. He knew now that he was accepted as his father's successor, and he felt purified of Adende's treachery.

"No, Bokou," he answered quietly, "it isn't possible. Not now. We are still too weak. My muscles are as flabby as the mole cricket's stomach. And we are so closely guarded. They would kill us easily with their magic weapons, or they would do to us what we have seen them do to others. Let us wait. Something will surely happen."

N'Gio didn't want to admit to Bokou that all his hopes lay in Yawana. He was afraid to tell him she was nearby, for fear she would be betrayed. If there was any chance of escape, he knew he must do it alone. Any attempt at mass escape was suicide. He was no coward, but he knew that to be true. Once he himself was free, he could rally support from friendly tribes and come to save his companions.

"What do they want of us?" asked Bokou in a voice that quivered with fear. "Do you think they will kill us? Do you think they plan to eat us?"

"I don't know," N'Gio said, discouraged, "but I don't think they plan to kill us. Otherwise, why would they have made us walk all that distance?" But in the darkness of his soul he too was afraid. His words were more reassuring to his companion than to himself.

They had to stop talking then, for the gate to the shelter was lifted and the village women came in, followed by the guards. Some carried heavy gourds and others wide hampers on their heads. They laid them down in front of the prisoners and handed out water, smoked fish, and manioc sticks rolled in banana leaves. The food was good and plentiful and N'Gio ate with pleasure. He was confused by the way they were being treated. First, constant beatings and curses; now the captors were leaving them in peace and treating them well, at least as well as was possible given the harsh fact of captivity.

When the prisoners had finished their meal they got ready to sleep, but the Bapounou had no intention of wasting such an able-bodied work force. They pulled out creepers and leaves and set them to work weaving straw roofs for huts. The women were given pandanus leaves to braid.

N'Gio got down to work. His companions were also happy to do something that would make them forget their misery for a while. Some of them even managed to hum songs and chants that gave rhythm to their work.

They were so involved in what they were doing that they paid no attention to the pandemonium that suddenly broke loose in the village. Cries and frantic barking from the dogs had awakened the other animals from their peaceful sleep and provoked a chaos of baaing and grunting and squawling. N'Gio heard all the noise, but wasn't very interested. At Mounigou this sort of cacophony always welcomed hunters when they returned to the village loaded with fresh meat. This echo of the past reminded him of the harsh reality of the present and he went on working mechanically. If he had only known that this time the hunters and their quarry were quite different from those of his memories, his heart would have stopped right then and there. For Yawana, caught and held, had just been brought into the village.

In spite of all her precautions, the kidnappers had became aware of her presence. Two days before, when she had spied on Ilali in the hut with one of the kidnappers, the slight rustle she made running back to concealment had not escaped the Bapounou, who had reported it to his leader, Mouele, as soon as he rejoined the others.

"I think I saw someone run away to hide," he said. "Should I organize a search?"

"No," said Mouele. "We're in a hurry. It must be the mate of one of these animals, who is trying to join him. If she's come this far, she'll come all the way. Let's wait until we get to the village. She's sure to come sniffing around and then we can get her more easily."

Mouele never guessed that it was N'Gio's wife he was talking about. Had he known, he probably would have gone after Yawana immediately. But as it was, he didn't think about it until he arrived back at the village. He spoke to King Minga about it, and the next morning everybody joined in a search of the countryside surrounding the village. That was how two adolescent boys came upon Yawana asleep in a plantation. They stopped, amazed. They were dazzled by the languorous grace of her sleeping body. Her face was resting on her arm. Her breasts gleamed in the gentle light and her smooth stomach, barely covered by her loincloth, rose and fell softly with the rhythm of her breathing.

The boys looked at each other, and crept back to the village to announce their find. A team was immediately put together and hurried to the spot where they had made their discovery.

Brutal hands grabbed at Yawana. She woke with a start and was terrified to see a group of men surrounding her, roaring with laughter. Before she had time to understand what had happened, her wrists and ankles were seized and she was lifted on the men's shoulders and carried at a gallop. Her agonized cries and desperate efforts to twist free were useless. At last she stopped fighting, almost suffocated by the huge sobs that welled up inside her. She knew she was lost, that it was all over.

It's dreadful, she thought. Why didn't I find a better hiding place? Oh, N'Gio, N'Gio! What will become of us?

She didn't even spare a thought for what might happen to her, she was so wrapped up in the despair of knowing that she had not saved her husband. As she wept, she saw the branches of the trees pass above her, and after a long jogging trip that bruised her and jolted her unbearably, she saw that they were entering the village compound. As she passed, she could hear shouts and animal cries, the same clamor N'Gio heard.

In the center of the village she was thrown roughly to the ground. Yawana didn't dare move a muscle. She crouched down in the dust and hid her head in the crook of her arm. A circle of curious villagers closed in on her as more and more came up to take a look.

Yawana felt so desperate that she couldn't even think beyond the immediate moment. She closed her eyes to shut it all out. Dogs were barking very close. Voices urged them on, and she felt them bite her legs. She flailed at them blindly with her arms and brought on another explosion of jeers and laughter. Her lips clenched to avoid crying out, Yawana lay under the nipping dogs, determined not to give the crowd any more amusement. Pebbles hit her, and children poked at her with sticks, shrieking with laughter.

All her hopes were gone. She knew that what she was enduring that moment was only the beginning and she could well imagine the tortures she would have to bear, for she had watched the cruelty of the rapists.

Suddenly she realized that the crowd had fallen silent, and she began to tremble with panic, certain that it augured some imminent disaster.

A harsh voice rang out and Yawana heard some shuffling as the tight-packed circle around her opened out. Feet advanced toward her and didn't stop until they were touching her body.

Mouele had alerted King Minga, and he now stood in silence gazing at the supine body of the beautiful young girl. He stared at her greedily. Then he put a foot under Yawana's stomach and turned her over. She shrieked and opened her eyes. A giant stood over her, his face hard.

"Stand her up!" he shouted.

Two men leaned forward and lifted her easily. Yawana, held stiffly upright, her arms and legs firmly pinioned, her feet hardly touching the ground, was terrorized by all the faces staring at her. Her eyes, large with fear, rose to Minga's face. As he stared at her, the huge man's lips drew back over his pointed teeth in a sneering grin. What she saw in his expression made her shudder. It held a cold ferocity, sparked with a violent lust that left no doubt about what he was going to do with her. She lowered her eyes.

Minga chuckled silently. He detached his whip from his belt, and keeping his eyes on the young woman's face, passed the thong over her body. Yawana felt the cold rough leather on her skin, and goose bumps rose on her flesh at the humiliating contact. She stared up at him again. Minga was still smiling. Then she felt the pressure of the whip increase as it slid between her legs. She was utterly revolted and tried to move to avoid it, but she was held too firmly and had to endure Minga's game. When she realized that, she forgot her fear and spat in his face.

"Pig!" she shouted.

Minga's face turned gray with rage. He wiped his wet cheek. He stepped back and without warning lashed the whip with all his might across the girl's stomach.

Yawana was unable to restrain a cry, as the tearing pain hit her. She contorted her body violently in an effort to get away, but the two men twisted her arms behind her back and lifted her above the ground. Her arms were pulled almost to breaking, and the pain paralyzed her completely. The whip slashed at her mercilessly. She screamed again and again but the blows redoubled.

N'Gio's name burst from her in a desperate shriek, as if only he would be able to save her from her torturers. Then she fainted dead away.

When N'Gio heard his name shrieked in such agony he leapt up, forgetting he was chained. The chain tying the collar to the stake was too short and he fell prostrate on the floor, half strangled. The other captives also heard, and froze where they stood.

N'Gio got up again. The screams ceased. His companions knew, as he knew, that only Yawana could have shrieked like that and they were all looking at him compassionately. He couldn't prevent tears from rising to his eyes. He fell to the ground, weeping and groaning, impotent and desperate. The most horrible thing in the world had happened: Yawana was at the mercy of those monsters.

Her anguished scream had calmed Minga's rage. He dropped his arm, rolled up the whip, and slipped it into his belt. He was panting from the effort of the whipping, and a white froth lined his lips.

"Let her go," he gasped.

The two men obeyed and Yawana slid to the ground, still unconscious. Minga turned to Mouele. "N'Gio! That must be the name of the husband," he said. "Do you know if we have him?"

"Yes, King Minga," said Mouele, "it's Adende's son, the old vulture. She escaped us when we were taking the village."

Minga had his breath back now. He pointed to Yawana.

"She's very beautiful," he said. "I want her brought to the feast of the ancestors tonight, to thank her for dropping in on us. Have her prepared by the women. And see to it that she doesn't escape again or you will pay with your head. Do you understand?" His voice was hard and Mouele shuddered.

"Yes, King Minga," he said humbly.

Minga turned on his heel and strode back to his hut. Mouele bent down and in an easy movement lifted the inert Yawana onto his shoulders and carried her to the furthest point in the village. The villagers assumed that the fun was over, and went their separate ways. Mouele went to the huts inhabited by old women who were only capable of the most sedentary occupations. He laid the young girl on the ground and, with his king's admonition in mind, bound her wrists and ankles with creepers. Then he went into one of the huts.

Two old women were sleeping there. Mouele shook them and told them to wash Yawana and prepare her for the king. The hags nodded, and when Mouele was sure that they had understood, he left.

One of the women fixed a creeper around Yawana's neck. The other took a gourd filled with water and emptied it over the girl, slapping her body all over. Yawana came to and sat up, eying the old women with disgust.

"Come now, stop your simpering and get up," said one of the women dryly. "Come and bathe yourself. And whatever you do, don't try anything clever because if you do, I'll make you sorry." And to show she meant it she whipped Yawana with a creeper as her companion took hold of the creeper around Yawana's neck and pulled on it, forcing her to follow.

Yawana was careful neither to answer nor to resist. She was too weak. She was already resigned to anything that might happen to her, reasoning that it was better this way. She was exhausted from the long journey and now she could at last be with N'Gio openly. Even if we are separated, she thought, at least I'll see him, I'll be able to talk to him.

The thought comforted her a little. As the creeper bit into her neck, she rose and followed the two women. Her bonds only allowed her tiny steps, but the women paid no attention to that. They hauled her across the village. Only a few grimacing children noticed them and seemed to get some fun out of it. They jumped about in front of them and made faces under Yawana's nose. She walked on, eyes lowered, pretending not to see. It was hard to walk. The bonds hampered her, the creeper hurt her neck, and the old woman whipped at her ankles.

The two women led her to the river and plunged her in, pushing her head underwater several times. She coughed spasmodically as they rubbed her vigorously with handfuls of grass mixed with sand. When she was finally rid of all the dust she had accumulated on her body since the morning, they pulled her out of the water and led her back to the village.

The walk in the sun was enough to dry her off. They pushed her into the hut and tied her to the central post, making sure that she couldn't move any more than was absolutely necessary.

They fussed over her young body, massaging it with a strongly scented oil. For a brief moment, Yawana relived the morning when Ivohino had prepared her for her marriage ceremony. One of the old women pinched Yawana's nipple, abruptly bringing her back to reality. Yawana moaned and tears welled in her eyes, bidden more by the memory of her mother than by the pain the old woman had inflicted.

They untied her from the post. Mouele came back to make sure that all he had ordered had been done, and replaced the creeper around her neck with a collar and chain he had brought. Then he untied her hands and ankles and showed her a mat on the ground. The young woman sat down.

One of the old women brought her a broiled chicken with fried bananas and some water. It was her first meal in days. In spite of her misery and fear, she ate everything put in front of her. Then she lay on the mat and, without another thought for past or future, fell sound asleep.

CHAPTER XXV

The prisoners were given food before nightfall. This time, N'Gio couldn't bring himself to eat anything, but Bokou, delighted with his luck, ate every scrap of N'Gio's smoked meat and boiled taro.

All day, N'Gio reeled under the blow of Yawana's capture. Bokou tried several times to console him, insisting that he had no proof that Yawana had been caught, and that he himself was not sure that he had heard N'Gio's name called out, but N'Gio finally told him to leave him alone, and the well-intentioned fellow let him be.

N'Gio's dark thoughts revolved endlessly around the same point. He had seen too much of the punishment meted out to prisoners to have any illusions about what awaited Yawana. Perhaps at that very moment she was in the clutches of the rapists, or being subjected to horrible tortures. Pictures whirled and multiplied in his exhausted mind. He could not imagine, of course, that she was sleeping peacefully, nor that what she would soon undergo would be infinitely more disgraceful and humiliating than anything he was fantasizing.

His companions dropped off to sleep one by one, but N'Gio, his eyes straining in the dark, found no rest. The beating of drums in the village announced the start of the feast. Flames leapt in great orange tongues against the sky. Insects buzzed and hummed.

The young man's intense exhaustion was about to get the better of him at last when a group of Bapounou armed with firebrands came into the shelter. They made straight for him. They examined his bonds, removed the wooden block and chain from the stake.

"Up!" said one of them.

N'Gio started to tremble. He was sure that if they had come for him at night in the midst of the festivities it could be for no other reason than to sacrifice him during the initiation rites. He would be strangled, burned, or buried alive, perhaps eaten. Bokou's anxious misgivings had been well-founded after all. He longed to wake him to say good-

bye, but the guards pushed him roughly and he was forced
to follow.

In the center of the village, the festivities were in full
swing. Dancers were tapping their feet rhythmically, turning and twisting as one, and drums throbbed urgently.
Everyone had already drunk a lot and their fixed, expressionless gazes showed that they had taken iboga.

The guards dragged N'Gio to the edge of the clearing.
An enormous pole, painted red and white, was standing
there with several people seated behind it. The young man
easily recognized King Minga, who was surrounded by
women. There also seemed to be a group of elders and a
man whose garb marked him as the witch doctor. Minga
was seated on a sculpted throne made from pink orere
wood, ornamented with ivory inlays. He wore a leopard-
skin loincloth and his head was adorned with a tiara of red
monkey fur. A huge necklace of human teeth hung over his
naked, well-muscled chest. His wrists and ankles were
weighted down with gold and bronze bracelets, and his
hand rested on the carved handle of an ebony cane. A
small drum of human skin interwoven with stems of sweet
lemon trees rested on his knee. One of his women, a very
young girl, knelt naked at his feet, pouring him drink every
time he asked for it.

The guards brought N'Gio before him and threw him to
the ground with a violent push. "Bow before King Minga,
dog!" shouted one of the guards. N'Gio, on his hands and
knees, lifted his head and threw a look of hatred at Minga.
Two hands seized him by the hair and rubbed his face in
the dust.

"Do you understand?" demanded the voice. "Bow before
Minga!"

Then the man pulled his head back and hit him hard.
N'Gio's mouth was full of blood and sand, but he didn't
make a sound. Minga stuck his cane into N'Gio's stomach.

"I accept your homage," he said sarcastically. "Welcome
to my village. This night you are my guest and you will
take part in my feast." He turned to his men and ordered
sharply, "Tie him up!"

The two men lifted N'Gio to his feet and pulled him
toward the post. They bound him to it in a standing position. N'Gio's arms were stretched back and tied with creepers that bit into his flesh. He had his back to the dancing,

which seemed to be getting more and more frenzied by the
minute, and he was facing Minga.

The king tapped the girl in front of him with his cane.

"More drink, Buanga," he ordered.

She filled a clay bowl and held it out to him.

Minga swallowed its contents in one gulp.

"Now for our guest," he said, holding out the bowl.
Buanga filled it again and got up gracefully. She went toward N'Gio, her hips undulating suggestively. The light
from the flames danced about her long legs. She held the
cup out in front of her like an offering and her eyes ran
approvingly over the young man's body. She found him remarkably handsome.

She lifted the bowl to N'Gio's split, swollen lips, but he
turned his head away. One of the guards grabbed the bowl
from her, pulled N'Gio's head back by the hair and forced
the liquid down his throat.

"More!" said Minga.

Buanga held out a newly filled bowl to the guard and
again N'Gio was forced to drink. The wine was acidly bitter, and the iboga in it soon began to take effect. N'Gio
could no longer feel the bonds eating into his flesh, and he
forgot the horror of his situation. The music seeped into his
body and thundered in all its fibers. Buanga held out one
more filled bowl, and this time he drank without protest.
His entire body was sweating profusely and the young girl
could not resist running an admiring little hand over the
rippling muscles.

Minga gave a short mirthless laugh and whacked her
across the kidneys with his cane.

"No, Buanga! Not with that dog! Not now!"

Humiliated and aching, she sat down at her master's feet
without a word. She would have loved for Minga to let her
have the handsome prisoner then and there, he looked so
strong, but there was nothing to be done.

Minga got up from his throne and came to stand in front
of N'Gio.

"What do you think of my hospitality?" he asked. "Is it
not worthy of the son of the great chief Adende?"

The wine had not affected N'Gio's hatred. "You are
nothing but a coward," he muttered indistinctly. "What are
you waiting for? Kill me now!"

"Kill you?" asked Minga in honeyed tones. "Oh, no!

There's no question of that. Your life is far too precious to me, as precious as your father's life. Did you know he sold you all? Unhappily for him he did not live long enough to enjoy it, poor man," and Minga grinned. N'Gio's face tightened at the thought of the old chief's treachery.

"I am the one," continued Minga, "who suggested the deal to him, and I must say, it didn't take much to convince him. But since you are his son, I have reserved a very special treatment for you. You must know that your wife is now in my hands. You must have heard her screams?"

With an evil leer, Minga observed the painful expression that crossed the young man's face. "Well, you can rejoice!" he said. "You will see the dear child. She is to take part in our festivities tonight. All you need now is patience," and he sat down again on his throne. No one paid any more attention to the prisoner. As the music beat into his brain, he wondered about Yawana's part in the festivities and a wild anxiety filled him, piercing through the effects of wine and iboga.

The dance went on for long hours, until suddenly Minga stood up and sharply hit his drum several times in succession. Immediately the drums began a long roll, and the dancers formed a swaying circle around N'Gio.

The throbbing became almost unbearable and N'Gio felt his whole body vibrate. They forced some more drink down his throat, and the thought crossed his befuddled mind that now they were about to sacrifice him, but he was floating in such a hypnotic trance that the thought barely affected him.

There was a movement from the edge of the village. All heads turned, and N'Gio too was able to turn his head sufficiently to see what the excitement was about. He saw a procession of women advancing, their loincloths gaudy, their heads adorned with waving plumes. They came nearer. Suddenly, N'Gio, instantly sober, was straining desperately at his bonds, for walking in the center of the group was Yawana, held firmly by two of the women. Unlike the others, she was naked from head to foot, although her arms and legs were ceremonially decorated with gold bracelets that jangled with every step. Her body had been oiled and the firelight danced off it as she came forward, straight as an arrow, her eyes glazed and totally void of expression. N'Gio realized that she too had been drugged.

He fought against his bonds but only managed to tighten them further.

The procession came to a stop in front of N'Gio and he and Yawana found themselves face to face. In spite of the drug she had been forced to take, Yawana recognized her husband, and tried to run to him, but the women held her back. Her lips began to tremble uncontrollably, as if she were trying to say his name, but no sound emerged. N'Gio also tried to say something, but emotion knotted his throat and he couldn't speak. They stared at each other and their eyes held the sorrow and suffering of an entire people. They were completely at the mercy of these unscrupulous kidnappers and there was no hope left of escape. Yawana lowered her head and her eyes filled with tears.

Minga came over and stood between them. Several times he banged on the ground with his cane and the drum roll started up again. Nobody danced, but the circle closed around them to better see what was to follow. Every face stared greedily at N'Gio and Yawana.

Minga spoke to N'Gio in deceptively mild tones. "The attack on your village unfortunately interrupted your wedding night," he said. "I owe it to you to rectify that, so if you will allow me, we shall carry on the ceremonies here, so that I can earn your forgiveness."

Yawana and N'Gio didn't really understand what he was getting at, but they knew full well that his gentle tone hid some cruel and horrible plan. It was not long before their worst fears were confirmed.

Slowly unfastening the leopard skin around his waist, Minga began to laugh. The two women tripped Yawana so that she fell to the ground, and two other women came to help hold her down. Before she could make a move to defend herself she was spread out, her arms and legs held apart by rough hands.

Minga fell on her and raped her brutally in front of his entire tribe, who were shrieking and yelling in a paroxysm of excitement. Then he got up.

Yawana had been expecting the rape, and she endured it with resignation. Above her she could see all the faces twisted into bestial masks of lust. She thought they would let her go, but she was wrong. Almost at once another body fell on hers, plunging into it. Then another followed, and another.

N'Gio, insane with impotent rage, twisted and turned, trying to free himself, shouting violent insults at his wife's rapists.

At first Yawana clenched her teeth and passively submitted to the torment. But gradually the drug took effect and each new violation brought the young woman a mounting pleasure she could not conceal. Pleasure flooded her in spite of her rage. N'Gio himself had never been able to bring her to such a height of prolonged and intense sensation. She had no way of knowing that her body was designed for sexual enjoyment, for unlike most of the girls in her tribe, she had not had her clitoris removed at birth. Her mother, Ivohino, who came from the Akanda tribe which did not know of this practice, had insisted that her daughter not undergo the ritual mutilation which would have deprived her forever of the full sensual pleasure of love. Yawana could no longer contain the moans that welled up in her and each cry pierced N'Gio's heart, for he could see and understand what she was experiencing.

Minga also saw what was going on and he rejoiced in it; it amused him to cause such a handsome young man to suffer. He approached N'Gio and almost touched him.

"You love her, don't you," he shouted in his ear to be sure he was heard above the excitement of the crowd. "You are suffering! See how she revels in her pleasures. Do you think she is thinking of you? That's right, each time one of my men possesses her, it is you she thinks of." And he laughed long and loud.

N'Gio literally frothed with rage. "I'll kill you, Minga!" he spat out. "One day I'll kill you." But he knew that he would never be able to make his threat come true. At last the men left Yawana alone. The women let go her arms and legs and she lay on the ground without moving. An enormous wave of shame engulfed her. Would N'Gio ever be able to forgive her for what had happened? She had gone out of control, and she hated herself bitterly for it.

As she lay there in desperate humiliation, the Bapounou were swept away in total frenzy. Women were tearing off their loincloths, and men were doing the same. Loud cries rose above the music and hurt N'Gio's eardrums. Young girls with their eyes almost popping out of their heads twisted their bodies in front of him. Young Buanga, braving Minga's rage, came close to the post. The king saw what she was doing, but far from discouraging her, he gestured to her to continue. An evil plan was forming in his mind. It would add spice to the evening's events.

Now that nothing held her back, the young girl began to caress N'Gio with a light touch. He could not long fight his arousal, perhaps because of all the wine he had drunk, perhaps because he had just watched his wife being raped by the entire village, or perhaps because of the couples twisting and turning in front of him in sexual frenzy.

Buanga laughed and laughed, and Minga laughed; everyone was laughing.

That was what Minga was waiting for. He shouted orders and two men leaned over and lifted Yawana. She let them do whatever they wanted. They carried her to N'Gio and placed her against him. Then they tied her there solidly, riding on him, as the crowd jeered and screamed in delirious abandon.

"She's all yours now," sneered Minga.

The two lovers were left in this humiliating position all night. Both were weeping, immeasurably saddened for themselves and for each other. Their physical closeness was little comfort after all they had been through.

At dawn they were untied and fell unconscious to the ground. N'Gio was taken to the shelter. Whips whistled about him, but he hardly noticed. The women tore the bracelets off Yawana and dragged her without ceremony to the area reserved for women prisoners, and left her there without even bothering to chain her. Her fate had already declared itself.

CHAPTER XXVI

N'Gio and Yawana stayed in the village for several days. The young man was in a deep depression that even Bokou's cheerful attempts at conversation could not dissipate. He lay in a corner all day and all night, unable to stop tortured flashbacks of what he had seen. In spite of his agony of mind, he did not blame Yawana for her part in the degradation they had just experienced. It was the conqueror's privilege, after all. He remembered having seen young girls taken captive and brought back to the village by Mounigou warriors. They, too, had been forced to submit, and they had then stayed on in the village and married, without ever complaining. At least Yawana was now close by. Even if he couldn't see her, he knew she was safe from the dangers of the jungle. It made him feel better, for he was sure that they would now be kept together. Yawana had regained her strength. Her fellow prisoners, impressed with her courage, lavished kind attentions on her. A vast sadness filled her, because she could not communicate with N'Gio.

Days dragged by monotonously, broken only by meals and the morning bath. The prisoners wove baskets or braided mats all day.

Luckily for N'Gio, the partition was high enough to block his view of the women's area, so he did not see the men come every evening to make their choice. The youngest were always chosen, and Yawana was chosen more often than any of the others because of her beauty. Usually she was taken to King Minga. He made her drink, and then made her dance for him before forcing her to do his bidding. In the morning she was ushered back to the prisoners' shelter.

One night, the prisoners heard dull crashes resounding from far away. They resembled the crashes that had so bewildered them the day of the wedding in Mounigou, and they realized beyond a shadow of a doubt that their tragedy was somehow linked to the strange sound. The crashes came again and again and N'Gio reflected that it did indeed sound like a giant drum announcing a feast at which they were all to be the sacrifices. They were being well fed, which reinforced their fear that they would soon be eaten.

One day, about twenty more men and women in chains were thrown into the shelter. The prisoners questioned them and found out that they were Vili tribesmen from the Bayandji tribe. Their village had not been at war with the Bapounou, yet they too had been attacked a few days ago. Their guards had been quick to give the alarm and they had fought valiantly, but their attackers were too many and possessed strange and wonderful weapons, and they had been conquered. Many of them had been massacred. These were the only survivors. They could not understand what had happened to interrupt the peaceful flow of their quiet days.

Their arrival brought an end to the respite. Very early the next morning, guards erupted into the prisoners' shelter and woke them all, lashing about freely with the whips if someone was a little slow to react. Yawana was one of the first to get up. They tied her to a group of other women and led them outside. Heavy hampers and bundles lay on the ground and Yawana's share of the load was a heavy basket of smoked meat. The endless walking was about to begin again. She hoisted the basket onto her head and followed her companions as the guards prodded and pushed at them. As she left the village, she saw N'Gio stumbling ahead, chained to the other men. She gave a sigh of relief. So he was coming, too. He saw her and made a small sign from far away, and she stared at him, her eyes luminous with tenderness. They crossed the village mechanically and took the path that led to the river. The women were shoved unceremoniously into the big hollow tree trunks that had so intrigued N'Gio, and they put their bundles down. Then the men were jostled in too. For a moment Yawana had the wild hope that N'Gio would be in her vessel, but he was one of the last to get in. Each of the prisoners was handed a long wooden stave and the canoes were pushed out into the stream.

The prisoners were terrified. They were all forest people and had never experienced such precarious water travel. When they had to use the river for transportation they used steady flat rafts and punted with long poles, so they had no idea how to use oars. The guards showed them what to do and after some awkward tries they got the rhythm of it and began to row together in a fairly smooth fashion.

The river suddenly widened round a bend, opening into a big lake. Whips whistled ceaselessly about their ears and kept them rowing furiously, with just a brief pause for food before the voyage resumed. By nightfall, they had crossed the lake and camped on the opposite bank.

Next day they left the canoes behind and the walk started up again. It was less painful here for the trail was well trodden. Whitened skeletons protruded from the grass here and there, and N'Gio and his companions worried more and more. Clearly they were not the first to trudge this path that led toward the setting sun.

At the evening stop, after she had eaten, Yawana heard a long low rumble from beyond the trees. She had no idea what it could be, and neither did her companions. It went on all night long, and although they did not know what it meant, it terrified them. Its roar was not unlike the heavy breathing of a gigantic beast.

The march continued next day, and the more they marched, the louder the sound became. Sensing that they were soon to meet their fate, they wondered anxiously what it could be. A huge plain stretched before them and was soon behind them. Later, they came across a field that had been burned, to renew feeding grounds for buffalo and antelope. The earth and sky teemed with game of all sorts. The path had turned sandy, cutting across a wood of stumpy trees. N'Gio, striding at the head of the column, suddenly felt a stinging wind hit him in the face as he stepped out onto a beach that stretched as far as the eye could see. The ceaseless swelling rumble they had heard earlier was clearly the sound of huge ocean waves plunging toward shore like packs of wild beasts. Spray flung high into the air, making a fine mist all about them and adding to the menace of the scene. Yawana had never before seen such vastness. It seemed to go on forever. She had always imagined that the edge of the earth would look like this. This must be the end of life and the beginning of death. From their faces, the other prisoners were clearly experiencing a similar awe, and as if to emphasize the grandeur of the moment, a beautiful rainbow rose right out of the water, spraying the sky with radiant color. They thought of the story of the m'bumba of the seven colors, symbol of the

power of life and death, which, legend had it, had been
vomited forth by a giant fish in primeval times. Panic
closed in on the prisoners when they saw this strange sight
and they refused to go a step further. Whips cascaded on
their backs with renewed vigor before they could be persuaded to go on.

There was a village by the dunes, its bark huts almost
hidden under a fringe of coconut palms. A noisy crowd
came running out of the huts as the column drew near, and
the prisoners and their guards were soon surrounded by the
bare bodies of a crowd of men and women. The children
poked and jeered at the prisoners as they were driven toward the seashore, where derelict huts awaited them. This
time they were left there without guards, for where could
they escape to? N'Gio tried to get his group to move with
him toward Yawana's group, but they were too tired and
refused to budge. He saw her stretching her tired body on
the sand far down the beach and he too gave up and lay
down.

Minga had followed the march, and the bearers carefully
laid his throne down. The village chief, a tall old man with
a noble carriage, came forward to meet him. A simple
straw loincloth swished about his legs and the only ceremonial insignia he carried was an elephant-tail fly switch,
symbol of oratory.

"May this be the best of days for you, King Minga of the
Bapounou," he said, bowing a head crowned with a bush of
pure white hair. His words were singsong and he barely
moved the lips under his heavy mustache.

"May it be even better for you, Wamba, venerable chief
of the Baloumbou," replied Minga warmly.

The two men headed for the village to discuss business
matters. They were close friends, even closer for the business ties that bound them. They had known each other
since childhood. The alliance between Bapounou and Baloumbou tribes went back many years to when their fathers,
and their fathers' fathers had begun to trade together. The
Baloumbou had come from the south in the distant past.
Led by Babinga the Pygmy, they had left Mongo country,
seeking a huge salt lake he told them about, which was so
enormous that one could not see the other side. They settled beside the ocean and soon learned to draw salt from
the sea, evaporating the water in large gourds.

About the same time, the Bapounou left the central lands and settled in the plains, calling the place Tchibanga. They heard about the Baloumbou industry and knew that salt was a rare and precious commodity for the peoples of the interior lands. That gave them the idea to act as traders between the two. They traded for goats, straw loincloths, and pots in the beginning, for their women were very skilled at the art of pottery. Then they resold the salt to the Akele, the Pahouin, and the other tribes of the great forests and plains. At times in the past they had also exchanged war prisoners or criminals for the salt.

This commerce had continued peacefully for years and might have gone on forever had not the white man come to explore the shores of Africa. They were half-gods, who brought with them invincible weapons, treasures of unsurpassed beauty, blazing jewels, wondrous fabrics, and brass pots.

The white men had no interest in salt. They wanted slaves, and more slaves in exchange for their treasures. The Baloumbou never asked themselves why, they just accepted that goats and clay pots would no longer do for trading, and that they now needed men. The Bapounou adapted to the new form of payment and organized bigger and bigger raids on both neighboring and distant tribes.

Minga and Wamba worked out their accounts as they smoked herbs and drank palm wine. They had every reason to be satisfied as they chatted under a leafy mango tree.

"You have brought me good strong men, Minga," said Wamba. "And the women are beautiful. The white Bitanda will be well pleased. I heard their big gun roar a few days ago. Why did you take so long this time?"

Minga took a long draught of the palm wine. "We had to go deeper and deeper and further away all the time," he sighed. "Those animals are getting wind of the danger and are deserting the villages we can reach easily."

A woman laid a fat grilled fish before them.

"I'm not surprised," said Wamba, tearing off a piece of gray flesh with his fingers and popping it into his mouth, "but there is no cause for you to worry. These tribes are split up into small villages and their villages are scattered in the forest. They will not get together to mount any sort of defense. My messengers will go out to the N'Komi tonight. The white men will give them the merchandise, and when they come to get the prisoners, we can divide it."

A gleam of pure greed lit Minga's features. "I want as many baskets of salt as you have fingers on each hand, for every man or woman," he said firmly. "I also need guns, powder, and lead, and don't forget the water that burns the throat. And then more iron bars. I'll wait here as long as necessary."

"Anything you ask, Minga," said Wamba, smiling. "You know you are my friend, and the whites will not refuse what I ask. They need us to provide them with men of our color. I don't know what they do with them. Do you think they eat them?"

Minga shrugged evasively, picking out a fishbone that had become stuck between his teeth. He didn't care what they did with the prisoners he turned over to them. All he cared about was what he got out of it himself, for it enabled him to dominate his own and other tribes.

"I suppose it's possible that they eat them," he said indifferently. "After all, we do that too. Less than the N'Komi of course, but meat is meat."

While the two chiefs were having their friendly discussion, Baloumbou women brought food for the prisoners: water, fruits, and huge baskets filled with large oysters. Yawana took one of these hesitantly. She had never seen one before. She broke it open with a pebble and found the inside slimy and revolting, but the smell was appetizing. She tasted the flesh and enjoyed the iodine flavor. The other women followed suit and they ate all they could manage. Huge pyramids of shells lay beside them, mute testimony to the many others who had passed this way and eaten of the same food.

N'Gio lay in the sand, gazing at the sky and thinking of Yawana. He would have liked to fly up into the blue with her and leave this accursed earth. He wondered if they could soon be together, but some instinct told him they were going to be taken far far away and that they would never come back. He did believe, though, that their lives would be spared. None of the tribes kept prisoners this long if they intended to kill them. Certainly they would never have made them come such a distance. He was sure that nothing in the future could be as bad as what they had already endured.

Yawana stared at the horizon, her stomach full. She had

never seen the sea, and never imagined that such a vast stretch of water could exist. Time and again, enormous waves crashed against the shore with deafening noise, and she saw shoals of translucent crabs riding in the foam. In any other circumstances she would have been enthralled by the spectacle, but she was so exhausted emotionally that nothing reached her or touched her anymore. She truly believed that she was drained of tears and laughter forever.

She knew now that there was nothing she could do to change the inexorable path of her destiny. Even if they set her free, she could never find her way back to Mounigou. The only hope that sustained her now was to be reunited with N'Gio. Perhaps they would be allowed to build a little happiness together wherever they were going. She shivered in spite of the hot sun, not knowing whether from fear or exhaustion.

All day the villagers forced them to reconstruct the ruined huts by the sea. They barked out guttural orders and beat the prisoners furiously. N'Gio worked hard, and soon there was shade for all under the straw roofs. Minga came to show off his catch to Wamba. They stepped among the chained bodies lying on the sand and Minga told the guards to check on the bonds as he dragged Wamba toward the women. Yawana saw them coming through her long lashes. Minga stopped in front of her, said a few words to Wamba, and the two men laughed. Yawana did not have to wait long to guess the cause of their amusement, for two men grabbed her and led her toward the village. She turned her head and cast a despairing glance at N'Gio as he watched her go, his heart in his eyes. She went, her head bent, to serve once again as her captor's plaything, hating the fate that had made her so beautiful and so susceptible to the pleasures of the flesh. N'Gio fell back to the ground and held his head in his hands, groaning and sobbing. He stayed this way for a long time, until well after nightfall, when huge fires had been lit to illuminate the beach and prevent any prisoners from attempting an escape. The armed guards were now Baloumbou, and they kept watch all night.

Many days passed. Every morning the prisoners went to bathe in the ocean. But they were fastened together in groups, weighed down by iron chains, and battered by the waves that terrified them, so they got no comfort from it.

Their food was almost exclusively oysters, and the pyramids of shells grew daily. Sometimes they were given coconuts, but they never had fish and hardly ever elephant or buffalo meat.

The Baloumbou went about their occupations as they waited for their messengers to return. Their women filled gourds with sea water which they then emptied into huge metal containers exposed to the sun. Next day they took out white powder, which they packed into tightly woven baskets. N'Gio realized that this was the precious salt the Bapounou had come to sell to his village. He had always wondered where it came from. Now he felt that it was responsible for the tragedy of an entire people and the massive uprooting of a race.

Yawana was nothing more than a curiosity for Chief Wamba. Minga had boasted about her and he just wanted to verify his claims, to see if it was really true that the Akanda women were lewd creatures. Yawana did nothing to confirm this, and he was very disappointed. He didn't tell Minga, for it might have made him lose face, but he had her taken back to the other women prisoners in the morning, and left her in peace from then on. While she was with him, she had dared to ask him what their fate was to be, but the old Baloumbou only stared at her disdainfully.

"Shut your mouth, stupid woman," he said. "You're no more than a piece of merchandise. In my eyes your destiny is no more important than that of the giant spider whose soft stomach serves as womb for the greedy wasp."

She had not pressed the point. Later, when Wamba had been somewhat softened by his lovemaking, he told her that they were being taken far far away, and that he didn't know more than that himself.

Once back with her companions, tied to them as before, Yawana tried to imagine where this distant land might be. This beach was like the end of the world to her. She told the other women what Wamba had told her, but she sensed a hatred in them that she could not understand. She knew nothing of jealousy. She had no idea that women she had always considered her friends might be jealous of her, for in spite of the dreadful circumstances, they were indeed secretly upset that it was she who was always chosen.

This life by the sea was calm. It almost began to seem secure. But a horrible scene served to remind the prisoners

of their desperate plight and showed them that the Baloumbou were as cruel as their kidnappers had been. One night,
one of the new arrivals, a Vili, managed to get out of his
chains. He should have escaped at once, but he wanted first
to see his wife. He crept over to the women prisoners who
told him that she had been taken away with some of the
others by a group of men. He guessed the reason for this,
and managed to crawl unseen as far as the village, where
he could hear cries coming from some of the huts. He crept
toward the one where he thought he recognized his wife's
voice. Like all the huts, this one had two doors facing each
other, to facilitate escape in case of danger. He chose the
back door and came upon his wife flat on the ground. Mad
with rage and grief, he plunged an assegai he found near at
hand into the muscled back which was riding up and down
on his wife. He plunged it in so hard that the iron went
right through the man and reached his wife's heart. They
let out a terrible dying shriek and the other villagers came
running. The Vili did not try to run away. He let them
capture him.

They tied him firmly to a coconut palm and, next day,
they assembled the other prisoners to watch his punishment. They tore out his tongue, then cut up his entire
body, pouring salt into the wounds and leaving him in the
broiling sun all day, crazy with pain, his mutilated mouth
emitting strange, animal sounds. When night fell they piled
wood at his feet and burned him alive.

One fine morning as N'Gio and his companions lay on
the sand, they saw the Baloumbou women drop their metal
containers and run to the border of the forest, followed by
the guards. There was a clamor of bells and all the villagers
hurried down the trail leading to the beach.

N'Gio raised himself onto his elbows and saw a long column winding its way out of the jungle. The villagers
greeted them with every manifestation of joy and excitement. Many of the newcomers bore hampers on their
heads, and they were surrounded by men who wore
brightly colored fabrics. It looked to N'Gio as if these men
had white clay on their faces, and he assumed that they
must be warriors returning from an expedition, bringing
back new prisoners. However, there were no whips, and he
could hear no rattling of chains as they walked. They were
too far away for him to distinguish anything more. The

group hurried toward the village and soon disappeared from view. N'Gio lay down again on the sand, resigned to await whatever would happen next.

Crushed by the heat, Yawana was sound asleep and saw nothing.

CHAPTER XXVII

"Vasco!" yelled Gomes for the second time, "where are you, you bastard? Answer me!"

Gomes was in a very bad mood. Jonathan's disguised threats the day before had made him very uneasy. What a good thing, he thought to himself, that he had the time and presence of mind to say a few words to Vasco. He could not bear to think what might have happened if the half-breed, drunk as he was, had chosen to translate the answers of the two N'Komi for what they were. Had the captain known his share in the attack on the ship, he would be hanging from a mast, of that he was certain. He shuddered, and poured himself a full tumbler of brandy. He really needed it. Vasco didn't answer, and Gomes wondered where he could be.

"He's never there when I need him, the donkey," he grumbled to himself. "He must be fornicating in some corner."

He wiped his fat, sweating face, remembering that he hadn't even felt like making love with his little black girl the night before. He was sick of her and had decided to sell her to Collins. He'd had her too long, and she no longer amused him, though she had been a good pupil. Taking a virgin and leading her down the path of vice and degradation was his only pleasure in this accursed country.

"Mother of God, where is that idiot! Why doesn't he answer?" he exploded. "Vasco!"

He rose heavily and went out on the porch of his hut. There was no one outside. He sat down again, thinking of his ruined plans. He had prepared his strategy so carefully, awaiting just such an opportunity for years. He was sick of Africa, the stifling heat, the mysterious diseases, but there was no question of returning to his own country, which had rejected him. He wanted to go to the New World countries where gold was easy to come by if one didn't have too many scruples. Of course he could simply have asked the crew of *The Sea Witch* to take him on board, but his greed had made him think up another way to leave. A few tumblers of tafia and promises of magnificent gifts had easily persuaded King Nkougou, who reigned over all the N'Komi villages of the lagoon, to participate in his plan. Together, they worked out the attack on the ship and decided that the entire crew should be massacred. Only the captain, his lieutenant, and the ship's doctor were to be spared. Gomes' men were to kill off all the sailors left on shore.

The Portuguese were for the most part retired sailors, and Gomes was sure that, under threats of death and torture, he could have forced the English officers to chart a course for them. Once he arrived he would kill them, of course. He would then have a ship stuffed with merchandise and slaves, for he had carefully not told Nkougou that part of his plan was to complete his cargo with as many N'Komi as he could stuff into the hold. The money from this haul should have enabled him to live a lavish life in the New World.

Now the beautiful dream was shattered and he could only hope that the stupid English captain would not go out and counterattack the N'Komi. That would be the last straw. For a moment Gomes wondered if he ought to warn Nkougou of this possibility, but then he reflected that Jonathan would probably do nothing after all. His company would not encourage an action that might cause enough trouble to close off the market. Had Gomes known of Jonathan's intentions never to return to Africa and to leave the slave trade forever, he might have felt less sure of himself.

At last Vasco appeared in the doorway.

"You called, Mr. Gomes?" he asked innocently.

"What do you mean, did I call? I've been yelling for you for two hours! How many times do I have to tell you that I want you to come the minute I call? You deserve a good hiding to liven up your filthy nigger skin a little!"

"I'm not really a nigger," wailed the half-breed. "Please, Mr. Gomes, don't do that. Don't beat me, I beg you."

"You're nothing but a filthy black!" yelled Gomes. "And if you ever do this again I'll tan the hide right off your back."

Vasco's eyes rolled with terror. He often whipped the slaves and he knew well the burning pain of the lash.

"Well, we'll forget it this time," Gomes went on, "but remember, don't do this again."

Shaken by his narrow escape, Vasco eyed the brandy bottle longingly. Gomes followed his glance. His valet was a beast of a man but he needed him, and knew how effective he was in bringing rebellious slaves into line. His voice softened.

"Take a drink and sit down. I want to talk to you."

Vasco filled a goblet and swallowed its contents in one gulp. He sat down on the floor.

"No news of the slaves?" asked Gomes. "Have you heard anything? They should be coming soon."

"No, Mr. Gomes," said Vasco, "I haven't heard a thing. I can go and see the N'Komi. They may have heard something."

Gomes gave it some thought.

"Good idea," he said at last, "go at once, and hurry back."

Vasco left and Gomes sighed. He was suddenly very tired. He laid his head down on his arms and slept at the table. His little black girl crept quietly into the room, not quite sure what to do. He treated her like a dog, and she was as attached to him as a dog to its master, in spite of his cruelty.

At about that moment, Jonathan's longboat docked. He jumped ashore, followed by Woolcomb, and climbed the path that led to the fort. Huge flowering hibiscus and tulip bushes bordered the sinister spot with brilliant color. As the two officers went inside the Portuguese guarding the entrance greeted them respectfully, to their great astonishment.

"Polite, today, aren't they," Woolcomb remarked.

"Yes. A little too polite, I'd say," Collins said with a grin.

When they reached Gomes, he was sleeping soundly. The little black girl fled when she saw them. Jonathan walked up to him and tapped him on the shoulder. The fat man started, then stared vaguely at Jonathan. Recognition dawned, and he rose hurriedly, a smile fixed on his lips.

"Oh," he said, "it's you, Captain."

"Good day, Mr. Gomes. You don't look too well. I hope you are not ill?" asked Jonathan, feeling like a hypocrite.

"No, no," stammered Gomes, "I feel just fine. A little tired, that's all. It's this dreadful heat. Will you have a drink?"

"No, thank you," said Jonathan, taking a seat. He took out his pipe and began to fill it. Turning toward Woolcomb, he asked, "Mr. Woolcomb, while I talk with Mr. Gomes, would you go down to the storeroom and see if there is any news of Matthew?"

"Certainly, sir," said the officer, walking toward the door. Jonathan carefully lit his pipe and drew on it luxuriously.

"Mr. Gomes, we are all ready to load up your blacks," he said. "Do you think they are still some distance away? I'd like to leave as soon as possible. I still have to see to taking on fresh foods, but I don't want to do that until the last moment." Gomes' anxieties melted in the rays of Jonathan's relaxed good humor.

"Exactly, Mr. Captain," he said in his most authoritative manner, "I just sent Vasco out to get us some news. I don't think the convoy can be very far. It's probably a question of a few more days, I promise you. Maybe three or four at most."

Two children came chasing into the room. Jonathan recognized the two half-breed lads Gomes had introduced as his own. Their giggles stopped when they saw the look on their father's face. Gomes started to rise to chase them out.

"Do let them be," said Jonathan, drawing the youngest onto his knee. "They're not disturbing me at all."

The child turned huge, fear-filled eyes toward him as Jonathan mechanically caressed the silky curls.

"I could sell you those two," said Gomes curtly. "They give me more worry than they're worth and I'd be happy to get rid of 'em. They're eight and ten years old. I'd sell you the pair for a sovereign, and believe me, you'd be getting a good deal. They're circumcised, what's more, the little toads. Show Mr. White Man that they cut your end off!"

The two children exposed themselves willingly, almost proudly.

"You see, Captain? They're all ready for selling."

"But they're your own children," Jonathan said in shock.

"Well," said Gomes uneasily, "they're mine insofar as I got them with a black female, but they're nothing but niggers. They do have a little human blood I 'spose, but they're niggers just the same. You can't change that. And then, look at 'em! They're sturdy, and good-looking. I'm told that out there in the Americas there are rich gentlemen who pay well for merchandise like that. I hear it's as good as women, although I've never tried it myself." He laughed coarsely. "I prefer women who've never felt the weight of a man before, y'see."

Jonathan stared at him in disgust. Every time he met him, the man became more repulsive. He reflected that Gomes would eventually sell them anyway, and that he might as well be the one to buy them. Wherever he took them, they could hardly be worse off than with this repulsive man.

"Very well, I'll take them," he said.

Gomes rubbed his hands with satisfaction. "You'll have to keep an eye on 'em all the time," he said. "They're vicious as they come, these little half-breeds. D'you want 'em on board right away?"

"No, not yet. They'll come with the others," said Jonathan hastily.

Footsteps rang on the wooden boards of the veranda and Woolcomb came in. "No news of Matthew," he said as he sat down. "He never said one word the whole time he was with the others. He wouldn't gamble, he wouldn't drink, and he wouldn't eat. They told me that suddenly one evening he just picked up his weapons and walked out. They didn't pay too much attention when it happened, but no one has seen him since."

"Send two men out to look for him, Mr. Woolcomb," said Jonathan somberly. "Try to find out if he borrowed a boat. We should comb the outskirts of the fort as well. He can't have gone far. I want him found."

Woolcomb was about to leave when an agitated voice came from the doorway: "Mr. Gomes, Mr. Gomes!" And Vasco came hurrying in. "Mr. Gomes, they're here! They're coming! They want to see you—"

"Who wants to see me?" interrupted Gomes curtly.

"King Nkougou. He's there, and there are some others with him. The Baloumbou. They've come from the coast."

Gomes' face cracked into a broad smile.

"What was I telling you, Mr. Collins? See? This is good news."

He turned to Vasco. "As for you, halfwit, you know that King Nkougou likes something to burn his throat. Take him to the veranda and give him something to drink at once, and get a move on or I'll get mad."

Vasco hurtled out of the room and Gomes turned to
Jonathan: "Would you follow me, Mr. Collins, and you
too, Mr. Officer? We'll greet them outside."

Gomes sat down on the steps and Jonathan and Woolcomb followed suit. Vasco came rushing out and laid a full
bottle at his master's feet, then stood silently behind them.

A group of blacks climbed the steps and came toward
the three whites. They were strangely dressed. Some wore
only loincloths of beaten fig-tree bark, others were decked
out in discarded military clothes or ragged shirts. One of
them stood out like a beacon. Tall and slender, he wore a
superb red coat too tight and short for his extraordinary
chest. A pistol and a short saber were slipped in the belt
and his genitals were tucked into a palm leaf corset. He
limped as he walked, for he had a high boot on one foot
only. To complete the singularity of his appearance, he was
wearing a long blond wig, topped by a battered three-
cornered hat.

"That's King Nkougou," explained Gomes, "those others
who are not wearing anything at all must be the Baloumbou messengers."

The king walked slowly to the foot of the steps and
gazed at the three whites. There was no respect in his
glance, just unadulterated greed. One of his men swept the
steps in front of him and put down a small carved wooden
stool, and the king sat down gravely, without saying a
word.

Gomes raised his arms in welcome: "Good day, King
Nkougou."

Nkougou grumbled in reply.

Gomes picked up the bottle at his feet, took a long swig
himself, and passed it to Nkougou, who quickly swallowed
most of its contents. Then he passed it to Jonathan. Jonathan hid his disgust and conformed to what he took to be
the local etiquette, muttering to Woolcomb to do the same.

The officer hesitated.

"For God's sake, pretend you aren't disgusted," whispered Jonathan. "And make it look genuine. His majesty
the king is observing you closely and if you don't get on
with it, he'll think we gave him poison!"

Woolcomb drank without enthusiasm, and Gomes took
back the bottle and handed it to the king, who grasped it
with undisguised satisfaction.

Then a long dialogue began between Gomes and Nkougou, partly in Portuguese and partly in an unknown language. Vasco broke in to interpret every now and then. Jonathan couldn't understand a word, so he watched the discussion and gestures closely. Sometimes the king got angry and voices rose, but Gomes didn't seem disturbed and held his ground.

At last, they seemed to agree. Nkougou put down the empty bottle with a look of regret and then rose with unsteady dignity. He turned his back on the three white men and moved away to talk with his companions. One of the men snatched up the small stool and hurried after him.

"Everything's fine," Gomes said happily. "They're two days' march from here, but that old bird is as shrewd as they come. He wants us to advance the merchandise to him so that he can take over the blacks from the Baloumbou. They probably don't trust him too much."

"We'll do what's necessary," said Jonathan, pleased. "I'll send Mr. Adams along to help Woolcomb. They'll settle with you what should be advanced. There's no time to lose. You should get them out on their way tomorrow at dawn. I presume you will be sending an armed escort, if only to make sure that the Negroes are really there?"

"Not to worry, Mr. Collins. I'll do just what you suggest."

"Did you ask him how many they have over there?"

"It's not easy to get figures out of 'em, but I think he said there are close to three hundred head, although I can't tell you how many male and how many female."

With the slaves already in the compound, this came to exactly the number Jonathan had in mind, and he answered Gomes with satisfaction.

"Perfect, Mr. Gomes. It's late, and I must get back to the ship, but I'll send Mr. Adams to you at once."

Turning to Woolcomb, he said, "I count on you to give me an account of the merchandise we advance, and for God's sake, don't forget Matthew."

Then he turned and strode purposefully toward the dock.

Gregory was soon there and followed Gomes and Woolcomb to the storeroom. His orders were to give Gomes whatever he needed, except for weapons and shot, which would be turned over the day the deal was consummated.

Gomes made his choice and the sailors pulled out the

merchandise Woolcomb indicated, a pile of assorted para-
phernalia: metal basins for the Baloumbou's salt, crates of
crockery, bottles of Barbados rum, hats and knives mixed
in with iron bars, bales of cotton, and glassware.

Gomes tried as hard as he could to obtain some guns but
Gregory was not to be swayed. The Portuguese was very
put out, knowing that Nkougou would give him trouble on
that score, but there was nothing he could do to counter-
mand Jonathan's orders. They worked late into the night
by the light of the flickering torches.

Woolcomb spoke to the sailors about the proposed
search for Matthew next day, and returned to the ship with
Gregory.

Later that night, Gomes and Nkougou talked things
over. As Gomes had anticipated, it was a stormy discussion. Nkougou was furious. He needed weapons for dealing
with the Baloumbou, and the Baloumbou needed them for
dealing with the Bapounou. Gomes had a hard time convincing him that the orders came from Jonathan, not from
him. At last, he exploded, "It's all your own fault! You
shouldn't have failed in your attack on the ship. If you
hadn't, they'd all be dead by now and you'd have all the
guns you wanted. Now the white captain is suspicious."

Nkougou had to admit that Gomes had a point here:
"You are a father to me," he whined. "You decide for me.
But those fellows, those Baloumbou and Bapounou, they'll
think I am trying to double-cross them. It's not good for
dealing."

"Well, you work it out with them," said Gomes firmly,
"they can just come and pick up their guns here, and
they'll see that it's no double-cross. Here, drink!" and he
handed him a bottle of brandy.

The gift of brandy calmed the king and the two men
parted.

"Don't forget to send some of your men to carry the
hampers," said Gomes. "You must leave at dawn tomorrow."

Nkougou promised to take care of it and returned to his
village.

Next day the long, heavily laden column left the fort.
The N'Komi bearers were surrounded by Portuguese men-
at-arms. Nkougou followed behind, carried on a throne by
his subjects and accompanied by two of his concubines.

Vasco went with them in case an interpreter should be necessary, and he was charged with keeping an eye on the
operation and seeing that all went well.

Gomes watched them disappear. Only a few days now
and all would be settled. He breathed a sigh of relief. He
would have to feed all these Negroes until they were taken
aboard. Slowly, he climbed the steps to his quarters where
the little black girl awaited him. Much later, stretched out
on his back as she ministered to him, he reflected that
there would undoubtedly be another ship anchored in the
lagoon one of these days. He swore to himself that next
time he would not fail.

CHAPTER XXVIII

Three days later the long column of bearers reached the coast. The Baloumbou ran to greet them with exuberant exclamations of welcome, although some, when they noticed the Portuguese soldiers, stopped in their tracks and retreated to a safer distance to watch the proceedings. The children ran from these strange white men like flocks of black birds. The Portuguese were quite pleased with the situation and they stayed in a close group, their faces full of scorn and watchfulness. They ordered the bearers to lay down their hampers in the shade of some coconut palms and sent Vasco to get them some food and drink. In the meantime, Nkougou, surrounded by Baloumbou tribesmen, entered the village.

He was received by Chief Wamba, and the two men congratulated each other and went to the large central hut where Minga was waiting. They bowed and greeted each other with customary ritualistic courtesy and then drank large quantities of fresh palm wine. When it was not fermented, the mildly acid beverage was very refreshing and had no intoxicating effects.

Nkougou came quickly to the point of his journey. Happily for him, and contrary to his expectations, the two chiefs did not fall into a rage when he told them that they would not get the weapons until later. They accepted his explanations without question. They didn't trust him at all, and the respect they showed him was a mere matter of politeness, but there was little they could do. He was more powerful than any of them. He reigned over a vast territory he had conquered by force and they were careful not to arouse his anger. Moreover, he was the one who dealt directly with the Poutou and the Bitanda, the white men whose glance was hard to meet, who had come to Africa from another world.

The Portuguese knew that it would be a long discussion, and they waited patiently, eating fruits and fish that Vasco had boiled for them on the coals. The leader, a small stocky man with a grim face, was not eating. He stood leaning against a tree trunk, anxious to leave as soon as possible. In spite of the armed men with him, he did not feel safe with these savages whom he knew to be no strangers to deceit. He heaved a sigh of relief as he saw the three chiefs making their way toward him.

Halfway there, Minga left Nkougou and Wamba and went back to the village. The negotiations did not concern him directly for the time being, and he knew that his own negotiation with the Baloumbou chief would come later.

Nkougou was the first to speak: "We go see the slaves," he said dryly to the leader of the escort.

He hated having to deal with one of Gomes' underlings whom he considered trash. Without pausing to see if anyone was following, he set out majestically for the beach, with Wamba.

The Portuguese spat on the ground, vowing to get his own back one fine day. He took Vasco and two of his men and ordered the rest to keep a careful watch over the goods and not let anyone near them.

By the time he had reached the two chiefs, they had almost come to the slave area. The sun's reflection on the white sand was almost blinding. He was hot and uncomfortable, and he cursed the foul life he was forced to lead, and the idiot Gomes who had let a prize like the British ship slip through their fingers.

He felt certain that it would have been so much simpler to do as he himself had suggested and drug the crew before killing them cleanly, rather than putting the affair into the hands of the fat black pig walking by his side. Now that the whole thing had failed so miserably, he regretted not having been more friendly toward the crew of *The Sea Witch*, and determined to treat them better when he got back. Perhaps, if it was not already too late, they might agree to take him on board ship.

Yawana was awakened by the noise. She raised herself up on one elbow. The sand pressed into her skin and itched. She brushed herself off as she watched the small group approach.

She was alarmed at the sight of Nkougou in his strange red garb with the one high boot and long blond wig. Then she saw the Portuguese. At first she thought they had clay on their faces, but when she realized that this was in fact their natural color, she was paralyzed with fear. She could never have imagined that such hideous beings existed. The pale skin was incredibly repugnant to her. Sometimes, in the forest, she had seen men with a reddish sheen to their faces, and with reddish hair, but they only came out at night for their eyes could not stand the light of day. If their parents failed to kill them at birth, they were chased from the villages and lived as recluses, usually dying very young.

But the ones she was looking at here didn't look degenerate. They even seemed dangerously powerful. Once her father, Isembe, had told her of white gods who had come at the beginning of time, but she had always considered the story a legend. Now she was seeing them with her own eyes, though she was sure these were no gods. They looked more like the children of a devil. Somehow, she knew that they were responsible for all her troubles.

The white men stopped a little to one side and the red-coated man came over and examined the captives one by one. He had the Baloumbou chief with him and another athletic-looking man dressed like the whites, but with darker skin, and negroid features. Yawana immediately sensed reserves of cruelty and evil in him. He was feeling all the women with evident enjoyment. When her turn came, he lingered longer, and she stood, paralyzed with revulsion as his hands roughly squeezed her breasts. All the women were submitted to a similar inspection and then the group went toward the men. She could see the men undergoing a similar but much briefer examination, and when it was over, Vasco went toward the Portuguese. She saw him talk animatedly to them, pointing first to the women, then to the men. Nkougou joined them and then Wamba hurried back to the village. They talked more, and the white men went away.

N'Gio was sure that the discussions held nothing good for him. Surely they were to be sold once more. He could see Yawana. She was so beautiful. He would have given anything for the strength to burst his chains and run to her. His predictions were fulfilled, for as soon as the white men went away, the man in red began to yell out orders and many men who had been standing at the edge of the forest came running. At the king's orders, the N'Komi bearers surrounded the prisoners and without provocation began to lash them indiscriminately with their whips. The prisoners

knew what was expected of them. They got up at once, and
began to move toward their fate.

Yawana wondered how many times they would change
hands, and where they would finally end up.

As they left the shore, the prisoners saw the villagers
throw themselves wildly on a mass of hampers, tearing
them open with eager cries. Minga stood there, ready for
his share, and seeing him, N'Gio felt a flood of hatred for
the man who had led his father into treachery and brought
them all to be herded from place to place like cattle. Then
the forest swallowed them up.

N'Gio and Yawana marched steadily for two whole
days. One evening they stopped at the mouth of a great
river. There was a long narrow village along the shore, and
a huge lake stretched before them, with many small islands,
each with leaping fires. Canoes paddled peacefully about in
the calm waters, some crowned with braided sails swelling
in the wind.

No guards were visible. It was clear that these people felt
so powerful they had no need of sentinels. They knew no
one would dare attack them.

As usual, the prisoners had to put up with the jeers of
villagers and blows from the children before they were
closed into a building with high walls and stakes. Once
again the women and men were separated by a partition.

Fruits were handed out to them. Nkougou wanted to be
certain that there would be no risk of escape and he came
himself to make sure the chains were secure, and doubled
them where he felt there was need. He ordered huge fires
lit so that the area was illuminated, and set guards all
about the enclosure.

N'Gio slept very badly. The mosquitoes, drawn by the
smell of fresh blood and dancing flames, bombarded him
all night. Yawana waited for them to come and fetch her,
but this time the women prisoners were left in peace; no
one came at all. Worn out by her emotions and the long
march, she fell into a deep sleep.

When they awoke, they were given small smoked fish on
wooden skewers. Yawana felt pleasantly rested. The brief
stay by the ocean shore had calmed her, and the diet
of fresh oysters had given her back her youthful vigor. The
men felt better too. They had not been too badly treated

and the recent march had not been as difficult as the previous one.

In the morning, Yawana and her companions were taken to the river to bathe. They hardly spoke to one another. Each was closed in her own particular agony. Some, the weaker among them, moaned ceaselessly, but most of them preferred to remain silent. The water was muddy and brackish. Pelicans perched on mangroves between fishing expeditions. A large crocodile lazing on a log, its jaws wide open, slid into the water.

Yawana rubbed her body with handfuls of sand. Then she rubbed the back of another young prisoner, who in turn did the same for her. She stepped out of the water, and an old woman handed her small sticks of wood and ash for cleaning her teeth. Then they were all taken back to the village.

They passed the men who were being led to their morning bath. N'Gio wanted to pause when he saw Yawana, but the guards prodded him on. Although they were so close, once again each was seized by an intense loneliness.

Back at the village they were told not to lie down on the ground. Some women busied themselves over Yawana, searching her body and hair for parasites. Then they rubbed her all over with palm oil, and twisted her hair into hundreds of tiny braids. The men were prepared in much the same way. With both sexes, white hairs were pulled out if there were not too many, or dyed if there were.

King Nkougou came often to supervise the preparations. The whole strange business began to trouble the prisoners considerably. N'Gio was convinced that they were being prepared for a mass sacrifice, perhaps in honor of the white men. Yawana had ceased to speculate about anything. Sometimes excellent care followed brutality, sometimes abundance came after deprivation; she didn't know what to expect, but she didn't think they were heading for death. She would not allow herself to lose all hope.

The N'Komi chief was very satisfied. This herd was of excellent quality. The females were beautiful and healthy and the children seemed not to have suffered unduly from their endless march. The boys looked strong, and the young girls were worth a lot of goods. As for the men, since the whites liked them strong, they would not be disappointed. And he planned that they would be as easy to

train as they had been to capture and lead this far. He was
sure that this group would calm Gomes' anger toward him
for what had happened at the English ship. He vowed to
keep all the weapons for himself and give none to Minga
and Wamba. If they weren't happy, it would give him an
excuse to make war on the Baloumbou. And then he could
sell them to the whites. He liked the idea. Once more he
looked over his victims. Their skin gleamed softly from the
oil; their defects were hidden so that the whites would
never notice them. He ordered small cotton loincloths
handed out, then left, shouting for them to start on their
way. This time the women and children were put at the
head of the column. Before them came the N'Komi musicians, and the rhythm of drums and strings filled the air as
they started on their way.

The wide trail wound along the riverbank, and then
along the borders of a misty lagoon. The musicians played
without stopping and their lively rhythm pulled the prisoners to a faster pace despite their chains. For a moment Yawana was able to forget her pain and worries and admire a
countryside more beautiful than any she had ever known.
N'Gio's mind scarcely strayed from the heavy yoke that
hurt his neck. All he wanted now was for this treacherous
journey to be over once and for all, whatever awaited them
at its end.

He was soon to know. As the sun accentuated the richness of the colors around them, they walked between tall
plantations. They were not, as in Mounigou, randomly
seeded here and there with a banana tree, a taro tree, an
igname, and a matadi in straggling confusion. Here there
were endless rows of neat vegetation.

After a vast palm grove, they came to a wall of tightly
packed stones. A door opened and the prisoners entered,
watched by silent, sad-faced blacks.

The place was teeming with white men. They surrounded the newcomers immediately and pushed them toward some windowless huts, shouting words they could not
understand. The huts were far bigger than even the
mbandja of the Bwiti. Yawana recognized the huge man
with the dark skin who had so frightened her on the beach,
but to her great relief, Vasco didn't seem to notice her.

Great cauldrons were steaming in front of the huts. The
young woman was led into an enclosure. The musicians

ceased their playing and rejoined the other N'Komi. Yawana turned her head and saw N'Gio being led into one of
the huge huts.

Before the doors clanged behind, the young man had
time to glimpse an enormous canoe with gigantic swaying
tree trunks on its deck floating on the great lake. It looked
very frightening. His yoke was taken off, and he was
shoved into the darkness of the hut. He stumbled over
sprawled bodies and managed to find a spot near a wall. A
greasy, nauseating brew was served to them, then the door
was shut, leaving them in total darkness.

Announcing a better tasting Kent.

25% Less tar.
Smoother taste, too.
Micronite II filter is why.

Kent. #1 selling low tar.
Now even better.

Newport

Newport

MENTHOL KINGS

Alive with pleasure!

Warning: The Surgeon General Has Determined That Cigarette Smoking Is Dangerous to Your Health.

CHAPTER XXIX

As soon as he got back on board after hearing that the arrival of the slaves was imminent, Captain Collins undertook a last-minute inspection of the vessel. The rigging had to be checked again, and he discovered a weakness in the mizzenmast. He saw to it that barrels of sweet water had been tarred and prepared in sufficient numbers to ensure adequate rations for five hundred people for four months. Pierre checked the state of preservation of the salt cod, wine, and flour, and threw out anything that looked rotten.

Gregory saw to the loading of all the goods he had been able to buy from Gomes. Huge bales of cotton were lashed to the maindeck, ebony, ivory, straw, wax, honey, and spices were packed into the storerooms in the center. The easily accessible storage space halliards were reserved for food and sweet water.

Later, Jonathan called a meeting of the officers. He wanted to give them his orders concerning the fresh food, and he asked Pierre to join them.

As he waited for them to gather he stared up at the sky. During the past several days it had became more and more cloudy, and a stiff breeze whistled around the ship. The dry season had started. He was pleased. Suddenly, Jonathan started. A huge praying mantis had settled on the sill and was staring at him, really staring, its triangular head turned to him and its huge green eyes looking him up and down. Its face was so sinister that Jonathán couldn't help a shudder of horror. In a sort of trembling rage, he crushed it with the butt of his pistol. He didn't know what it was he had felt, but it was a horrible feeling. He decided that his nerves must be in very bad condition for a harmless insect to affect him so strangely.

The noisy arrival of Woolcomb and Clark made him feel better. He told them to pour themselves a drink. Simon MacLean arrived next, followed by Gregory. Pierre then came in bearing with great pride a coconut-milk blanc-mange he had made, and they tucked into it with gusto.

The chaplain was not there. In fact, it would have surprised them to see him, for they were now more accustomed to his absence than to his presence.

"Gentlemen," said Jonathan, "the slaves will be here in five or six days. As soon as they have been branded we shall set sail. We must expect about three months to reach Louisiana. We'll stop first in São Tomé, but who knows what we shall find there. I want every care taken about the food from this moment on. I want all the crew to help stock up the ship, and no stealing. Do I make myself clear?"

"You've nothing to fear on that score, sir," said Gregory. "The sailors are so eager to leave this country that they won't cause any problems."

"Good!" exclaimed Jonathan.

He turned to the young doctor. "Mr. MacLean, will you take care of the water and see that it is safely brought in from land? We need a barrel per man, including the Negroes. See that they're completely waterproof. You can let them swell and only bring them on board when they are sealed. Make sure that the water is pure and has no bad taste. Try it out with alkaline if necessary. Anyway, you know what to do better than I do. Take care of it today."

Simon MacLean was delighted to be given such responsibility and left the cabin at once. The others could hear him briskly giving orders outside.

"Mr. Clark," continued Jonathan, "you will choose the best shots on board. Give them guns and powder and let them take pistols too. I want them to go out hunting every day. Kill everything you can get, buffalo, antelope, wild boar. Bring iron-bound barrels for salting meat on board. You must ask Mr. Gomes to give you guides and bearers. If you come across some elephants, it's good meat for the Negroes. You can get the men at the storerooms on land to smoke it; it'll keep them busy."

William Clark hurried off to get to work.

"As for you, Mr. Woolcomb," said Jonathan, "Pierre will tell you what fresh fruit and vegetables he needs. Don't forget that we need as many lemons as possible to avoid scurvy. Get together all the live animals you can find. You can put the goats in the battery and the chickens in pens on deck. Scrounge everything you can from the villages surrounding the fort. I hope we have more luck with these than we did with the cow and pigs we brought with us on the outward journey. They didn't take at all well to the ocean!"

Pierre dragged Woolcomb with him to the storeroom, leaving Gregory and Jonathan alone. "Have a drink," said Jonathan.

The two men drank in silence, relieved to be so close to departure.

"I've already brought in plenty of kindling wood for the kitchens and I have a crew still chopping. We never have enough, and Pierre will need it," said Gregory.

"That's true. I'd forgotten about that. Thank you for taking care of it. By the way, Gregory, have we found young Matthew?" Jonathan sounded anxious.

"No, sir," Gregory said quietly, "he seems to have completely disappeared. We haven't turned up a trace. Gomes has assured me that he looked into it at his end but no one knows anything."

"God! What a mess! Well, we'll have to consider him a deserter unless he proves us wrong. I'll log him in as a deserter. Divide up his possessions among the crew."

For the next few days there was constant activity on board *The Sea Witch*. As Gregory predicted, the sailors attacked the work with gusto and cheerfully accepted every chore that came their way.

Hunters left every morning before dawn and barrels of salt meat piled up in the holds. The hunters were inexperienced and wounded several elephants that escaped, but they finally managed to kill four. Their meat was smoked and sewn into linen sacks, then hung from the masts. Mac-Lean had found a spring, and barrels of water were piling up.

Pierre watched the growing mounds of bananas, lemons, bitter oranges, and mangoes. They were all laid out on screens in the holds so that the air could pass around and under them. Breadfruit and coconuts were piled on the floors. Woolcomb had also brought in a sizable stock of smoked fish and was lucky enough to catch about twenty big turtles. They stored them between the guns along with the goats. A sailor was assigned to see that they were kept wet every day, to keep them alive.

This flurry of activity lasted several days, during which Jonathan didn't go ashore once. Gomes was more affable

than ever and assured him that the slaves were on their
way and that he would let him know as soon as they arrived. He tried to get Jonathan to come to dinner, but the
captain had decided that he could not bear to be with the
Portuguese after what had happened and he refused point
blank.

One evening, Jonathan leaned on the bridge rail, reflectively smoking his pipe as he watched the sunset. The sky
was a dazzling green, turning purple and then violet. He
thought about what he would find across the ocean. His
sexual abstinence was beginning to weigh upon him and he
thought of his beautiful Aurelia. This country could be a
vision of splendor if only she were here to share it with
him. He was deep in his reverie when he noticed an unusual bustle on shore. The rising rattle of many voices
reached him across the water. He gave a sigh of relief. The
slaves must have arrived.

Soon after, Woolcomb confirmed his guess. He came in
on a boat almost sinking under the weight of the fresh
fruits he had found.

"They're here," he yelled from the boat, "there are lots
of them! The fat fellow said to tell you that he wants you
there tomorrow."

Jonathan leaned down and gave him a hand up on deck.
"Good news, Mr. Woolcomb," he said, beaming, "come to
my cabin. This calls for a celebration."

Woolcomb told his men to unload the fruits and followed
his captain.

"Have you finished provisioning the ship?" asked Jonathan as he poured the drinks.

"Yes, sir. That was my last trip ashore. I think Clark has
filled all the meat barrels and the doctor has finished loading the water."

"Good!" exclaimed Jonathan. "We can load at once
then. Tell Pierre to prepare food for the slaves tomorrow
night. We'll load them as they are ready and we'll leave
very early next day to take advantage of the tides. Have
you seen the reverend ashore?"

"Yes, he's there with Gomes," said Woolcomb. "When I
left them they seemed to be involved in a sort of drinking
tournament."

"I do hope he won't be too drunk tomorrow," said Jonathan wearily. "I need him. When it's over, please see that

he gets aboard even if you have to use force. I don't want to have to go looking for him just as we're about to leave."

Gregory came to join them a little later on. Clark had stayed on shore with MacLean, and Collins asked Gregory to see that they returned to the ship that evening. As soon as they arrived, he asked them all to dinner in his cabin to iron out the last problems concerning the trip. Then the five men went their separate ways.

Jonathan undressed and lay on his bed. Tomorrow would mark the beginning of a new period. The melancholy notes of a tune hung on the night air, filtering in from the deck, and soon a song rose in the night:

> *Rule Britannia, Britannia, rule the waves*
> *Britons never shall be slaves*

In view of the circumstances, the song brought a sardonic smile to Jonathan's lips. It was a long time before he was able to fall asleep. He could not stop thinking about Aurelia. He knew he must put her out of his mind, but doubted that he would ever be able to do that. Those dazzling moments he had spent with her were too vital a part of his being to be pushed aside.

CHAPTER XXX

"Mr. Gomes, Mr. Gomes! You must get up! It's almost day."

Vasco leaned over his master's couch and shook him vigorously. The little black girl was asleep in a corner of the bed and she instinctively curled up tight. The Portuguese opened his eyes with difficulty. It was still dark. He sat up and rubbed his eyes.

"What?" he mumbled. "Wassa matter?"

"It's me . . . Vasco! Mr. Gomes, you must go to the barracks."

"Very well, very well! I heard you. It's not worth shouting. Get out of here and wait for me at the barracks."

All excited, Vasco left at a run, and Gomes, noticing the young girl crouched in a corner, gave full rein to his temper. He pushed her brutally and she fell on the floor.

"You, get a move on!" he shouted, "and get the hell out of here! I never want to see you again! Understand?"

The girl ran out, sobbing loudly.

Time to sell her, thought Gomes. She no longer gave him any pleasure at all; he hardly even wanted to touch her. He decided to put her in the bunch he was selling this time. He would surely find a young female to his taste among last night's newcomers. It had been too dark when the column arrived at the fort, and he hadn't had time to examine the slaves, but he resolved to make his choice that day. The thought of smooth new flesh calmed his early-morning irritation.

He had asked Vasco to wake him early, because he wanted to see whether any of the slaves had defects that would have to be hidden before that damned English officer turned up.

He stretched. He had drunk a lot the night before with the chaplain. His head felt heavy and there was a bitter taste in his mouth. God! That Ardeen was some drinker! It was a pleasure to find a drinking partner worthy of the name among the crew of *The Sea Witch*. He resolved to try to persuade Ardeen to stay on until the next ship.

He summarily sprayed a little water over himself and went out to join Vasco at the barracks. Vasco had awakened the guards and they were warming themselves around a fire. They looked grumpy, dirty, and ragged. Gomes saluted them vaguely and they answered with grunts.

"Get a move on and open up those rooms," he said. "I want to see what that carrion looks like."

The guards exchanged looks. One of them nodded his head and the youngest got up clumsily, spat a stream of tobacco, and dragged his way to the largest barracks. Then he raised the bar that held the door and opened it.

N'Gio had been awake all night. The stink made it almost impossible to breathe. They were packed in so tight that it was impossible to find a comfortable position. A rush of fresh air dispelled the stench a little and two men stood in the doorway silhouetted against the red flames of the fire. They grumbled curses he did not understand and pulled out one of the prisoners. After a while they came back, and another man was dragged outside.

Gomes, helped by Vasco, was conducting a careful examination of the slaves. If there seemed to be any small defect he had the man put aside and then indicated what should be done to disguise the problem.

N'Gio didn't have to be persuaded to come out of the barracks when they came for him. Day was dawning. He breathed the pure air deep into his lungs as two white men held him firmly and the third, a small fat man, his face all pitted, examined him by the light of torches.

The man felt him all over, made him turn around and kept saying incomprehensible words to the tall dark-skinned man N'Gio had noticed on the beach. Then N'Gio was taken to a corner near the fire where some of his companions had been herded together and were now sitting on the ground. A little further on, some white men seemed to be doing some mysterious thing to a small group of prisoners. N'Gio gave up trying to understand what was going on. He sat there a long time, hoping they would leave him outside forever, but it was not to be. He was taken back to the barracks and the door closed him into stinking darkness once again.

When he had inspected all the men, Gomes went to the women's and children's quarters. To his great satisfaction, most of the adolescents had already been circumcised, so

there would be no bargaining him down on that score. The
little ones were rather skinny but they seemed to be in excellent health. They hugged at their mothers' legs as the
Portuguese handled them without attempting to be gentle.

He took his time over the women. Some of them were
pregnant, and he was delighted, for they would bring a particularly good price. Yawana, half asleep, watched this brutal examination. This obese white man was much uglier
than the others, she thought to herself. His way of touching
her companions, particularly the very young ones, was dis-
gusting and she hated the constant leer on his face. She
knew she would not escape his attention, and sure enough,
when Gomes stood in front of her there was a look of lustful greed in his eyes that made her recoil in revulsion. The
huge white man burst out laughing. Here was the girl he
had been looking for. In all his time in Africa he had never
seen such a beauty. His eyes glittered and he ran his hands
all over her body. Though her body had been manipulated
and slobbered over many times, for Yawana, this was the
worst yet. His hands became more and more probing and
insulting; he smacked his lips and swallowed with a sicken-
ing sound as he touched her.

Gomes dropped his hands regretfully. He would have
liked to take her to his quarters at once, but Collins was
sure to arrive soon and he would be distressed if Gomes
were not there to greet him. He would have to wait. He
reflected that he did not want the English officer to set eyes
on a female of such unusual quality or he would be sure to
want to purchase her.

"Vasco," he said in a strangled voice, pointing at the
young black girl, "take that one out of the group and put
her to one side. I don't want them to see her. Hide her
away somewhere and don't bring her out until that filthy
ship has left the lagoon. Understood?"

Yawana hadn't understood a word but she somehow got
the gist of what was going on. She found it hard to keep
back tears. It couldn't be possible, she could never let that
revolting creature possess her, she would kill herself first.

"Yes, Mr. Gomes," said Vasco. "I understand, Mr.
Gomes. I'll hide her away for you and bring her out when
the ship leaves."

But the half-breed had already decided to do nothing of
the sort. He didn't care a damn what his master wanted.

He had had enough of being treated like a slave by this swine. His hatred had swollen beyond the bounds of tolerance and he knew he would soon have to give it free rein. He had other plans now.

Gomes continued his inspection desultorily. He had lost interest now that he had found someone to replace his little black girl. He was rubbing his hands in delight as he walked back to his quarters. "God!" he muttered to himself, "they're a damned fine herd, all right. Collins will have to pay well to have them. There are a few that the doctor will probably reject, but I'll find a buyer for them later. There's no lack of buyers."

He thought of Yawana again and excitement rose in him. He would make her do everything he wanted. He had read the disgust in her eyes and it delighted him. It would be all the more challenging to tame her. After a good beating she would be as compliant and docile as a lamb.

He had barely walked into the room when a man came running in, calling, "The longboats are leaving the ship, Mr. Gomes."

"So what? We were expecting it, weren't we?" grumbled Gomes, snatched from his erotic fantasies. "Give the blacks something to eat and tell Vasco to bring me food. It'll take some time before they get here."

The man left the room and Gomes suddenly spotted his little black girl huddled in a corner of the room. Rage welled up in him and he leapt across the room and slapped her. "What did I tell you?" he screamed. "I don't want to see you anymore. Get out!"

Just then Vasco came in with some cold meat and eggs.

"Vasco!" he shouted. "Put that down and get this bitch out of here. Put her in with the others. Chain her and give her a little taste of the whip so that she gets the message."

The half-breed grabbed the girl and dragged her outside, ignoring her sobs. Gomes sat down calmly to his meal, knowing that Collins would not be there for a while.

Jonathan had rung the ship's bell well before dawn. He told the officers to dress well, so that the blacks would understand that they were dealing with a different kind of white man from the Portuguese ruffians. He himself wore a navy coat, white trousers, and gleaming black boots.

All the longboats were lowered. Gregory had seen to it that the chains and bracelets made by the armorer and his mates were in one of them. The others held guns in large crates, barrels of powder, and bags of lead.

All the sailors piled into the boats, except a few men left behind to guard *The Sea Witch*. MacLean was carrying his medical instruments, a measure, and a scale. Jonathan had also asked him to take all he needed to record the sales on the Company Register. Jonathan had his branding irons with him, and he waited while a small coffer of gold pieces was lowered on a rope, and a sailor placed it carefully in the bottom of the boat.

As he was about to move away, the captain was amazed to see the chaplain gesticulating from the front deck. "Ho! You in the longboat!" yelled Frank Ardeen. "Wait for me!"

"What is that idiot doing?" exclaimed Jonathan, highly annoyed. "I thought he had stayed ashore. Come on, hurry up and get in!" he shouted at Ardeen.

As usual, Ardeen's descent into the boat caused riotous merriment among the sailors. He fell without dignity into the boat, rose, lost his balance, and fell on the oarsmen, who pushed him off. He ended up by sitting disconsolately on the bottom.

It was not a sudden surge of religious zeal that propelled Ardeen to return to shore. He had got drunk with Gomes the night before, but had suddenly realized through his fog that he had work to do and that Jonathan had taken him on board to do it. He was wary of the captain's reaction and didn't want to stay and rot in this country if a disgusted Jonathan decided to leave him here. So he made sure that he was taken back to the ship and that he had the things necessary for baptism with him. He tried to explain this to Jonathan, but the captain paid no attention. His mind was on other things. Ardeen had no way of knowing that Collins didn't care at all about the souls of the men he was transporting. The rules required a chaplain on board, so he had one, and that was all he cared about.

As they reached shore, Jonathan told the men to check their weapons, and then he unloaded the boats under the indifferent gaze of a small group of Portuguese who had come to watch them land.

It all took time and when the crates and the rest had been taken up to the fort, it was already well into the day. The fires under the giant cauldrons had been doused and Jonathan concluded that Gomes was economizing on food for the slaves. It would probably be better this way, for they would be more docile and easier to load.

Gomes arrived at the same time as the English captain and his crew. He brought as many men as possible with him to lend a hand should any trouble develop.

"Good day, Mr. Collins," he greeted him with false friendliness. "You will be pleased. I've looked them over and I can promise you, you won't be disappointed. That you won't. It's the best herd I've ever seen. Where would you like to start? Males or females?"

"I'd prefer to start with the men," Jonathan answered quietly.

Meanwhile, MacLean had laid out his instruments while a sailor lit a small brazier for the branding. He put the register and writing instruments on a crate in the shade of a mango tree. The armorer set up his forge in an enclosure reserved for the purpose and Gregory gave instructions to the sailors for the transfer of the Negroes to *The Sea Witch*. Frank Ardeen, no doubt exhausted from his unaccustomed exertions, lay dully in a corner, his eyes bleary.

Seeing that all was in order, Jonathan turned to Gomes. "Whenever you are ready, Mr. Gomes," he said.

Gomes barked out orders and three of his men went into the barracks in a tight semicircle, weapons at the ready.

A black man appeared in the doorway. He stumbled as one of the Portuguese pushed him. The man's eyes rolled in terror, his lips emitting a wail of fear. He tried to slide to the ground, but one of the men lashed at his legs. Vasco approached and spoke to him harshly. He lowered his head and let himself be led to MacLean. Jonathan sat down and chose a quill with a fine point. MacLean, filled with a sense of the importance of his job, examined the slave carefully. He measured and weighed him, each time telling Jonathan the figure to be inscribed in the book. He made him open his mouth and inspected his teeth. He made sure there was no film over his eyes, counted his fingers and toes, and examined the abdomen for signs of hernia. He felt all the muscles to judge their elasticity and lifted the loincloth to examine the testicles and penis. Then he gave him a push, turned him around, and examined his rectum. Satisfied at last, he told Vasco to tell the man to jump up and down in one place several times. The man began to jump up and down awkwardly.

"He's fine," said MacLean to Jonathan. "I give him about thirty years. He's a nice piece. There's only one tooth missing."

Collins observed that the doctor did a very careful job and said, "Keep it up, Mr. MacLean, that's good. There, now you can brand him."

Gomes had been watching the examination anxiously. That young devil of a doctor was shrewder than he would have thought. He swore under his breath. The touching up he had done that morning on a few doubtful specimens would not go unnoticed.

MacLean gave an order and two sailors seized the black, who was paralyzed with fear. They dragged him to the brazier. MacLean grabbed the iron Jonathan held out to him. It was a fine silver plaque attached to a metal rod with a wooden handle. He heated it over the brazier.

The two sailors forced the black man to get to his knees and held him like that while MacLean rubbed his upper thigh with a tallow-treated rag. He laid a piece of greased parchment on it, pressed the metal plaque to it and held it there a brief moment.

The black man tensed under the pain of the burning metal, but the sailors held him firmly and he couldn't move. MacLean pulled away the rag and parchment, and the letters RAC appeared in indelible swellings on the black flesh: the initials of the Royal African Company.

The black man was led to the armorer who riveted iron bracelets to his wrists and ankles. A chain was passed through them and he was left to the sailors. Just then, King Ngoukou, whom nobody had noticed, appeared as if by magic. He leapt on the prisoner and snatched off his white linen loincloth. Jonathan watched from afar, shrugging his shoulders in disdain. He knew that it was customary to deprive slaves of every possession, but unable to accustom himself to such greed, he shuddered inwardly.

Another slave was brought out to MacLean. He was getting ready to begin when a howl made everyone jump. Reverend Ardeen was standing, turning like a top, snatching madly at his coat and shirt. They thought he had gone mad, but they understood what was tormenting him when a huge black centipede dropped to the ground. Vasco tried to crush it with his heel but it escaped with startling swiftness and disappeared under a pile of dead leaves.

Ardeen was wailing and swearing for all he was worth, the curses falling from his lips more worthy of a sailor than a chaplain. The crew reveled in the richness of his vocabulary and were loud in their admiration, but Gomes was shocked. A long red mark on Ardeen's back showed the burn left by the insect.

Now Ardeen was completely conscious. He put his clothes back on and decided against lying on such inhospitable ground. He grabbed his crucifix and the other ritual objects nearby and hurried angrily toward the spot where the newly branded Negro was being held. Jonathan could hear him muttering indistinguishable words as he went, and concluded that he was starting his work.

By the end of the morning, MacLean had examined almost half the prisoners. He rejected some who looked a little doubtful, one with a collapsed bridge which seemed to indicate pian, an African form of syphilis, and one who had been carefully doctored by Gomes but clearly had dysentery. The Portuguese had simply shoved a handful of grasses up his anus to hide the problem until he was loaded onto the ship. MacLean grabbed Gomes and took him aside in anger. This was no joking matter. The man had a violently contagious disease. Jonathan would have preferred to wait for nightfall before loading the slaves, to avoid their having to see their country from the decks of the ship, their country which they would never see again. But he thought it preferable to send Gregory out immediately with the first boatload. Soon after, the sound of clanking chains told him the slaves were on their way to the dock.

Jonathan knew that he could not finish before nightfall, but he was determined to get through the males that day. He refused to stop for lunch and asked Gomes to see that a light meal was served to him and to the men where they sat.

MacLean continued to work feverishly. Sometimes there was a scream from one of the more terrified prisoners as he was branded, but all in all the day passed without incident.

N'Gio crouched in the stench of the dark barracks and watched as his companions were led out one by one. He was starving. A nauseating brew the night before and a banana that morning were all he had eaten recently. Sometimes N'Gio heard a scream after a man was taken out. He was haunted by the thought that the white men wanted to eat them and the screams seemed to confirm his fear that the prisoners were being put to death. The more he tried to block out his anguished speculations, the more they swarmed into his mind.

They came for Bokou at last, and N'Gio knew that he would be next. "Farewell, N'Gio," Bokou found the strength to whisper as he was being dragged through the door.

N'Gio could hardly answer. He sensed that the end was near and he was empty of all feeling. He suddenly grew very cold and began to tremble uncontrollably. He was going to be killed. He knew it. Yawana would be killed too. He cursed his father and the day he was born. He wanted to vomit. He resolved to make a dash for freedom, whatever the cost, but when he saw four white men come for him, instead of the two who had come for the others, he knew that there was no hope of escape. Vasco had warned Jonathan of the young man's phenomenal strength. N'Gio let them drag him outside, resigned to death.

White men were milling about everywhere. He saw two of them, standing near a fire, holding Bokou in a strange curved position. A third one was bent over him and from where N'Gio stood, it looked as if he were wielding a weapon. Bokou arched his body and gave a great shriek. N'Gio thought it was a death cry, but to his surprise he saw that they were picking him up and dragging him further away. He felt greatly relieved. Clearly, the men were not being killed. He let MacLean examine him without twitching a muscle.

The white man with wispy hair the color of dry-season grass made him bend over and stared into his mouth. Then he squeezed his body everywhere, and spent a few minutes on his privates, but it all seemed to be done without brutality or evil intent. Sometimes he talked to another white sitting under a tree, and they exchanged a few words. Without knowing quite why, N'Gio was aware that he was being admired, and he stood up straighter.

"Magnificent," muttered MacLean, "this one is exceptionally fine. Take a look at those muscles and that build. There isn't a single thing wrong with him!"

"Really magnificent," admitted Jonathan. "What a shame they aren't all like that! If we weren't in this particular part of the country, you could almost take him for a Mandingue. How old would would you say he is, Mr. Mac-Lean?"

MacLean thought for a moment. "I'd say twenty, not a day over."

Jonathan nodded. "Brand him with my mark," he said. "I'll keep him as part of my own personal share."

N'Gio saw him scratch at something laid out before him, and then the man who had examined him led him to the fire and made him kneel and bend over, as he had seen Bokou do. He wasn't worried. He felt something greasy on his thigh and all at once he felt a strong burning sensation. MacLean had branded him with the letters J.C. for Jonathan Collins. His skin tightened but he clenched his teeth to keep in the cry. He was determined to show these white men that he was the son of a chief, and that he did not fear pain.

When he had been branded they took him into an enclosed area where he saw Bokou and some of the other prisoners. They welded some iron bracelets on him which hurt less than the ones he had been carrying so far, and then they sent him on to join his companions.

Bokou was whimpering, holding onto his thigh where a sort of tattoo had been stamped. All the others bore the same mark. Only N'Gio's was different. He reflected that this must be a ritual tattooing and that the whites had understood that he was the son of a chief and had shown this with a sign. Usually, however, this kind of initiation was accompanied by all sorts of endurance tests, much more painful than the burn he had just suffered. It had nothing in common with the three Isis cuts he had seen once on a man from the Fang clan. The man told him that for his initiation he had had his skin rubbed with spice and been made to pass through a leafy tunnel, through huge ant heaps, broken shells, and bamboo spikes. While he was crawling through, assegais poked through the foliage and nicked him repeatedly. He had borne the trials bravely and when he emerged from the tunnel, he was proclaimed *nyamoro,* a real man. Then they had made three cuts on the back of his neck to symbolize the coat of the antelope, *soo,* and this gave him the privilege of always being able to eat of its flesh. But how far away all this seemed to N'Gio now.

"Bokou! Stop wailing like a goat before a python," he

said sternly to Bokou. "Where are all the others? I don't
see everyone here."

"I don't know, N'Gio," answered Bokou in a shaking
voice. "They are probably dead."

"You're more stupid than a turtle," said N'Gio, annoyed.
"The white men could have killed us already if they had
wanted to. All they did was make a ritual mark on us."

But Bokou had ceased to listen and was whimpering
again, and N'Gio, discouraged, stopped preaching at him.
There was nothing to do now but wait. They would soon
see what was to happen. Anyway, nothing mattered anymore. Nothing at all.

Other prisoners were brought to where they sat. The
black chief, still ridiculous in his red coat and blond wig,
continued systematically snatching the loincloths from the
slaves. He came over to N'Gio and snatched at his. N'Gio
spat into the air and regretted only that he had no pepper
grains to add strength to his curse.

"May your penis shrivel and your wife give birth to
monsters," he hissed at Nkougou.

The N'Komi king went gray under the vehemence of the
malediction. He restrained himself from hitting N'Gio, only
out of fear of the white men, and beat a hasty retreat as the
other prisoners threw a stream of curses at his back.

Another white man came into the enclosure. N'Gio
could see from his stagger that he was drunk. Around his
neck he wore a shiny talisman and held a metal receptacle
in his hands. The tall half-breed joined him, taking the
metal bucket in his hands. Reverend Ardeen stared vaguely
at N'Gio and the other prisoners. He made a great effort to
concentrate and opened his arms wide.

"Canaan be accursed!" he declaimed in a resonant voice.

He stopped short, not knowing what to say next. Noah's
curse on his grandson seemed to let loose a flood of ideas
in his head, for he grabbed the brandy flask from his coat
pocket and took a long swig. This seemed to revive him,
and he continued: "The Lord," his eyes rolled upward and
contemplated the heavens, "The Lord made you this color
to make you slaves to the whites. But you are lucky that
He has sent me to you. Thanks to me, you will be more
than miserable animals, you will be privileged to serve the
whites in Paradise. A marvelous destiny awaits you," he

hiccupped and lost the thread, then continued: "You will soon be in a dreamland. You will eat good Christian food, and prayer will elevate your primitive souls. One day your children and your children's children will bless your memory for having enabled them to rise faster than if you had stayed here, bowing to idols and practicing your pagan rites." He turned. "Pass me the holy water," he muttered to Vasco.

Vasco handed him the bucket. Ardeen dipped his hand into it and moved among the prisoners, spraying them liberally with water.

"Now I baptize you in the name of the Father, the Son, and the Holy Ghost," he intoned majestically, "and the Devil take you all!"

Vasco translated all that Ardeen had said and the two men left.

N'Gio was bewildered by what he had heard. The tall man with the dark skin must be very important, since he seemed to turn up everywhere, and he had said things which were hard to accept. How could anyone promise paradise to men in chains, and promise them a dazzling future that had begun with a massacre, with tortures, curses, and blows? All he wanted was for them to take away his chains and set him free. There was no paradise greater than the forest, his birthplace, with Yawana at his side. The strange incantations made a ceremony of what was taking place, but it was a ceremony far different from the ones he had known in Mounigou. He decided that the white man who spoke must be some kind of witch doctor.

He was hungry and thirsty, and longed to lie down in the shade and sleep. His reflections were interrupted by the arrival of sailors from *The Sea Witch*. His chains were fastened to those of another man and he was shoved out of the enclosure. Jonathan had forbidden his men to use whips, except in extreme cases, for he did not want the slaves' skin marked more than it had been already. Instead, they were persuaded to walk faster by punches and slaps.

N'Gio resigned himself. Here were more days and days of walking opening up ahead. The journey would never end. He sighed deeply. But it was only a few minutes' walk to the dock. He would have liked to walk into the lake and

bathe to get cool, but they didn't give him time. He was
pushed into a canoe far bigger than the one the N'Komi
used, and the whites themselves did the rowing.

It was hard to climb into the boat with the chains. One
prisoner who fell into the water was barely saved from
drowning to the accompaniment of shouts and curses from
the whites.

N'Gio found himself on the decks of *The Sea Witch*. At
last he could examine the strange craft he had seen from
the fort. It was huge and everything on it was huge. He
couldn't understand what the smooth tree trunks with creepers dangling from them could be doing there. The prisoners were grouped under these trees on a wooden deck,
where they were given a thick hot soup, fragrant with
spices. The young man thought it delicious. He was very
hungry.

Then they were given some water and told to stand up.
One by one they were sent down a dark hole that led to the
insides of the ship. N'Gio, chains clanking, felt as if he
were entering a tunnel, but this tunnel smelt of pitch,
sweat, and fish, and its exit was invisible to him, for it led
far far away to the other side of the ocean, to a country
N'Gio or his descendants might one day call home.

He emerged into a large dark chamber, where the ceiling
was so low that he had to bow his head to enter. The other
prisoners were there, and he was pushed ahead and made
to lie down. His chain was fixed to a metal bar running the
length of the wall, which left him just enough freedom of
movement to lie on his back, squeezed between two of his
companions. The whites left, and he heard a trapdoor open
and close. Darkness closed in around him. He gave up
trying to find out if Bokou was also there and closed his
eyes, trying not to hear the wailing and groaning that surrounded him.

As he planned, Jonathan managed to get all the males on
board before nightfall. All that was left now was the formal
purchase of the women and children. He was determined to
finish it all the next day, and asked MacLean to be a little
quicker in his examinations. Gomes had regained some of
his jauntiness. It had gone very well; there had been few
rejects. Jonathan seemed to have forgotten the incident of
the doctored black, and even complimented the Portuguese
on the quality of his merchandise. They decided to start on

the selection of women very early the next day, and Gomes invited Jonathan and his officers to dine at the fort.

During the meal, the chaplain, stimulated by his baptisms, was in great form and would not be quiet. He spent the evening relating some of the "marital" problems confided by his female parishioners back in Chester. Jonathan laughed until he cried. The only one of the gathering who didn't seem to find this very funny was Gomes, who suddenly felt an irrational fear that the indiscretions he had confessed to the priests of his own faith while still a young man were being made sport of at a dinner table somewhere in Portugal.

The gathering broke up early. Gomes called for Vasco several times before he went to sleep, but Vasco never came.

CHAPTER XXXI

Gomes never woke up cheerfully and this morning was no exception. He bitterly reflected on the moment when MacLean discovered that he had tampered with a sick prisoner. The little doctor annoyed him, with his airs and pretenses. He had humiliated Gomes in front of everyone when he could just as easily have dealt with it discreetly. What did he think the slave traffic was, anyway?

"What do you think you're doing?" the young man had asked in his disagreeable voice. "Don't you know this is a highly contagious disease?"

Gomes had been so surprised by the attack that he had fumbled around for an excuse to justify his deception: "I thought it would be for the best, Mr. Doctor, I corked him up so he wouldn't leave a train of shit wherever he went. I swear it, Mr. Doctor, I never meant any harm!"

"Let's just drop the whole matter," Jonathan had cut in. "I'll give you some interesting information, though, Mr. Gomes. An epidemic of that kind could kill off an entire crew. Luckily, there's no harm done this time. But I warn you that a repeat of this incident or one like it will certainly be taken into account in our final reckoning."

Gomes had been furious, and a good night's sleep had failed to erase his rancor. He supposed it would all be over by nightfall. The ship would leave tomorrow and he could go back to his old way of life. He thought of the beautiful Negress he had picked out. She would surely make him forget all these annoyances. He planned to tell Vasco to bring her to him that night. She must not put up too much resistance, he thought, just enough to add spice to it all.

He had planned to be the first to arrive at the women's quarters, but Jonathan and his entire team of experts were there before him.

Gomes assumed a falsely jovial air and said, "Ah! Mr. Collins! I see you're already at work. Well, I think you'll be pleased. The females are of as high a quality as the males."

"I certainly hope so, Mr. Gomes," said Jonathan.

Vasco arrived with Frank Ardeen, lending support to the faltering chaplain.

"Good day, Reverend," said Gomes cheerfully, "I see that Vasco has taken good care of you."

"Good day . . ." mumbled Ardeen grumpily.

Jonathan ignored Ardeen as Vasco helped him into the enclosure and propped him up against the inner wall. He certainly didn't look very brisk, but there was so little for him to do. . . .

Gomes sent his men in to open the door. They poured into the shelter. The women prisoners were terrorized when they saw the troupe of white men. They all leapt to their feet like a herd of hunted antelope. Mothers tried to calm small children, who clung to them, howling. The other women shrank against the walls and corners of the enclosure, and some of the bigger children hid behind them.

Jonathan watched all this without expression, waiting for MacLean to proceed. Then he called to Vasco: "Vasco! Come here!"

The half-breed came running. "Yes, Mr. White Man."

"Vasco, listen to me. I want you to translate what I'm about to say for these women, all right?"

"Yes, Mr. White Man. It's all right. I'll tell them everything you tell."

"You will tell them that I wish them no harm. I just want to find out if they're sick. Afterward, they will be sent to rejoin their men."

"Yes, Mr. White Man," repeated Vasco eagerly, "you won't hurt them, and after they can go make love."

Jonathan smiled. That wasn't quite it, but he supposed it was better to let Vasco explain it in his own way. The important thing was to still the panic and make the women trust him.

"Tell them, too, that we won't separate them from their children. Did you get that?" Jonathan continued.

"Yes, Mr. White Man. They keep children," repeated Vasco.

"Good!" said Jonathan with satisfaction. "Now run off with you and see to it."

Puffed up with importance, Vasco hurried into the women's enclave and talked long and loud. Yawana, who stood in the middle of the huddled group, understood only one thing. She was soon to be reunited with N'Gio, and for her, nothing else mattered. She didn't care where they would be taken, and she didn't care what they planned to do with her once she got there. An overwhelming joy possessed her and tears welled in her eyes, but they were tears of happiness. Since her arrival at the fort she had been haunted by one fear only, the fear of having to endure the lust of the hideous, obese white man with the revolting leer who had roughly pawed at her body.

"N'Gio, my fine N'Gio," she murmured to herself, "at last I'll find your strong arms again, and I'll never leave you again. Never!"

Her companions in misfortune must have been thinking along the same lines, for they quieted down and the children stopped their wailing.

These white men were nothing like the others Yawana had seen. They wore very beautiful clothing on their bodies. The one who stood out the most was the man who seemed to be in charge, a tall slim man with clear light eyes. Her eyes lingered on him. He made her feel less frightened. He was talking to a man with red hair and there was something soothing about the way the words fell from his half-closed lips.

The tall man who had spoken to them told them to sit while they waited, and Yawana crouched down with the others while the whites called the adolescents forward one by one.

MacLean worked quickly, as Jonathan had requested. He was getting rather tired of counting teeth and toes. The children looked frightened, but he was a gentle man and soon reassured them. He separated the boys and girls into approximate age groups. Three eight-to-fifteen-year-olds were worth two sovereigns and a pair aged three to seven were worth one sovereign. Later he planned to look at the smallest children who would be thrown into the same lot as their mothers.

"Are they all circumcised?" asked Jonathan.

"Nearly all," said MacLean. "I can do the rest during the crossing." He prepared to brand them all on their buttocks, and laid them in a row, face down. The children were terrified by the white men and the burning iron. They howled and yelled throughout the operation. When it was over they were not chained, but left loosely tied by a cord about their waists. The sailors then led them toward the enclave where Jonathan asked Gomes to bring them food.

The children's screams had greatly agitated the women prisoners, some of whom added their lamentations to those of their children. They were not only upset at the treatment their children were receiving, but they were also terrified for themselves. Yawana resolved that she would not cry out. She was sure that this could be no worse than the tattoos and mutilations she had seen inflicted upon young girls in her own village. Nonetheless, she wondered what it could possibly mean, and why it was being done.

Aziza, Adende's little concubine, had been so shocked by the ghastly death of the old chief, that she had no reaction to anything anymore. Since her capture and the violence she had had to endure, she merely sat day after day, her gaze blank, without a word, a perpetual smile on her lips. Sometimes she hummed songs for hours on end, or muttered jumbled words that had no meaning. Yawana envied her. She was in a world of her own where pain could no longer reach her.

Jonathan pulled off his coat and turned the page on the register.

"Ready, Mr. MacLean?" he asked. "I'd like to get the women done now."

A sailor brought some wooden buckets and MacLean washed his hands carefully. "Now we can start. Bring the first one," he ordered.

The woman they pushed toward him was young. She had tiny breasts and wide hips. MacLean took off her loincloth and flung it aside. Jonathan had been so revolted by Nkougou's behavior the day before that he had forbidden his presence at the examinations, and arranged for the bits of fabric he seemed so concerned about to be returned to him later.

At first the woman stood in frozen silence. Then, seeing that MacLean wasn't going to hurt her, she stared at him boldly. MacLean was always shy around women, particularly if they were young and nude. In spite of the fact that this one was black, he felt uneasy and found it hard to carry out his examination calmly, particularly when he had to determine whether or not she was pregnant. Jonathan and the crew watched, grinning widely. Gomes, who had been totally uninterested in the examinations of the children, looked on and leered.

"Let's get a move on, Mr. MacLean," said Jonathan. "At this rate it'll take us a whole week to get through."

MacLean blushed painfully. He finished, and made the young woman lie down so that he could brand her on the shoulder blade. She let out a piercing scream, for the paper slipped and the iron came into direct contact with her skin. He sent her to the enclosure and she threw him a look of hatred as she walked off, clutching her stinging shoulder.

The women came out one after another. MacLean had regained his composure and worked calmly and methodically, maintaining his conscientious approach in spite of Jonathan's request for speed.

They came for Aziza. Yawana watched her walk out, the smile still on her lips. To MacLean's surprise, she continued to smile throughout the examination and during the branding, and walked off, still beaming, with the crew's amazed and admiring eyes on her. She had lost her mind but certainly not her beauty.

Gomes had his back to the prisoners and was talking to Jonathan when Yawana was brought out to MacLean.

"You see what fine quality we have here, Mr. Collins?" he said. "There isn't one yet that you've had to reject. Do you think . . . ?" He stopped short. Jonathan hadn't been listening too carefully. Gomes realized that the eyes of crew and captain were all staring at a spot behind his back with a sort of wondering amazement. The sailors' rough jokes had trailed off into silence. Gomes turned slowly and saw Yawana. He thought he would choke with rage. He sought out Vasco with his eyes, but Vasco had prudently vanished.

Gomes realized that Vasco had gone against his orders and he was in a froth of fury. It was surely too late now. That devilish Englishman would never let her go. Perhaps he would even keep her for himself. He began to regret having sold his little black girl, but it was also too late to rectify that, since she had been inspected by the doctor some time ago and was probably on the ship by now. He swore to himself that Vasco would pay for this insubordination.

Yawana stood before MacLean with lowered eyes and bowed head. At last she let herself peep from under her lashes to see what was going on. She could barely suppress a smile when she saw the young white's startled expression as he stared at her, his eyes round, his mouth half open, looking as if he'd been struck dumb.

Jonathan realized what was happening to the doctor, and laughingly needled him, "Come, come, Mr. MacLean. Whatever is happening to you? My word! One would think you had never seen a black girl before."

"Well, you see . . ." stammered MacLean, swallowing hard, "you see, she's very . . . she's very beautiful. Really very beautiful."

"Yes. I'll grant you that," said Jonathan gruffly, "she's very beautiful. So what?"

The young doctor flushed to his ears and swore softly when he realized that he hadn't hidden his admiration and left himself an easy mark for the others' jokes. The captain was right, of course, it was only a black girl and he must examine her as he had the others. He flung off her loincloth and set to work.

While he was touching her, Yawana watched everything he did. She understood that she had had an extraordinary effect on the young man, and she was flattered by it. He didn't frighten her at all. His hands were very gentle, he didn't treat her roughly, and even when his fingers explored her body, her flesh didn't shrink from his touch.

She realized that she was the focus of everyone's admiration. She was getting used to these white men, and already she found them less ugly. The tall slim man was staring at her, but how different was his gaze from that of the horrible fat man with the shifty piglike eyes.

Jonathan felt a strong surge of feeling as he looked at the young girl. As he had said to MacLean, she was nothing but a Negress, but he was unable to take his eyes off her—the pure lines of her body, her elegant carriage, and the dignity of her movements. It seemed somehow incongruous to see such exquisite beauty in such a primitive creature. He looked at the flat stomach and long slim legs, and then his eyes moved upward to her face. She was gazing at him with such a strange expression that he looked away. When Yawana's eyes met his she felt a shock run through her. She had never felt anything like it and she didn't know what it meant. She looked away at the same moment Collins did.

Gomes, in the meantime, was experiencing far more

earthy reactions. He couldn't bear it another minute. Taking his courage in both hands he said, "No use to do any more with that female, Captain Collins. I forgot to tell you, that's the one I'm keeping for myself."

Jonathan raised his eyebrows, surprised, as if he were noticing the Portuguese for the first time. "What are you burbling about?" he asked coldly. "You're here to sell your blacks, aren't you?"

"Well, yes, of course," said Gomes in a conciliatory tone, "but as far as that one goes, I told Vasco to put her aside for me and he didn't do it."

"Well, I'm so sorry," said Jonathan hypocritically, "but you'll be sure to find another one in the group. Listen, I'll be a good sport. If there's one in the enclave you like you can take her back. They haven't all boarded yet."

"You don't understand, Mr. Collins," replied Gomes, barely able to contain his anxiety, "it's *that* female I want, not another. I must have her. That's the one. No other will do."

Jonathan stared at the fat man, his purple face sweating from the heat. He probably would have given in to his plea if the man had not looked so repulsive. He could not bear to see that haughty beauty in the grubby hands of this vice-ridden wretch of a man.

"No, Mr. Gomes," he said firmly, "sorry, I'm keeping her."

As MacLean continued to feel her all over, Yawana followed the heated exchange without understanding what was being said. Instinctively, she knew that it concerned her and her heart froze. She knew now that she wanted to leave, to go anywhere that these white men would take her, anywhere, do anything they wanted, rather than stay to become this monster's plaything.

"I beg you, white man, don't give. Don't give me to that man who is worse than a monkey," she whispered a faint prayer.

"Mr. Collins," begged Gomes, "leave her for me. What can it matter to you to take one less?"

"Well, if you really want to know she's too fine a piece for me to pass her up," said Jonathan. He was becoming quite irritated by the man's insistence.

"Listen here, Mr. Collins," Gomes continued, losing all control, "I'll give you three sovereigns for that girl. How does that strike you? That's a good deal, wouldn't you say?"

"Well for goodness' sake, Mr. Gomes," said Jonathan in a bored tone, "why does this matter to you so much?"

Thinking that Jonathan was going to let him have the girl, Gomes lost the last remnants of his dignity. "I need a woman, you see, Mr. Collins," he said. "I haven't got one anymore. I sold you mine and this is the one I want. I need her. I absolutely must have her."

Jonathan looked pensive for a moment. He was pleased to see this swinish man reduced to a pleading suppliant and he wanted to make the moment last. Gomes was watching him, his face full of hope.

"That's all right then," said Jonathan in a pleasant voice, and Gomes thought for sure that he had won. "I'll see to it you get your woman back. I'm afraid this one is really too beautiful for me not to buy her."

Gomes realized that Jonathan had been making fun of him and he pummeled the crate in front of him with his fists.

Yawana was no longer the only one watching the exchange. The crew and Portuguese men-at-arms were watching eagerly as Gomes' unbridled bursts of rage alternated with Jonathan's dry tones. The tension grew between them, and the sailors slowly drew closer as they saw that the discussion was getting more heated. Gregory pulled out his pistol and held it loosely in his hand, pointing it as if by chance in the general direction of the Portuguese, but they decided it would not be sensible to take sides with their captain, and held their peace. Reverend Ardeen, drawn from his sleep by the noise, came over to see what was happening and stood watching, a vacant expression on his face.

"You have no right!" shouted Gomes. "You haven't paid yet, and until you pay, all these Negroes are mine. I can do whatever I like with 'em, and it's none of your business. I shouldn't even be discussing this with you!"

Trying to hold onto his temper, Jonathan rose suddenly, towering over Gomes.

"Enough," he said succinctly. "Be quiet. Since you talk to me in this way, let me advise you to keep out of my way until we are through here. We shall meet for the final payment when I send you word."

Jonathan sat down again and ignored Gomes' presence completely. Green with fury, Gomes turned on his heel and stalked away, followed by his men.

"Keep an eye on them," Jonathan advised Gregory. "I think that Gomes isn't about to forgive me and I don't trust him, or his henchmen."

Yawana saw the fat man hurry off in a temper and she understood that she was safe. She was very grateful to Jonathan for not giving her to the fat man. She would have liked to show him how she felt, but he was talking to the young man who had examined her and he seemed to have forgotten her.

MacLean had already finished his examination but he preferred to wait for the end of the argument before making his comments to the captain.

"She's a very beautiful—" he began, but Jonathan cut in with a gentle voice, "Yes, I know, Mr. MacLean. That's enough of that. We still have many more to see, and after what has just happened I am all the more eager to finish before nightfall."

"Very well, sir."

"I'll take her as my own personal lot," added Jonathan, "brand her with my brand. Or rather, don't brand the girl. It would be a shame to spoil such a beautiful animal. Mr. Adams!"

"Yes, sir," said Gregory, hurrying over.

"Mr. Adams, on your next trip to the ship be sure to take this girl to my cabin and chain her there solidly. I'm not having her branded and I don't want anyone else to brand her with another mark. I'm referring to those Portuguese, of course. They're shifty enough to try to steal her from me. Did you see Gomes?"

"You can count on me, sir," said Gregory, "I was just about to take a boatload over."

"Go on, Mr. MacLean," said Jonathan.

The strange man with the red hair walked over to Yawana and motioned to her to follow him. Passing in front of Jonathan she looked full at him, but he took no notice. She was taken to the enclosure where the other women prisoners were waiting. The red-haired man had bracelets of iron welded onto her and passed chains through them. Yawana watched the procedure impassively. The women around her all wore chains just like hers.

Gregory began herding the women together to get them to the dock, when Ardeen came puffing up. "Wait!" he shouted, "I must baptize them. Vasco! Hey, Vasco! Come and translate my sermon. Where is that halfwit? How can I baptize them if they don't understand what I'm saying? They must know that I'm saving them from the fires of Hell."

But in spite of Ardeen's frantic calls, Vasco did not come.

"I've got no time to lose, Reverend," said Gregory bruskly. "Baptize them or not as you wish, but I have to get them on board."

"Very well," said Ardeen, resigned, "then I'll do it without the half-breed. The good Lord will manage somehow to make them understand, I suppose."

Yawana had no idea what the white man with the crazy look was doing as he waved his arms about and said words she didn't understand, nor could she make out why he sprayed water all over them. Then he suddenly waved an object that hung about his neck over their heads, and walked away with dignity.

Later, Yawana found herself chained to an iron ring in Jonathan's cabin. She was too depressed to wonder about N'Gio or look at her new surroundings. She hungrily ate the greasy soup a sailor brought her and sat pensively staring out the porthole at the land she was about to leave. It seemed to float up and down in her vision. How distant were the days when she had known happiness. They were as dead as Ivohino and Isembe, Adende, and all whom she had ever loved. The crack of the whip had destroyed the harmony of her existence. Even were she to find N'Gio again one day, it would never be the same. She was soiled forever by the hands that had made use of her body again and again.

On shore, MacLean continued his examinations. Gomes came back, calm now, a contrite expression on his face. He apologized to Jonathan for his behavior. He had lost the girl, but he knew that he should try to serve his interests and he wanted to make sure that Jonathan's anger would not influence his final negotiation. Collins was pleased and accepted the apology with good grace.

With relief, the young doctor saw the last prisoner brought out. He branded her and she went to join the final group to be rowed out to the ship. Vasco still hadn't turned up, and Ardeen skimmed quickly through his collective baptism.

Then Gomes brought out his two children. He held them by the hair and they fought like wildcats against his firm hand. Jonathan felt like slapping the man's face, but he reflected that he had angered him enough for one day, and restrained his disgust.

"Don't brand them," he said hastily to MacLean, "I'll take them on my share. They're really much too white to be considered Negroes."

MacLean found the children in excellent health. His gentle manner calmed them, and they followed Gregory without a fuss. Jonathan asked him to see that they were taken to the cook.

Jonathan was pleased with himself. Naturally, he had taken the best for himself, but nobody could deny him that, for the black athlete, the young Negress, and the two adolescents together made up exactly the three sovereigns' worth to which he had a right in his contract. Adams, Clark, and Woolcomb had each chosen a woman prisoner as their share. They would make money out of her on arrival and would enjoy the added pleasure of using her during the journey.

Ardeen hadn't said much until then. Suddenly he began to behave in a manner most unbecoming to his calling. He clearly and without equivocation offered to exchange his cross and silver baptismal bowl for a very young black girl in Gomes' keeping. Gomes was about to accept, but Jonathan stepped in and formally opposed the transaction. Thereupon the reverend had a horrifying fit, no doubt provoked by his intemperate indulgence in alcohol under the blazing sun. He rolled about on the ground, frothed at the mouth, and shouted incomprehensible words until he finally lost consciousness.

"I don't need you anymore, Mr. MacLean. Would you be so kind as to go back to the ship with that drunken sot and give him a little medical attention?" asked Jonathan.

Two sailors put together an improvised stretcher and carried Ardeen away on it. Disappointed, Gomes watched them leave. It looked as though he would not be able to keep his drinking companion after all.

"Let's go and work out the money," said Jonathan,

breaking into his thoughts. "In the meantime, Mr. Adams will see that the merchandise is taken out of the store-room."

Before following Gomes up to the fort, Jonathan motioned to a couple of sailors to accompany him. The settlement took place without incident. The total sovereigns accounted for on the register corresponded closely to the terms of the agreement. Jonathan filled in the difference with gold pieces and paid for the goods and food furnished by the Portuguese in the same coin.

He could see sailors through the door, in consultation with the N'Komi chief, and concluded that they must be trying to buy some young Negresses from him in exchange for wigs and brandy. He decided to close his eyes to what was going on, and resolved to ask MacLean to do a rapid check on their health before allowing them to board.

The world was turning brilliant orange under an evening sky. Jonathan closed his register and rose to his feet. Gomes stopped him as he was about to leave. "Let's have a last drink together, Captain," he suggested.

Now that Jonathan was about to leave, he felt a surge of sympathy for the fellow, but there was no real reason to prolong a meeting with a man he despised. Gomes knew that once the ship left he would find himself alone, very much alone, perhaps more so than he had ever been. There would be many moments when he would only want oblivion, to bang his head against the walls and drink himself into a stupor of forgetfulness. He wanted to do anything he could to delay that moment.

Jonathan was polite enough to accept, and saw the first honest smile illuminate the face of the fat Portuguese.

"Vasco," he called, "bring us something to drink!"

He called again and again, but the half-breed didn't turn up. He would be punished severely; he had become totally disobedient in every way.

Gomes hurried off to get the drink himself, and then the two men toasted each other in feigned friendship.

Then Jonathan took his leave, eager to get back aboard. He had barely reached the dock when he heard a lively argument taking place between the Portuguese and the N'Komi chief. It did not sound as though they were coming to any kind of agreement. Jonathan shrugged, it was not his concern. As his longboat glided toward *The Sea Witch,* he experienced an incredible sense of relief to be leaving those accursed shores.

He called a meeting of the officers as soon as he boarded the ship, and announced that all must be ready to leave at dawn. Then he took Woolcomb and Gregory to one side: "I don't want to leave without having a crack at the natives who wanted to massacre us," he said. "Take some men. I want you to destroy the village they came from. Take as many prisoners as you can and leave for the attack as soon as it's dark."

"Yes, sir!" said Gregory.

"One more thing, Mr. Adams," continued Jonathan. "Be sure to do it as quietly as possible."

"Don't worry about that, sir," said Gregory with a grin.

As soon as night fell, four longboats, packed with sailors armed to the teeth, silently detached themselves from the flanks of the ship and glided toward the end of the lagoon. Jonathan watched them leave. He could hear groans and weeping coming up through the vents. A light gust of wind set the rigging creaking and shook the hull. If all went as smoothly as it had gone so far, the departure should be calm and easy, Jonathan reflected as he strode back to his cabin.

CHAPTER XXXII

The opaque mist hovering over the lagoon turned white with the coming of dawn. Night noises faded, one by one. A few resounding splashes indicated the presence of hippos, who were leaving their cool mud to come and frolic in the waters. Then the coast of Africa plunged into a deep silence.

Jonathan was on the bridge, watching the preparations for departure. He could hardly distinguish the foredeck of *The Sea Witch*. Clark shouted orders and sailors scurried up the mainstays to free the sails. Others were winding the anchor chain around the capstan and fastening it with gaskets.

Suddenly a smothered cacophony could be heard through the fog. It grew and grew and the longboats appeared, heavily laden, low in the water. They came to rest beside the ship and Gregory scrambled aboard.

Jonathan leaned over the rail and saw the boats full of chained blacks and animals. As he had hoped, the expedition had been a huge success. Gregory came to find him while Woolcomb loaded the prisoners on board.

"I see you did a good job," said Jonathan.

Gregory's face was etched with fatigue as he answered, "It could have been worse. We settled our accounts with these people, as you wanted. We managed to catch them by surprise. I've brought you about thirty young 'uns, all males."

"Well, now," Jonathan said delightedly, "we've made a nice little profit for the company. We'll set sail as soon as they're on board. Then you can go take a rest."

"There's one more thing, sir," said Gregory, his face grave, "we found young Matthew, or what was left of him. They must have eaten him. We saw several of them wearing bits of his clothing. Because of that I ordered the village burned to the ground."

With these words Gregory left to help with the unloading, and Jonathan swore at the stupidity of the young sailor. He had paid for it dearly, with a hideous death. As the last of the new prisoners disappeared down the hatch, orders rang out and the ship became a hive of activity. Some sailors sang out lusty sea chanties as they hauled the cable and others hovered around the capstan to weigh anchor. Sails swelled with the breeze and *The Sea Witch* began its majestic passage toward the straits.

The fort was still asleep and the ship turned as it came opposite. There was a billowing black cloud of smoke rising from behind Nengue Sika's sinister shores. They could hear the relentless throb of a hollow drum tapping out an indecipherable message. Soon, the ship disappeared behind a jutting point of land and the masts faded into the trees.

The lagoon was still and empty when Gomes awoke. Now that they didn't have to keep a close watch on the imprisoned slaves, the men had spent a wild night, carousing and drinking till dawn. Since he couldn't have the gorgeous creature he had set his heart on, Gomes had grabbed the first black girl he came across. He had searched everywhere for Vasco, determined to make him pay for repeatedly flouting his orders, but Vasco had evidently found an excellent hiding place. At last Gomes had turned all his frustration and fury on the black girl. He had rained blows on her first, and then made her submit to odious brutalities, rendering her almost unconscious by the time he fell heavily asleep.

When he woke up that morning he again shouted for Vasco, with no more success than the previous evening.

But there was little time to worry about Vasco's whereabouts, for a volley of shots and screams came to his ears. Before he even realized that the fort was under attack, a band of blacks erupted into his quarters and fell on him. The last he saw of this world was an axe poised above his head and a spreading red mist.

The Sea Witch deployed all sails as it reached the open sea. Jonathan had no idea that Gomes had been sacrificed to the N'Komis' hysterical vengeance for the previous night's attack. He calmly watched the land fade, the land he considered a hotbed of treachery, greed, and murder. He thought that Hell itself could hardly be much worse.

He decided to wait until they were out of sight of the coast before bringing up the slaves to feed them, for he was afraid of their reaction if they saw their land disappearing in the distance. It could lead to suicide or rebellion. While he waited, he asked MacLean to examine the N'Komi captured during the night, and to brand them.

The smell of food floated from the galley where Pierre watched over his steaming pots. The sailors not on duty slept and watched the sea froth as the stem cut through it. A sailor stood on the topmast, chewing tobacco, his eyes on the horizon. The helmsman steered a careful course. The sea, with its huge waves, was magnificent, and the wind was steady. Jonathan reflected that it should not take them more than two days to sight São Tomé.

His anxieties soothed at last, he started toward his cabin when the sound of a fall came from the forecastle. Almost at once he saw two sailors come out holding a squirming figure whom he recognized as Vasco. The half-breed stopped struggling and let them drag him to Jonathan.

"What are you doing on my ship?" asked Jonathan abruptly. "Why did you leave your master?"

Vasco fell on his knees.

"We found him hiding in the front hold, Captain," said one of the sailors.

"Good. You can leave now," said Jonathan. His eyes came to rest on the half-breed.

"Mr. White Man, I want to leave with you," he begged, "I don't want no way to go back to Mr. Gomes. He'll kill me because I didn't obey him about the female."

"What female?" asked Jonathan.

"The pretty Negress you took for yourself, sir. Mr. Gomes wanted her for him. He told me to take her out of the barracone and I didn't do that. He was not happy."

"Well, why didn't you do it?" asked Jonathan, a little mollified.

"For revenge, Mr. White Man. He's a bad man. He wanted to get you killed by the N'Komi."

"You surely don't expect me to sail back for you?" asked Jonathan.

Vasco rolled on the floor in dramatic despair.

"Then you're going to throw me to the sharks! Oh, Mr. White Man, please don't do that! Whip me, beat me, do anything you want with me, but not the sharks."

"Get up, you idiot," said Jonathan, grinning. "I won't do any of that."

Jonathan had just made up his mind that the half-breed could be very useful to him on board ship. He was familiar with the various tribal dialects and he knew their customs. In fact his presence would be a real boon and would make it much easier to communicate with the prisoners. He turned to his chief naval officer.

"Mr. Woolcomb, take care of this man. Get him a decent pair of pants and a clean shirt. And find him a corner to sleep in between decks. He'll keep an eye on the slaves."

Vasco bounded to his feet joyfully. The white man was giving him responsibilities; he had confidence in him! He thought that perhaps they might set him free wherever the ship was going. He had heard that in some distant islands, half-breeds were privileged people.

"They'll explain what you have to do," continued Jonathan, "and if you ever get wind that something is brewing tell me at once. But let me warn you, at the first sign of a problem from you, we'll have you chained with the rest."

Vasco stuttered with eagerness, "I swear, Mr. White Man, I'll do everything you say. Vasco knows all about the niggers. He knows how to hit them when it's necessary. Vasco doesn't want to be branded and thrown in with the rest; they'd kill me for sure."

Woolcomb dragged him away and Jonathan went into his cabin.

Yawana was crouched in her corner as Jonathan entered and shut the door. She stared at him, her eyes huge. She had never seen him so close before. She was sleeping when he got back from the fort and he hadn't disturbed her. He left the cabin before she awoke. She had been alone ever since, chained to the iron ring. The ship's first movements terrified her as she watched the land disappear through the porthole.

Jonathan came forward slowly. His walk was ungraceful. Yawana couldn't bear the gaze of his clear blue eyes and hid her face in her hands. He laughed, and she felt him unchaining her and pulling her to her feet. Then he moved her hands away from her face and smiled at her. She lifted her head and dared to take a good look at him. He was as tall as N'Gio, but of a slighter build. His hair was long, and curled at the ends. It was gold, and so was the light fluff that showed in the open neck of his shirt. She didn't know why, but she wanted to touch it. His smile reassured her and she wanted badly to tell him how grateful she was that he had not abandoned her back there. He left her and went to the door, opening it and shouting, "Pierre! Come here!"

The cook appeared at once.

"Pierre," said Jonathan, "you're French, so you un-doubtedly know what one does with women. You see this Negress? Give her something to eat. Then warm some wa-ter and scrub her all over until her skin nearly comes off. Rinse her hair with vinegar and make sure that she has no lice, and then you can bring her back."

Pierre gazed admiringly at Yawana and clasped his plump hands. "Oh! She's so fine, so delicate! I don't know where you found such a beauty, Captain. It's a shame they aren't all like her. I'll be sure to get her cleaned up for you."

Jonathan smiled and thought of Gomes' two children.

"What did you do with the two little mulattoes?" he asked.

"They're as cute as can be," said Pierre. "Poor things, they're just skin and bone. I stuffed them, all right. They're still asleep. I settled them in the storeroom."

"We'd better find names for them, I forgot to ask Gomes their names."

"That's not much of a problem," Pierre said. Then he took Yawana by the hand. "Come with me, little one," he said kindly.

Yawana went. She felt there was nothing to fear from this pleasant little man. He was as fat as the horrible white at the fort, but his smile, his laughing eyes, and the funny brush of a mustache that jumped up and down when he talked made him appear harmless.

Pierre took her to a room that opened onto the deck. The walls were covered with shiny utensils and there was a wonderful smell in the air that made her stomach ache with hunger. He sat her down and gave her a goblet of red liq-uid and a bowl of beans with a piece of chicken.

Yawana drank the wine. It was good and warmed her body. The food was delicious and she ate it rapidly. While she was eating, some sailors came in and emptied huge buckets of steaming water into a big brown tub, and as soon as she had finished eating, Pierre showed her the wooden tub and said, "Jump in!"

Then realizing that she couldn't understand him, he took her by the hand and led her into the water. It was her first hot bath, and she hesitated before stepping in, but Pierre nudged her and, once in the water, she found it pleasant. Not for long though, for Pierre, armed with a brush and soap, started to scrub vigorously at her skin. He went at it with gusto, taking pleasure in the feel of the smooth young body that squirmed under his hands when he scrubbed too hard.

He rinsed her off and began again. This time he ducked her head several times and soaped her hair. Yawana got soap in her eyes and it stung and she couldn't see a thing. She could feel Pierre drying her off. Sometimes he rubbed too hard, and she gave a small squeal that made Pierre cluck in distress.

He talked to her ceaselessly. She didn't understand a word, but she knew that his tone was not insulting or harsh. Perhaps, after all, these white men were less cruel than the blacks. She had eaten well since she had been with them, and nobody had beaten or raped her. She had no idea that only her beauty had saved her and that the other prisoners were crammed into the smelly suffocating holds, undergoing a very different experience.

At last she was able to open her eyes. Her whole body tingled from the scrubbing, and she felt extraordinarily well. She touched her skin and found it softer than it had been before. Some sailors lounging against the doorpost were watching her, laughing. Pierre leapt for them, dishrag at the ready. "Go and work, lazy good-for-nothings," he shouted. "She's not for you. She's much too beautiful."

The sailors pretended to be terrified and left, joking as they went.

Yawana was ready. Pierre fastened a slip of red fabric around her hips and took her back to Jonathan. He was working on the maps when they came into his cabin. He raised his eyes and this time looked at her long and carefully. Her wrists and ankles were incredibly delicate, and her high breasts were so perfect that he found himself comparing them to Aurelia's. He had to admit to himself that the young Negress was second to no one in that regard. It was as if a heavy burden had been lifted from his shoulders and he laughed gently to himself.

"See how clean she is, Captain," Pierre said proudly. "Would you like me to fasten her?"

"No," said Jonathan, "it's not worth it. She won't run away."

"Of course she won't, Captain, but she shouldn't wander about the deck. The sailors find her a very tasty piece."

"You're quite right, Pierre," said Jonathan. "Listen, why don't you find me Vasco. I could use him."

As soon as Pierre left, Jonathan got up. He grabbed Yawana under the armpits, lifted her, and chuckling, spun her round and round. Then, when she was dizzy, he put her down and gave her a smacking kiss on each cheek.

"Hm! Perhaps you'll be able to help me," he said aloud in a pensive tone, thinking that the long voyage ahead might indeed hold some fun, and there would be plenty of time. Of course Yawana understood absolutely nothing of all this, neither his words nor his actions. She was more and more puzzled. She sat on the floor and stared up at him. He was at the table again, scratching at something with a bird's feather. She thought he must be completely mad.

Woolcomb came in with Vasco. She started in fright when she saw this man who seemed to follow her everywhere like a bird of ill-omen. She immediately noticed the whip in his belt and wondered if he had been called in to punish her for something. The white man with him had a long beard, and he seemed quiet and pleasant enough.

"I brought him along to you, sir, as Pierre asked," said Woolcomb. "I took him down to the holds and he translated for the slaves what they would have to do during the crossing. He seemed to do a good job and, what's more, they seemed afraid of him, which is a good sign."

While the two men were talking, Vasco sneaked several glances at Yawana, who pretended not to notice. He was very proud of his new duties and sported a clean brown shirt and blue trousers that Woolcomb had found for him. He was hoping that he'd have the use of the women prisoners and he did with Gomes, but he doubted that this one would be within his reach.

Woolcomb left and Jonathan addressed Vasco: "Is this the Negress you told me about?"

"Yes, Mr. White Man, that's the one. Mr. Gomes was angry because I didn't put this female aside for him."

"Listen," said Jonathan, irritated, "I want you to stop calling me Mr. White Man. You're on a ship here, and you can call me 'sir' or 'Captain' when you speak to me, and stand up straight!"

"Yes, Mr. White—er, Mr. Captain," said Vasco, standing at attention.

"Ask her her name, and ask her whether she has a man among the ones we took on board."

Vasco spoke to Yawana and she answered him briefly. He relayed to Jonathan what she had said: "She says her name is Yawana. She thinks her man is on the ship. She says he is called N'Gio, and that he is the strongest."

It could only be the magnificent black that Jonathan had branded for himself. Without knowing it, he had bought a couple—and what a couple!

"Tell her that she will live with me and take care of my things. She will not be allowed out of here without my permission, or I shall chain her up all day. Tell her that she won't see her husband during the crossing, but they will be reunited when we arrive. Did you get that?"

"Oh, yes, Mr. Captain, sir, Vasco understands everything," and he started to translate.

Yawana listened to him carefully and her face lit up when he said that she would be reunited with her husband. When Vasco finished, she spoke eagerly and volubly.

"She said," translated Vasco, "that she thanks you and she won't move from here. She'll do whatever you wish."

"Good," Jonathan said with satisfaction. "Now listen to me carefully, Vasco. I will need you here every day. I want you to teach her my language. But I warn you of one thing. If you ever try to touch her I'll have you whipped raw and thrown to the sharks."

"Yes, Mr. Captain," Vasco said hurriedly, "Vasco doesn't want to be eaten by the fish. He won't touch the girl."

"Well, you can go now. Do everything Mr. Woolcomb tells you and all will go well for you," said Jonathan, turning away.

Vasco hastened out of the door. The captain frightened him.

By now, no trace of land was visible from *The Sea Witch*. Jonathan felt it was time to let the prisoners get some air, and he left the cabin to give the necessary orders. Yawana was alone. She didn't know what to do. So N'Gio was aboard, and perhaps not very far away. The white man said she would see him again at the end of the journey—

perhaps that was not very far away. She wandered around
the cabin and, noticing interesting objects in it, she timidly
passed her hand over some of them. It was all so new to
her. Looking at these things, she began to want to know
what they were, and what they were used for.

Between decks, N'Gio stretched his stiff limbs. His whole
body ached from having spent so much time without being
able to move at all. The roof over his head was too low for
him to stand upright, and the heat was stifling. He had had
nothing to eat since they put him in the hold. At first he
was so exhausted that he slept, but not for long. His
companions suffered as he did and their wails and moans
swept about him in a disturbing cacophony of distress. He
was terrified of the sudden movements of the ship and he
was also nauseated. The air had become foul, and the only
light came from the edges of a panel that had been used to
close the opening after them.

At last a large square of light opened and N'Gio saw
several men fix up a ladder and slide down it. Immediately
the hold was filled with cries. The slaves were made to get
up and N'Gio was reminded of the fact that he was chained
to another man. Woolcomb, with Vasco, was checking
their bonds at the foot of the ladder and N'Gio in turn was
pushed toward the opening and made to climb to the open
air. As he came out of the hatchway he was blinded by the
sun and blinked, bewildered.

He found himself in an enclosure set up on the maindeck. His group was tied together with a long chain which
was attached to the mainmast at one end and the capstan
at the other. N'Gio didn't realize that at the first hint of
revolt, the chain could be pulled tight, immobilizing them
immediately.

Jonathan had had the deck cleared of all tools or any
object that could serve as a weapon, and the entire crew
stood at the ready, armed with guns.

Through Vasco, Gregory explained to the slaves how the
cannons posted at the four corners of the maindeck could
be used, and to demonstrate their effectiveness, he put a
straw man in the center of the deck. He shouted an order,
a member of the gun crew set fire to the fuse, and there
was a tremendous explosion. When the blacks had got over
their fright they saw that the straw figure had been blown

to bits. Vasco explained to them that this was what would
happen to them if they disobeyed. The idea of provoking
such a brutal punishment caused revolt to flee far from
their minds and hearts.

Jonathan was chatting with the ship's carpenter, keeping
an eye on what was going on above and below him. At last
he spotted N'Gio, whose height and breadth were really
impressive. The fact that he owned this magnificent creature gave him great pleasure. The women and children
were then taken out of their compartments and grouped on
the quarterdeck. The men strained to see their women but
a high tarpaulin stretched across the handrail prevented
them from seeing anything. As soon as they had all calmed
down, Jonathan ordered food distributed to them, and
Pierre filled bowls with fish soup and highly spiced manioc.
He had prepared it with great care, for he loved to cook
and didn't care whether his food was to be eaten by whites
or blacks so long as it was enjoyed.

Jonathan stared at the sky.

"Gregory," he said to his first mate, "I wouldn't be surprised if we get a bit of a wind coming up. I don't think we'll
have time to let them wash. Have the tubs emptied overboard."

"Yes, sir," said Gregory, "you're right. I'll see to it at
once."

He took a few slaves who had finished eating and made
them tip the tubs of water overboard. He had the portholes
opened to air the holds and Woolcomb undertook to provide some ventilation shafts.

A strong wind began to blow and the sea opened in deep
furrows, causing the vessel to roll violently. Without wasting a minute the sailors hurried the slaves back into the
holds.

N'Gio took one last look at the quarterdeck. It was so
long since he had seen Yawana. He wasn't even sure she
was on the ship. Then he plunged into the murk of the
hold.

"We shall leave them out longer if it's fine tomorrow,"
said Jonathan to Gregory, "otherwise we'll have to wait for
the stop at São Tomé."

The wind was just as strong the next day and it rained
heavily, so the slaves had to stay in their quarters below

decks. They were given a little meat and fruit and tiny rations of brandy.

As Jonathan predicted, on the morning of the third day the dark mass of São Tomé appeared on the horizon.

CHAPTER XXXIII

Jonathan went ashore with Gregory after ordering everything to be prepared for the disembarkation of the slaves. The port of São Tomé looked inviting. Small stone houses stood in neat rows, their windows bulging out into curved iron grills. Somehow such orderliness seemed out of place in this part of the world. A motley population of whites, blacks, and mulattoes milled about in the streets. Jonathan and Gregory crossed a colorful marketplace, asked an anxious-faced white man for directions, and found their way to the governor's mansion.

It was a severe structure, softened by the luxurious vegetation that surrounded it. They were led into a dark room. A gray-haired man who was seated behind a desk rose as they came in.

"Your Excellency," Jonathan began, "I am Captain Collins, commander of *The Sea Witch* of the Royal African Company, and this is Mr. Adams, my first mate."

The governor bowed slightly and held out a manicured hand.

"I am Miguel de Ferreira," he said. "Welcome, Captain, and you too, sir. To what do I owe the pleasure of your visit to my island? Do sit down, I beg of you."

He sat down behind his desk and the two Englishmen sat opposite him.

"I'm transporting some Negroes I bought on the coast, at Fernan Vaz," said Jonathan.

Miguel de Ferreira smiled wryly. "Then you must have dealt with that toad of a fellow, Theophilus Gomes," he said.

"Yes, indeed, your Excellency," Jonathan said. "Do you know him? He is indeed a very disagreeable character."

"Unfortunately, Captain, in this kind of business there are few gentlemen of honor," said Ferreira. "Of course I do not say this of yourself," he added quickly.

Jonathan ignored the remark and continued, "I need to stay here for a week, your Excellency. I need lodging for my crew and a place to leave my Negroes."

"I think I can be of help, Captain. I'll call my secretary." De Ferreira shook a small silver bell and a young man came in. He was of mixed blood, but his skin was very fair. Jonathan raised his eyebrows, and the governor noted his expression.

"Yes," he said. "It surprises you, Captain. Here, we often give the half-breeds responsibilities. Actually, Alberto is a quadroon. There is even a quadroon on the Council of the island."

Jonathan thought he detected in the quadroon a faint resemblance to the governor.

"Alberto," the governor said affectionately, "please look after these gentlemen. They need lodgings and they need a place for their cargo. I count on you."

"Yes, your Excellency," the young man replied respectfully.

The governor rose.

"Alberto will take good care of you," he said. "When you are settled, would you do me the honor of lunching with me? I am having a few friends to luncheon and I should like you to meet them."

"I accept with great pleasure, your Excellency," said Jonathan, "but I would first like to discuss my anchoring privileges with you and the cost of lodging my men and slaves."

Ferreira waved his hand. "Later, Captain, later," he said. "There is no hurry."

Jonathan realized that the man wanted to be alone and did not insist.

Alberto was very efficient. He showed them a large comfortable building where they could house all the crew of *The Sea Witch*. Then he took them into the fort that defended the port. There was an open courtyard surrounded by high walls and an iron gate, and there was room enough for the slaves.

When Alberto left, Jonathan decided to go to the governor's luncheon and left Gregory to see to the details of the accommodations.

"It's a safe place," he said, as he was leaving. "You can leave a very small contingent on board, and the others can all come ashore. But make sure that there are always some men available for guarding our Negroes. As for the Negress I bought and the two children, I want them kept on board.

They haven't been branded and if anyone notices them they can just kidnap them and put their own brand on them, and there's nothing I could do about it."

"Just as I planned, sir, don't worry about a thing," said Gregory cheerfully. "Enjoy your luncheon. I'll manage very comfortably, with Clark's and Woolcomb's help."

Jonathan was the first to arrive at the governor's mansion. Miguel de Ferreira received him in an austere sitting room, and his wife joined them there soon after. She was a woman of indeterminate age, and so drab that even her husband barely seemed to notice her presence once she had been introduced to the captain.

"I'm so happy to receive a gentleman," sighed the governor. "Since we've had all these revolts here in the islands, all the decent people have left. The heights are inhabited by Jewish colonists and deported criminals, and I hardly ever have the chance to talk to someone from a good background."

Jonathan assured him that the pleasure was also his. Just then, they were interrupted by the arrival of an elderly man who had lived on the island for a long time. He was a merchant and seemed more anxious to converse with the governor's wife than with the governor. Once he had greeted the two gentlemen, he became involved in a low-voiced conversation with Mrs. de Ferreira.

Then a couple came in. The man was called Antam Cacheo. He was the founder of a prosperous sugar plantation and seemed happy with the life he led on the island. His wife Teresa was much younger than he, and was endowed with a heady beauty that quite took Jonathan's breath away. She seemed absentminded, and slouched languidly in an armchair, fanning herself nervously.

"My wife can't stand the climate here," Antam explained, as though trying to excuse her to Jonathan.

It turned out to be a lively meal. Alberto kept watch over the black servants and was at the governor's beck and call. The food was excellent and the comfortable, civilized atmosphere about the whole thing gladdened Jonathan's heart.

The old merchant never stopped talking to Mrs. de Ferreira, who listened intently, quite overcome by all the attention he was paying her. The governor was discussing the island's future with Antam Cacheo and Jonathan listened absently, more interested in the tasty pork stew than in their conversation. Teresa never uttered a word during the entire meal. She didn't eat a thing, and several times Jonathan caught her gazing at him. Each time he looked, she lowered her eyes at once. The cloth in front of her was covered with tiny pellets of bread she had nervously torn and kneaded with her fingers.

"Captain, why don't you come and stay with us during your stop here?" asked Antam at the end of lunch. "We have a beautiful house and it will be a change for you from life on the ship." He turned to his wife. "What do you think, Teresa?"

Teresa, who was devouring Jonathan with her wide eyes, started visibly.

"I think it's an excellent idea," she answered, and turned to Jonathan. "Captain, will you come?"

"My God, madam, it would be impossible to refuse such an irresistible invitation. I accept with delight."

"Good," said Antam, pleased. "When you have seen to your business here, let's meet and I'll take you to my plantation. It isn't far."

Jonathan took his leave of the governor and his wife and guests, and decided to go and see how Gregory was faring. He found him at the fort. All the slaves had been settled and he was assigning the various watches to the sailors.

Jonathan gave instructions for the next day and then told him that he would be staying at the Cacheo plantation. He asked Gregory to see that his things were brought to the governor's mansion from the ship. Then, after making sure that his crew were decently lodged, he wandered about the little town for a while before meeting the settler and his wife.

Yawana stayed on board ship, as Jonathan had decreed. All morning she watched her people being taken from the ship in boats. She caught sight of N'Gio in his chains, but he was too far away to hear her cries. She wondered sadly where they were going, and if they were to be sold once again. The infernal circle had no end.

She tried to make sense of her feelings for the white chief. He never tried to touch her. He never beat her, and when he spoke to her his voice was gentle and there was a kind look in his eyes. The day after their departure he had a small adjoining cabin prepared for her, and for the first time in her life she slept in something other than on a mat on the floor. The bunk was soft and she lay there for hours watching the horizon rise and fall through the porthole.

Vasco also left the ship, which pleased her. She hated him and his deceitful eyes, but he came each day to teach her the white man's language. She listened to the words he tried to teach her, but she was not yet able to reproduce any of them.

An unaccustomed calm descended on the ship. A few sailors stayed behind, along with Pierre the cook and the two mulattoes whom he had triumphantly baptized Starboard and Larboard, and who trembled in fear of his gruff voice.

While the ship was berthed at São Tomé, Yawana felt that she had entered another world. Pierre let her roam around the deck freely, and she spent her time watching the sailors splicing rope, repairing sails, or polishing wood. The cook had taken her under his wing and made it clear that anyone who touched her would have to deal with him. The young girl sensed that he was her ally and did everything he wanted. He stuffed her with delicious food, made her scrub herself every day, and talked endlessly in a strange singsong tongue that was different from the language used by the other whites.

Sometimes he burst into great gales of laughter, which usually ended with affectionate pats on her bare bottom. She soon realized that the paddling was intended as a gesture of affection rather than a punishment.

They really wanted to understand one another and Pierre's basic good nature cemented an unspoken friendship between the two. When he finished preparing the meals for the sailors or scolding Starboard and Larboard, he revealed talents other than the one for fine cooking. He loved to comb and style Yawana's hair. He decked her out in glass trinkets or scraps of rags and lace borrowed from Jonathan's shirts. She let him do whatever he wanted, happy that someone was paying attention to her, and even learned to pronounce his strange-sounding name.

One day, when he felt particularly proud of his efforts as a hairdresser, he put a mirror in front of her. She was so frightened by the face that seemed to start out from nowhere that she ran into her cabin. Pierre went to fetch her and explained that there was nothing magical in it. At last she felt reassured enough to look again, and she found her image so lovely that she didn't want to stop looking at it.

While Yawana was being tamed, the other prisoners endured a vastly different way of life. They ate as much as they wanted, but the food was not intended for their pleasure. It was solely to improve their physical condition enough for them to be able to endure the long voyage ahead, whose interminable span they could not even imagine.

Woolcomb and Gregory, followed by Vasco, made them get up very early each morning. They were given a bowl of gruel and then taken on a long walk that led to the beach. There, they were kept chained, and forced into the water to wash and then to rub themselves dry with sand. Back in their prison they were given plenty of meat, fruit, and vegetables. MacLean visited them daily to take care of any minor health problems. He had examined the N'Komi prisoners their first day aboard, and found them all healthy. When he branded them he left the branding iron on their skin a moment too long, fully intending to provoke the pain and cries that followed.

Jonathan had authorized the men and women prisoners to be together to have sexual intercourse among themselves, thinking that would make them calmer on the journey.

N'Gio could not understand why he did not have the same right as the others. He had heard from women prisoners that Yawana was on the ship, but no one knew where she was. He was beside himself with anxiety. From the very start of the tragedy he was by far the most ill-treated, and he felt he couldn't bear this new deprivation. Every day he watched the couples embrace while he remained alone. There was also the horrible servile man the whites called Vasco who never lost an opportunity to push him around and insult him, and whenever possible to give him a taste of his whip. N'Gio had no way of knowing that the half-breed knew he was Yawana's beloved husband, having heard it from her own mouth. Vasco desired Yawana, yet knowing that she was inaccessible to him, he never missed an opportunity to turn his frustration on the young man.

Reverend Ardeen, who considered that he had now accomplished what he had set sail for, refused to lift a finger

or take part in any of the ship's activities. Jonathan's refusal to allow him to trade his religious objects for a Negress had made him stubborn and resentful. He frequently
retreated into bad-tempered sulks and waited for Jonathan
to leave the ship in São Tomé before leaping into the first
longboat. His drunkard's sixth sense quickly led him to the
one tavern on the island, the Blue Dolphin, and he had
remained there ever since. Sailors dropping by for a drink
found him in a state of permanent collapse on one of the
tables, a look of depression and dissolution on his face.

At last Jonathan was far enough from his responsibilities
to get a little rest. His only contact with *The Sea Witch* was
Gregory's daily visit to tell him how it was all going. From
the time of his arrival on the island, his host had done
everything he could to make his stay a pleasant one. His
wife Teresa seemed in better spirits, and her husband was
delighted. She had found her sparkle and gaiety again and
no longer complained about the heat all the time. Jonathan
soon discovered that her languid manner hid a passionate
nature.

The Cacheo house was built on a hillside and was spa-
cious and cool. Jonathan stood on the veranda gazing at
the sugarcane-covered hills and valleys stretching before
his eyes in all directions. Everything was quiet. Antam had
gone out on the plantation and would not be back before
nightfall.

A light rustling behind him made him turn and he saw
Teresa, leaning against the doorpost, looking at him. She
wore a long prune-colored taffeta gown that showed off her
shoulders and breasts. Her black hair, usually rolled into a
severe knot, tumbled freely about her shoulders and delicate neck, around which she wore a gold medallion.

"Good day, Captain," she said.

Her voice was low and musical and her unfamiliarity
with English made her pronunciation hesitant and charming.

Jonathan rose at once. He was at her side in two steps
and bent over the hand she held out to him. He felt her
shiver as his lips touched her flesh. Carried away by a wave
of intense emotion, he turned her hand over and kissed her
palm.

"Captain, please!" Teresa whispered unconvincingly, as

her other hand crept to his neck and her fingers caught at his blond locks.

He straightened then and took her in his arms. She pressed into him, trembling, and they found each other's lips. Jonathan stepped back and read years of frustrated desire in her luminous black eyes.

"We're alone," she whispered, her voice pleading.

Jonathan lifted her and carried her to her room.

That night at dinner, Teresa was so sparkling and her eyes glowed so in the flickering candlelight that Jonathan was afraid that her husband would suspect something, but he didn't seem to notice any change in her.

From then on, as soon as he left to attend to his sugar works, Teresa came to Jonathan. She gave herself to him with passionate abandon and he responded with equal intensity.

The slaves were regaining their strength. N'Gio had resigned himself to his situation. At least he ate well here, and he was not whipped so often.

One fine day, Gregory came to tell Jonathan that all was ready for the journey. The ship was in order. Clark had added a whole herd of goats and pigs to their livestock and there was plenty of fresh water. They could leave whenever Jonathan wanted.

"We'll leave tomorrow morning," Jonathan decided. "Start getting the Negroes back on board."

"I've already started," said Gregory. "What time will you be coming aboard?"

"Have a boat wait for me just before sunset."

"Very well, sir, I'll send one of the sailors to get your trunk."

After lunch, Antam left, saying good-bye to Jonathan, for he had work to do outside and was afraid that he would not be back before Jonathan's departure. Jonathan thanked him warmly for his hospitality and told him how sorry he was to leave. Teresa excused herself while the two men were talking and after Antam had left, Jonathan was alone. He felt rather heavy from the excellent grilled suckling pig with banana fritters, and decided to take a little rest. He went up to his room, threw his clothes off, and lay down.

A warm breeze rustled the leaves on the trees outside his window. He was just falling asleep when the door opened and Teresa came in. She was barefoot, her hair loose and curling about her shoulders, and she wore only a transparent chemise.

Jonathan leapt up.

"Aren't you afraid that the servants—?"

She cut in with a clear laugh as she smilingly removed the chemise.

"Don't worry, Jonathan dear, I sent them off to sleep and that's not an order they would dream of disobeying."

She was naked now as she stood before him, breathing heavily. Her rather heavy breasts rose and fell and her eyes pleaded. Jonathan found her very beautiful.

"You're leaving tonight," she said. "I want to be with you one last time."

Her smile faded and her eyes filled with tears. Jonathan held his arms open and she ran into them, sobbing.

Much, much later they stood together on the porch. A sailor sat on Jonathan's trunk as he waited for his captain at the foot of the stairs. Teresa wore a chaste dress of white cotton and her hair was caught up under a lace coiffe. She laid her hand on the officer's arm. "Jonathan, my dear one, I shall probably never see you again," she said. "Bless you for all you have done for me." She lifted her arms and undid the medallion at her throat. "Here, take this. I want you to keep it always and always remember me, your days in São Tomé, and our love. Will you promise?"

"I promise, Teresa," said Jonathan solemnly. She put the jewel into his hand and closed his fingers over it. Then she stood on tiptoe and kissed him passionately. "Farewell, my gentle friend," she said. "I shall pray to the Virgin to keep watch over you."

"Farewell, Teresa, I shall never forget."

The young woman turned and fled to hide her tears. Jonathan walked pensively down the steps. The sailor, who had watched their parting, hoisted the trunk onto his shoulders and the two men trudged down an avenue bordered with leafy mango trees and toward the sea.

Teresa, hidden behind the blinds, watched them go. She was sobbing, her soaking handkerchief pressed against her lips to silence her despair. She hated this country, she hated her husband, and she hated this man who had just left her to endless loneliness.

A boat was waiting for Jonathan at the port. Gregory

had come to meet him and he took the trunk and helped the sailor settle it in the boat. The Reverend Ardeen was sprawled on the dock, dead drunk, with two other sailors. Jonathan jumped aboard.

"I found all three of them at the Blue Dolphin," said Gregory, pointing to the three bodies. "They'd still be there if it weren't for me."

Jonathan grunted as the boat left the mooring ring.

"Did the loading go all right?" he asked.

"Yes, sir, very well indeed," answered Gregory. "The slaves are asleep. They're as fat as pigs, and this respite has calmed them down."

"I hope so," said Jonathan morosely.

He was thinking of the interlude with Teresa and didn't want to talk.

The boat came alongside *The Sea Witch*, whose lanterns twinkled cheerfully in the twilight. Jonathan was happy to get back. He was really rather bored with his idleness and the fiery Teresa.

"We'll leave at sunrise, Gregory," he said.

"We're all set, sir. The wind is right and it looks as if this weather is here to stay."

The men on deck were finishing their evening meal. As the sun reached the horizon, a green fire lit up the sky. Jonathan went down to his cabin. He was relieved to be back in familiar surroundings. He wanted to be alone a while and hoped that Pierre had prepared a fine meal for him, a pleasant change from the Portuguese cooking, which was too greasy for his taste.

He pulled off his boots and coat and poured a generous tumbler of wine, sipping it with a satisfied sigh, reflecting that the life he led did have its pleasant moments.

Just then, a singsong voice behind him said, "Good day, Captain."

He turned. "What . . . ?" The words died on his lips and his mouth fell open. Yawana stepped out of the shadows and stood before him in a white dress, her bare shoulders gleaming as they emerged from a cloud of foaming lace. "Good day, Captain," she said again, smiling.

Pierre came in with a steaming soup tureen. He put it on the table and surveyed the scene before him with evident delight. He had made Yawana's dress himself and had

spent many hours teaching her to say those three words to
Jonathan upon his return.

Jonathan shot a suspicious glare at him. "Did you do
this?" he asked, pointing at Yawana. Pierre rubbed his
hands together and smiled.

"Yes, that was me, Captain," he said proudly. "Don't
you think she looks pretty like that?"

Jonathan was suddenly filled with an uncontrollable anger. "I think she's a little savage," he exploded. "And that
she must stay a savage and not dress like a white woman.
As for you," he turned to Yawana, forgetting in his rage
that she couldn't understand him, "take that off at once!
You're nothing but a Negress, do you hear? Nothing but a
Negress!"

Without understanding the words, Yawana knew that he
was angry. Unsure of what else to say, she timidly repeated
the only words she knew, "Good day, Captain; good day,
Captain?"

Jonathan made a tired sweep with his arm. "Oh," he
muttered, "stay as you are."

He began to eat his pumpkin soup. Pierre was so taken
aback that he didn't know what to do.

"Are you angry with me, Captain?" he asked anxiously.
"I just thought it would please you."

"No, Pierre, I'm not angry. I ask your pardon. I don't
know why I flew into such a temper. You did very well,
she looks charming like that. Listen, let it pass, will you?
Let her keep the dress, but take her away now. I want to
be alone. I think I must be very tired."

"I made you some roast lamb and crêpes," announced
Pierre, pleased to see his captain return to his usual mild-
mannered self. He slipped out of the cabin, motioning to
Yawana to follow.

Jonathan stayed alone, lost in contradictory thoughts.
After eating very little, he went straight to bed.

Yawana found herself back in her small cabin. She felt
infinitely sad, but somehow it had nothing to do with her
captivity. Something else was welling up from deep inside
that she could not understand. Moonlight streamed through
the porthole. The young woman removed her dress and
folded it carefully before lying down naked on her bunk.
She wondered why the white man had looked at her with

the spark of desire in his eyes and then suddenly started to shout without cause.

"N'Gio, my N'Gio," she whispered, the tears streaming down her face. "I do so wish you were here. I hate the white man. I hate him."

CHAPTER XXXIV

After *The Sea Witch* left her berth in São Tomé she plunged into a turbulent ocean and had been flung about by giant waves ever since. The sky was clear, but there was so much wind that Gregory ordered the sails reduced. The ship continued at a fast clip, great green walls of water flooding the decks as Woolcomb set the slaves to working the pumps.

Jonathan was concerned about the weather because it prevented the blacks from going out on deck. Unused to the pitching and rolling of the vessel, they were terrified in their windowless prison. A more violent roll than most knocked over one of the toilets and neither the ventilator shafts nor white-hot irons dipped in vinegar nor constantly burning incense and juniper succeeded in removing the dreadful stench.

N'Gio, whose berth was in the center of the ship, didn't suffer from the widespread seasickness, but he was beset by painful cramps and couldn't move or get up. He had neither the strength nor appetite to eat the bananas which were the blacks' only food because the ship's jerky movements prevented Pierre from heating anything in the galley.

The sailors were more hardened to weather fluctuations and were not affected by them, but William Clark, for whom this was the first sea voyage, spent a lot of time retching on his bunk, emptied of all energy. The reverend wasn't much better and gave up drinking, and MacLean ordered turtle soup for them all, to calm their stomachs. Unfortunately, the remedy seemed to have an opposite effect.

Yawana suffered a little at first but soon adapted to shipboard life. She had the advantage of being far more comfortable than the other prisoners, for she had some freedom and could breathe fresh air every day.

She rarely saw Jonathan, who was very busy, and she suffered secretly as a result. In spite of the bad weather, Vasco came every day to give her English lessons and she was improving rapidly. Now she could exchange a few words with Pierre. The two brothers, Starboard and Larboard, were also learning quickly, and used their newly acquired skills to beg sweetmeats from the Frenchman. They were no longer afraid of his scolding or the beating he threatened them with when he caught them stealing something.

At last, the wind dropped and the ocean calmed. Gregory ordered the sails unfurled and *The Sea Witch* regained her steady majestic gait.

The prisoners were enormously relieved. As soon as the deck had dried, they were taken from their holds and brought up on deck. N'Gio stepped out between decks and filled his lungs with clean air. The heat inside the ship had been so heavy that he now felt very cold. He sat on the deck without daring to look at the rippling immensity beyond the ship. It made him nauseous. He wondered how long he would have to endure this hell. Every time he thought he had reached the depths of unbearable suffering a new trial proved to him that he could go lower still. Was this voyage to last for all eternity?

Women's and children's voices made him lift his eyes to the back of the ship. He was still hoping to catch a glimpse of Yawana, but was disappointed each time he was sure an opportunity was at hand. He so wanted to see Yawana, his little antelope. Once he even lowered himself to the extent of asking the man who was neither white nor black and who ceaselessly persecuted him, if he had seen his wife, since the white men seemed to let him roam about at will. Vasco laughed long and loud. But he didn't answer, he only delivered a well-placed kick to N'Gio's shins. N'Gio wondered sadly who would be able to give him news.

When she saw that the weather had improved, Yawana felt sure the slaves would be taken out on deck, and she hoped she would see N'Gio. But Jonathan's prohibitions were still in force and to be certain that she wouldn't try to disobey him, he had locked her in the cabin. He was particularly anxious that the other Negroes should not realize that she was receiving favored treatment, and he feared that if her husband saw her dressed like a white woman he might be so angry that he would start a revolt. It was very important to avoid lowering the already low morale of the prisoners.

Huge copper cauldrons steamed on the maindeck. Pierre

lovingly stirred away at their contents, little Larboard at
his side, ready to help.

"Come on, Starboard! Where's that ladle?" yelled Pierre.
He turned to Larboard and muttered, "Listen, you, instead
of picking your nose, why don't you go and see what your
brother's doing?"

Larboard hurried off to the storeroom in a gale of laughter from the sailors, who were vastly amused by the names
given the two children. Soon after, he returned with Starboard in tow. The child handed Pierre a ladle almost as big
as himself and Pierre growled at the two of them, "Get me
those bowls and get a move on."

The children obeyed, and Pierre carefully ladled some
pieces of boiled elephant meat and puree of manioc into
each, then hurried the boys off to give it to the slaves,
while Vasco surveyed the scene, fingering his whip.

N'Gio was very hungry. The fresh air had dispelled his
nausea and aroused his appetite. It was so good to smell
something other than the stink of the hold. He ate silently,
laboriously chewing the stringy meat. When he had finished, they gave him water from huge earthernware jars in
corded covers.

Jonathan and Gregory leaned on the rail and watched
the deck. Pierre ladled out the last of the soup and poured
boiling sea water into the cauldrons to clean them.

The smell of the sweating blacks was so strong that it
rose as far as the bridge despite the reverse wind.

"God! As soon as they've finished eating, get them thoroughly washed off," Jonathan said. "They stink to high
heaven."

"You can say that again," Gregory responded.

"Then they can have a sleep. It's beautiful weather, so
leave them out on the deck all day. You can give out a
little tobacco for each, but no pipes. I don't want any risk
of their setting fire to the ship. They can chew on it instead."

Jonathan was silent for a moment, and then went on,
"Leave the men naked, but you'd better give the women
some strips of rag for the sake of hygiene."

"Don't you think, sir, that they could use some exercise?" Gregory suggested. "They've been tied up without
moving for several days. I could make them sweep up the
deck."

"No, leave them alone today. We'll see to that tomorrow." A thought struck him, and he continued, "On the other hand, we could make them dance after dinner tonight."

"What a good idea," Gregory said. "I found a few drums when we destroyed the N'Komi village."

"Very good, Gregory," Jonathan said with a smile. "I leave it up to you, then."

The swelling sails spread undulating shadows on the deck. The helmsman leaned on the wheel to keep the ship on course in spite of the tailwind that made her dance capriciously. Gregory went to the maindeck and had the jutting planks of the bulwark adjusted. Some men then attached pulleys to them to send down buckets and draw up sea water.

Woolcomb lined up the slaves and the sailors poured big buckets of sea water over their heads. When they found them clean enough, they let them dry themselves and then the slaves were ordered to rub palm oil into their skins. MacLean checked quickly to make sure that they were all in good health, and made them rinse their mouths out with lemon water. During this time, a team of blacks, N'Gio among them, had gone down to the holds. After the clean air he had been breathing with such pleasure, the young man thought he would vomit from the stench. Two slaves worked the pump and poured salt water on the planks, and N'Gio and his companions scrubbed the floors. The toilets were full to overflowing and they were pushed to the openings and emptied into the sea. At last, to their great relief, they were allowed to go back up on deck.

N'Gio absentmindedly took the piece of tobacco handed to him. He didn't really want it. He threw it to Bokou and fell into a heavy sleep. Soon, only the N'Komi were awake. They were seething with rage at having been kidnapped and forced to endure the same fate they had long inflicted on their less fortunate black brothers. They were huddled in an aggressive little group, plotting in an undertone. Gregory noticed and called Vasco.

"Go and tell them to be quiet," he said, pointing to the group, "and quick."

Vasco hurtled down the ladder and rushed toward the N'Komi, his whip at the ready. He didn't use it, but shouted a few words at them and they stopped talking at once. His next words were harsh and nobody saw one of the N'Komi smile.

Jonathan ate with his officers. Pierre had prepared a fine meal, for fresh foods soon spoiled and it was advisable to eat them as quickly as possible. Figuring that pigs and chickens were better able to stand the voyage, he served goat stew, boiled taro root, and to the immeasurable delight of the assembled gentlemen, some salad and tomatoes that Clark had discovered on São Tomé.

The captain then soaked in a hot bath for a while, trying to relax. As soon as he was dried and shaved, he told Pierre to bathe Yawana while the water was still warm and soapy.

"Then shut her up in her cabin," he said. "I don't want her running off trying to find her man."

The cook hurried to get the young girl, who had been imprisoned in her cabin since morning. She was happy to see him, and stayed in the water until he came back to tell her to come to the storeroom with him for her food.

By midafternoon Pierre was again laboring over his cauldrons. The slaves ate greasy soup and bananas for their evening meal. Then Gregory had the drums brought out and Vasco explained to the prisoners that the captain would allow them to dance, and that if they had any objections, he would use his whip to change their minds for them. He had some difficulty finding musicians, for they did not come forward, but the threat of no food for anyone next day propelled three men to the fore and they grudgingly picked up their instruments.

N'Gio, awakened by the noise and the whip that Vasco had hastened to apply to his back, couldn't understand what was wanted of them all. There would be no joy in dancing by force, and still less by the threat of violence.

The musicians, nonetheless, tested the tautness of the skins on their drums and then began to play. They played mechanically at first, but then their fingers began to move instinctively to forgotten rhythms. The slow dull sounds hurt N'Gio. It seemed as if he were hearing the heart of his village beating from far away. The others shared his pain, and they demonstrated a melancholy which was exactly the reverse of what Jonathan had intended.

"Woolcomb!" he shouted. "Don't let them get away with it, man! They look as if they're asleep. Shake 'em up! Otherwise they won't even be able to walk when we get them there."

Encouraged by their commanding officer, the sailors went into action. They kicked the slaves to make them get up, while Vasco cracked the whip above their heads. The children on the quarterdeck needed no such encouragement. They responded spontaneously to the music and began to dance in time to the rhythm of the drums.

Suddenly, the throbbing began to wipe out the present reality. The drum players lost all sense of the moment as their palms tapped out the vibrant rhythm, and the masts of the ship became tall trees reaching for the sky. The sounds that came to them from their ancestral past made them forget the chains that clanked at their feet. The music soaked into N'Gio's soul and reached his innermost heart. He was the first to rise and his body followed the hesitant movements of his head. Watching him, the women grew braver, and soon the entire ship seemed to be swaying in rhythm.

The sailors found it an astonishing spectacle. They didn't feel the strong call of the music, but they were very amused by the wild contortions of the slaves, which they thought a supreme example of their savagery. They thought of the slaves as slightly superior monkeys, incapable of feeling, and they clapped along indulgently.

Jonathan's reflections were more complex.

"I don't agree with those who say that the blacks have no soul, what do you say, Gregory? This is beautiful music. It comes from somewhere. I wonder who taught it to them?"

"I must admit, sir, I've never given it a thought," returned Gregory. "But I do think you're right. The way they play and dance must mean something."

"There now," said Jonathan with satisfaction, "now they seem to be enjoying themselves at last. It's calming them down. We'll have more of this whenever the weather permits."

A lone, deep voice rose in song above the drums. It was N'Gio's. The sailors fell silent and the blacks shuffled their feet in accompaniment. He verbalized all the images that the music had awakened in his mind and that each beat of the stretched drumskins brought to life in his heart. A tornado rose from the depths of his throat and shook the tall

trees and made waves leap up on the rivers. He called up
the trail, sliding like a snake through the forest, and the
silent step of the leopard before its leap. He made night
fall, and summoned genies and gods whose whispers in the
dark he no longer heard. He sang of the silky flight of the
eagle and of the terrifying scuttle of the iguana.

They were all listening to him now, their minds lost in
visions that flashed before them as swiftly as dreams, and
between the words of his song they interjected muffled exclamations that sounded like sobs.

N'Gio sang of neither hatred nor blood. He sang only of
lost things, the way one sings of a lost love. But at the end
of his song he threw out a supreme curse against those who
had tricked him, bought him and sold him, and he spat
into the air with all his strength. And all the slaves did as
he did.

Obviously the significance of this was lost on the white
men, but Vasco understood the gesture very well indeed. It
opened up new horizons for him. He reflected that if he
maneuvered N'Gio efficiently, he might serve his own
plans, as would the N'Komi warrior who had whispered to
him that he was the son of King Nkougou. The time was
not ripe yet for his crazy scheme, but later these two men
would be easy to manipulate.

N'Gio sat down, exhausted. The others began to dance
again with renewed vigor to forget what they had heard.

Yawana heard N'Gio's song. She knew that his words
were for her. They hammered into her skin and her body
shuddered. She recognized in the beat that throbbed
through the walls the music that accompanied the erotic
dances in her village, and she began to respond to it as she
had done on the night of the Ndjembe. Her breasts hardened and her loins were on fire.

She began to dance slowly and then faster and faster. She
tore off the fabric that covered her and let herself respond
to the wild rhythm. She lost all sense of place, and was
overwhelmed by a driving desire to find N'Gio. He alone
could calm the fire raging in her. She hurled herself against
the door, battering it with her fists and screaming.

Just then, Jonathan walked in. He heard the screams and
frantic shrieks from Yawana and opened the door. She retreated when she saw him and hid in a corner of her cabin,
her eyes unfocused and drugged.

Under Jonathan's astonished gaze she gradually began to come to her senses.

"What on earth were you yelling about?" asked Jonathan.

"Yawana want to dance," she whispered.

It was the first time she had said anything more to him than "Good day, Captain," and it made him laugh. He didn't want her to go to the others, but he felt it was unfair to stop her.

"Well," he said cheerfully, "if Yawana wants to dance, dance she shall!"

He came and took her by the hand and dragged her into his cabin. She stood in the center, dazed, and naked.

He took the wine flask and filled two glasses. Taking up his own, he handed the other to her.

"Here, Yawana, drink!" he said.

The young woman took the glass and without a thought drained it at once. For her, drinking and dancing went together, and she did not linger over the sweetish taste of the wine. Jonathan poured her another glass but stopped her from draining it as she had done the last.

"Gently, now," he said. "By God, you drink like an old seadog!"

She didn't understand the words, but from the gentleness of his tone she sensed that they were not bad.

The throb of the drums permeated every inch of the ship. Yawana put down her half-empty glass and voluptuously gave herself to the magic of the dance. She swayed gracefully, and her eyes filled with a mysterious sensuality. Her movements grew more and more frenetic until she was wildly twisting and turning, arcing her body and rolling it into a tight ball only to arc again.

Suddenly her desire to be in N'Gio's arms flooded her again. She needed desperately to feel his hard stomach against her own and she needed to clamp her thighs about his strong back. Her hands stretched out to him blindly, but there was nothing but emptiness before her. There was nothing but the dim silhouette of Jonathan before her.

Jonathan was stunned by the overt, overflowing sensuality of the young woman's dance. He had never seen anything like it. He had never seen a woman display such unabashed eroticism. Yawana, her lips half open, had gone way beyond the real world, and he realized that she wanted to take him with her.

Jonathan never knew quite what it was, the obsessive beat of the drums, the sweat running down the bare body that gleamed excitedly in the candlelight, or the subtle musky smell that arose from her body. Yawana was watching him from under half-closed lids and as he came to her, her lips curled back over coral gums. She threw herself back to take in the white man, and she forgot N'Gio.

Jonathan felt her nails in his back and heard her deep groan. She had no idea what name she cried, N'Gio or another. All was lost in the thunder of the drums and faded into the sunset that illuminated the prow of *The Sea Witch*.

CHAPTER XXXV

The scratching of sand on lathes accompanied the chants of the slaves as they scraped the deck. N'Gio did not sing. He simply moved his lips from time to time to avoid the sailor's kick.

The sand cut painfully into his tense palms as they clutched the piece of wood he used for the scraping process. It was the same every day. He was luckier than his friend Bokou, who was sent every day to clean between decks and to empty the bowls full of excrement.

Gregory toured the decks and the large hold. The planks had whitened from continuous scrubbing. He knew it would be easier and faster with iron scrapers but he didn't dare put them in the hands of the slaves, for they could be used as murderous weapons.

N'Gio saw him stop in front of him and forced himself to join in the singing. The officer stared at him for a few moments and then resumed his tour of inspection. N'Gio waited until he was some distance away and then stopped singing and slowed down the pace he had accelerated while the officer watched. He felt even more naked and defenseless, for a few days ago they had shaved his hair after the daily bath. They shaved every hair on his body and cut his nails to the quick. They had done the same to the women he glimpsed from time to time, and he tried to imagine how Yawana would look without her hair.

Almost as though Vasco had guessed his thoughts, he came close to the young man, looked about to make sure that there was no white man in the vicinity, and almost without moving his lips, he muttered, "I'll come and see you this evening and give you news of your wife."

He slipped away before N'Gio could answer.

N'Gio was more and more disconcerted by the change in the half-breed's attitude. Before, Vasco had never lost an opportunity to hit him or kick him, and then suddenly, one day, he stopped. In fact, he even arranged for him to have less work and easier tasks. He couldn't understand what could have caused such an about-face. But knowing there would be news of Yawana that night swept all doubts to the wind. He wanted to know what she was doing, and how she was weathering these strange days on the ship. He was so happy that he began to sing with the others, and this time it was not merely to avoid the beatings.

The constant fine weather and steady wind made it possible for the slaves to be out on deck all day long and to keep the holds relatively clean and livable. The journey was not causing too much discomfort and Jonathan was pleased. He leaned over his map and plotted the ship's course, and then straightened up, and stretched comfortably. *The Sea Witch* was already past the halfway mark, and so far there had been no incident to interrupt the peace of the voyage, except that this morning MacLean had come to tell him that five blacks were sick with something or other, he didn't yet know quite what. The slaves seemed to have adapted to shipboard life. He himself watched to make sure that they were well fed and he had formally forbidden any brutality or whipping unless it was absolutely necessary.

"I'm convinced," MacLean said to him with admiration, "that you are among the rare few who adhere to the instructions given slavers."

"Well, don't have any illusions on that score," said Jonathan, almost as if he were afraid of being too careful in adhering to the rules. "I don't do it out of humanity. I have simply found that it would be stupid for me to damage the market value of my blacks by starving them and whipping them into a sullen stupor. Anyway, Doctor, it seems to me that you, too, take your duties seriously?"

The young doctor blushed. "Well," he stammered, "it just helps me to put into practice the things I've studied. And then, Captain, I do love my work, and it makes the long sea voyage seem shorter."

"I'm with you there," said Jonathan. "I, too, find it a long voyage. Don't say a word to anyone, but I've determined that this will be my last voyage."

"You're not going back to England, then?"

"No, Mr. MacLean, no."

Seeing the reserved expression on Jonathan's face, MacLean restrained himself from asking for more explanations. The man must have his reasons for not wanting to return to his homeland. There was nothing stopping the young doctor from going back home, but there was nothing to draw him there either, and he made a sudden decision.

"I think I'll do the same, Captain," he said suddenly. "There's sure to be less competition for me out there in New Orleans. Back home you need a lot of money to set up a doctor's shingle, but I guess folks are not so difficult in the New World."

The two men agreed to keep in touch once they had settled into their new lives.

The deck was scrubbed spotless and it was time for lunch.

With the monotony and regularity of the voyage, surveillance of the blacks, while not ostensibly relaxed, had somehow become less strict for the past few days. The prisoners seemed very calm. The sailors still watched over the slaves during their meals, but their fingers were no longer clenched on the guns they carried.

There was no fresh meat left. The only food now was salt cod and gruel, and since this was Sunday, N'Gio and his companions each received a tiny ration of brandy to supplement their food. The young man enjoyed the strong-tasting salt fish, the highly spiced gruel, and the alcohol that warmed his blood.

As soon as he had eaten, he took a packet of straw given to him by a sailor and began to fashion a hat, as he had been taught to do. He was anxious for the day to end. It was the first time that he longed to find himself chained in discomfort down in the hold. Vasco's promise to come and talk to him about Yawana made him impatient for the moment to come.

A few sailors stayed to keep guard and others left to get their meal. Pierre, helped by the inseparable Starboard and Larboard who followed him like twin shadows, handed out dried beef in a sauce, and lentils with lard.

"Say, old bird," grumbled one of the sailors after tasting the wine, "what are you serving there, vintage vinegar? It's already bad enough, thanks to all that water you put in it, but this time, it's revolting!"

A chorus of voices joined in and there was suddenly chaos. Protests poured in thick and fast.

"He's right . . . It's true . . . We've had enough of this . . . It's a disgrace . . . We're treated worse than those blacks . . ."

Pierre waved his chubby hands to quiet them.

"Listen to me, fellers," he said. "Now don't get annoyed. It's not my fault. I'll open another barrel."

But the new barrel he pierced had also turned sour. He tried a third, and found that none of the wine was drinkable.

He came back and announced the distressing news. There was nothing to be done, and since the sailors loved their cook, they calmed down and decided to make do with beer. Pierre then had the clever idea of fermenting the spoilt wine with bananas, oranges, and sugar.

Luckily for the officers, their wine was in bottles and couldn't spoil. Ardeen had turned up from some obscure corner for the Sunday meal and was sitting at the table with Jonathan. He rarely showed up there for meals. He said he had not yet recovered from his seasickness and preferred to stay in his cabin. Jonathan never tried to discover why, if this were true, the reverend spent so much of his time on the forecastle, where the ship's lurch was so much more pronounced. Had he done so, he might have observed that while Ardeen was drinking less, he was indulging another of his obsessions, and the sailors were shamelessly exploiting it.

They had bought three weak little Negresses who were too frail to pass MacLean's inspection, for some baubles, and stowed them away on board ship. The poor girls were hidden in the anchor pit and their owners only took them out of there to rent them out. Naturally, this was all done without the knowledge of any of the officers. There would have been hell to pay had any of them found out. Frank Ardeen descended to the pit on a regular basis.

Ardeen was the first to leave the table. Clark and Adams followed soon after, and Woolcomb joined them. Jonathan thought that they must be going to take a rest, unless they planned to send Vasco to get the women who bore their brands.

He lit his pipe, and Yawana slipped into his cabin. She was now free to come and go as she pleased as long as she didn't appear on deck when the slaves were out getting their airing. Pierre had taught her to sew, and she made herself dresses with odd bits of rag and fabric he managed to find for her. She seemed to do it quite well, judging from the long slender yellow tunic she was wearing.

Jonathan smiled at her.

"Here, Yawana, eat!" he said, pointing to the remains of the fine Sunday meal.

Yawana didn't wait to be asked twice. She fell on the food and cleaned off the plates. Jonathan poured her a glass of wine. He had to admit to himself that he found her company enjoyable and a fine weapon against loneliness. She could not wipe out the memory of Aurelia, but her singsong voice and her laugh comforted him. She asked question after question, and this insatiable desire to learn touched him deeply.

"Yawana want to smoke," she said, setting down her empty glass.

Jonathan held out his pipe. She took it and began to smoke gravely, her eyes on his.

He was so kind to her. His eyes shone with a gentle light. Sometimes as she watched, she saw a flicker of pain cross his face. He suffered somewhere, deep inside. As for Jonathan, he was becoming more and more attached to her delicate face and the gaze she so often fixed on him, which always seemed to hold a mute question. She was as disarming and delightful as a child.

A cabin boy came in to clear the table. Jonathan got up and went to the window, staring out to sea. Yawana joined him, and gave the pipe a few quick taps to empty out the ash.

"I want to take a rest," said Jonathan. "Do whatever you have to do."

Yawana sensed his sadness. She wanted to stay close to him, but she gave a deep sigh, and moved away, putting the pipe on his desk and picking up all his dirty linens for washing.

In the storeroom, Pierre gave her all she needed, and while she was scrubbing away at the clothes, her arms deep in soapy water, she, like N'Gio, let her fantasies go to the evening ahead. A sort of ritual had sprung up between her and Jonathan. Every evening after dinner, while the slaves danced for their exercise, Jonathan made love to her. The first time she had sought him almost unconsciously, but it was now a sort of communion that bound them together and they looked forward to it with ever-growing impatience.

Jonathan, stretched out on his bed, his eyes on the ceiling, was thinking of the same thing. Three lonely creatures were waiting eagerly for the end of the day. Yawana was the focus of both men's thoughts, N'Gio's tinted with anxiety, Jonathan's anticipating pleasure.

The young woman rinsed out the table linens several times and gave them to Starboard to hang up to dry. Then she washed herself carefully, and massaged herself well. She had barely dressed and returned to Jonathan's cabin, when the first notes rang out on deck.

She found Jonathan waiting for her. Seeing his bare chest in the twilight, her body was overcome by an intense wave of desire that seemed to deepen with their every encounter. At first, she had found it difficult to accustom herself to this large white body with its fishy smell, but now she loved it and desired it with all her being.

She stripped off her clothes and began to dance. She knew now how to control her movements and temper them with subtlety. She jerked spasmodically, or moved with calculated languor, watching Jonathan's eyes all the while for the fires she lit in him.

Jonathan played along with her and delayed the moment of taking her in his arms as long as possible, fascinated by the wild grace of her body. Her woman's instinct had taught her to prolong pleasure to the limits of the endurable, to the finest point of ecstasy.

So deep were Jonathan and Yawana in their own storm that they never heard the drums cease. At last, panting and exhausted, they lay on the bed together, their breathing gradually slowing down to normal. Yawana lifted herself on one elbow to look into Jonathan's face.

"Otangani," she said, using the word for "white man." She had never been able to pronounce "Jonathan." "Otangani, are white women like Yawana?"

Jonathan gave a muffled chuckle. "White women can't be like Yawana," he said, using her simplified sentence structure. "Yawana is black."

Yawana lay on her back, annoyed, and didn't say another word. Jonathan sat up and stroked her cheek. "But Yawana is a very pretty black girl, and she knows how to make love," he added.

She felt better, but a nameless sadness swept over her.

"One day," she said softly, "you will tell Yawana to go away, and she be very sad."

"Yes," said Jonathan gently, "one day I'll leave. A white man can't stay with a black woman."

Suddenly he felt angry, as much at himself as at her. "Now, be quiet," he said gruffly, "and don't talk of that again. Otherwise I'll send you back to the other women."

Then he fell asleep, and Yawana hardly dared move for fear of waking him.

As soon as everyone was asleep, Vasco took the lantern and hurried to the center of the hatchway. Nobody paid any particular attention; he went down every night to make a last tour of the holds.

N'Gio was waiting anxiously. He saw the hatch lift and a ladder appeared, followed by a beam of light. The light wavered its way to the corner where the N'Komi were housed, paused there a few moments, and then came toward him.

Vasco bent down and crawled to N'Gio. He clearly planned to keep his promise. At last N'Gio would know what was happening to Yawana.

The half-breed held the lantern up to N'Gio's face to make sure it was he, and then placed it on the floor. "Your wife, Yawana, is not unhappy," he whispered. "She is even very happy."

"Where is she?" asked N'Gio breathlessly. "Have you seen her? What is she doing?"

Vasco gave a silent laugh.

"She is the captain's woman."

"What are you saying?" cried N'Gio.

In his fury he tried to seize Vasco by the throat, but he forgot the low ceiling in the hold and banged his head brutally, then fell back to the floor.

"Calm yourself, N'Gio," Vasco said in a falsely soothing voice. "Aren't you happy to know that your wife is free, and well treated? Of course, she is absolutely obliged to fornicate with the white man, but don't you worry about that. The moans she gives are not moans of pain."

Destroyed by this information, N'Gio could not say a word.

"Well?" asked Vasco with heavy sarcasm. "Don't you even thank me? I promised you news of your wife, didn't I? I'm your friend, you know."

For some time he stared at N'Gio, a nasty smile on his

face, but the young man sat with his head in his hands, saying nothing. Vasco left. Soon after, he climbed the ladder and closed the hatch behind him.

N'Gio sat in the dark. Huge tears ran silently down his cheeks. He would have preferred that his wife share the fate of the other women prisoners than to know that she was taking pleasure in the arms of a white monster. His mind balked at it, it couldn't be true; Vasco must surely have lied in order to hurt his spirit since he had ceased to hurt him physically. All the same, the thought of Yawana naked, making love to the white man, loomed larger than any other. A wild rage grew in him then, a rage that tasted of blood and bitterness.

Vasco settled the hatch back in place. The ship was still. The sails stood pale against the starry sky. He hurried to his sleeping quarters in the forecastle. He could hear Ardeen's groans and grunts and the girl's moans. He would dearly have liked to use one of the little Negresses from time to time himself, but since that was out of the question, he crept in and watched the reverend at his games. He always enjoyed seeing how he handled the young girls.

By the time he went to bed, he was feeling very pleased with himself. N'Gio had reacted exactly as he had hoped. He had easily sown the seeds of hatred in his heart and he planned to reap them. There hadn't been any problem with King Nkougou's son and the other N'Komi, but he needed the support of others too, and he needed N'Gio on his side. Soon, he would be master of the ship, and then Yawana, with all her airs and graces, would have no choice but to submit to his lust.

CHAPTER XXXVI

Its belly plunging through the foam, the ship looked like a huge bird settling into a down-filled nest. So far, *The Sea Witch* hadn't crossed any other ship on her path, and except for a few minor skirmishes that exhaustion and close quarters had provoked among the crew, she was steadily heading for her goal, majestic and imperturbable.

Jonathan left his desk just as MacLean came to the door asking to see him.

"Two slaves died from dysentery this morning," he announced grimly.

"Couldn't you save them?" asked Jonathan.

"No, sir, I tried everything. Nothing worked."

"Bloody nuisance," Jonathan grumbled. "What about the others? Are they all right?"

"Yes, I got them out of it. I fed them banana and salt cod broth with a good dose of pepper, and their pains stopped."

"Well, we must throw the dead out to sea as soon as possible," Jonathan said. "I don't want an epidemic."

"I've already given the order, sir," MacLean replied.

"Let's go and see about it." The two men left, Jonathan still barefoot in his trousers, with no shirt. They reached the deck just as the two bodies arrived, carried by a group of blacks.

"See that?" exclaimed MacLean, pointing to sharp black fins cutting the water beside the ship. "You'd think they can smell it, wouldn't you? They've been following us for two days."

"I know," said Jonathan. "Well, it won't do any harm. It'll show the blacks what will happen to them if they try to jump overboard."

Woolcomb was hurrying the men. The two bodies were freed of their chains and pushed overboard. N'Gio had been one of the blacks carrying his unfortunate companions, and he saw the sharks leap for their prey. There was a revolting mess of foam and blood and soon there was nothing left in the wake of the ship but a faint red stain. Jonathan told MacLean to be sure to have all those who had come in contact with the corpses thoroughly washed, then he went back to his cabin.

Yawana was leaning against one of the windows, gazing at the horizon. For the past few days she had seemed sad. It was probably the enforced captivity and the knowledge that her homeland was fading further and further with each passing day. But Jonathan didn't like to see her depressed.

"You'd better get on with cleaning up my cabin instead of dreaming," he said bruskly. He was upset at the loss of his two slaves.

Yawana turned, and he saw that her eyes were filled with tears.

"What's wrong?" he said, his voice softening. "Are you sad?"

Yawana shook her head. "No, Otangani," she said. "Yawana not sad. Yawana is happy with you."

"Good," he said, reverting to his gruff tone. "Then if you're not sad, get busy. Go on with you! Get to work! I want to see this cabin spotless when I get back."

"Yes, Otangani," she said listlessly.

Jonathan left, and Yawana started to put the place in order. She really enjoyed the work. What Jonathan had assumed was sadness was in fact something quite different. Yawana was merely upset by the certainty that she was with child. She had had her suspicions for a few days, but now that the full moon was past she had no doubts. Also, she knew it could only be the white's man's child. During the long stop in São Tomé, she had realized with joy that she was not pregnant. After the repeated brutal rapes she had endured, she would not have known if her child were N'Gio's or not. And she wanted N'Gio's child, and only his. On this strange day she was no longer sure whether she should weep or rejoice over what was happening to her.

Vasco came in for her daily English lesson and her time for dreaming was over. He closed the door and leaned against it with a look of vicious triumph. As he did every day, he stared at her with an insolent lust that made her shudder with disgust.

"I saw N'Gio," he said at last, in her language. "He is well. I talked to him of you."

His tone was such that Yawana said defensively, "And what did you tell him?"

Vasco sneered. "Nothing much. I told him you were well."

Yawana gave a sigh of relief.

"Yes," continued Vasco slowly, "I told him you were very well and that you fornicated with the captain every night."

He watched for her reaction with half-closed eyes.

Yawana went rigid. "You are more poisonous than a spider crab." She spat at him in a wild rage. "Why did you do that?"

Vasco assumed an innocent air.

"I can't really remember why," he said. "I thought it was the right thing to do. I wanted him to know that you were not mistreated like the other women."

Yawana was desperate. If N'Gio lost faith in her, what had he left to sustain him in his pain?

"You're revolting," she said at last. "What will become of him now? I'll never dare to see him again."

Vasco giggled nervously. "Yes," he said, "to tell the truth, he was furious."

"What shall I do?" Yawana whispered to herself. She turned on Vasco: "Go and tell him that it isn't true, that you lied."

"Too late," he said dryly. "But he will forgive you on one condition."

"Tell me," she said, beginning to cry.

"Come, come, it's not so bad," Vasco said in a falsely reassuring tone. "If you do as I tell you everything will be all right." He lowered his voice. "Every evening I go down to see the prisoners and when I come back up I must remove the ladder. Tomorrow evening I'll do as usual, but I will not remove the ladder. In the meantime I shall free N'Gio and the rest and they will be able to come out. But we need weapons, and your husband is counting on you to help us. The captain wears a key on his belt. It's the key to the armory. You will steal it from him while he sleeps. I'll be waiting outside the door and you will give it to me. That's all I ask of you. We'll see to the rest." His tone grew threatening. "It's in your interest to obey me, or you can be sure that N'Gio will kill you sooner or later."

Yawana was sure he was mad, for how could they possibly win against the white men? And even if they won, who would be able to guide this enormous vessel? They would all be lost forever on this endless lake. Furthermore, she distrusted the man intensely, and some instinct warned her that N'Gio would not come out of this alive. It seemed wiser to play along with his game, however, so she answered in a deceptively submissive tone, "I'll do as you say."

She had enough good sense to grasp the situation much more clearly than Vasco himself. His plan was doomed to failure. He'd decided to revolt when he saw the half-breeds in São Tomé in positions of power and responsibility. He wondered why he himself could not do the same. It would be better to turn around and go back to Africa than to sail to the end of this miserable voyage and be given a dismal job. They might even sell him. He could kill Gomes and take his place, and that would give him power.

His plan seemed incredibly simple to him. He hadn't told Yawana the whole truth. He was indeed planning to go down to the holds and free N'Gio and the N'Komi, and then he planned to take an axe he had managed to hide from the sailors from under his mattress, and kill the two men on the night watch. Next, with the key he wanted from Yawana, he planned to give out arms to his accomplices who would catch the crew by surprise and kill them all. Once the ship was under his command, the rest of the prisoners would be thrown into the sea, and N'Gio with them, so that he could have Yawana all to himself. It would be child's play, he thought, to get the ship back to Africa. He had seen how to steer it. All he had to do was glance at a small bronze box every now and then, and an arrow would tell him where to go, and then he could point the ship in that direction. The sails were all set, so it would be easy to turn around and sail for Africa.

He left the young woman, sure that she was sufficiently in his power to do his bidding. Yawana wept when he left. She wept for N'Gio, for her captive friends, for the baby in her womb, and a little for herself. Then she pulled herself together.

The more she thought of it, the more Vasco's plan seemed absurd. Even if there was a chance that it might work, in view of Vasco's untrustworthiness, what would become of her and of N'Gio? They would undoubtedly fall into the hands of other cruel greedy people before they could make their way back to their village. From what she had seen of the way her friends were being treated on board ship, even though they hardly lived comfortably, as she did, there was no comparison with the way they had been treated by their own race. They were no longer tortured, or murdered, or constantly raped. Anyway, it seemed obvious that Vasco was playing a double game. Why should he suddenly want to free them all when he had always taken pleasure in beating them down?

All that day she was tortured by questions, and when the drums began to beat for the evening dance, she made her decision.

Jonathan was surprised to find her standing motionless, as though immune to the rhythms that usually moved her so deeply.

"What is it, Yawana?" he asked. "Why don't you dance?"

"No, Otangani, Yawana won't dance. Yawana worried," she said. Jonathan was alarmed at her tone and questioned her teasingly. "Well, well! Fancy that, now! Yawana worried, is she? Why are you worried?"

Suddenly Yawana saw clearly her real reasons for wanting Vasco's plan to fail. She loved Jonathan. She didn't want anything to happen to him. She didn't want him killed. She stared at him intently, amazed at the feelings she had just discovered in herself.

"Yawana is afraid for you," she said. "Vasco is bad. Very bad. Vasco wants to kill all the white men and take your boat."

Jonathan suddenly realized that she was serious.

"When does Vasco want to do this?" he asked, his voice hard.

"The night after this night. Vasco tell me, 'Take the key from the captain. The key for the weapons.'"

Jonathan's hand flew straight to the ring of keys on his belt. His sea-chest keys were there, and the keys to the armory and the munitions storeroom. Only Gregory had duplicates of those keys. He looked at Yawana, all coldness gone from his eyes. She had never seen such tenderness in them. He was wondering why she had warned him. She was only a slave, and he had never hidden from her that this was how he considered her, and that the circumstances

that bound them together would end. She knew he would
sell her one day, as he would the others. Why had she
saved his life and the lives of his crew? He laid his hands
on her shoulders, his face grave. "Thank you, little Yawana," he said in an infinitely gentle voice. "I shall never
forget what you've just done. We'll settle this affair, and
then I promise you that your husband will get better treatment. You must pretend to obey Vasco. I'll give you a key
for him tomorrow night. Don't worry about me anymore."

Yawana hadn't understood it all but she sensed a change
in him. She gave him an odd look and tore off her clothes.
"Otangani, take Yawana. Now," she said. Her tone was
beseeching, but there was a thread of imperiousness running through it. She sounded almost desperate. Jonathan
bent down and picked her up. He carried her to the bed.
The throb of the drums seemed to fill the room. They
stayed together a long time, Yawana clutching him in painful torment, cries of pleasure mixing with her sobs. She
thanked Jonathan in her soul for what he had given her
and begged N'Gio's forgiveness for the intense pleasure it
gave her.

The next day, Vasco came to see her and repeated his
instructions.

"I saw N'Gio," he said. "He knows now what you will
do to save us all. He told me to tell you that he forgives
everything."

It was clearly a lie. He had managed to speak to N'Gio,
but only to tell him that they would carry out the plan that
night and that he would have the opportunity of killing the
captain with his own hands.

"Don't worry," she said. "I want to be free, too, Vasco.
I'll give you the key this evening. He'll never notice. I
know just what to do to make him sleep."

Vasco sneered and cast a possessive look at her. "Very
good, Yawana," he said. "I see you've understood. You're
a real chief's daughter."

In the afternoon Jonathan called his officers to his cabin
and told them what he had learned. "As I feared from the
start, gentlemen," he said, his brow furrowed with anxiety,
"there is a slave revolt brewing for tonight. I didn't warn
you sooner because I didn't want those responsible to know
that we're aware of it." With a nod in Yawana's direction,
he added, "she's the one who tipped me off, luckily for us.

From what she tells me, Vasco has masterminded the whole affair. She couldn't give me any details but it's easy to guess at what he plans. He'll free some of the males, try to get at the guns, and kill us all. More wine, anyone?"

Woolcomb filled the glasses and Jonathan sipped his wine thoughtfully.

"Now, gentlemen," he said after a brief pause, "here's what we're going to do. First, it's imperative that Vasco suspect nothing. As soon as the slaves are taken down for the night, I want you, Woolcomb, to deploy your sailors on the quarterdeck and the bridge, hidden in the longboats. Gregory, you and your men hide behind the handrail. As for you, Clark, I want you to see that there are men posted all around the powder and armory storage rooms."

He paced up and down the cabin.

"These are simple precautions," he added. "But we'd better be careful, since we don't know exactly what they have in mind. I'm sure that Vasco will make his move when he goes down, as usual, for his final tour of inspection in the holds. As soon as he reaches the quarterdeck, jump him, chain him well, and tie him to the mainmast. We'll take care of him at daybreak."

He had barely finished talking when a sudden concert of howls and exclamations came to their ears, followed almost immediately by gunshots. Jonathan and the officers sprang from the cabin as one man, leaving Yawana beside herself with fear and worry.

Neither Jonathan nor Vasco had anticipated that there might be a third individual with plans of his own. The son of King Nkougou of the N'Komi, mad with rage at having been captured as a slave, had decided to take matters into his own hands and started the revolt with his tribesmen, without waiting for Vasco's help.

As always, the crew were gathered on deck, but they weren't paying much attention, since the slaves' behavior was usually so calm. They were taken completely by surprise. Pierre, with Starboard and Larboard at his elbows, had already served some of the slaves with soup. He dipped his ladle into the cauldron and unconcernedly poured some into the bowl of the N'Komi who stood in front of him. As soon as the bowl was full, the man flung the boiling liquid into Pierre's face. His hands covering his cheeks, Pierre staggered away. Without wasting a second the N'Komi was

upon him, snatching the knife from his belt and stabbing
him repeatedly in the stomach. Pierre gave a dreadful
shriek and crumpled in a torrent of blood.

The savage murder was so swift that the amazed sailors
didn't react fast enough. Seeing their bewilderment, the
N'Komi sprang for them and grabbed their guns. Starboard
and Larboard fled, shrieking in terror.

Using their chains as weapons, the slaves cracked the
heads of two sailors. Vasco was furious to see the situation
pass beyond his control, but he flung himself into the fray
anyway. The gunnery crew rushed to the fore to prepare
the cannons for firing, and the men at the capstan abandoned their posts in a panic. Others rushed to the quarterdeck for safety, and that's where they met their officers,
running out of the captain's cabin.

"You pack of grisly cowards," yelled Jonathan. "Get to
your posts!" He brandished his pistol. "I'll kill the first
man who retreats," he shouted.

His officers followed suit and the sailors turned back to
the fight. With the clear orders they received from Jonathan and Gregory they were soon in control. Steady gunfire
pushed back the attackers. Sailors climbed into the rigging
and fired above the slaves' heads. Some of them, like
N'Gio, had not taken part in the uprising. They lay head
down on the deck. N'Gio huddled against the taffrail and
didn't move a muscle.

The gunshots died down and the rebels were soon forced
into a tight group. Nkougou's son, seeing that there was no
hope left, leapt onto the bulwark and jumped into the sea,
dragging his chainmate with him. They sank at once.

Sailors were milling about everywhere. Vasco saw that
he was lost, but he was too much of a coward to attempt
suicide, so he ran in circles, not knowing where to go. A
blow on the head knocked him out and he was dragged
away with the rebellious N'Komi. Seeing their chief dead,
the N'Komi were rolling about the deck, beseeching the
sailors to have pity on them. The sailors were far from gentle. Their fright pushed them to brutality and Woolcomb
had to intervene to prevent a full-scale massacre.

At last the ship calmed down. It had been a brief turmoil, but it cost six lives among the slaves and four from
the crew. Two had been killed at the beginning, then one
had been strangled and another's throat had been slit. As

for Pierre, they carried him to the galley, but in spite of all MacLean's efforts they were unable to bring him back to life. The two little mulattoes who adored him watched it all without understanding that they had lost their best friend, possibly the best friend they would ever have.

Jonathan stared bitterly at the mess on deck. Cauldrons had been upturned in the melee and the soup was everywhere, mixing with the blood of the dead and dying. He was furious that his crew had allowed themselves to be taken by surprise. Many had displayed unpardonable cowardice, which could have caused disaster for them all. He swore to take action once the worst was over.

"Gregory," he called, "separate the rebels from the ones who didn't try to rebel, and take them down into the hold. I want them bowed down with chains."

Gregory barked out some orders and the sailors, delighted to show some zeal after their abysmal behavior, hurried to obey.

"What shall we do with Vasco?" asked Gregory.

"Tie him up solidly," said Jonathan angrily. "We'll get to him soon enough. But now get that deck cleaned up and throw the Negroes' corpses to the sharks."

Prodded by the sailors, N'Gio and his companions quickly cleared up all signs of the fight.

The four dead sailors lay forward, sewn into sailcloth. Jonathan had wanted to proceed at once with the funeral, but the chaplain was dead drunk. Even the noise of the mutiny hadn't awakened him. Since he wanted to give the sailors a Christian burial, Jonathan put the funeral off till the following day, hoping that by then Ardeen would be in a fit state to officiate.

"Bring Vasco, and let's get it over with," Jonathan said. "I want all the slaves to be present at his execution."

Clark lined up all the blacks and Vasco was dragged to where Jonathan stood. Hung about with chains, he had regained consciousness. One of his eyes was half closed from a blow in the face and blood dribbled from his mouth. He had lost all his brashness. He knew well what awaited him, but he still hoped somehow to avoid it.

The sailors hurled him roughly at Jonathan's feet.

"Forgive me, sir! Forgive me, Mr. Captain," he wept.

"Vasco," Jonathan said coldly, "you are guilty of mutiny and murder."

"Oh no! No, Mr. Captain. Vasco just wanted to kill the filthy blacks that murdered the cook. He never wanted to do the white men any harm."

Jonathan didn't believe a word of it but he wanted to be fair. He turned and asked, "Did anyone see Vasco fight against the blacks?"

"It's not true," said one of the sailors indignantly. "He's the one who killed Martin. He slit his throat with a knife."

"You see?" said Jonathan to Vasco.

"No, Mr. White Man," sobbed Vasco, clutching at Jonathan's feet. "No. Vasco never did that. Vasco loves the whites."

"Sure," Jonathan said sarcastically. "That's not quite what Yawana told me. You told her to get my key from me so that you could get weapons, only your plan misfired. Your accomplices couldn't wait."

Faced with Yawana's betrayal, Vasco realized that he could do nothing to save himself. He began to wail in despair. Jonathan hardened his heart and meted out the sentence.

"Vasco," he said gravely, "you will be hanged for the crimes you have committed." He laid an hourglass on the floor and added, "When the sand has run out, you will be executed."

Death seemed a certainty, but Vasco tried again.

"Mr. White Man, I beg you, don't kill Vasco. Vasco would make a good slave. You can sell Vasco for much money. It would be a waste to take his life."

Jonathan found it quite a convincing argument. It was true that Vasco would probably fetch a good price, and it might be a pity to kill him in the circumstances. But his crime was too serious, and he had to be an example to the others. If his life were spared it would only encourage another revolt.

Vasco began to hope again as he saw Jonathan hesitating. "Have pity, Mr. White Man," he cried. "Vasco does not want to die!"

But Jonathan's face had hardened. He was staring at the sand running through the hourglass. The half-breed realized at last that there was nothing more to be done. His eyes wide with terror, he too stared at the sand in the glass. He didn't even react when a sailor came up behind him and slipped a rope under his arms.

N'Gio was watching all this without quite understanding what was taking place. When Vasco had come to him and assured him of his freedom if he killed the captain, and told him that he would have Yawana back, he had accepted at once. But now that he saw how badly everything had turned out he was glad that he had not taken part in the revolt after all. As the last grain of sand trickled through the hourglass, Jonathan signaled to the sailors.

"Now!" he said.

Vasco was paralyzed with fear and the sailors had to carry him to the front. They slipped the rope through a pulley and quickly hauled him up the yardarm of the foremast. When he saw how high he was, Vasco began to wriggle and scream, his eyes rolling madly.

Gregory got together ten sailors in a semicircle at the foot of the mast. By now Vasco had screamed so much that only the faintest of cries came from his open mouth. The men loaded their guns, took aim, and at Gregory's terse command, fired. Riddled with bullets, the half-breed's body jerked and was suddenly still, swinging from the rope like a puppet. The sailors hauled down the corpse and threw it to sea at once.

"Well, I hope that made them think a bit," Jonathan said as Gregory came forward. "Have them taken below again. They'll have to manage without dinner since they knocked over their soup. We'll leave them below decks all day tomorrow. That should calm them down."

"I'll just keep a few up here to scrub the deck," said Gregory.

Jonathan pointed to N'Gio.

"See that big Negro over there? That's Yawana's husband. He had nothing to do with the revolt. Take him back down and give him something to eat. I want him treated very well."

When N'Gio saw that he was being separated from the others he thought he would also be killed, so he was most surprised when he was led to the galley and given a copious meal.

Jonathan gathered all the crew below the bridge. He went up and leaned on the rail, and addressed the men in a firm voice.

"Now you see where your stupid negligence has led us," he said. "Where do you think you are?"

Ashamed, the men lowered their heads and those in the front row turned to face their comrades rather than meet Jonathan's stern eye.

"What's more," Jonathan continued, "I noticed that several of you ran like rabbits. Your cowardice cost the lives of four of your comrades, and our cook, Pierre. I shall not punish any of you this time, but I shall not again tolerate such carelessness and cowardice. Have I made myself clear? Very well. Break up now."

The men dispersed silently and went back to their posts.

"Double the guard tonight," said Jonathan to Gregory, "and I want armed men in the holds."

He strode back to his cabin. Yawana greeted him joyfully. Throughout the explosions and chaos of the fight she had stayed close in the cabin, torn with desperate anxiety for N'Gio and for Jonathan, the two beings she loved in such different ways.

"Pierre is dead," said Jonathan dully. "One of the N'Komi murdered him."

The girl felt a huge sadness take possession of her. Pierre was the first person to give her a few moments of happiness since her capture. He was so kind to her. He always treated her like a human being.

"Vasco paid for his treachery," continued Jonathan.

But this death of a man she despised and hated left her indifferent. She was about to ask for news of N'Gio, but Jonathan spoke first.

"Your husband will be well treated now, Yawana," he said. "He won't stay with the others any longer. If you like, you can see him once a day."

He knew that in saying this he was depriving himself of the young woman's company, and although his heart was heavy, he felt he owed her that, at least. Perhaps Yawana sensed his sadness. She turned her head away and gazed out to sea.

"Don't you want to see your husband?" asked Jonathan. He was surprised to feel a sliver of joy piercing his heart.

Yawana gazed so deeply into his eyes that he could hardly bear it.

"No," she said at last. "Yawana not want to see N'Gio." Her voice was faint and breathless. "Not now. Not on your ship. Later."

"Whatever you like," he said.

Then she slowly slid into a small heap at his feet. She clasped her arms about his legs and rested her cheek on them. It was almost impossible to bear so much joy and so much sorrow, all at the same time. Her shoulders shook and she sobbed convulsively.

CHAPTER XXXVII

It was as if the revolt had been a prelude to a period of calamity, for a violent storm struck *The Sea Witch* the next day.

It lasted three days, and during those three days the ship was tossed about the ocean like a cork. There was no question of emptying the toilets. The ventilation shafts were kept closed all the time, but huge waves of sea water came in all the same. It was a dreadful torture for the slaves, chained in the holds, lying in a revolting mixture of salt water and excrement. The stench was beyond belief, and their wounds, caused by rusty chains, burned and swelled from the salt in the water. Food was scarce.

The second day, a gust of wind stronger than the rest broke a yardarm which fell on a sailor's leg and crushed it. MacLean had to amputate to prevent gangrene, but in spite of his cauterization of the wound with a red-hot iron, it became infected and the man died the next day.

Then, suddenly, calm returned to the ship, and it continued for the rest of the voyage.

A good strong wind sent the ship speeding on her way and as soon as the mess left by the storm had been repaired, life on board resumed its careful routine.

The slaves had been afflicted by dreadful bouts of seasickness. Their failed revolt seemed to have finally resigned them to their fate.

N'Gio was free to come and go on the decks and was chained only at night, in a small alcove in the forecastle. He now ate the same food as the sailors and helped them in their tasks. His extraordinary strength amazed everyone. He spoke little, and was very docile and amenable.

He wasn't quite sure why he was getting this new treatment, but suspected that Yawana was at the bottom of it. He didn't blame her anymore. On the contrary, he had managed to convince himself that she was better off with the white man than suffering the same dreadful rigors of the voyage as the other black women. He still suffered over his inability to see her, and his suffering would have been

immeasurably greater had he known that she herself refused to see him. He wondered if they would ever be together again. He enjoyed the tasks he was given. They
helped him to forget his gloomy thoughts, but at night,
alone and in chains, the last weeks of his life played before
him remorselessly. He kept seeing the unbearable moments
when Yawana was repeatedly raped before his very eyes,
every detail forever burned in his memory. When he remembered his physical response to the scene, which he had
been unable to control, he was tortured with remorse and
shame. The most painful memory was of the moment when
the vile thieves had taken advantage of his state and tied
Yawana, panting and almost unconscious, to him. He relived the night they spent in that humiliating state, taunted
by their captors. It was the last night they ever spent so
close to one another. His depression became so severe with
these memories that he wanted to die.

Yawana caught a glimpse of N'Gio once, when she was
on the bridge during the day. She hid quickly so that he
would not see her. She could have run toward him and
thrown herself into his arms, but something stopped her.
She knew she would never be able to confront him as long
as she was on the ship, because she knew that if she did, all
would be over between her and Jonathan and she wanted
to delay that painful moment as long as she could. She
wanted to be near the father of the child growing in her
womb, whose existence he would never know about. She
never quite dared to admit to herself that besides the love
she bore the captain, she felt an immense gratitude toward
him for having treated her so well. By his behavior when
they were together in bed, he had somehow purified her
body of the dreadful degradation of the rapes she had been
forced to endure.

Jonathan now let her live in his cabin with him. Perhaps
he needed the company after Pierre's death. The Frenchman had left a great emptiness and the young man who
replaced him in the kitchen was no substitute, although he
did his best. As for Starboard and Larboard, they had got
over their grief, and the new cook had to contend with
their mischievous pranks.

The crew never complained about the stringent discipline Gregory now enforced on board ship. He ordered maneuvers every day and shooting practice on empty bottles

thrown out to sea. Ardeen was plunged into a permanent state of apathy and only rarely appeared on deck. No one took any notice of him.

Almost four months had gone by since *The Sea Witch* had left the coast of Africa. Jonathan calculated that they would soon see the Islands and planned to berth there for as long as it took to stock up on fresh food and water. If the wind held, it could be only a matter of days now.

As if to confirm his conclusions, MacLean came into his cabin one morning, eyes gleaming with excitement.

"Sir! Sir!" he shouted. "Come and see! Birds! We can't be far from land."

Jonathan stepped out on the bridge and saw large white birds, undoubtedly some species of gull, gliding above the ship to the accompaniment of cheers from the sailors, some of the more practical-minded of whom had already set up traps to catch some.

"Well, that's excellent news!" exclaimed Jonathan. He leaned over the rail and called for Gregory. The first mate raised his head. "Yes, sir?"

"Gregory, we must celebrate. Have a ration of brandy passed around to the men."

A redoubled cheer greeted this remark. N'Gio reflected that these birds must be of good omen for the whites to greet them so enthusiastically.

The sailors managed to catch about a dozen birds. The flesh was very tough and tasted very fishy but it was a change from salt cod. The birds raised their morale. Soon they would go ashore. All that day and the next they were in good spirits and went about their tasks with renewed vigor.

A few days later, the sailor in the mast stared intently at a speck on the horizon. "Ship ahoy, to starboard!" he shouted.

Gregory grabbed his spyglass, but the ship in question was too far for him to distinguish its nationality. It was probably a merchant vessel. Nothing more natural or less worrisome, since they were now approaching the coast. Nonetheless, he thought it wise to warn Jonathan. The captain was of the same mind and the two men forgot about it.

Jonathan didn't tell Yawana that the end of the voyage was drawing near. Unconsciously, he must have sensed how much pain this would give her. After all, he thought, a captain of a slaver should not have to worry about the feelings of a Negress.

Next day, Gregory came to find Jonathan. He was worried.

"It's strange, sir," he said. "But the ship seems to have drawn much closer during the night. I would almost say it's following us."

"Let's take a look," said Jonathan. "I'll meet you on the bridge."

He pulled on his boots and left the cabin.

"See for yourself, sir," said Gregory, handing him the spyglass. "She's still about three miles away, but she must be pretty fast to have caught up that much."

Jonathan put the spyglass to his eye. The sun was low on the horizon and he couldn't see too well. Nonetheless, he was able to make out that the ship was a three-master. He put down the spyglass and nervously snapped it shut.

"Doesn't mean a thing, Gregory," he said. "She's just on the same course we are. Let me know if she gets any closer."

The sailors were leaning on the rails making comments about the other ship. It was the first one they'd seen for quite a while.

The slaves were brought up on deck and washed, and then put to their usual scrubbing tasks.

By midday, the strange ship was much closer. Without knowing why, Gregory was much less relaxed about it than Jonathan. Without telling Jonathan of his fears, he called Clark.

"I want you to get your gun crew ready and set them to doing combat maneuvers," he said. "That ship behind us may be perfectly inoffensive, but I'd rather we were ready for anything. Tell your men it's just a maneuver. We don't want to alarm the rest of the crew."

"You can count on me, sir," said Clark smartly, his whistle already at his lips.

Gregory hurried off to find Jonathan.

"That ship's pretty close now, sir," he said. "We should be able to identify her."

"You look worried, Gregory."

"Yessir!"

"Bah!" exclaimed Jonathan. "It would be far stranger if we were alone in these seas!"

The two officers came out on the maindeck where the women prisoners were eating their meal, their children playing about their feet. The laughter and conversation ceased as the two officers came up.

Jonathan leaned against the rail and pointed the spyglass at the other ship, adjusting it to get a clearer view. He swept the deck from stem to stern. There was no officer on the bridge, but it was lunchtime. He was probably eating. One man was at the wheel. Everything looked very calm and normal. The weather was so pleasant that it was likely that most of the crew was off somewhere taking a well-earned nap. His spyglass came to rest on the flagstaff and he smiled. It ran the Union Jack.

It was as he had thought, a merchant vessel probably, and an English one to boot. Perhaps it would bring fresh tidings from Britain. Jonathan began to look forward to the meeting he would probably have with the captain. He was just about to tell Gregory to give the order to heave and wait for the encounter when a glint of something metal caught his eye. He looked close and noticed that the portholes were slightly raised, which was unusual on a merchant vessel in full sail. He swept the deck again with the spyglass and then noticed men hidden in numbers behind the rails. They were very well hidden, but one had been careless enough to let the tip of his gun show.

Jonathan swore through clenched teeth.

"By God, I think you're right, Gregory!" he muttered. "It's sporting the Union Jack, but I'd be very surprised if she's one of ours. Clear the decks for action and alert the men."

He spoke in a low murmur, as though afraid of being overheard by the pursuers. "Have all the men at their posts double quick and get those slaves below decks at once. Load the cannons and muskets and put us under full sail. We must do everything we can to avoid being boarded."

Suddenly The Sea Witch became a hive of noise and activity as the sailors ran for their battle positions and the slaves were pushed unceremoniously back into the holds.

Gregory was pleased that he had already warned Clark, for the portholes slid open at once and the cannons squeaked into position on their wooden wheels.

Someone on the other ship must have been watching The Sea Witch, and seeing the agitation, concluded that the ruse was over, for the British flag came tumbling down the staff and the Spanish flag rose in its stead.

Jonathan ran past the galley. He paused a minute to tell the young cook to take Starboard, Larboard, and Yawana down to shelter.

N'Gio was in a panic at the sudden tension and chaos. He was sure that something very serious was happening and he ran to the foredeck to hide. Just as he was about to climb into his alcove, he bumped into Ardeen, bumbling along to see what all the fuss was about. He was hastily fumbling with his trousers.

"Take shelter, Reverend!" shouted a sailor. "There's going to be some fireworks any minute and we need you to save us all from Hell."

Courage was not Ardeen's most developed virtue. He turned at once and hid in the safest place he could find.

Yawana, dragged by the young cook, found herself in a dark room that smelled of rope and pitch. The two young mulatto boys clung to her skirts. The sailor told them not to move from there whatever happened, and left them to go up on deck. Yawana tried to comfort the children, but was terrified herself.

It all looked more dangerous than anything else they had experienced so far. These white men suddenly looked terribly fierce. She began to tremble along with the two little boys, wondering if she would ever get free of the constant threat of violent death for herself and those she loved.

On deck, Woolcomb was distributing powder and shot. Jonathan, his spyglass glued to his eye, was watching the maneuvers of the other ship as it approached. He could now almost distinguish the men's features as they lined the rails, no longer trying to hide their intent, grappling hooks at the ready.

"That's a fine band of ruffians there," he said to Gregory angrily. "They're all ready to board us any minute."

"We must avoid that at all costs, sir," said Gregory. "If they get their grappling hooks on us we won't be able to hold out long with the men we have."

Jonathan ran a critical eye over his assembled crew. It was not a reassuring sight. They looked fierce enough, but somehow he felt their hearts were not in it. He thought of their inglorious behavior at the time of the slave revolt and knew that a confrontation would mean a bloody massacre.

"You're right," he admitted ruefully, "they'll give themselves up at once, given half a chance. They could even kill us if they thought it would help them save their own skins."

"The only ones we can count on are Clark's gunnery crew," continued Gregory. "They're professional soldiers and quite a different caliber from the rest."

The Spanish vessel was getting closer and closer. It was going to be difficult to keep out of her line of fire. Jonathan could only think of one way of maintaining control over the situation.

"Tell Clark to come here on the double," he said to Gregory.

The first mate hurried to the gundeck, where he found Clark well organized and comfortable in his own domain. The fuses were lit, the cartridge paper was rolled and ready beside the guns, and a few goats still tied to the stanchions bleated noisily.

"Captain wants to see you on the double, Clark," said Gregory.

In a few seconds the officer stood in front of Jonathan.

"Clark, it's going to be a quick one, and I won't have time to tell you what to do, so I want it all straight now," Jonathan said tersely. "In a few moments we'll turn about to larboard to cut off her path. Bear in mind that we'll take a twenty-degree turn, and set your guns to shoot down her masts and prevent her from maneuvering. Shoot as soon as you sight your target. We will then turn about again to starboard and when you sight her again, send some fire into her front storeholds. If you make your mark, that should stop her dead. If not, God be with us!"

"I'll lay my bets on my gun crew," said Clark, smiling. "When will we begin?"

Jonathan glanced at the distance separating the two ships.

"When there's nothing but a cable-length between us," he said, "and that doesn't give us much time!"

"Aye aye, sir!" said Clark. "I'll be ready."

He turned on his heel at once and hurried back to the gundeck to set the sights at the necessary angle.

Jonathan leaned against the bridge rail. Woolcomb had stationed men all along the larboard rail in the shrouds on the same side. He took his speaking tube and shouted into it, knowing that the wind would not carry his orders to the enemy vessel. "We're going to turn to larboard. Shoot anything that moves and aim well. Recharge your weapons immediately and turn them to starboard to do the same again. Got it, all of you? Try to be accurate and we needn't fear a boarding."

The men seemed comforted by this promise, and with satisfaction, Jonathan saw them hold their arms with more confidence as the moment for using them approached. Perhaps they'd make good fighting men yet, he thought to himself.

There wasn't a second to lose. He went close to the two men at the wheel and watched tensely as he tried to help them effect an accurate, rapid turn. He would have to be alert to the exact right moment, for the slightest error in judgment would be fatal. If it were too soon, the enemy would be able to try the same maneuver and put *The Sea Witch* in open danger of her guns, or come up behind and cut her off. If it were too late, they risked being rammed. ·

Gregory lifted his speaking tube to his mouth and waited for the captain's signal. Shouts of victory were already ringing from the decks of the enemy ship.

"Make your turn," shouted Jonathan.

"Haul in the square sheets and unfurl the mainsail," shouted Gregory.

"Starboard all!"

As he shouted the order, Jonathan lent his strength to the helmsmen to give the wheel a strong turn. *The Sea Witch* groaned and shivered as her wood took the brunt of the shift. She picked up speed and sailed across the assailant's path. The maneuver was so quick and so well thought out that by the time the Spaniard understood what was happening, it was too late. The wind whistled through the gundeck, through the open portholes, and the gun crew waited, fuses in hand. Clark saw the enemy prow cut into the first porthole. "Fire!" he shouted.

His order and the subsequent explosion happened almost simultaneously. Then the second crew rushed in and fired another round, and so on to the last.

A cloud of smoke and acrid fumes from the powder blinded the gun crews for a moment and made them cough. The frantic goats tugged at their ropes, bleating pathetically.

"Larboard all!" shouted Jonathan.

"Haul in the mainsail and unfurl the square sheets!" yelled Gregory.

There were a few last crackles of musket fire.

The two helmsmen strove against the wheel with all their might to change course as Jonathan heard exclamations of joy from the crew. He turned his head. Clark had done his work well. Flames were leaping everywhere on the Spanish vessel. The bowsprit mast was cut down at the first fire and hung in front of the prow. The foremast had collapsed and the mainmast was split down the middle. Torn sails dangled with bits of rope and yardarms. Cries of rage and shrieks of pain could be heard distinctly. Men were crushed by the masts, caught up in the collapsing sails, and hit by flying metal and shot. Only the mizzenmast was left standing, and there was nothing now that the enemy vessel could do to defend herself.

The Sea Witch completed her majestic turn to attack from the other side and the crew hurried to reload their weapons. A rain of musket fire from the Spanish ship mowed down several sailors. Three of them fell and didn't move again, while the others dragged themselves moaning to the shelter of the bastingages.

"Don't show yourselves, for God's sake!" yelled Woolcomb.

The men ran for cover and continued to load their muskets from a crouching position on the floor. In the gundeck, the gun crew, their faces blackened with powder, were already loading the larboard guns. They were too tense to enjoy their success, but their grins were evidence enough of their satisfaction with their performance so far.

"Prepare the guns and muskets for the foredeck!" shouted Clark. "Aim the back guns full into the hull!"

The Sea Witch was back on course. The Spanish ship had hurriedly brought a gun to its foredeck. A bullet whistled past the English deck. The enemy was trying desperately to turn sideways to be able to use its full gunnery. At last *The Sea Witch* was ready.

"Fire!" shouted Clark.

The bullets crashed full into the prow, shattering the figurehead and broaching a huge hole in the fore of the ship. The musket fire scythed the decks, breaking limbs and peppering men with bits of metal. Flames leapt high on the deck. Water rushed in and the vessel began to list heavily. There was a huge explosion and more holes gaped and more water rushed in. Men were flinging themselves into the sea, throwing in everything they could find to help them keep afloat.

The Sea Witch sailors leapt about, shrieking with the joy of victory, and made a perfunctory show of reloading their muskets.

N'Gio had never heard such a dreadful din. Throughout the entire battle, he sat crouched, head in hands, imagining with each burst of gunfire that the end had come. Yawana, huddled in the back hold with the two children clutched to her, had never heard anything like it either, not even when in her village tremendous rolls of thunder accompanied violent tornados and seemed to run into one horrible threatening growl from above. In the close dark room where she sat, she reflected that death must be something like this, a sudden horrible encounter in the darkness.

The ship fell silent. Light opened above her head and she saw the young cook who had brought her there, his jolly face framed in light.

"Come on up. It's over," he said.

She wanted to laugh and cry at once. Up on deck all the men were singing, laughing, and embracing each other, although two sailors lay dead in a puddle of blood and MacLean was on his knees attending to the wounded. She passed Jonathan and saw that he was grinning from ear to ear. There was an extraordinary expression on his face. His hair was tangled, and his eyes shone with surprising fire. She loved him so much at that moment that her throat ached. She was convinced that if the mighty architect of the universe and supreme king whom her father Isembe had called Ngwe Apombo existed, he must look just like Jonathan at that moment, superb in the ecstasy of his victory. She had to restrain herself from prostrating herself at his feet.

Before going back into the cabin, she looked out to sea toward the ship that had been following them. She was a dilapidated skeleton in the distance, sinking slowly into the sea, with tiny black dots swimming frantically all around it.

"Should we go out after the survivors?" asked Gregory.

"Do you think there'd have been any survivors at all if

they had boarded us?" asked Jonathan. "No, Gregory, they tried to get us by a ruse and they got what they deserved. Anyway, we wouldn't have enough to feed them, too."

Gregory knew Jonathan was right. He didn't insist.

Soon the sharks and exhaustion took their tolls of the swimmers.

The slaves were brought up on deck for air. They were still greasy and trembling with fear. They were not made to dance that day, and to strengthen their spirits Jonathan even ordered a portion of brandy to be served to them after their evening meal.

Ardeen turned up, pale from his close encounter with death. He insisted on giving a funeral oration for the two dead sailors and accompanied their disappearance into the depths of the ocean with a very suitable *De Profundis*, unspoiled by any of his usual embellishments. Jonathan and the other officers were stunned, for during the dinner held in celebration of their victory he never touched a drop of alcohol and he retired solemnly to his bunk as soon as the meal was over.

"Keep an eye on him, Mr. MacLean," Jonathan said when the clergyman left. "If he doesn't take at least one drink tomorrow, the man's sick!" Everyone roared with laughter.

Later, when Jonathan was alone with Yawana, he was too tired from the emotions and excitements of the day to notice the almost religious fervor with which she gave herself to him. The incantation she intoned seemed to him like modulated moans and cries.

The Spanish vessel's treachery set Jonathan to thinking. Obviously, in these waters, all methods were permissible for trying to get hold of another ship's cargo. Thanks to his quick action, it had turned out all right, but he might not always be lucky enough to send an adversary to the bottom of the ocean so quickly. He got Gregory to take an inventory of the food and water remaining, and then called a meeting of his officers.

"Gentlemen," he said, "I have decided to avoid berthing in the Windward Isles after all." He laid out the map in front of them. "Therefore we must change course and go more to the north. We'll run down the coast of Florida and sail straight for Louisiana. It's a dangerous route, there are shoals and reefs, but at least we won't risk any more encounters with those rogues."

The officers bent over the map, following the route traced by Jonathan's finger. He went on: "That will mean that we must cut down our rations, but we should have sufficient. How are your wounded doing, Mr. MacLean?"

"Much better, sir," answered MacLean. "They'll make it, I think. The blacks are also fine. As long as we have enough lemons left I see no reason to object to this change of plan."

"And you?" asked Jonathan, turning to the others.

None of them had any objections.

"Good!" exclaimed Jonathan. "Inform the crew of the new orders. From now on I want a stringent watch over the water barrels. Mr. Adams will see to the rationing himself, and water will be distributed only once a day. Anyone caught stealing water must be put to death immediately. And I don't want the slaves to get too much exercise. We must keep their appetites down. Just keep them scrubbing the decks as they have been doing."

The crew greeted the new situation grimly, but they resigned themselves to it once Woolcomb had explained that these measures were intended to avoid more encounters of the kind they had just experienced. Their lack of fighting spirit won out over their love for creature comforts and they settled into the new routine without fuss. The officers were good about setting an example, and ate the same food as the crew.

Jonathan's attention was taken up with the difficult navigational task he had set himself. Yawana seldom saw him. She realized that he was worried so she didn't suffer too much from his absence and abstraction. Her breasts were often painful these days, and her stomach was beginning to round out. She prayed that he wouldn't notice, for she was terrified that if he realized she was pregnant, he would have her put in with the other women. When she was alone she talked quietly to the child in her womb. She wondered if she would give birth to a daughter, with her father's blond hair and blue eyes.

The Sea Witch continued her peaceable path in an incredibly translucent ocean. The sailors caught plenty of fresh fish, which everyone enjoyed eating. The young woman noticed they passed more and more islands. She

wondered sadly what land awaited her. Would it be worse
than what she had already experienced, or would she find
peace there? She was haunted by the thought of finding
herself reunited with N'Gio. Her love for him was as strong
as ever, but it had been so bruised. He would have to understand what she had been through, and accept the white
man's child.

A heavy heat settled over them. N'Gio was becoming
more and more useful. He had learned to splice rope well
and the sailors treated him kindly. He had stopped wondering about the future. He was simply marking time. Waiting
for something to happen.

One of the women gave birth. It was MacLean's first
birthing and he was proud of his part in delivering the little
boy. The next day, Ardeen, forced into sobriety, christened
him "John." It was the first name he thought of. The
mother was taken from the other prisoners and put in a
more comfortable place where she could nurse her child in
peace.

At last, one night, the slaves couldn't hear the rush of
the water past the ship's hull, and they realized that their
prison was stationary, floating smoothly. *The Sea Witch*
had weighed anchor at the mouth of the Mississippi Delta.

CHAPTER XXXVIII

Jonathan would have preferred to wait for dawn before going into the unfamiliar sandy shallows. He had given orders to weigh anchors at ten knots, quite far from shore.

Leaning on the rail, he gazed at the land he planned to make his home. It was warm and humid. The moon seemed to be racing through the clouds which were smeared across the sky. Every now and then she found a gap in them and illuminated a flat, low coastline, with fires glowing here and there. There were the faint humps of a few islands to the right, and dancing lanterns in the distance showed the presence of other anchored vessels.

The sailors took in all the sails and went below decks. They hardly spoke. Like them, Jonathan was immersed in a tremendous lethargy now that the long voyage was almost over. Gregory came to rest his elbows on the rail at his side. His face, illuminated by the yellow gleam of the poop lantern, looked exhausted, but content.

"Well, here we are," he said to Jonathan at last.

"Yes, here we are," echoed Jonathan, rubbing his hands over his face. "For the first time in a month we can sleep without fear of ambush or attack."

"I sent a few men down to guard the slaves."

"Will you have a drink?" asked Jonathan.

"No thank you, sir," answered Gregory politely. "If you don't mind I'll go right to bed."

Jonathan grunted.

"I think you're right, Gregory. I'll do the same. We'll have a very busy day ahead of us tomorrow."

"Good night, sir."

"Good night, Gregory."

The first mate left and soon after, Jonathan made his way to his cabin.

As he undressed, Yawana lay on the edge of the bed, her arm bent. He stared at her a moment before blowing out the candle and climbing into bed, taking care not to wake her.

The young woman was not asleep, but she didn't want him to see her tears. She heard the springs creak as the big naked body stretched out beside her own. She was longing to press her body close to his. She heard his breathing become slow and regular. Then she turned over on her back and looked at the sky through the porthole. She did not want to see this country which she knew was the last stop. Not yet. At first, she had so longed for the end of this journey, but not anymore. This was where Jonathan would leave her, sell her. And she would never see him again. She would so have liked to stay with him always. For a long time she lay listening to the creaking of the ship, the hiss of the wind through the rigging, and the slap of the water against its sides.

She was already up when Jonathan awoke the next morning. She stared at him, her eyes huge with the tears she had shed in the night.

He got up, pulled on his pants, and went toward her.

"We've arrived, Yawana," he said gently.

She didn't answer. He moved over to the window, where the land, though veiled in a light mist, was visible.

"Come and see."

Yawana crouched close to the wall, her back to him.

"Yawana not want to see," she muttered obstinately. "You will leave Yawana and she is sad."

Jonathan forced a laugh. "But you will be reunited with your husband," he said.

"You will sell Yawana," she whispered, with a sob she could not contain.

"Well, of course I'm going to sell you. But I plan to sell you with your husband."

She wiped her eyes and rubbed them with the back of her hands.

"Why don't you keep Yawana?" she asked in an almost inaudible tone.

"Come on now, stop crying," he said crossly, trying not to show her how much her distress moved him. "I can't keep you. I was able to keep you on this ship, that was different. But on land, that's another matter. A white man doesn't live with a Negress."

Yawana couldn't understand why this made any difference.

"I'll see about selling you both to a good white," Jonathan continued. "You and your man. I promise that you won't be unhappy."

She almost told him that she was carrying his child, so great was her desire to stay with him always, but she knew it could change nothing. Blacks were cattle to the white men; she had learned that. She had seen how her people were treated. Only her beauty had saved her from similar treatment so far. She had always known how their relationship would end, so there was no point in saying something that he would probably mock. He was right. She was only a Negress. The time they were to spend together was over. But she still wanted to extend it for as long as she could. She didn't want to see N'Gio yet.

She sniffed.

"Yawana doesn't want to see N'Gio. Not yet. Wait a little."

"Fine," he promised gravely.

He was beginning to realize the extent of her love for him and it made him annoyed with her, and with himself. It suited him to wait a little bit before getting rid of her. The disembarkation and the sale of the slaves would undoubtedly take some time and he had to get hold of the authorities in New Orleans and find a berth for the ship. It would all probably take two or three more days.

He took her by the shoulders and looked into her eyes. Then, without understanding quite why, he held her in his arms and kissed her very tenderly on the lips. Yawana responded to his kiss with desperate passion and pressed closer to him. At last he pushed her away. He pulled on his shirt and left the cabin without looking at her.

Once outside, he took a deep breath. I wonder what's got into me, he thought angrily. It's only a black girl. Nothing but a little black girl.

He rattled down the ladder and reached the bridge, where some sailors were gazing at the flat gray scenery.

"Gregory!" he shouted.

"Yessir!" said Gregory, appearing immediately.

"Gregory, have them bring the slaves up on deck, and feed them. Then see that they wash and get a shave, and tell MacLean to examine them."

"Aye aye, sir," said Gregory, turning smartly.

"Wait!" called Jonathan. "Get me a longboat. I'm going

ashore to that island marked 'Massacre' on the map. I'll
bring us back a pilot."

"Would you like me to come along, sir?" asked Gregory.

"No, it's not necessary. I'd rather you stayed here. Have
the crew clean up the ship and get them to wash themselves too. We must show these Frenchmen that an English
ship is not a scruffy raft manned by ruffians."

It was now well into the day.

Before leaving *The Sea Witch,* Jonathan raised the flag
to the masthead and the bridge flagstaff. Then, out of courtesy, he had the French flag also raised, to a burst of cannon fire. Immediately, the other ships all sported the fleur-
de-lys, and answered his salute.

The mist had lifted, replaced by a sticky heat. The longboat cut through yellow waters made turbulent by the ebb
tide. He passed close to the French ships. Their names,
Eléphant and *Dromadaire,* made him smile. Sailors hung
over the rail and grinned as they passed. There were men
among them who didn't look like sailors at all. As they
passed a third vessel, a schooner called the *Gironde,* they
were astonished to see women on the quarterdeck. They
looked sad, and responded halfheartedly to enthusiastic
greetings from *The Sea Witch* sailors. The comments flew
thick and fast in the longboat.

Jonathan directed them toward the entrance of what
seemed to be a small port. His sailors, exhilarated by the
sight of women, were singing their heads off. They looked
good in their clean trousers and shirts. Gregory had been
so strict with them that they had all shaved in a hurry and
sported a variety of nicks and cuts.

Some men on shore waved frantically. Jonathan understood that this was where he should land and changed
course. Soon, the longboat's bow hit the sand. He jumped
ashore, and went in up to his ankles, the sand was so soft.
He told one of the men to wait in the boat and took the
others with him.

The French soldiers greeted him and invited him to follow them. Their uniforms were scruffy and far from clean.
Jonathan thought to himself that his own sailors, even
when they were dirty, were more presentable than these
men.

Preceded by the Frenchmen, Jonathan and his sailors
climbed a small pine-covered hill and found themselves fac-

ing a long, low wooden barracks. The soldiers stood aside
for them to enter. Jonathan stepped into a mud-floored
room which was well aired by large windows open toward
the sea. An officer got up as he came in and walked toward
him, hastily buttoning up his coat. Unlike his men, he was
impeccably neat. He held out his hand to Jonathan. He was
a tall lad with a melancholy face, and couldn't have been
much older than twenty.

"Lieutenant Morange, in charge of the guard of the Dauphine Island," he said. "Welcome to Louisiana."

Jonathan warmly shook hands with him.

"I'm Captain Collins, commander of *The Sea Witch* of
the Royal African Company," he said. "Pleased to meet
you, sir."

"Would you please be seated?" the young man suggested, then called over one of the soldiers. "Soldat Per-
loup! Bring wine and give these good people a drink, they
must be very thirsty."

The sailors sat down outside and began a long discussion
with the soldiers. Jonathan could hear their voices but not
what they said. He had no idea that the burning subject
under discussion was the women they had glimpsed on
their way in.

The soldier brought in a bottle of wine and left. As they
drank, Jonathan explained to Lieutenant Morange that he
came from Africa with a cargo of slaves for Louisiana.

"I'd like to disembark my Negroes as quickly as possible," he said, "and get them sold. I'll need a good pilot to
take me up the Mississippi to New Orleans."

"You could do that, of course," said Morange. "But I
don't advise it. The waters are low just now, and with all
the fallen trees there's some danger. To my mind, the best
you could do would be to anchor in Lake Ponchartrain. It's
not far from there to New Orleans by road, and I'm sure
that Mr. de Pailloux, the governor of the town, will furnish
you with the means of transportation. He'll be all the more
delighted, because he has Mr. de Bienville, governor general of Louisiana, as his guest right now. They will receive
the news of your arrival with joy. We really need field
hands here in Louisiana."

"Well, that's good to hear," said Jonathan. "I shall bow
to your judgment."

"It's low tide just now and it won't turn for another four

hours. I suggest that we lunch together, and then a pilot will take you back to your ship."

"I accept with pleasure," said Jonathan, happy to eat something besides salt cod for a change.

"Wonderful," said Morange with a wide grin. "Would you like me to take you around the island in the meantime?"

"I'd be delighted," said Jonathan. "It's been a long time since I walked on anything other than a ship's planks." As they walked he asked, "Tell me, sir, you mentioned a while back that this island is called Dauphine, yet on my map the name is Massacre."

The young lieutenant began to laugh.

"Yes, that used to be its name. You see, when the island was discovered, it was littered with human bones and skeletons. It must have been the scene of a tremendous battle between Indian tribes long ago. That's where the name came from."

"Are they still around? The Indians, I mean?"

"God, yes! The Natchez. They live along the riverbanks. They're peaceful enough and we hear good things from the people living in the area. We've even given their name to a village further north."

By now they had reached the port where Jonathan planned to disembark. It was completely surrounded by sand banks, and a few dilapidated ruins attested to the fact that there once was activity there. Morange explained that the port had been blocked by a hurricane in a single night, and that it was impossible to clear it.

Back at the post, Jonathan told his men that he was staying to lunch with the lieutenant and that the soldiers would take care of them.

The meal was quite a feast. There was roast wild turkey, roast leg of venison, and to Jonathan's great delight, fresh salad and bread. The wine was mediocre and Morange apologized for it. Jonathan promised to send him over some choice bottles of the Bordeaux he still had in stock on board ship.

Jonathan, like his sailors, was also intrigued by the women they had seen on the decks of the *Gironde*. Unable to contain his curiosity any longer, he asked about them.

Morange blushed to the roots of his hair.

"They're . . . well, how shall I say . . . they're ladies

of leisure, sir. They send them to us here to marry them off to the settlers."

"Well, judging from their unhappy looks, the prospect does not seem to please them," remarked Jonathan.

Morange looked stern.

"Oh sir! The life that awaits them here could hardly be worse than the debauched life they led before. They're lucky to be here. Do you know that they make them travel from Paris to Le Havre chained to carts, and sometimes walking?"

Jonathan raised his brows. He was revolted at such treatment for white women, however corrupt they might have been.

"I hope they can at least choose their husbands?" he asked.

Morange looked surprised at the question.

"Absolutely not!" he exclaimed indignantly. "The governor decides. Listen, I'll tell you a story that was told me recently. A young man who claimed to be of noble extraction came here one day with one of these women and pretended to be married to her. It was not true, and the governor at that time was quite right to be angry at such a flouting of his authority. He called the young wag up to his house and told him that the girl belonged to the colony and not to him, and that he could now dispose of her as he pleased. He had decided to give her to his nephew who was in love with her. In a blind rage the young man wounded the nephew in a duel and fled with the woman. She died of exhaustion during the flight, and is buried here somewhere in the sand. She was called Manon, or so I was told. No, sir, these creatures have no say in the decision, and it's only fair."

Jonathan was beginning to be very irritated by the young man's narrow-minded self-righteousness, but he was still curious to know more.

"Why don't the settlers come with their wives?" he asked.

"The settlers? They're the worst dregs of humanity you can imagine," sneered Morange. "They're contraband salt dealers, smugglers, or outlaws whom the regent has ordered deported. Of course there are some in the lot who've never done anything wrong, but the constables in charge of picking them get a ransom per head. Put yourself in their

place. They sometimes pick someone up in the street—
anyone, you know, and they're forced aboard the ships," he
laughed. "That's why they call those constables the Mississippi gamekeepers. That's why!"

Jonathan had to restrain himself from showing his disgust and anger. Here he was, arriving in Louisiana with a
boatload of Negroes, and simultaneously a French ship was
bringing French men and women, snatched from their
homeland in chains, beaten and captured against all honest
principles by their own people. All this just to settle a hostile
land not their own. It seemed that the blacks had no worse
a fate than the whites in this regard. If the motives were
different, the methods employed to capture and bring them
over were similar, and just as cynical and cruel. He was
beginning to wonder if anywhere in the world there was a
spot where he might find peace.

Nonetheless, he restrained himself from showing the little Frenchman what he was thinking. He was planning to
settle in this country. It would be better not to draw the
animosity of the authorities. And then what right had he to
judge anyone for trafficking in a business in which he himself stood to make money.

However, he made a mental note to forget to send over
the bottles of wine he had promised this pompous young
officer.

He was relieved when he saw the pilot arrive. He was a
sturdy fellow from Brittany, now long in Louisiana but
seeming to have settled in well. He assured Jonathan that it
would be easy to guide his ship between the sand banks.
Jonathan took his leave of the French lieutenant and, without regret, departed the island of Dauphine to return on
board ship.

The slaves were all out on deck, most of them asleep.
N'Gio stared reflectively at this unknown country whose
forests and oppressive heat seemed so like his own, with its
great river biting into the land. So it was to bring him here
that they had destroyed his village, killed his family, raped
his wife, and forced his father to betray his tribe. He fig-
ured that he must be on the shores of a great lake. He
wondered if perhaps he could follow the shoreline and one
day come back to the village where he started out. For the
moment he was too tired to think about it. He had only

one wish left. He wanted to leave the ship and find Yawana
and sleep until death came to him.

Yawana was in the cabin. She smiled at Jonathan. She
was wearing the dress that Pierre had made for her. The
few hours she had spent alone had given her time to think
and to fortify herself for whatever lay ahead.

Jonathan was delighted to see her in better spirits. He
filled two wineglasses and offered her one. She was really
very beautiful. Then he left her and went to give orders to
weigh anchor.

CHAPTER XXXIX

The Sea Witch set sail and passed the Island of Ships. The pilot, as he had promised, was so familiar with these waters that he ignored the sounding ropes and threaded them in and out without hesitation. They benefited from the turn of the tide to enter Lake Pontchartrain without incident.

As the sun began to set, the ship cast anchor for the last stage of its journey, less than a cable's length from shore. The waters were smooth and calm. The muddy bank was bordered with mangroves.

That night, Jonathan invited the pilot to share dinner. He turned out to be a much better pilot than a conversationalist, and when he went to the cabin Woolcomb had prepared for him, the ship's officers knew little more of Louisiana than they did before.

The night was a torment for them all. Hundreds of mosquitoes attacked the ship, getting into every cranny and sticking to the sweating bodies. They tortured slaves and sailors alike with their burning bites, and continued their attack until the first light of dawn.

As they were making ready to go ashore Jonathan sent for the doctor.

"Mr. MacLean," he said, "I'm going to the admiralty to ask for a health visit. Please have everything ready by the time I come back. Do we have many sick?"

"Apart from the wounded, who are getting better, there is no one sick among the crew. As for the Negroes, sir, some are not too well, but it isn't serious. They're suffering from the aftereffects of seasickness, that's all."

"If you think one of our blacks seems to show any symptoms of a contagious disease, arrange to have him removed before the visit," said Jonathan. "These damned Frenchies are capable of stopping us from unloading the rest of the cargo."

"Don't worry about that, sir. That creature Gomes showed me what's to be done!"

With that, the two men began to laugh, and recollected

the uncomfortable moments spent in the company of the Portuguese. Jonathan finished dressing as they talked. He pulled on high black boots with silver buckles and white trousers.

"I do want to thank you for the way in which you have discharged your duties, Mr. MacLean," he said formally. "I must admit that I have been pleasantly surprised by you. You have a skill that I never imagined."

The young doctor reddened.

"I did what I could, sir," he said. "It was a pleasure to work under your command."

"Now we're quits," said Jonathan, grinning, "but I do want to say that thanks to your excellent care, our losses have been minor, and they would have been even less had we not had the revolt and the attack."

As soon as MacLean had left, Jonathan placed a three-cornered hat on his head, attached his sword to his belt, and put on a dark blue coat edged with gold braid over a shirt foaming with lace. It was too hot for a wig, so he just tied his hair back with a black ribbon.

He looked at himself carefully in the mirror. Perhaps if the governor saw him like this he would forget that he was a slaver and treat him like a man of quality. His fingers felt something hard in one of the pockets of his coat. It was the medallion Teresa had given him. He opened it. A small curl of black silky hair fell out. He picked it up and put it back in the locket, staring at it reflectively. For a quick flash, he saw again the passionate body of the lovely Portuguese woman arching voluptuously in the heavy heat of São Tomé. Teresa. Teresita, as she made him call her when they made love. One more memory to shy away from, just like all the others: so many flowers pressed carefully in the pages of a book, leaving only a dried-out skeleton between two soiled pages. There were so many accursed memories that he wanted to banish beyond the borders of his consciousness. He never wanted to step into their deathly world. In a state close to rage, he hurled the jewel into a drawer.

Yawana caught the gesture and vowed to herself to look at the talisman some other time. She watched closely while Jonathan dressed, full of wonder at the transformation. She had never seen him look so handsome. When he left the cabin to rejoin Gregory, she sighed deeply. Starboard and

Larboard came tumbling merrily into the room and dispelled her gloomy thoughts. She found it simpler to call them Star and Lar. They had often been her only companions during the long voyage and she had come to love them. As they usually did, the three of them set about tidying the cabin together.

The children had never seen women anything but naked and they were very impressed whenever they saw Yawana in a dress. Through her close association with Jonathan, there had been a profound change in the young woman that showed even in her gestures. She had blossomed from a little Negress whose only task was to care for the plantations and bear children, into a breathtakingly beautiful woman, dressed elegantly, glowing with a deep beauty that was enhanced by her early pregnancy.

While the boys were exclaiming over the strange objects in Jonathan's cabin, Yawana couldn't restrain her curiosity and went to look at the mysterious locket. She opened it and found the lock of hair. Immediately she understood that it concerned a woman, a woman in love. She was suddenly prey to an unknown pain that gnawed at her. Jealousy, something that had no name in her own language, had come to torment her. She grabbed the curl and threw it out of the window into the lake. Then she took the scissors and with difficulty chopped off a little of her own hair and put in the locket. She had never learned the maledictions that were said to cause the deaths of faraway people, so she could not use it on this rival she did not know, but on the off chance that it would work, she spat in the locket before closing it up and replacing it where she had found it.

When they reached the bank, Jonathan and Gregory were pleasantly surprised to find a coach waiting for them. A black man with gleaming white hair, dressed in rumpled livery, was drowsing on the driver's seat up in front. A slim, elegantly dressed man leapt to the ground, said a few words to the startled coachman, and moved toward them.

"Good day, gentlemen," he said to the two officers. His voice was clear as a bell but his English was hesitant. "I am Mr. Chassin, commercial administrator. The governor, Mr. de Pailloux, got word of your arrival and sent me to welcome you."

"I'm Captain Collins, sir, and this is my first mate, Mr.

Adams. I am most grateful to see you. This heat makes walking uncomfortable."

The three men shook hands.

The administrator settled them in the back seat and sat down opposite them. The coachman flapped the reins and the carriage rolled way. The path was muddy and overrun with nettles, so the horses had to walk until they reached a height where the ground was harder and they could move ahead at a brisk trot.

"It's a very bad road," apologized Mr. Chassin. "It's an old Indian trail that leads to the river. But we won't have to use it much longer. Soon the Mississippi will be navigable as far as New Orleans."

Then he asked them all sorts of questions about the journey. Jonathan listened absently and let Gregory do all the answering.

The road wound into a dense forest of sycamores, almond trees, and chestnuts. Here and there tall cypresses made a darker smear in the green. The branches of enormous oaks hung with moss that drifted in the breeze.

The forest lightened and gave way to fields of tobacco. At last they saw the first houses, little hovels with irregularly nailed planks and bark roofs held down with large stones.

The carriage turned onto a road between two rows of better houses. Many of them were timbered, with tile roofs. And they were all surrounded by fences.

"Gentlemen, we are in New Orleans," announced their guide.

Jonathan and Gregory couldn't help exchanging a surprised glance. So this was all there was to that French town with the fancy name! A few peasant cottages along a dirt road.

"The blacks won't feel strange here," Jonathan couldn't help saying rather sarcastically.

"This town has just been settled," returned the administrator, annoyed. "Give it time to grow. Soon this will be the largest commercial port in the whole of Louisiana. The plans are being drawn up and work will begin here soon."

Jonathan was sorry he had spoken, but it was too late to apologize. He muttered, "Interesting!" and fell silent.

The little settlement stretched along the Mississippi

where it swept into a wide curve. The carriage rolled a little farther and then stopped before a one-story stone building. Two soldiers with bored expressions stood guarding the entrance.

"Here we are, gentlemen!" said the administrator brightly.

He got down, followed by the two Englishmen. The three men went inside, saluted listlessly by the guards. They hurried down a long corridor and the administrator opened a door and stepped aside for them to enter. A man got up as they came in. He came around the desk at which he had been working and walked forward to greet them. He was of medium height, with a kind face. He wore a black coat over an embroidered waistcoat. His blue trousers were worn over white stockings and his feet were encased in pumps with silver buckles.

As soon as Mr. Chassin had introduced everyone, Mr. de Pailloux shook hands with them. "Welcome to New Orleans," he said in impeccable English. "Sit down, gentlemen, and tell me what I can do for you."

"I have a contract to deliver my Negroes to your colony, Mr. Governor," said Jonathan. "I'd like a doctor to come aboard so that I can receive authorization to disembark my cargo as soon as possible."

"Certainly, Captain, I understand," said de Pailloux.

He turned to the administrator.

"Where can we reach Dr. Thibaut, Mr. Chassin?" he asked.

"I think he must have finished his visits to the *Eléphant* and the *Dromadaire* by now," said Mr. Chassin. "I expect he's taking care of the girls on the *Gironde*."

"Ah, yes, of course," said Mr. de Pailloux, smiling at Jonathan. "As you can see, Captain, our colony is getting settled little by little." More seriously, he added, "Chassin, see that he's told to go aboard *The Sea Witch* as soon as he's finished."

The administrator assured him that he would see to it.

"Thank you," said Jonathan. "I'll need quite a large depot for my slaves."

"We have just the thing," said de Pailloux. "I can put a West Indies Company store at your disposal. It's empty at the moment. How many do you have?"

Jonathan looked at Gregory inquiringly.

"More than three hundred," said the first mate.

"It should be large enough then," said de Pailloux. "When do you want to hold the auction? Or had you planned to sell off first come, first served?"

"Oh, no, certainly not first come, first served," said Jonathan hurriedly. "We plan an auction, and as soon as possible. I once saw a first-come, first-served sale in Jamaica and I've never seen anything more revolting than all those people hurling themselves on the slaves to lay claim to being first. No, I must prefer an auction."

"Well, then," said the governor, "I'll have more posters made up and distributed in the town, and I'll send soldiers to alert the more distant settlers."

"Do you think we could auction the day after tomorrow?" Jonathan asked. "Is that too soon?"

"Absolutely not too soon, Captain, absolutely not! Everyone here needs field hands and they already know of your arrival. Don't you worry, you won't have any problem selling them. However, may I ask a small favor?"

"Certainly, Governor."

"It's like this," said the governor. "Some of the plantation owners are friends of mine. They're not all deportees, you know. These are good people who came to settle here of their own free will."

"Without the help of the Mississippi gamekeepers?" Jonathan couldn't resist interjecting.

De Pailloux coughed with embarrassment. "Ha!" he said. "I see you know about that. No, as I said, these people settled here of their own free will. I'd like them to get priority treatment, as you might say. What I mean is, you must have some pieces on board that are of exceptional quality, and I should like these people to be able to benefit before the public auction."

"I see no reason why not. Quite the contrary," said Jonathan, thinking of the promise he had made to Yawana. "That's settled, then. Tell your friends to come aboard tomorrow morning and they can take their pick. How many will there be?"

The governor's face lightened at Jonathan's cordial tone.

"I should think there'll be four of them," he said. "And one of them may bring his wife and daughter."

"In that case, Governor, would you be so kind as to extend my invitation for them to have luncheon with me?

And may I have the pleasure of counting you among my guests?"

The governor smiled. "Why, with great pleasure, Captain. Particularly as I can't stay long with you today. Unhappily, your visit has coincided with that of our governor general and I must look after him."

He turned to the administrator.

"Mr. Chassin, could I ask you to show these gentlemen the depot? And then, take them to the inn."

The governor rose and held out his hand to Jonathan.

"Mr. Collins," he said warmly, "you are a real gentleman. It's a great pleasure to meet seafaring folk such as yourself. I'll see you tomorrow, then."

The three men left the room and stepped out onto the main street. It was now crowded with sailors, settlers of all sorts, and a few women decked out in velvet and ribbons despite the intense heat. Some of them were followed by Negroes or mulattoes carrying packages. Yet in spite of all this activity, the town still looked grubby and pathetic.

A traveling coach passed in a cloud of dust. Jonathan caught a glimpse of a woman's face behind the glass. An appreciative glance came his way from under a powdered wig and he thought he caught the shadow of a smile as the coach swept by.

"That's the governor general's wife," said the administrator.

Reflectively, Jonathan continued his walk.

They turned left toward the river. Flat-bottomed boats were gliding on the water and the banks were laden with piles of wood and building materials. To the right, by the riverside, stood a large hangar built of planking, on a stone foundation. A massive iron door bore three heavy locks, which the administrator unbarred. Once opened, it revealed an enormous depot. The beaten-mud floor was dotted with wooden posts holding up a framework that supported the shingle roof. The few openings near the roof had iron grills across them. Jonathan examined it critically.

"I think this will do very well, Mr. Chassin," he said. "What do you think, Gregory?"

The first mate was testing the locks. He turned. "Yes, it'll do fine, Captain."

Mr. Chassin beamed.

"Well," said Jonathan, "come back this afternoon with all you'll need to fix the cannons."

"Very well, sir, I'll bring the furnaces and the cauldrons."

Jonathan addressed the administrator: "Is there anything here that resembles straw? I'd like the Negroes to be able to have some bedding."

"As much as you could wish for. We have plenty of straw. I'll have some brought in during the day. I'll also have a small cart put at your disposal and I'll leave you my coach and coachman."

The three men returned to the town, well pleased.

Chassin invited the officers into the Old Brittany Inn, and told them to wait while he saw to their needs.

The tavern was furnished with few clumsily carved wooden tables and some wooden benches. Sailors were quaffing mugs of wine and conversing noisily. The arrival of the two Englishmen and Jonathan's elegant clothing must have impressed them considerably, for they fell silent at once, and only began talking quietly again after they had taken time to examine the newcomers from head to foot.

Jonathan and Gregory settled down at a table to the side. There was an appetizing smell floating about the place in spite of its unprepossessing aspect. The whole of one wall was covered by a large open hearth, on which chickens were roasting on a spit, turned by a dog in a wooden wheel.

A very young girl came over to see what they wanted. She had a heavy face surrounded by unkempt blond hair, but her ragged dress showed a well-formed body and generous breasts. She stood in front of Jonathan and stared at him admiringly. Jonathan smiled at her, pleased to see a white serving girl.

"Give us some wine, miss."

She didn't move. She just stared with her mouth agape.

"Hey! Wake up, my beauty," said Gregory, grinning.

She turned to him and he put out a hand to touch her. She stared at him with a distracted air and scurried to the back of the room just as a booming voice rang out, "Well, then, Rosalie, what're you waiting for?"

A huge man came out. He advanced toward her with a furious look and slapped her across the buttocks with a large hand.

"Get yourself into the kitchen," he said nastily.

She ran off, her eyes filling with tears.

"She's a little dim-witted," he said, his voice turning obsequious. "What can I get for you gentlemen?"

"Some wine. And make it good wine," said Jonathan shortly, irritated by his manner.

"Yes, sir, right away, sir," said the innkeeper, bowing. "Will you be staying for lunch?"

"Yes," answered Jonathan, "but we're waiting for someone."

"Certainly. Certainly. Take your time." The huge man ambled back to the kitchen.

Raised voices told the officers that the jealous innkeeper didn't like the girl to hang around the customers too much. "Why do you think I married you . . . ?" The rest of the sentence vanished as a door banged shut.

She came soon after, bearing a pitcher of wine that she placed on the table with two steel goblets. She left at once, without daring to look at Jonathan. He noticed her red eyes, and the imprint of five fingers on her cheek.

Jonathan and Gregory drank the fresh wine as they waited for Chassin.

"I want you to know that I'm planning to settle here," said Jonathan. "So I shall leave you in command of *The Sea Witch.* I hope you will get her back to England without any trouble. I'll give you a letter for the Company, and I'll give you the monies from the auction. They'll be delighted with the expedition and with the merchandise that we bought in Africa."

"I think so too, sir," said Gregory. "I shall miss you. I sincerely hope we'll meet again one day."

Jonathan drank some wine and put his goblet down on the table.

"Who knows?" he said. "If I may give some advice, Gregory, take Woolcomb as first mate. He's very capable. And don't forget to stop off in Cuba; you have a sugar cargo to take on."

There was a short silence and then Gregory said, "What will you do here?"

"I don't know yet. I'll see. I think I'll manage all right with these Louisiana Frenchies. I might set myself up as a planter or become commander of one of their coasting vessels, I just don't know, Gregory. Honestly. Anyway, for the

moment all I care about is forgetting for a while that I was
an Englishman and a slaver."

Gregory chatted on and Jonathan answered his questions
vaguely. His mind was elsewhere. Perhaps he was thinking
of Aurelia, or perhaps Teresa, or perhaps even Yawana, or
the mysterious woman who had smiled at him in the street.
Perhaps he wondered if her name also ended in the letter *a*,
which seemed to dog him in his unhappy loves.

The administrator arrived and put an end to his melancholy thoughts. He seemed very hot and bothered as he sat
himself down beside the two officers.

"All set, gentlemen," he said. "Your Negroes will get
straw and water, and your carriage awaits you." He wiped
his forehead with a lace handkerchief he pulled from his
sleeve. "Now let us forget your worries," he added, "let's
drink and eat. The cuisine here is excellent. The innkeeper
has a vile temper but he knows about cooking."

Rosalie came up and prepared to wait on them and
Chassin greeted her. "How are you, Rosalie?"

"Very well, thank you," she mumbled, keeping one eye
on the kitchen door.

"Stay and talk with us a little."

"Oh, no, Mr. Administrator!" she gasped. "My husband
will beat me!"

Chassin ordered the meal and Gregory waited till she
had gone to ask Chassin how she had come to this country.

"She's an orphan," explained Chassin. "She arrived here
about a month ago on the cargo boat *Baleine*, with ninety-
seven other orphans. Three Ursuline sisters came with
them. It was the regent's idea to find them husbands here.
Rosalie is the prettiest of the bunch. I can tell you, it wasn't
easy! The settlers preferred the prostitutes from the general
hospital. They're less virtuous. The poor girl really suffers
with that innkeeper."

The lunch was every bit as good as Mr. Chassin promised. The roast duckling's skin crackled to their heart's delight and the haunch of venison was tender. While they ate,
Chassin told them that gold, silver, and tin were to be
found in the area. France's plan for Louisiana hinged on
some of these untapped riches.

"Have you already found some?" asked Jonathan, interested all of a sudden.

"Actually, no," said Chassin, "but we are almost certain

it's there. But if it's not, plans will have to be changed.
Cane sugar doesn't grow here and the tobacco and indigo
industry isn't developed yet. Silkworm-rearing is beginning
to show something, but nothing can equal mineral riches."

The conversation continued, turning about the future of
the colony.

The meal ended with a basket piled high with sweet wild
grapes, and the innkeeper, in apology for his brusk welcome earlier, insisted on giving each of them a complemen-
tary glass of brandy.

It was time to return to the ship. Jonathan rose, and
Chassin threw a gold piece on the table as the three men
left. The carriage was waiting in front of the door, along
with a cart drawn by two mules. A young black, wearing
an unraveling straw hat, held the reins.

Jonathan and Gregory climbed into the carriage. Before
leaving them, Chassin gave the old coachman his instructions.

"Noel, you stay with the white gentlemen and try not to
doze off on the way." He turned to Jonathan with a grin.
"He's old," he said by way of explanation, "please don't
hesitate to wake him if you see you're slowing down."

The old coachman nodded his snowy head with a wide
smile.

"Never you fear, Mr. Administrator, Noel won't sleep."
He slapped the reins on the horses' flanks and they left at a
smart trot, with the cart following behind.

Halfway through the afternoon they arrived back on *The
Sea Witch*. While they were gone, MacLean had had the
slaves rubbed with oil and their bare black bodies gleamed.
They waited lying under large tarpaulins on the deck.
N'Gio had been put with them and chained, but the young
doctor had decided not to put Yawana and the two little
mulatto boys in with the rest for the French doctor's inspection.

Jonathan hurried to his cabin and removed his heavy
clothing with relief. He slipped on some light cotton trousers and a linen shirt. Yawana gave him a drink. She was
neatly groomed and fully dressed.

The French doctor arrived as day was waning. Jonathan
let MacLean greet him on board. The two doctors spoke
together and then went to the slaves. Dr. Thibaut was a

middle-aged man who had arrived in Louisiana a few months previously. He began his inspection at once.

MacLean, watching him, reflected that he had rarely seen such incompetence. Clearly the man wanted only one thing—to be done as soon as possible. He passed rapidly among the bodies stretched out on the deck, emitting grunts that he probably thought professional and profound. His visit took no more than fifteen minutes, and during the entire inspection he held a handkerchief delicately to his nose.

Thibaut was sweating profusely. MacLean asked him down to his cabin. Visibly delighted to have finished his task, the French doctor signed the log and wrote out a certificate to the effect that there was no contagious diseases on board ship that could impede immediate disembarkation. He refused the glass of wine MacLean offered him and left the ship in a hurry, as if he thought it would explode under his feet. He had hardly spoken a word all the time he was there.

MacLean turned in his report to Jonathan.

"If all Louisiana doctors are like him," he muttered, "I should do pretty well!"

Jonathan was about to answer when Gregory came in, to say he was going back to town.

"Take our cook with you," said Jonathan. "We're having guests tomorrow, and I'm afraid we have little fresh food on board. Let him buy anything he needs."

At that moment, the reverend made an appearance. The officers were surprised to see that he wore clean clothes and seemed sober.

"Reverend! What a surprise!" exclaimed Jonathan.

Ardeen looked disgruntled.

"There's been nothing to drink on this ship for the past eight days," he muttered. "Does that answer your unspoken question, Captain? I'm going ashore with Mr. Adams. I'm sure I can turn up at least one lost soul there."

"Or a drinking companion," said Jonathan. "Try the Old Brittany. I think it's the only tavern in the area."

Ardeen's eyes glistened angrily but he didn't answer.

"Will you honor us with your presence at luncheon tomorrow?" asked Jonathan. "The governor will be coming with some friends of his."

"Count on me, Captain," said Ardeen. "I wouldn't miss it." He suddenly took on a humble air and added, "But you're mistaken about me, you know. This voyage brought me closer to God and I've decided to go on the wagon."

He turned his back on them and followed Gregory, who was climbing into the longboat. As he watched them leave, Jonathan wondered if Ardeen had been making fun of him.

CHAPTER XL

By the time the longboat which had been sent ashore to pick up the guests returned to *The Sea Witch,* it was close to midday. Jonathan, in full dress uniform, inspected the ship to make sure that everything was spotless and in order. The deck was still damp from the morning mist, but the brasses gleamed, the ropes were impeccably spliced, and the ship was an honor to the best traditions of Royal Navy discipline.

Each of the slaves had been issued a piece of cloth in the interests of decency. They were chained to prevent any incident and armed sailors stood guard.

N'Gio hadn't really understood why they'd chained him to his companions again. He tried to speak to them, but the long voyage had crushed everyone's desire to communicate. Each of them, even Bokou, was immersed in his own misery. Physical suffering had given way, little by little, to an absolute certainty that they were nothing at all, not even animals. Their only desire was to leave that dreadful ship and the stinking air of the holds and to step on land again and smell the scent of wet grass. N'Gio was not much better. He had reached a point where he couldn't remember Yawana's features, it was so long since he had seen them. He had even stopped looking toward the back of the vessel in the hope of catching a glimpse of her. He waited, that was all. His past seemed so far away that he had begun to wonder if it had ever existed. He was like a pebble on a trail, just as hard, and just as insignificant.

Jonathan went down to the gangway to greet his guests. The men managed to climb aboard easily, but the women had a difficult time of it. The three of them in their elaborate dresses had to be hoisted aboard by the sailors. The crew was delighted at the novelty and watched the laborious ascent, joking and laughing and making remarks that were not always in the best of taste.

At last everyone was on deck, breathless, but safe and sound, and Mr. de Pailloux made the introductions.

"Captain Collins," he said, "I want you to meet Mr. Hubert. Jonathan shook the hand of a stocky man, getting on in years. Hubert was elegantly dressed and the man's open expression pleased him at once. His handshake was direct and brisk.

"Happy to meet you," he said cheerfully. "This is my wife, and my daughter Virginia."

Jonathan bent over Mrs. Hubert's hand. She was a full-blown woman, a little frightened at finding herself on a slave ship. She answered the captain's welcoming speech with a shy smile.

Then Jonathan turned to the young girl. Virginia had thick auburn hair and her face, while not classically beautiful, showed a lively sensuality barely held in check. She couldn't have been more than eighteen. Her yellow satin dress showed off her voluptuous young body to perfection and her square décolletage did not hide her full, tender breasts.

A black velvet ribbon was tied around her neck. Her slightly bulging brown eyes stared insolently into the officer's blue ones. She held out a small soft hand and was not embarrassed to show him with an insistent pressure that she liked what she saw.

"Mademoiselle," said Jonathan, "welcome aboard *The Sea Witch*."

"What a superb ship!" she said in an affected voice. "Does it belong to you?"

"Unfortunately not," answered Jonathan, laughing.

Mrs. Hubert kept looking uncomfortably at the slaves, but her daughter wasn't the least bit embarrassed by their presence and gazed at them with cold, appraising eyes.

Another settler, Mr. Debreuil, came with his wife. She was made up like a floozy and she immediately asked Jonathan to stop calling her Madame and simply call her Margot. Her dress was dark red and quite revealing, and her vulgar tone clearly indicated that her path to Louisiana had not been a virtuous one. Jonathan suspected that she must have been one of a load of girls similar to the ones on the *Gironde*. She seemed very comfortable with her new position, and her husband, a shrimp of a man, gazed at her constantly with a hangdog look.

Finally, Mr. de Pailloux introduced Mr. Laville, a slim man dressed a little too carefully, a rich merchant from New Orleans. He languidly held out to Jonathan a slim, well-manicured hand heavy with rings, and thanked him in an affected tone for his hospitality.

In turn, Jonathan introduced his officers, the doctor, and the reverend, who true to his word, was sober. Then he suggested that they go to table before looking at the slaves, an invitation they all eagerly accepted.

The table was laid out on the bridge, shaded by a tarpaulin. Jonathan sat at the head with Mrs. Hubert and her daughter on either side. Gregory sat between Virginia and Margot, and Ardeen, by chance or design, sat beside Margot. MacLean sat between Hubert and his wife and the others placed themselves wherever they could, leaving the governor to take the end of the table opposite Jonathan.

Jonathan asked Yawana to take care of the service, helped by Starboard and Larboard. She was wearing her prettiest dress for the occasion, the one Pierre made for her.

As she brought the drinks in, the first person she saw was Virginia. Her woman's sixth sense immediately alerted her to the fact that the girl would do all she could to entice the captain. She was irritated to see Jonathan smiling at the girl and listening attentively to her chatter. She forced herself to calm down and filled the glasses carefully, so no one noticed how her hand trembled.

It was the first time she had seen white women so close. Jealousy gave way to curiosity. She stared avidly at their faces, their silky hair, and brilliant clothing. The men interested her less and she hardly noticed the appreciative glances they gave her. When everyone was served, she stepped back and waited for Jonathan to give the order for the meal.

The guests were drinking and chatting. The chaplain was unrecognizable in his fine clothes and the elegant bearing he had affected to go with them. However, he couldn't hide the desire he felt for the flashy Margot, and it was obvious that he wouldn't wait for the end of dinner before suggesting he was available for spiritual counseling. MacLean was listening sympathetically as Mrs. Hubert discussed her health with him. Her husband was deep in conversation with Gregory. Their words were lost in the general clamor of voices. As for Jonathan, he politely answered Virginia's insistent questions as she devoured him with her eyes.

"What is your first name, Captain?" she cooed, setting down her half-empty glass.

"Jonathan, mademoiselle."

Virginia looked at him with open-eyed admiration, as if she had just learned the most extraordinary piece of news.

"Jonathan!" she exclaimed. "What a wonderful name! May I call you Jonathan?"

Her mother threw her a disapproving glance but she didn't seem to notice.

"I must seem very immodest to you," she said. "But here we are so far from all the social observances. So will you let me?"

"But of course, Miss Virginia," said Jonathan, grinning.

Virginia quickly lifted her hand to her generous décolletage to make sure it was having the desired effect and, reassured on that score, clapped her hands joyously like a child. "Then, Jonathan, you must call me Virginia." She managed to put all the seduction she was capable of into those few words.

"I'll be delighted to, Virginia," said Jonathan, and they both laughed.

Jonathan was enjoying the game. It was pleasant to flirt with a lovely young girl after so long. He knew very well what she was up to, but he was enjoying talking about something other than Negroes and splicing.

Encouraged by his responsiveness, Virginia managed to let her tiny foot slip against his, quite naturally.

Yawana was observing all this in a fury. A dull anger filled her, but what she resented even more than the obvious ploys the young white woman was using was the way Jonathan seemed to be accepting her advances with such pleasure, seemed even to encourage them. The white girl was like a bitch in heat. Yawana would have liked to tear out her silky hair and give her to the ants to eat.

"Yawana!" called Jonathan. "You can serve lunch now."

She came forward at once. "Yes, Otangani, Yawana will get it at once." She leaned over the rail and called, "Ho! Star and Lar! Quick, bring eat!"

Then she went into the storeroom to make sure they heard her. A few minutes later, she came back with the two children ahead of her, each bearing different platters. If Jonathan had any doubts as to the excellence of the meal, he was soon reassured. The young cook did not have

Pierre's extraordinary touch, but he had managed pretty well. The pumpkin soup was followed by a fish stew garnished with lemon and discreetly spiced. Then there was *daube de boeuf sauvage* with rice, followed by roast quails with prunes, salad, and fruit. The aromatic Bordeaux wines went well with all the dishes, and put two red flowers in Virginia's cheeks.

The reverend, as was to be expected, fully honored the wine and his lusty humor provoked coarse chuckles from Margot as her frail husband looked on disapprovingly.

Mr. de Pailloux joined in all the conversations and never missed an opportunity to show Jonathan that he held him in some respect.

Hubert was in the process of describing his tobacco plantation to Gregory, describing the blackberries that bordered the Mississippi north of New Orleans, and discussing his theories about raising silkworms, while his wife continued to drown MacLean in her problems. As for Laville, he was pleasantly chatting with Clark and Woolcomb and never missed an opportunity to pass his hand caressingly over the heads of the two young mulattoes every time they came near him.

Yawana was busy filling glasses and making sure that Larboard and Starboard did their work correctly. She did all she could to stay near where Jonathan was sitting. Virginia, her eyes shining, was talking a mile a minute, showering Jonathan with questions about his life and adventures. From the start of the meal there seemed to have developed a sort of instinctive rivalry between her and Yawana. Virginia was well aware of the smoldering looks the young black girl threw her way and was vastly amused by them. Every time she could, she peeped at Yawana to see her reactions, but Yawana sensed that these glances were without malice. Sometimes there was even a sort of shyness, and Yawana had the distinct impression that the young white girl was examining her with friendly eyes, as if she hoped to make an ally of her. Yawana was puzzled, and forgot her wish to spill wine on her dress.

After lunch, Jonathan suggested that his guests choose their slaves. He made it quite clear that he would prefer the women to stay on the bridge and they accepted, except for Virginia, who absolutely insisted on going down to the deck with him. He left Mrs. Hubert discussing her vapors

with MacLean, and Margot's throaty giggles punctuating
each of the reverend's obscene remarks. De Pailloux apologized that he couldn't stay longer.

"Mr. de Bienville, the governor general, is leaving us today and I must discuss some of the plans he is implement-
ing for our town before he goes," he explained to Jonathan.
As he left, he assured him that posters had been put up
everywhere announcing that the auction would take place
the following day. He was sure that there would be many
buyers, for the news of *The Sea Witch*'s arrival had spread
throughout the country like a forest fire. Once again, he
thanked Jonathan for having received his friends so gra-
ciously, and left for shore.

N'Gio watched the group approach. He was resigned
that he would be sold again, and he was past caring. It
would have been quite different had he known that Jonathan had already made his decision about him and Yawana. From the little he had been able to observe, the captain was sure that Mr. Hubert was the kind of man in
whose household the slave couple would be the happiest.
He couldn't force him to buy them, of course, but the man
would have to be stupid not to want to buy superior creatures.

Jonathan was not mistaken. N'Gio aroused the most interest. To avoid any ill-feeling he decided to take the initia-
tive. After all, N'Gio was his personal property and that
gave him the right to dispose of him as he thought fit.

"Mr. Hubert," he said, pointing to the young man, "I
recommend this fellow. He is quite an exceptional piece.
He's in excellent condition, strong as a horse, and easy to
manage."

Without saying a word, Hubert approached N'Gio. He
lifted his eyelids, inspected his teeth, and felt him all over
with the sure hand of a connoisseur. Then he felt his testicles.

Virginia stood beside Jonathan watching this examination and her breathing became more rapid.

"Yes, a very fine male indeed," said Hubert at last. "I'll
take him. How much do you want for him?"

"At least two hundred piasters," said Jonathan, "but he
has a wife and I don't want to separate them."

"May I see her?"

"You already have, sir. She's the young black girl who served us at table."

Before the settler could say one word, Virginia broke in. "Oh yes!" she cried. "Do take her, Father, she's very pretty."

Jonathan stared at her, surprised at the unexpected pleading in her voice.

"I didn't think you wanted to get rid of her," said Hubert. He turned to his daughter and added, "I'll get her for you, Virginia, you need a servant."

"I'll sell you the two for five hundred piasters," said Jonathan. "It's a high price, but the girl isn't branded. It would have been a shame to do it."

"It's yours, Captain."

Virginia flung her arms around her father's neck. "Oh! Oh! Thank you, Father."

The girl's attitude surprised Jonathan but her bizarre behavior at dinner must be the explanation. Her childish joy astonished him, nonetheless.

"I will ask you one thing," said Jonathan to Hubert. "This Negress warned me about a revolt that was brewing on board my ship. She and her husband deserve humane treatment."

"I can promise you that, Captain. On our plantation, the work is quite bearable, and I am not in the habit of mistreating my hands. All other considerations aside, I pay dearly for them. I make it a point of honor to respect His Majesty's edict on the matter."

"She'll be very happy, I promise you," added Virginia. She smiled at Jonathan and he caught a gleam in her eyes that could have been mockery.

Hubert chose three other slaves, among them, Bokou, N'Gio's companion. Jonathan gave them to him for eighty piasters and the Frenchman seemed very pleased with the deal. The frail Debreuil took ten of the N'Komi, and Jonathan hoped to himself that they wouldn't give him too much trouble. He forgot that Margot would be there to add her weight to their management. As for Laville, he showed no interest in any of the males and still less in the females. Only young boys seemed to interest him, but in the end he didn't choose any of them.

"Didn't you find anything you liked?" asked Jonathan anxiously.

"You know, Captain," said Laville, "in my line of work I don't need field hands. I am more in need of a couple of young lads for work about the house. Something like your two young mulattoes, for instance."

"Oh, you mean Starboard and Larboard? But I'll sell them to you if you like them."

Laville restrained his expression of intense satisfaction with difficulty.

"I'll take them if they're for sale," he said in a tone he strove to keep indifferent. "They're very handsome."

This last remark made Jonathan wonder for a moment about the purity of his intentions, but he finally decided to accept the deal. The boys were very young, and only a slightly tinted complexion betrayed their Negro blood. Perhaps it would be an opportunity for them to get an education that would save them from the hard plantation life. The important thing was that he had been able to keep his promise to put Yawana and N'Gio in good hands. With Hubert, he was sure that there would never be a problem, and he could see no reason why Virginia should mistreat the young woman.

When they were all agreed, Gregory prepared the bill of sale. Jonathan signed it and sealed it with the Company seal. It was agreed that the owners would come and take over their property in two days, after the auction.

It was time to part company. They found Mrs. Hubert and MacLean with the Reverend Ardeen and Margot. Debreuil had some difficulty persuading his wife to leave. She was absolutely set on staying on board. She finally agreed to leave the ship when Ardeen, at her insistence, agreed to go ashore with them.

Virginia said good-bye to Jonathan at the gangplank.

"I'll come to the auction tomorrow if I can," she said eagerly. "It must be fun. I've never seen one. Otherwise, I'll come with my father to fetch his slaves."

"See you soon, Virginia," Jonathan said, smiling, as she prepared to descend the hull.

Everyone piled into the longboat. As usual, Ardeen managed to distinguish himself by his mode of descent. Margot's descent caused great amusement among the crew. She cursed like a trooper and insulted her husband for all she was worth. The others left *The Sea Witch* with more dignity, and Jonathan, relaxed at last, watched them row toward the bank.

"Well, that didn't go too badly," said Gregory, who had come with him to see them off. "They were delightful, particularly that young girl."

"Yes," said Jonathan. "She knows what she wants all right."

The two men climbed to the bridge silently.

"Don't be too long," advised Jonathan. "If you plan to get the blacks into the town it's time to begin disembarking them."

"I was just about to do it, sir. Everything there is ready to receive them. I'm taking the cook so that he can prepare a soup right there for them. I'll come back with him later."

"Take as many sailors as you need to guard them," added Jonathan. "We'll start the auction in the morning, so we'll leave very early tomorrow."

"The administrator has left us his cart," said Gregory.

"Ah! Excellent! Gregory, don't forget to leave the blacks I sold today on board. They can stay out on the deck a little longer, and then get them down in the holds for the night."

"Yessir."

Jonathan was quite pleased with the results of his day. Virginia could turn out to be quite interesting if he decided to settle here. The others were all pleasant people. He might be very happy, living in this country.

He took advantage of the fact that the table was still laid to help himself to a glass of wine. Gregory was already on deck, grouping the slaves and giving orders to the crew. It was very hot. Jonathan suddenly felt very tired. He left his empty glass on the table and went into his cabin.

Yawana was waiting, seated on the bed. She didn't say a word. He read in her eyes that she suspected something, but he decided not to tell her yet that he had sold her. There would be time for that when Mr. Hubert came to pick them up. Actually, he was wrong. Yawana suspected nothing; she was merely jealous of Virginia and couldn't hide it.

He began to undress, and when he was entirely naked he walked toward her. She hadn't moved. Her hands were clasped between her knees and her face was expressionless.

Without seeming to notice, Jonathan slid behind her and lay on the bed. In her white dress, she looked tiny, and she didn't move. Jonathan watched, and saw her shoulders shake with sobs. She cried and cried, without moving from where she sat. Gradually she calmed down. Then sniffing and drying her eyes, without turning to face him she asked, "Otangani loves the white girl?"

Jonathan raised himself on his elbow and placed a strong hand on her shoulder.

"That's it, then, is it?" he asked in a serious voice. "You're jealous. No, Yawana, I don't love the white girl."

In a great rush of tenderness, Yawana turned to him and buried her face in his chest. "Yawana loves Otangani," she murmured. "She knows that she will leave you, so she has pain, and it is for this that she cries. She is sorry."

Jonathan caressed her face gently. What could he say? She was right. Yawana understood his silence and didn't press him for a reply, and he was grateful.

She moved quietly away from him and slowly removed her dress, pulling it up over her head. She stood before him, naked, vulnerable. In her eyes he read such a fervent prayer that he sat up and held out his arms. And she threw herself into them with abandon.

Their moment of passion was brief, but they had never before shared such intensity of feeling. It was as if they wanted to mark each other indelibly with their lovemaking.

These two creatures, so far apart at the beginning, had been thrown together into a world of hate and blood, and had discovered there a violent, impossible love. Now the outcome was inevitable. Yawana would rather she had died and Jonathan had never lived.

In the night, with infinite care not to wake him, Yawana took the scissors and very carefully cut a small lock of her lover's hair. She wrapped it in a tiny rag and hid it under the bed.

CHAPTER XLI

N'Gio watched his friends leave one by one, the friends with whom he had come such a long, desolate way. They exchanged no good-byes. Then it was time for the women and children to disembark. Two slaves left on board recognized their little family and threw themselves into the water, trying to rejoin them. They were fished out and pulled back on deck, where they were well chained in spite of their mournful cries. N'Gio didn't see anyone who looked like Yawana, so he thought she must still be aboard, but out of sight.

He, Bokou, and a few others who were chosen by de Pailloux's friends spent the rest of the day scrubbing the decks. It was a tiring, dreary job. The sailors wouldn't let them rest. Woolcomb had told them they wouldn't get paid until the ship was scrubbed from top to bottom. They had grumbled a bit, but the prospect of the revelry they would be able to enjoy went a long way to resigning them to the task at hand, although they were liberal with kicks and curses to speed up the slaves.

That evening, *The Sea Witch* was spanking clean. Woolcomb had discovered the two young girls hidden in the anchor pit. He dragged them off to Jonathan. They were nothing but skin and bones after the treatment they had received throughout the trip, and it was impossible to find out who was responsible. The captain had Yawana scrub them down and they were served up a fine meal. They could hardly force the food down. He decided to give them to Hubert, if he agreed to take them in. He was sure that in his hands they had a fair chance of regaining their health.

At last, N'Gio and the other slaves were given their evening meal and taken down to the hold. For once the air was not foul there and N'Gio found a place to lie down comfortably.

During this time, the other slaves were coming into New Orleans. The few hours' march had worn them out. Their sweating bodies were covered with dust their dragging chains had stirred up on the trail. The administrator's cart had been used to carry small children and pregnant women. The silent parade, escorted by the sailors, excited much curiosity along the way. They wound their way down the main street between two motley rows of people who had gathered to watch their progress. It was a great event. The announcement of the auction had drawn in settlers from the surrounding country, and the merchants were delighted. The Old Brittany tavern had been full to the rafters all night.

Gregory had arrived earlier in the carriage, and was waiting for them in front of the depot. Cauldrons were steaming on open hearths and the cook was ready to ladle out the evening meal.

As soon as they arrived, the sailors had to form a protective cordon about the slaves to prevent prospective buyers from crowding around, trying to make an early choice. The slaves were led into the depot and fastened there with thick chains running the length of the walls. Each was given a bowl of soup, and then the door was locked and the sentries posted in front of it to discourage the enterprising onlookers. The crowd gradually dispersed.

For once, the slaves slept comfortably on a thick matting of straw.

Next day, Yawana was awake very early. Careful not to make any sudden movements, she got up and slipped out of the cabin, completely naked. She crept out onto the bridge. The deck was strangely calm and still. One sailor stood, his gun between his legs, drowsing against an open hatchway. The lake was reddening under a huge sun. A waterfowl followed by a band of chicks wrinkled the glassy surface as they passed in a flutter of feathers. The ship was absolutely still.

She yawned and stretched. She felt calm, and ready to accept her fate. She knew she would soon see N'Gio but she couldn't quite bring herself to imagine their meeting. There would be time to worry about that later.

Two men appeared on the forecastle and greeted each other casually. Yawana backed away and hurried to the galley. Starboard and Larboard were sound asleep on the ground next to the two little Negresses. She washed carefully, draped a piece of cloth around her loins, and lit the furnace. She heated water and brought it to a boil, then infused the tea leaves. She carried the tea with biscuits to Jonathan's cabin.

He was up.

"Tea, Otangani," she said.

"Very good, Yawana," said Jonathan, smiling.

He drank the burning beverage in small sips and stared gravely at the young woman over the rim of his cup.

"Now," he said gently, "you must promise me not to cry."

His words stabbed Yawana's heart like a dagger. So the moment of no return had arrived. Earlier, she had felt ready to confront it with courage, but now she felt horribly desolate and her legs were weak. "Oh, Otangani!" she wanted to cry, "keep me, I beg you," but she didn't flinch and went on staring at him calmly.

"Yawana promises," she said bravely. "Yawana cannot cry anymore. There are no tears left."

Jonathan felt ashamed. He coughed, embarrassed. He began to prowl about the cabin on bare feet, not knowing where to start. At last he spoke in a voice he strove to keep natural.

"Yawana, I have given you to some whites." Instinctively he used the word "given" rather than "sold." He continued: "They will come and fetch you and N'Gio tomorrow. I have kept my promise to you. Are you pleased?"

The young woman lowered her eyes.

"Yawana is pleased," she murmured. "What whites?" Her voice was so low that he had to strain to hear her voice.

"The white man with the two women."

Yawana stared into Jonathan's eyes. "The white girl who was making smiles at Otangani?"

"Hm!" said Jonathan, embarrassed. "Yes, to her and her parents."

For a moment Yawana was silent, and then to Jonathan's surprise, her face cleared.

"Yawana sad," she said in a firmer voice, "but they are good whites and Yawana is pleased."

What else could she say? She loved him. She would have chosen to be his dog lying at his feet every night of his life, always, for the sake of a stray look or smile. But she wasn't even as much as a dog. She was just a Negress who was not supposed to be able to love a white man.

"Do you want to see N'Gio now?" asked Jonathan, hoping to ease the tension between them.

"No, Otangani," she said, her voice pleading. "Yawana wants to stay with you more. Tomorrow, yes, if you wish."

Jonathan didn't answer. Without a word, he dressed in light clothes, took his cargo register, and left the ship in Woolcomb's hands.

Yawana watched the longboat move away. She would have one more night with him, the last one. Tomorrow she and N'Gio would be reunited. So many things had happened since they were separated. The long march in Africa and the sea voyage had changed her forever. Jonathan had been a sort of shining light in the tragedy of her life, and she would never forget him. But the man she was about to meet again and whom she had loved with all the strength of her young girlhood had not been given the same opportunity. She would have to fill the gap that had been dug between them, that gap that had deepened and widened day after day.

As she had said to Jonathan, she had no more tears and wanted no more, ever.

Sadly, she began to bundle up her few possessions, Pierre's dress, a few strips of cloth, a broken comb and a small mirror that Jonathan had given her. From under the bed, she took the small lock of blond hair, sewed it into a small linen pouch, and hung it about her neck with a piece of string. Then she woke Star and Lar and the two little girls. She did not want to be alone. She gave them fruit to eat. The little mulattoes, still half asleep, gnawed on bananas. As for the girls, still dazed and listless, Yawana gave up trying to make them eat anything and dragged them out on the bridge, where they sat, mute, in the sun.

Then Starboard and Larboard followed her into the cabin and helped her to straighten up, their cheerfulness and affection helping to dispel her sadness.

Gregory and Captain Collins were ready for the carriage ride into town. The driver, Noel, had been completely awakened by all the comings and goings. He whistled between his teeth and the horses set off at a smart clip.

For the moment the officer was dreamy, his thoughts on Yawana, the little Negress who had looked so sad. Then he forgot about her. He had other worries, and no time to dwell on her in this way.

"Well, Gregory?" he asked. "Everything ready?"

"Yes, sir, you'll see for yourself. The town is teeming with people. I think we can finish the auction this morning."

"All those problems, all that unhappiness and all that voyage just for this," mused Jonathan. "Strange, isn't it?"

"Yes, I suppose so."

It was a beautiful morning and they passed scores of people heading for the town. Many were on foot; others rode mules or horses. A few carriages moved to the side to let them pass. Some men wore a whip in their belts or rolled to the pommel of their saddles. The blacks followed behind, wearing short trousers and buff shirts, with large straw hats on their heads.

Here and there, posters were stuck on tree trunks, announcing a large auction of male and female black slaves. Mr. Chassin had certainly advertised thoroughly.

The first houses appeared. Their flowering gardens and neat white fences made them look cheerful and welcoming.

It was like a holiday. The streets were noisy and crowded with a reveling crowd dressed in their Sunday best. Noel was obliged to slow down in order not to hit anyone, so they ended their journey at a slow walk.

The plaza in front of the West Indies Company depot crawled with people, and the sailors had a hard time keeping them back.

The crowd parted to let the carriage through and the coachman drew up in front of the door, where Chassin and Clark were waiting. Their arrival brought enthusiastic greetings. Many prospective buyers had been waiting since dawn and were becoming impatient.

Jonathan got down from the carriage and greeted the administrator and gunnery officer as the door was being opened. All four men walked inside and the door closed again behind them.

The slaves watched them in total silence. They recognized Jonathan and realized that they had reached the end of the road. Perhaps it was the end of the mistreatment, but perhaps it was the start of another ordeal. Worse tortures might keep them awake at night until death dispersed them in a wind unlike any that blew over their forests, or their bones might rot in a land unknown to their gods. The crowd roaring outside terrified them; it sounded like a pack of wild animals..

The slaves had been washed very early in the morning, and their toilet bowls were emptied and their bedding thrown into the river. In spite of it all, there was a penetrating odor of sweat in the depot. Jonathan had all the ventilators opened as wide as possible to air the place before the auction.

Gregory had a barrier built that divided the depot in two. In the center, there was a small platform with a table and two chairs. Jonathan surveyed the place and seemed pleased with the arrangements. He was in a hurry to finish this business, so that he could settle down somewhere, anywhere, and rest.

"Terrific, Gregory! Get it all set now. We'll start as soon as you're ready."

"Very well, sir."

Gregory turned to Clark.

"Go on, old fellow. Get the blacks grouped behind that barrier, the men in front and the women at the back."

Jonathan laid his register and inkwell on the table.

He addressed the administrator. "Would you care to take charge of the auctioneering, sir?"

Chassin was flattered and he preened himself slightly.

"It's a great honor, Captain. I'll do it with pleasure. But why wouldn't you yourself . . . ?"

"You know all the people here," Jonathan said. "It would be easier for you to follow the auction. I don't really understand much about commerce. That's your specialty."

The administrator was all smiles. This wouldn't do his reputation in the town any harm at all, and if he were the auctioneer, no one would dare doubt the honesty of the transactions.

During this time, Clark had got the big chain from the wall and the slaves had been pushed to where Gregory wanted them, guarded by the sailors. The door opened and MacLean slipped in. He came to supervise the branding, in case one of the buyers wanted his slaves branded as soon as the deal was made. Dr. Thibaut accompanied him, but merely as an observer.

"I have your doctor's certificate of health," Jonathan explained to the administrator. "The children have all been circumcised and the women are healthy. And so that they will be in accordance with the laws of your kingdom, they were all baptized before we embarked them."

"That's all very good indeed," said Chassin.

He climbed onto the platform and sat behind the table, ready to start the proceedings.

"I'll help you," said Jonathan.

He left him and went toward the door. The sailor on guard duty was about to close it behind him, but Jonathan stopped him.

"No. Leave it wide open. It stinks in here."

Jonathan made a conciliating gesture to the crowd shouting its impatience for the proceedings to start.

"In one moment, ladies and gentlemen. I beg your patience for one more moment, just so that we can finish getting it ready for you."

His strong authoritative voice and his towering elegance calmed the loudest voices in the crowd, and a relative silence fell over the buyers. They were twisting their necks to catch a glimpse of what was going on beyond the barrier of sailors.

Clark approached Jonathan.

"It's all ready now, sir," he said in an undertone.

"God! Let's wait a moment to get the smell aired out," said Jonathan, also in an undertone. "With this heat and this crowd, it'll be intolerable otherwise."

"I haven't seen the reverend," said Clark. "Do you want me to send someone to find him?"

"What for? We really don't need him. Leave him wherever he is, I'm sure he's just fine." Jonathan couldn't hide a smile. It was easy to imagine what Ardeen might be doing at that moment. He was probably with the eager Margot. The husband's supply of liquor and the wife's newfound virtue were both likely to be subjected to rude assaults by the shameless chaplain.

Clark returned to the depot and came back in a few minutes.

"It's fine now, sir," he said.

"Then let's begin," said Jonathan.

He addressed the crowd. "The auction will begin," he shouted in a sonorous voice.

The sailors stepped aside and there was a rush for the depot. Everyone tried to get in at once. The dealers were the most determined to get into the front row. People pushed and shoved and shouted without shame. Jonathan, who had tried to find a safe spot where he would avoid being trampled, elbowed his way to the platform. He climbed up and stood beside the administrator, waiting for the din to subside before he spoke. Seeing that it kept on as loud as ever, he banged on the table several times with the flat of his hand and sternly surveyed the gathering.

There were still a few women's laughs, some murmurs, and then the depot fell into silence, broken only by coughs and the sound of feet shuffling.

"Ladies and gentlemen," said Jonathan, "we are about to sell, in your august company, a cargo of males and females loaded up on the coast of Africa. The males will be sold individually, the young ones in lots of two or three according to age. Females with children younger than three years old will be sold in the same lot with their children. As soon as a slave has been sold, it will be the sole responsibility of the new owner, and we will not be responsible for guarding it. If any of you wish to keep the chains, they will cost you one piaster extra. These Negroes, Negresses and the young black girls and black boys were all taken aboard ship in the Gabon. They are all healthy. Their bodies are in good condition, they have been baptized, and the males are circumcised."

An approving murmur greeted his announcement. Jonathan raised his hand. "Please," he said, "I haven't finished. The auction will be to the highest bidder, and it will be on sight only. No touching. Mr. Chassin will be our auctioneer; he is commerce administrator of your town."

Chassin smiled and bowed slightly.

"The sales will be immediately recorded and exchanged against a bill of sale, and there will be no returns. And now, before we begin, I must ask you to be absolutely silent, so as not to interrupt the auction. If there is the slightest incident, we will suspend all sales."

There was some applause while Jonathan returned to his seat and latecomers continued to dribble in. The blacks crammed at the back of the depot gazed with horror at these white men in their bizarre clothing, and their women with painted faces, eccentric dresses, and complicated coiffures. But the eyes fixed on them were what terrified them the most.

Jonathan, too, was struck by the passionate expression that deformed most of the faces. They looked intensely greedy, the look on the faces of gamesters at the table. He looked for Virginia in the crowd and saw with relief that she was not there. The spectacle about to take place would not be a pretty sight. It was to be the last degradation, but also the dirtiest. It would take a lot of time to wipe all that out; perhaps there would never be enough time.

Some of the small blacks began to cry, sensing instinctively that something horrible was about to happen. Their mothers managed to quiet them down and everyone, white and black, awaited Jonathan's signal.

"Mr. Clark, bring in the first one."

Clark opened the barrier and a sailor pulled out a black and kicked him up onto the platform. The slave, his wrists and ankles chained, stood with bent head.

The administrator read what Jonathan pointed to in the register. "One piece of India, about twenty-five, second choice. He has two teeth missing and one toe missing on his left foot. Traces of lash marks on his back. Who will start this one at one hundred piasters?"

"One hundred and ten!" shouted a tall man in the first row. His insolent air and loud clothing marked him out as a slave dealer. Two tough-looking individuals stood at his sides.

"One hundred and twenty!" said someone from the back.

The price went up to one hundred and sixty piasters before the black was sold to the man in the front row. He gestured to his companions. One of them paid out the money on the table and took the receipt that Jonathan held out to him. The other removed the chains, threw them on the ground, and replaced them with the ones he had brought with him. Then he dragged the slave out to the door and made him climb into a cart, where he chained him well before returning to the depot.

Meanwhile, a second black had been led to the platform.

"Ah!" said Chassin, "a superb piece. Twenty years old. Fine merchandise. All teeth, no scars. Strong, and well built for reproductive functions. We'll start him off at one hundred and fifty piasters."

The young slave was a magnificent specimen of manhood. He had wide shoulders and narrow hips. The sailor who held his chain made him turn slowly and everyone admired his build. At his least movement, all his muscles rippled and his skin twitched like a thoroughbred bothered

364 NO RIVER SO WIDE

by a horsefly. He stared out over the crowd with huge, fearless eyes.

The price rose rapidly, but this time, the first bidder didn't get him. There were many who wanted him, and each time the price went up a woman's high clear voice immediately exceeded the price with a higher bid. The dealer turned to look at the determined buyer. It was a woman of about forty, dressed all in black. She looked at him defiantly. He shrugged and whispered something into the ear of one of his henchmen.

"That's the Baron widow. She's desperate for a male. She won't let this one go. Never mind, let's drop it."

"Two hundred and fifty piasters, does anyone say better? Sold to the lady in the center," said Chassin.

The widow came forward and quickly placed the sum on the table. She took the receipt held out to her with her eyes fixed on her purchase.

"Will you keep the chains, madam?" asked Jonathan.

She seemed to come out of a dream.

"No, thank you. I don't think I'll need them," she said with a thin smile.

"Unchain him," said Jonathan to the sailor holding the slave.

The widow took the young black by the arm and dragged him away. He followed docilely. There were a few sneering murmurs in the depot as they passed, but she seemed not to notice. She had just sunk all her savings into her purchase. It was so long since her husband had died. Four months. Four long months, during which the hot Louisiana nights had given her no relief for her burning body.

She made the slave climb into a cart, pulled by one mule. She hoped that they hadn't lied about the merchandise. She snapped the reins and they started off. The administrator had said he was well hung; she'd see about that later. She let out a small giggle, suddenly feeling very young. She laid a delicate hand on the young slave's bare leg, but he didn't move, his eyes lost in visions that would only be dream or nightmare to him from now on. "You must be hungry," she said in a gentle voice. She snapped the reins again and drove off with her prey.

The sales continued smoothly. The dealer left after having bought about twenty males. He crammed them into his cart and everyone in the depot could hear the curses and blows he was handing out as they left.

The auction brought in better prices than anticipated, and the piles of gold coins grew, to Jonathan's great satisfaction. The slaves all reacted differently. Some seemed distant and dreamy and let themselves be led about in a daze. Others manifested their despair noisily, calling to their wives, and provoking a concert of lamentations that the sailors had a hard time quieting. When that happened, Jonathan had them pull out the wife and tried to sell them as a couple, but he soon gave up, because it was not always what the bidders wanted and the situation only got more desperate when the woman was pushed back in among the others.

The last male left in a clanking of chains and then it was time for the adolescents. It was even worse there, when they were separated from their mothers, and once again, the sailors had to intervene. Then, realizing that their piercing cries would not stop their fate, the young slaves stopped their tears and sobered into a morose silence.

There was less lively bidding because of their youth, which meant that much labor couldn't be expected from them. The dealers got some good buys, for they had time to raise them to adulthood.

The atmosphere got more heated again when the women came onto the block.

Offers crossed and sometimes the administrator had difficulty following the agitated bidding. The youngest and prettiest provoked such passionate responses that it was almost like gambling, and sums far surpassing what was bid for the men began to fly about.

The last sale of the morning was Aziza, still as beautiful and as impenetrable, with the wide smile that had not left her face since she left Africa. There were few buyers left by then, and she fell to a couple of settlers who made the highest bid. They refused to chain her, and when they took her off, having seen the way they kneaded her buttocks and breasts and whispered to one another conspiratorially, Jonathan wondered what they planned to do with her.

The depot emptied and everyone left. There was a dreadful din of grinding spindles, whips cracking, boots tramping, and a tumult of other noises, and the slaves set out for their new lives. For some it was to be a prolongation of their sufferings, perhaps even a worsening. For others it would be sweet, and peaceful. Everything depended on who had bought them.

As the sailors were cleaning up, Jonathan and Gregory counted the money. The total sales surpassed their wildest hopes. The Royal African Company would not be displeased. Jonathan took out his own share and the shares of the other officers. He wanted to pay Mr. Chassin for the trouble he had taken, but he refused to accept any money.

"Nothing at all, Captain," he insisted. "I want nothing. I did it to help you and it was a pleasure. It is my duty to serve the colony. The labor force you have brought us will allow us to work to bring out the full potential of this country, which badly needs it."

Jonathan realized that it would be in poor taste to insist. He added up the total and made Gregory sign.

"From now on," he said, "this is your responsibility."

It took Gregory and two men to load the heavy coffer into the carriage. Clark went off with his sailors. The administrator retired. Jonathan was alone. He gave a last glance at the empty depot. Nothing was left of the long voyage. Nothing but a few rumpled papers, some garbage, a closed register, and a pervasive smell that resembled musk. It was as if the whole expedition had never happened. There was nothing left for him to do now but go back on board ship. Tomorrow he would say good-bye to the crew. He felt terribly weary.

CHAPTER XLII

". . . I am therefore leaving the command of *The Sea Witch* to Mr. Adams, and I wish you a good voyage."

Jonathan ended his farewell speech to the crew who had gathered on deck. They took the news with total indifference. The only thing that interested them at that moment was the extra pay they had been promised which would ensure them a good time ashore. They didn't care about a change of captain; that wouldn't change the conditions of their life on board ship.

Jonathan didn't care either; he had not expected any regrets from a crew of men for whom he had nothing but contempt. These men were no longer his concern and he parted from them with happiness.

N'Gio, Bokou, and the few other slaves left on board participated in the farewell ceremonies. They had been brought out from between decks and, still chained, were waiting for their buyers to come and get them. Of course, they had no idea what was awaiting them. Nobody seemed to pay much attention to them anymore, and they barely got any food at all that day. The N'Komi had lost all their aggressiveness. Bokou didn't complain anymore. As for N'Gio, he was no longer capable of imagining that he would see Yawana, or he might have tried to prepare himself for their reunion.

Jonathan left Gregory to his new responsibilities and went to his cabin to get ready for his own departure. He began at once to stuff his belongings into the chests. He was so concentrated on his luggage that he didn't notice Yawana's absence. The young woman had taken refuge in the galley. She was naked, except for a narrow band of cotton tied about her hips. This was her way of indicating that she no longer considered herself anything more than a slave, like all the others, and would wear nothing different from what they wore. She waited, her meager possessions tied into a small bundle at her feet. Star and Lar, usually so cheerful, were very quiet, knowing from her sad look that she was soon to leave them. The two little girls were clasped in each other's arms, staring uncomprehendingly about them.

Jonathan folded his parade uniform and put it on top of the rest. He would probably never wear it again. He closed the lid of the chest and was just twiddling the key in the tricky lock when Gregory came in.

"One of the buyers has come with his wife," he said. "The chaplain is with them."

"Well! Well! The chaplain! I know who it must be. Good, Gregory. I'll wait for them here. Mr. Debreuil took ten blacks if I remember. Get them into the longboats. You register the sale, take the money, and don't forget to give them the bill of sale. Would you also be so kind as to bring us something to drink?"

A harsh laugh accompanied the flouncing entrance of Margot, more extraordinarily got up than before, in a dazzling green dress with frills.

"Ah! What a *drôle* you are, Chaplain!"

She became more serious when she caught sight of Jonathan.

"Oh, good day, Captain Collins. Do forgive me. Frank is so amusing."

So she called the chaplain by his first name! Jonathan had no time to answer her, for the reverend came in close on her heels, followed by Debreuil, who looked more self-effacing than ever.

"Good day, Captain," trumpeted Ardeen. "We've come for the husband's Negroes."

"Good morning," Jonathan was finally able to say.

Margot turned to her husband.

"Go and look after your Negroes, dear," she ordered. "You'll come back when you've finished."

Debreuil left without a word as the cabin boy came in with a flask of wine and served it to the assembled company.

"Tell me, Reverend," said Jonathan, "you seem in a good mood!"

Ardeen refilled his empty glass before answering.

"Imagine, Captain, Margot—Mrs. Debreuil had a brilliant idea. She's a great lady, and her kindness of heart is as great as her beauty. But I prefer to let her tell you about her plan."

Margot held out her empty glass and the cabin boy hurried to refill it. She and Ardeen were definitely two of a kind.

"Well," she said modestly, "it was really Frank, really the chaplain who had the idea. You know that the *Gironde* brought out some poor girls, outcasts from society. They disembarked them, but they didn't find them any husbands. I should explain that many from the last lot were sick and the men hesitate to start a family under those conditions. On the other hand, they wouldn't be adverse to a few . . . shall we say, temporary encounters?" She giggled.

"That's right, and it's a scandal," said Ardeen seriously. "We have decided to take in the poor, lost creatures. Madame Debreuil has a very large house outside the town on the river. It's quite beautiful. I advised her to take in the young women so that they can find shelter and comfort."

Jonathan stared at him suspiciously.

"You mean you are prepared to put them up like that? With no payment? Just to do nothing? You are really extraordinarily charitable, madam," he said. "And extraordinarily wealthy."

"Yes," said Ardeen. "Of course we would ask then for some small participation." He had the grace to look embarrassed. "A sort of contribution, so to speak. I mean to say, when they have friends over, they might ask them to participate a little in the household expenses."

Jonathan couldn't believe his ears. He could hardly keep from bursting into uncontrollable laughter.

"Well, I do congratulate the two of you," he said, somehow managing to keep a straight face. "You are very pious indeed, madam. As for you, Reverend, I recognize well in this the charity of your spirit and the kindness that has always been your predominating trait. May I ask what you intend to call your hou—your foundation?"

"We don't know yet," said Margot, pouting. "But I'm sure that the chaplain will find a name for it."

"I have no doubt he will," said Jonathan, smiling.

Gregory and Debreuil came back and put an end to the discussion of the grandiose plans of the reverend and his patroness. Jonathan reflected that perhaps the girls would find their new life no worse than the one they had left behind, although it would certainly be no better.

"Are you pleased, Mr. Debreuil?" he asked.

"Yes, Captain, I thank you," answered the other. "I'll go

back ashore now." He turned to Margot and asked, pointedly ignoring Ardeen's presence, "Are you coming?"

"Yes, we're coming," Margot said impatiently. "Good-bye, Captain."

Jonathan bowed. "Good-bye, madam." He shook hands with Ardeen. "I wish you good luck, Reverend. I have a feeling you'll find clients for Hell rather than for Paradise."

"The road to Hell is paved with good intentions," said Ardeen sententiously. "Don't forget that, my son."

He winked at Jonathan and followed Debreuil who was walking out with bowed shoulders.

Margot, sprightly and delighted about her new activities, so similar to the ones she had abandoned, walked ahead of them both.

They had hardly left the ship when Laville was announced. Jonathan received him cordially and offered him a drink, but he declined politely.

"You are too kind, Captain. I'd love to accept, but I want to get back to New Orleans as quickly as possible. My business awaits me. Where are the children?"

Jonathan poked his head through the door.

"Yawana," he called, "bring Starboard and Larboard. Hurry up!"

He turned around and smiled at Laville. "They won't be a minute."

Laville, seeing he would have to wait anyway, accepted a glass of wine to please Jonathan, who wanted a drink but didn't enjoy drinking alone.

Yawana started when she heard her name. She took the two boys by the shoulders and gave them a little push. "Come, Star. Come, Lar," she said. "Come and see your new master."

"Do you think he'll beat us?" asked Larboard. Starboard began to cry. Larboard, the older of the two, tried unsuccessfully to look brave. Yawana shook her head.

"No, he will not beat you," she said. "This white is not like the others. He does not look bad. Come, Star, do not cry."

The three of them went into the cabin. Jonathan was surprised to see Yawana naked. He frowned, but Laville hardly seemed to notice. His attention was entirely on the children. He came close to them and stroked their cheeks.

Then he pulled his purse out of his pocket and laid it on the table.

"That's the full sum, Captain," he said. "Please count it."

"Of course not, sir," said Jonathan, handing him the deed of sale.

"I do want to thank you for something, Captain," he said. "I see that you didn't brand the boys. It shows an aesthetic sense of a kind one meets very rarely, and is entirely to your credit. It would have been a crime to spoil such pretty lads." He took the children's hands. Starboard had stopped crying. Yawana watched them leave. She was sure they would be happy with this man, seeing how gently he treated them. As for Jonathan, he was not quite so sure.

As soon as they left the room, he turned to the young woman. "Why are you naked?" he asked. "Where is your dress?"

"Yawana is slave now," she said simply.

He didn't know what to answer and went on packing. He understood what she wanted to say and while he didn't feel any shame, he felt a veiled sense of remorse, knowing that he was hurting her, and hating to do so. He hoped the Huberts would come quickly and that it would all soon be over. He preferred to wait for a third party to be present before uniting Yawana with her husband. Without quite knowing why, it was a moment he dreaded.

N'Gio watched as the longboat that had taken away the ten N'Komi returned to the ship. There were two whites in it, one of them a woman. He looked around at Bokou and the others and wondered whose turn it would be this time. Was he to stay alone for the rest of his life?

Yawana also watched the boat come in. This, then, was the end. She longed to throw herself into Jonathan's arms one last time. But she knew she must be brave. She was pleased that she didn't feel like crying.

As he had done earlier, Gregory came to tell Jonathan, "The Huberts have come, sir."

"Get their slaves on board, except for the big strong fellow. Take his chains off and bring him here," said Jonathan, looking at Yawana.

He went on deck this time, to greet the visitors. Mr. Hubert had brought his daughter. It was terribly hot, but she was elaborately dressed, clearly hoping to dazzle the captain. She was wearing a pink silk dress that mostly left her shoulders bare. Her face was protected from the sun by a straw hat with a wide brim.

"Here we are at last, Captain," said Hubert. "I wanted to come sooner, but one of my horses was limping and I had to go to the smith first."

"Good morning, sir, good morning, Virginia," said Jonathan.

The young girl gave him a dazzling smile.

"I was eager to see you, Jonathan," she confessed, dancing about from one foot to the other. "Your ship is so, is so . . ."

Jonathan never found out what his ship was, but it was probably unimportant. He led them to his cabin, which was cooler than the deck.

When they entered, Yawana stood straight and still by the map table. Her arms hung loose at her sides. She felt strange in this cabin now; she didn't belong anymore.

Virginia danced through the door in a rustle of perfumed freshness. She was so intent on getting and holding Jonathan's attention that she didn't immediately notice the other young woman.

"But this is charming, Jonathan!" she cried. "Is this where you live?"

She caught sight of Yawana and stopped short.

"Oh!" she exclaimed. "There's the Negress you bought for me, Father."

"Yes, that's her," said Jonathan.

Virginia stared at Yawana with an amused smile. She turned to Jonathan.

"But she's really very pretty," she said. "I like her better like this than in the dress she was wearing the other day."

Yawana was like a statue and Jonathan couldn't help once more admiring the pure perfection of the body that had given him so much pleasure. Yawana let him look and didn't flinch.

"Yes," he said in a dull voice, "she's very pretty."

Yawana began to feel embarrassed with so many eyes fixed on her.

"I must say," said Hubert, "she's a very rare piece. I'm delighted that you let me have her, Captain." He turned to his daughter: "She's for you, Virginia, just as I promised."

"What's she called?" asked Virginia. "If she has a name."

"Her name is Yawana," said Jonathan.

There was something in the way he said her name that surprised Virginia. She studied his face, but saw nothing that showed any kind of emotion. On the other hand, Yawana had understood the spoken message and was comforted by it, seeing that she still meant something to him.

Virginia approached the young black woman with a hard, possessive look that softened as she came nearer.

"She's healthy, and neat," said Jonathan to Hubert, "and she's also intelligent. She learns very quickly."

From the gestures and words she understood, Yawana realized that she was now the property of the young white girl. She watched her advance toward her. Virginia smiled at her, and some of Yawana's tension eased. Slowly, she tried a small smile, but she was still on the defensive. She only knew the women of her own race, and her experience with them since her capture had left her wary of women altogether, and warier still of the white women of whom she knew nothing.

Virginia laid a gentle hand on her shoulder. She trembled from the contact, but not from fear.

"Don't be afraid, Yawana," said Virginia, misunderstanding. "I won't do you any harm."

Yawana noticed that the girl's voice was rather throaty and she liked the way she pronounced her name. Jonathan and Hubert were not paying attention to them. They were talking of Jonathan's plans.

"Don't listen to what they tell you," said Hubert. "They're crazy. They imagine that this country is stuffed with gold and silver. God! Why not diamonds, while they're about it? Listen to me. There's nothing here and you'd be wasting your time."

"But what can one do here, then?" asked Jonathan.

"I don't know, you could plant rice, or wheat, or indigo plant, or you could raise silkworms."

Virginia and Yawana weren't listening. Without either of them quite realizing it, something was growing between them. The ties between Yawana and Jonathan, her position as a slave, and her extraordinary beauty touched something in Virginia's heart and struck a chord in her sensuous na-

ture. Her extreme youth made her sensitive to instincts that
her education tried to cramp.

They stared at each other silently, studying each other
and judging each other in the same search. Yawana didn't
flinch under her steady examination, and this strength of
character astonished the young white girl. She gave Yawana a slight push and made her turn and come to a stop
facing her. Then a gleam danced in her eyes and she
dragged the young woman toward the window.

"You are very beautiful," she said, unable to resist the
wild charm that came from the graceful body. Her hand
caressed Yawana's shoulder and dropped to her breasts,
touching them lightly. Yawana let her do as she wanted, but
shut her eyes under the touch. Under her lowered lids she
was surprised to see the expression that came over Virginia's
small face. Did the Ndjembe rites exist among white women
also, she wondered? She opened her eyes.

"You, too, very beautiful," said Yawana,

Virginia gave a muffled giggle and pinched the other
girl's waist lightly.

"You must say 'Mistress,' " she said softly to Yawana.

"Yes, Mistress. Mistress very beautiful," said Yawana
and she looked resolutely into Virginia's eyes. Virginia was
the first to look away.

She managed to regain control of herself and taking her
hand away, she turned to her father, leaving Yawana re-
flective. The two men were still talking about plantations
and the future of Louisiana. They had missed the exchange
between the two women.

Gregory came in. "The blacks are in the boat, sir," he
said. "All except the big one. Do you want me to bring him
in, now?"

"Yes," said Jonathan. "Bring him in."

"Is that the husband?" asked Hubert.

"Yes, that's the husband," returned Jonathan. "It's the
first time he and his wife are seeing each other since their
capture. I hope everything will go all right." He got up.

"Yawana," he said, "N'Gio, your man is coming."

The young woman felt very faint. Here at last was the
moment she had longed for and feared so long. She rushed
to the furthermost corner of the cabin and stood there.

CHAPTER XLIII

N'Gio, pushed by Gregory, had to stoop to get through the door. He had grown thinner during the crossing, but all the same, the room suddenly seemed smaller when he stood to his full height.

He advanced a few steps into the cabin, mechanically rubbing his wrists from which the chains had been removed. His head was close to the ceiling. He looked at the white men staring at him silently. His eyes rested briefly on Virginia and then on Jonathan. He wondered what they wanted of him.

He exuded a tremendous sense of strength and power. His body had the well-muscled perfection of an ancient athlete. He was unafraid. They had removed his chains, and he felt sure they meant him no harm. He was amazed at himself for feeling no anger against this man he had hated to the point of wishing to kill him. He hadn't yet spotted Yawana.

The young woman's heart started to beat so fast when she first caught sight of him, that her entire body resounded with its thudding. How beautiful he is, she thought to herself. His features had hardened and there was a bitter twist to his mouth, but his gaze hadn't lost its pride and his noble bearing was arresting. She realized how ridiculous it was to have worried that she might no longer be able to love him. Her love remained as strong and as pure as it had begun. She was suddenly afraid that if she waited another second, she would lose him forever. She plunged impetuously toward him in a rush of eagerness.

"N'Gio!" she cried, sobbing.

He saw and heard her at the same moment and thought he would die for joy. His face lit up and he opened his arms as she flew into them, her head against his chest. He held her so tight that she almost suffocated.

Their joy was beyond words or reason. Everything they had suffered since the accursed day of their marriage was swept away. The ship, the chains, the kidnapping, the white man, murders and tortures—all vanished in a whirl of ecstasy. Nothing existed but the two of them, alone.

N'Gio couldn't contain his tears. They fell and mingled with hers.

"Yawana, little antelope," he whispered, again and again, as she wept, "N'Gio! Oh my N'Gio! Don't ever leave me again."

And they whispered forgotten words that only the trees and forests and river birds had heard before.

They were nothing but black slaves, primitive creatures, and yet Jonathan was deeply moved by the intensity of their reunion. Virginia also seemed very affected by it. Only Mr. Hubert appeared unimpressed.

"Come," said Jonathan, turning to the settler and his daughter. "I'd like to show you something. Two little black girls I want to give you." He didn't want to say he was eager to leave Yawana and N'Gio a little time alone.

Desperately clinging to each other, the two young people didn't notice that the whites had left. As soon as they were calmer Yawana gazed at N'Gio, trying, without words, to say things she could not express. In their silence, she understood that never in moments of joy or sadness would either of them ever mention the events they had lived up to this moment, and when she knew that N'Gio too had understood, she smiled.

Meanwhile, Jonathan had found it easy to persuade Hubert to take charge of the two young girls, and a sailor put them in the longboat. He came back to his cabin.

"It's time," he said simply, to Yawana.

She took N'Gio's hand and dragged him forward. He let her do as she wanted. Jonathan hadn't waited for them. He had already rejoined Hubert and his daughter on deck.

"I've been thinking," said Hubert. "Why don't you come to us while you're trying to decide what to do? You need a rest after your long voyage and it would give you time to think."

"You're very kind, sir," said Jonathan, "and I greatly appreciate your offer. But I have a few things to settle, and—"

"Oh, please Jonathan, do come!" interrupted Virginia, her imploring eyes fixed on him. "It's so beautiful where we live. Come and see!"

"What's more," Hubert continued persuasively, "if you

like the place, you could settle there. It's good land and I could use a man like you. We could do great things together."

Jonathan was tempted, but he had no intention of working for Hubert, and still less of falling under Virginia's spell. He could see what tall plans for the future she was building, with her pretty little face, her languorous eyes, and sensuous mouth. He didn't want to admit it to them, not even to himself, but he had no wish to prolong this phase of his life by spending time under the same roof as Yawana and her husband. It would be an unbearable situation. The memories of the voyage were still too vivid and it would take time for them to fade.

"Really, sir," he said, "I haven't made up my mind yet. I need to find out what I really want to do. Perhaps later, if—"

"As you wish," said Hubert. "I just want you to know that you'll always be welcome."

"Oh, it would have given me sooo much pleasure," breathed Virginia.

Jonathan smiled at her.

"I will come, Virginia, I promise," he said. "I'll come soon."

Yawana and N'Gio appeared on the bridge and slowly descended the ladder. The young woman was clutching the bundle she had left in the galley. The small twist of linen with Jonathan's lock of hair in it hung about her neck. They had their arms about each other's waists, oblivious to the world about them. They walked slowly toward the gangplank.

A sailor was keeping the longboat from banging against the hull. Another was pulling on the rudder. Hubert climbed down first and Virginia took Jonathan's hands in hers.

"Come soon, Jonathan. Don't wait too long," she said in a small voice. "I'm so bored there, so lonely."

Jonathan kissed her hands and she pulled them away as if his kiss had burned her.

"I won't be long," he promised.

Yawana saw the exchange and smiled to herself. Whatever might develop between the white girl and the captain, he had been hers first.

Jonathan made sure that Virginia was safely settled and

then signaled to N'Gio to climb in. The young man started down the gangway, turned his back to the water, one hand on the rail and one on the tiller, and stared at Jonathan penetratingly before he climbed down. Jonathan never knew what lay behind that look. Then N'Gio turned away and went down.

"Your turn, Yawana," said Jonathan.

She threw the bundle into the boat and a sailor caught it. Looking deep into Jonathan's eyes, she said, "Thank you, Otangani." She climbed down quickly without another word. Jonathan leaned over and watched until she was settled in the boat. The sailors began to row away from *The Sea Witch.*

The sun was very high. Huge white clouds massed here and there in the blue sky. A cool wind was rising. Jonathan shivered, but not from cold. Soon, he too would leave his ship never to return, and he didn't know whether to be happy or sad. For so long *The Sea Witch* had been home, country, and friend to him.

The longboat diminished to a speck on the horizon. Virginia sat in the middle, next to her father. She was furious that Jonathan hadn't been more eager to accompany them. She was the one who had insisted that her father invite him, and she had hoped until the last moment that he would change his mind.

From the first moment they met, she longed for him to take her in his arms. She was beginning to find her virginity a burden that clashed with her passionate nature. She wanted to marry, not to spend feverish nights tossing and turning in her lonely bed. The naked slaves always milling about the big house kept her in a strange state, and Jonathan was just what she needed.

If only he came to her father's plantation, she was sure she would be able to keep him forever.

Yawana crouched in the front of the boat. N'Gio had his head on her shoulder, his eyes closed. She watched the ship grow smaller and smaller. It was the first time she really saw it from the outside, and she had trouble realizing that this was where she had spent so many days in love and suffering.

She didn't know where she was going, and she didn't care. At last, she had reached the goal she desired on a tragic morning in the ruined, corpse-strewn village of Mounigou. Now she was with N'Gio. He looked exhausted. The shock of emotion had been too much for him. He was sleeping. She cradled him closely in her arms. She planned to care for him and love him as if he were a child. Together, they would forget everything else and think only of themselves, and perhaps they would at last find happiness.

These white people didn't look bad. She'd be able to manage them. When the young white woman touched her earlier, she saw a gleam in her eyes that opened up a future filled with possibilities. She stared at the girl's delicate neck. Yes, she would know how to deal with her.

Far away she could still make out Jonathan, silhouetted against the sky, motionless. ——

"Good-bye, Otangani," she whispered.

Suddenly it seemed to her that there was a flutter in her womb, and she smiled, her white teeth gleaming. She still had something belonging to the white man, something of her own. One day she would have to tell N'Gio, but not now. There was time. Her sigh was lost in the sound of the oars slapping the waters of the lake.

The irresistible love story
with a happy ending.

THE
PROMISE

A novel by
DANIELLE STEEL

Based on a screenplay by
GARRY MICHAEL WHITE

After an automobile accident which left Nancy McAllister's beautiful face a tragic ruin, she accepted the money for plastic surgery from her lover's mother on one condition: that she never contact Michael again. She didn't know Michael would be told that she was dead.

Four years later, Michael met a lovely woman whose face he didn't recognize, and wondered why she hated him with such intensity . . .

A Dell Book $1.95

Dell Bestsellers

REMEMBER IT DOESN'T GROW ON TREES

**ENERGY CONSERVATION -
IT'S YOUR CHANCE TO SAVE, AMERICA**

Department of Energy, Washington, D.C.